A *Kiss* of Adventure

Praise for Catherine Palmer's Books

"Each of the Treasures of the Heart books is a delightful read. The energy, adventure, and romance kept me intrigued to the end. I will definitely recommend this series to my friends."
— Francine Rivers, best-selling author

A Kiss of Adventure

"This entertaining book is hard to put down."
— *CBA Marketplace*

"Elements of *The African Queen* and *Romancing the Stone* blend in this action-filled romance. Light, romantic fun."
— *Library Journal*

"I had trouble putting it down! I look forward to reading your next book."
— Jo Anne Cottone; Raleigh, North Carolina

"Your characters catch my interest from the beginning, and the background material is wonderful, but to have all of that with a Christian message is more than I usually hope for."
— Virginia Carney; Newport, Arkansas

"Your characters are so honest in their feelings toward God. I also like the fact that your books tackle tough issues, which helps me in my own walk with God."
— Sandra Grahl; Bear Lake, Michigan

"Touched me with the miracle of how God works. I needed to hear the words you wrote."
— Bridget S. Langdale; Houston, Texas

"Excellent! Filled with adventure, romance, danger, and God."
— Heather Vickers; Fremont, California

A Whisper of Danger

"At last, a Christian romance with real emotions. The only negative side to your books is that I can't get enough of them!"
— Liz Hunt; Glasgow, Scotland

"It is sometimes hard to find books that are both spiritually uplifting and entertaining. Your books are both!"
— Angela Martin; Fredricktown, Missouri

"Full of suspense and action. I had a hard time putting it down."
— Cherie Wallace; Sellersville, Pennsylvania

"A delightful romance! I was especially touched by your insights into God's will."
— Patty Goodman; Minneapolis, Minnesota

Prairie Rose

"In Rosie, Palmer has created an entertaining and humorous character. Highly recommended."
— *Library Journal*

"Begins with a bang and doesn't let up till the end. The author expertly presents the tragedy and triumph of the human experience."
— *A Closer Look*

Prairie Storm

"A fine addition to the entertaining series."
— *Library Journal*

"[This] bittersweet romance takes on themes of forgiveness and reconciliation with spiritual tenacity."
— *Romantic Times*

Finders Keepers

"A romance that tackles deeper issues."
— *Library Journal*

A Victorian Christmas Cottage

"[An] engaging seasonal collection of novellas. Entertaining."
— *Library Journal*

HEART
QUEST®

romance the way it's meant to be

HeartQuest brings you romantic fiction
with a foundation of biblical truth.
Adventure, mystery, intrigue, and suspense
mingle in these heartwarming stories of
men and women of faith striving to build
a love that will last a lifetime.

May HeartQuest books sweep you
into the arms of God, who longs for you
and pursues you always.

A Kiss of Adventure

CATHERINE PALMER

Romance fiction from
Tyndale House Publishers, Inc.
WHEATON, ILLINOIS

www.heartquest.com

Visit Tyndale's exciting Web site at www.tyndale.com

Check out the latest about HeartQuest Books at www.heartquest.com

Originally published in 1997 as *The Treasure of Timbuktu*.

HeartQuest is a registered trademark of Tyndale House Publishers, Inc.

Designed by Melinda Schumacher

Library of Congress Cataloging-in-Publication Data

Palmer, Catherine, date
  A kiss of adventure / Catherine Palmer.
    p. cm. — (HeartQuest) (Treasures of the heart ; 1)
  ISBN 0-8423-3884-5 (sc)
  1. Africa—Fiction. 2. Tuaregs—Fiction. 3. Kidnapping—Fiction. I. Title. II. Series.

PS3566.A495 K57 2000
813'.54—dc21   00-056768

For my parents, Harold and Betty Cummins,
missionaries to Bangladesh
and Kenya from 1959 to 1991

Don't store up treasures here on earth,

where they can be eaten by moths and get rusty,

and where thieves break in and steal.

Store your treasures in heaven. . . .

Wherever your treasure is,

there your heart and thoughts will also be.

—Jesus Christ (Matthew 6:19-21)

Prologue

"What is the treasure of Timbuktu?" Tillie asked as the purple African twilight gave way to an onyx night. In the secluded clearing she could no longer hear water lapping the banks of the Niger River, but the mosquitoes whining around her head and the bullfrogs croaking their throaty love songs told her the river was not far away.

Graeme squinted once more down the dusty road they had followed; then he leaned back against the fallen branch of a giant baobab tree. "I'm not sure. It could be a number of things. Right now that's not important. What is important is that you understand your role."

"I'm listening."

"Two hundred years ago, Mungo Park left Scotland to explore this river. He vanished, leaving only that scrap of a diary you're holding. I don't know what he meant by writing about a tree-planting woman. I have an idea, but I'm not sure."

Gently rubbing the aged, crumbling paper between her thumb and forefinger, Tillie pondered the fragile mystery it held. "Go on."

"When I first found out about the journal, the Tuareg tribe had it. One Targui in particular: Ahodu Ag Amastane. He's the *amenoukal,* the chieftain, of a large federation of

Tuareg drum groups. And he's not someone to tangle with. *Ruthless* and *bloodthirsty* are the best words I can think of to describe the guy."

Tillie straightened on the fallen log and listened for any sound of pursuit. "Our friend on the camel?"

"The same."

"But if the document was his, why did he let the little boy give it to me?"

"I think the boy was sent to find out whether you're the tree-planting woman."

"Yes! That's what he asked when he gave me the amulet!"

"When you acknowledged it, the next step for the *amenoukal* was to abduct you from Bamako."

"Why?"

"Because of the curse. For some reason the Tuareg believe the document is cursed—and so is the treasure. No one can handle it but the tree-planting woman." He took the paper, refolded it, and slipped it into the locket. Then he opened her palm and set the amulet in it.

Tillie felt the hair rise on the nape of her neck. Her eyes lifted to meet his.

"Me," she whispered, slightly stunned. "I'm the tree-planting woman in the legend."

ONE

"Nothing happens." Tillie Thornton slipped her hands into the pockets of her pale blue cotton skirt and frowned. "You know what I mean, Mama Hannah? My life here is always the same, day after day. What am I doing?"

"You are walking through the market with me to buy some fruit and perhaps a good yam."

Tillie glanced at the elderly African woman—her companion, caretaker, and best friend since her mother's death so many years before. Never tall, Hannah lately had taken on a pronounced stoop, as though she were always walking into a strong head wind. Tillie knew that the old woman had spent her youth carrying hundred-pound loads of firewood, and that beneath her bright yellow scarf Hannah's forehead bore the indentation of the leather strap that had steadied the burdens.

But Tillie suspected her *ayah*'s stride had less to do with weighty cargo than with an unfaltering sense of purpose. Hannah never varied from obeying the God-given command to look after her *totos,* the four Thornton children placed in her charge. Shoulders bowed and neck arching forward, she strode Bamako's dusty streets with no less determination than a mother hen with chick in tow. At twenty-five, Tillie was certainly no fledgling, a fact that mattered not at all to the older woman.

Hannah's high cheekbones, ebony skin, and large earring holes testified to her Kikuyu heritage, yet she was every bit a mother to the four ivory-skinned siblings she had reared. Practical, pedantic, God-fearing, and blessed with a wry sense of humor, Hannah had been the serene eye in every storm that had whipped across the family through the years. There had been many.

"'When the whirlwind passes, the wicked is no more,'" she liked to remind the children, "'but the righteous has an everlasting foundation.'" Solomon's proverbs were nourishment to Hannah, and she doled them out like precious cups of water to the thirsty.

Looking over a box of yams in the Bamako market, the old woman squinted and tilted her head first one way and then the other. "Small and mealy," she pronounced. "Come, Tillie. We shall search until we find better yams. 'The Lord will not allow the righteous to hunger.'"

A heady scent, sweet and overripe, saturated the dry air in the marketplace. Rows of stalls displayed pyramids of fruit and vegetables, sacks of yellow and white corn, lumps of peanut paste, rocks of salt, heaps of fragrant herbs and spices. Like fat black raisins, flies seeking moisture stuck to everything.

While children played in the folds of their skirts, women in flowing dresses and heavy necklaces haggled over prices of silver filigree rings, amber beads, carvings, woven blankets, and cotton fabrics printed in bold patterns and brilliant colors. Their good-natured bartering mingled with the squawks of scrawny chickens and the bleating of tethered goats.

Unable to put aside her nagging discontent, Tillie touched Hannah's arm. "I know where I'm going today, of course. How could I not know? It's always the same. I know I'll fill this basket with bananas and coconuts. I know we'll walk back to the house and cook supper. Tomorrow morning, I'll get up and drive out to the compound to check on my neem trees. I'll talk to my gardeners, prune the trees, plant the three new species that were flown in from South America, eat my lunch—"

From down the row of stalls a swift dark movement caught Tillie's eye, and she broke off. As she turned, the shadow darted behind a pyramid of long green plantains. "What was that, Hannah?"

"What, *toto?*" Her companion glanced about the market, then shook her head. "Your peace has been shaken by the disturbance last night."

"Disturbance? Someone tried to break into our house, Mama Hannah! If I hadn't thrown my shoe at the window and scared him off—"

"God watches over us, doesn't he?" The elderly woman smiled, her face softening into a familiar grid of gentle lines. "'The name of the Lord is a strong tower; the righteous runs into it and is safe.' Your unease disturbs me far more than a thief at the window, Tillie. You always wanted to help people, and now you are. Planting trees to hold back the Sahara sands and put food in the mouths of the hungry is a good thing."

Tillie stopped, her basket of woven palm leaves dangling against her skirt. How could she explain the turmoil in her heart? At her feet, dust from the dry street settled onto her sandals and bare skin. She sucked in a deep breath of arid, ninety-degree heat and brushed at the flies dancing about her face.

Lifting her head, she searched for a way to make Hannah understand. Above her, two-story houses—crumbling whitewashed memories of Mali's long French occupation—blocked what little breeze might drift from the Niger River a few city blocks away. Laundry strung overhead from balcony to balcony hung motionless in the still afternoon.

"Yes, planting trees is a good thing," Tillie acknowledged finally. "I can't deny that." Though the capital city lay in the Sahel, a zone just south of the Sahara Desert with the river to provide fish and irrigate crops, she knew the threat of famine always hovered. The few native kapok, baobab, and shea trees that studded the shimmering landscape seemed to cry out in thirst.

"But, Hannah," she went on, "is this God's choice for me?"

"Once you thought so. I remember how your eyes shone when you tore open the letter from the Pan-African Agriculture Council. When you read that you had been given a job in Mali, you cried, Tillie. Even your father smiled at your happiness."

"And when you agreed to come here with me, everything seemed exactly right. I'd prayed so hard to find something useful to do with my life, and I felt sure this job was the last piece in the puzzle. My plans all made perfect sense."

"*Your* plans? 'Many are the plans in a man's heart, but the counsel of the Lord, it will stand.'"

"I thought coming here was God's plan, too. What could be more logical?" Tillie let her basket drop at her feet and held up her left hand to count in the African way Hannah had taught her. She wrapped her little finger with her right hand.

"First of all, I grew up in Africa. Even though Kenya is on the other side of the continent, I knew I'd adapt to life in Mali better than I ever did to college in the States." She gripped her ring finger. "Second, I speak three African languages. I felt sure I could learn another." The middle finger disappeared. "Third, agroforestry is my passion. Holding back the desert with trees to help people grow food was the perfect vocation."

"Then what troubles you?" The elderly woman took Tillie's hand and cupped it inside her own dark chocolate fingers. "You have always been the surest of the four *totos* God gave me to bring up. You are calmer than Jessica, bolder than Fiona, and more faithful to the Lord than Grant. What is this distress I see in your eyes?"

Tillie picked up her basket. "Oh, Hannah. I've been here almost a year, and I'm sure I haven't touched a single life. I'm not even certain my trees will grow. PAAC won't let me drive up north to choose planting sites until I've finished all my experiments down here in the capital. I've told them Bamako has different soil from Timbuktu and the rest of the Niger River basin, but they—"

Again, a quick movement snared her attention. The shoppers in the market moved as languidly as the stifling air, but someone . . . something . . . didn't feel right.

"Did you see that?" Tillie whispered. "Over by the sandal stall. Someone's following us and then hiding when I look up."

Hannah touched a yam. "It is not every day a white woman with long golden hair walks through Bamako market. Probably a curious child is tagging after you."

"Maybe." Tillie scrutinized the stall a moment longer.

"Anyway, I don't see how I'm supposed to spread agro-forestry techniques to the people of Mali unless I can spend time with them. My employees have taught me only a smattering of the language because they want to practice their English all the time. And then there's Arthur. . . ." Her voice trailed off.

"A Christian man. A man who wants to marry you, Tillie."

"I've prayed about Arthur Robinson until I'm blue in the face. I just can't make up my mind."

"Your mind?"

"I mean I can't read God's will in this. What does he want me to do with my life?"

"He wants you to walk in him one day at a time."

"Easier said than done." She flipped her braid over her shoulder as she bent to inspect a stack of mangoes. Selecting one, she held it up to the late sunlight and pressed her thumb against the flesh to see if it was firm.

Hannah tugged on the green leaf-spikes of a pineapple. Dressed as always in a colorful cotton shift and narrow belt, with a bright scarf covering her hair, the old woman seemed as much at home in the middle of Mali as she had been in Kenya, so many miles away. How did she do it? Where did that peace come from?

"Do you think God wants me here planting trees and helping people?" Tillie asked.

"I think he is the vine and you are only a branch. If you remain in him and he remains in you, you will bear fruit as big and sweet as this." Hannah held up an enormous ripe pineapple. Her face broke into a warm smile, brown eyes crinkling at the corners. "But apart from Christ, Tillie, you cannot do a thing."

Tillie set the mango back on its pyramid. Her own words echoed. *I've been here almost a year, and I'm sure I haven't touched a single life.* Could her failure to bear fruit, her inability to make a difference in the lives of those she touched every day, mean she had grown apart from Christ?

"God will work his purposes in Mali whether you are here or not," Hannah said as she set the pineapple in Tillie's basket. She picked up a coconut from another pile. "With him acting through you, you can do anything. But you have to learn to bend like the coconut palm."

"I know you're right. It just seems like nothing ever happens."

"Something is happening now."

Tillie swung around. A dark figure slipped behind a door. "I'm telling you! There he is again."

"It is only Arthur."

"Arthur? No, it's—" She turned to find Hannah gazing in the opposite direction. At the opening to the market, a tall man in a crisp gray business suit lifted a hand in greeting.

Tillie let out her breath. "Yes, here comes Arthur. But, Hannah, someone's in the shadows down at the other end of that stall."

"A street urchin looking for a pocket to pick." She added the coconut to Tillie's basket. "Poor child."

Tillie watched Arthur's progress, noting his frown as he skirted a tethered donkey on his way down the long, straw-littered aisle. *In spite of his training in diplomacy, he never feels comfortable in the poorer sections of the city,* Tillie thought. *He's so much better suited to his air-conditioned office in the British embassy.*

During the past year, Tillie had come to enjoy her

adopted home. Ever adventurous, she went on lone expeditions, exploring the back alleys of Bamako, drinking cups of steaming, sweet, mint coffee on street corners, trying on the strange silver rings and necklaces sold by street vendors. She had made it her business to absorb every scent, every sound, every taste of Mali's fascinating desert land.

"Matilda!" Arthur caught up with her and swept his hat from his head. Light brown hair scattered across his damp forehead. "The guard at your house told me you'd walked down to the market. I've had some wonderful news."

"Let me guess. You've figured out who was stealing rare books from the library in Timbuktu and selling them in London?"

His mouth hardened. "Not yet, but we're close."

"You got the reassignment you'd applied for?"

"Indeed I did." His face beamed. "I'm to be transferred back to England in less than a month. I'll work in downtown London. Television, cinemas, warm baths, the tube . . . humidity!"

Tillie laughed. "I could do with a little rain myself."

"Could you?" He searched her eyes. "Tillie, I've come down to the market because I have something important to talk to you about. This position is the answer to my prayers in more ways than one. May we speak in private?"

Knowing exactly what he wanted to discuss, Tillie glanced at Hannah. The older woman was pulling her little cloth money pouch from her bodice. As usual, Hannah looked as though she hadn't heard a word. Tillie knew better. Hannah heard everything, her sharp brown eyes missed nothing, and her lips were ever ready to voice her opinion.

"Please, Tillie." Arthur took her hand in an uncharacteristic public display of affection. "I've come all this way to speak with you. I must have your answer."

She gulped down a bubble of air. *Think . . . pray . . . run . . .* "I'm sure I saw some tree-shaped carvings in one of these stalls," she managed to mutter. "Umm . . . Hannah, would it be all right to separate for a few minutes while Arthur and I look for carvings?"

"Give me the basket. I will meet you at the house at suppertime."

"I hate to leave you alone after what happened last night and . . . and everything." She searched the street for signs of the person she felt sure was following them. "You'll be OK in the market by yourself?"

"I am always OK. You know that." Dismissing her with a wave, Hannah went back to counting out coins to pay for the produce they'd chosen.

Yes, Hannah was always OK. Slipping her arm through Arthur's, Tillie turned him away from the main market area. She needed time to think. Would it be disobeying God to reject Arthur's proposal?

It did seem they'd been thrown together by a divine hand. Like two pale birch trees in a forest of hardy African baobabs, they never could have missed each other here in Mali. They found they had much in common. They both enjoyed travel, reading, playing Scrabble, gardening. They liked to sample exotic cuisines and collect indigenous art. And they were Christians.

But could she really imagine being *married* to Arthur? Upright, uptight, oh-so-British Arthur, with his business suits, Eton ties, and polished shoes. Arthur with his Dictaphone and two-pound, leather-bound daily planner. Could she marry a man who ran his life by a strict schedule when she had always followed her heart?

It didn't feel right, but maybe feelings weren't all that important. "'Trust in the Lord with all your heart,'" Hannah would say, "'and do not lean on your own understanding.'"

Oh, Hannah. Why is trust always so easy for you and so hard for me?

"Darling?" Arthur had pulled out his planner and was flipping through the pages as they made their way between the stalls. "I see I'm to be back at the embassy in twenty-seven minutes for an engagement. I've so little time, and really, we must talk. I'll come back to the market another day and get a carving for you, shall I? I'll bring it with me when I pick you up for our dinner this weekend."

"I want a kapok tree, and you won't know what they look like. Come on. You can talk while we walk."

He shrugged in resignation, and they edged between rows of stalls stacked high with blue-black dates, green plantains, dried fish, yellow papayas, and bananas. Arthur was a rock of stability, a reminder of the security Tillie had longed for since her mother died. Hannah had provided that stability for years—but where Hannah's loving determination had been an anchor for Tillie's drifting family, Arthur's persistence felt like manacles she couldn't wait to escape.

"I must know what you're thinking, darling," he said, stepping over the carcass of a goat. "I'd appreciate not being kept in suspense about this."

"I was thinking of the day we first met. That party at the embassy. Remember?"

"How could I forget?" Arthur's pale blue eyes went almost green in the slanting sunlight. "You, in that black dress with your hair hanging loose about your shoulders. Your arms tan and your legs long and slender. I thought I'd died and gone to heaven."

"Do you remember what we first talked about? Those stories you told me?"

Arthur shook his head and grinned. He caught the heavy golden braid that snaked down her back and gave it a tug. "What stories are those?"

"You told me the history of Mali," she reminded him, a little irked that he'd forgotten. "You talked about the wonderful old library in a mosque in Timbuktu. You described the ancient books someone has been stealing, and you told me how you're helping the Malian government track down the thieves. You told me about the Tuareg tribesmen who used to raid the salt caravans on their way to Timbuktu. The 'blue men.' You said you'd even met a Targui once. And you told about the British explorers who came here to trace the Niger's course."

"Mungo Park and that lot?"

"Yes, Mungo Park. Don't you remember? I was so thrilled, I could hardly go to sleep that night. The stories were about Africa—Africa at her rawest and most beautiful." Her troubled eyes searched his face. "I was sure you loved Africa as much as I do, Arthur."

His smile was indulgent. "I think I actually told you those things to frighten you. Perhaps I thought you'd look to me for protection while you were here. How little I understood you in those days." He paused and gazed at her. "When I began to realize how comfortable you were in Africa, my first thought was to change you, to remake you into a version of myself. Instead, you changed me. I've learned to appreciate the people here. I'm even used to the heat. I honestly can say I know now why God brought me here. I was led to you."

Understanding his confession—but hardly comforted by it—Tillie looked away to watch the women, all dressed in heavy black-veiled burkahs, complete their transactions for the day. Chickens flopped at their moorings, unaware of their impending fate. Mangy brown dogs rooted in small piles of trash and rags in hopes of finding a bone or a scrap of meat.

Tillie worried her lip between her teeth, glancing almost absently across the sea of faces—until she saw a small shape dart behind a booth. She frowned and silently voiced a prayer for protection. Curious in spite of her nervousness, she felt half-inclined to investigate. Arthur would have a fit over that. She tugged him toward an aisle between the stalls.

"Of course, life in London could be rich as well," he was saying. "Think of it. Breakfast in a tea room. The smell of fresh bread baking. Beautiful dresses in glass shopwindows. Churches with proper ministers, songbooks, and organs. A flat with a television, a laundry, a well-stocked kitchen. Can you see it?"

Tillie could, and she wasn't at all sure she liked what she saw. They stepped into a narrow cobblestone street, nearly empty of Bamako's usual odd assortment of old trucks, bicycles, and oxcarts. Sagging houses leaned toward the street. Wooden and iron balconies hung lopsided overhead.

Tillie glanced into open doorways at the lounging grand-

fathers and children who stared as she and Arthur walked
by. She lifted a hand to wave at a little girl peeking at her
from behind the trunk of a scrubby palm. Again, she sensed
movement behind her. She stiffened and whirled. A small
ragged figure darted into an alley. She caught her breath and
grasped Arthur's hand.

"What is it, darling?"

"Let's get out of the market." She started away from the
passage where the figure had vanished.

"Matilda!" He protested as she pulled him along. "What
about those tree carvings you were so determined to find?"

"Later." Annoyed with herself even more than with him,
she dropped his hand and hurried down an alley alone. As
she emerged onto the next street, she caught another
glimpse of the scurrying little figure, now moving in the
shadows on the other side. Her heart beating in rhythm
with her footsteps, she watched as the dark shape slipped
into a tiny fabric shop.

"Darling, for heaven's sake." Arthur caught her wrist and
pulled her up short. "What can you be thinking of, rushing
about in this heat?"

"Someone's following us," she whispered.

"Who? Where are they?" Scowling, he peered across the
street.

Tillie nudged his elbow and pointed with her chin in the
direction of the hidden figure. "I keep seeing someone in
the shadows. At the marketplace . . . and now here."

"Don't be ridiculous, darling! No one's following us.
You've let your imagination run away with you."

"It's not my imagination. I wouldn't doubt it's the same
scoundrel who tried to break into the house last night and

rob us. I'm going to put an end to this nonsense." Lifting her chin, she started across the intersection. At that moment, a ragged child flew into the afternoon sun. Like a fluttering bird, he flung himself onto Tillie. She staggered under the impact, groping for a handhold and finding nothing but the boy's scrawny shoulders.

As they struggled to regain balance, he grabbed her face with bony little fingers and pulled her ear to his mouth. "You are Tree-Planting Woman?" he whispered in broken English. "You are Tree-Planting Woman?"

"Arthur!" She pushed at the child's hands. "Get him off!"

"I'm trying!" Arthur wrestled with the clinging boy, grasping at flailing arms and trying to pin kicking legs.

Tillie broke loose and stumbled backward. The child flew at her again, grabbed her braid, and shouted out his question. "You are Tree-Planting Woman?"

"Ow! Yes, I plant trees!" she gasped. "In the PAAC compound. Pan-African Agri—Ouch! Let go! I plant trees, OK?"

In the next instant, the boy threw his arms over her head, tossing something around her neck as he did so. Then he dodged out of Arthur's grasp and bolted away down the street. Tillie lurched toward Arthur, her pulse hammering in her temples as she grabbed for his arm. "Arthur?"

His expression stopped her. Arthur, his cheeks drained to pale white, gazed into the distance. "Tuareg," he mouthed.

Rags flying behind him and thin black legs churning, the little boy ran toward a tall, white single-humped camel. "*Amdu!*" the child shouted. "*Elkhir ras!*"

High on a large leather saddle sat a man, all but his dark eyes veiled in indigo blue cotton. Two multicolored silk sashes crossed his chest and ended in rows of tassels at his hips. Wearing a stone bracelet, a silver ring, and an elaborate wrought-iron key, he carried a wicked-looking spear, a steel broadsword, and a large, decorated-hide shield. A small dagger was strapped to his arm above the elbow.

"*Enkar!*" he snapped at the boy as he reached down and yanked him onto his dromedary. "*Io!*"

"Tuareg," Arthur repeated dully. "Here . . . in Bamako."

As the boy's excited cries filled the air, the Targui suddenly lunged forward. "*Tek! Tek!*" he commanded, dark eyes on Tillie as he spurred his camel.

"He's—he's coming after . . . me!" she screamed.

"Don't run!" Arthur threw one arm around her and pulled a pistol from his jacket. He leveled it at the charging Targui, but before he could fire, the camel rammed into him. The weapon clattered across the street.

Strong charcoal-hued fingers snaked around Tillie's arm and jerked her into a dragging stumble beside the loping dromedary. As the Targui lifted her into the air, a battered Land Rover with a canvas roof rattled around the corner. Spooked, the camel skittered and stopped.

"*Tek! Tek!*" the Targui shouted and flailed at his beast with the reins as he struggled to maintain his grip on Tillie.

"Help!" she screamed. "This guy's trying to kidnap me!"

The Land Rover swerved toward the balking animal, then slowed as it drew alongside. The driver dove at Tillie, wrapped an arm around one of her legs, and pulled. "This way!" he shouted. "Hop into the truck!"

"Are you crazy?" she shrieked. "Let go! You're . . . you're tearing me in half!" Suspended between the white camel and the Land Rover, she spotted Arthur. He had retrieved his gun and was aiming it at the Targui. As Arthur fired, the warrior dodged, and Tillie was jerked from his hands.

An iron arm locked around her waist and threw her into the Rover. Blue sky whirled overhead, and she glimpsed the rough stubble of a beard and a tangle of black hair as she slammed onto the vehicle's steel floor behind the two front seats. She rolled onto her knees and lunged for the open side.

"Arthur!" she bellowed, thrusting her head and shoulders out of the opening.

"Get back inside! You want to tear your head off?" The driver reached behind, grabbed her, and held her down with one rock-hard arm as he steered through the crowded street. Coughing and choking back hot rage, Tillie watched as Arthur ran after the Land Rover.

"Matilda! Stop! Get out of there!" he cried, his features contorted. "Darling!"

The Targui had regained control of his dromedary, and it moved past the Englishman, gaining on the Land Rover. As the vehicle swerved around another corner, Tillie tumbled and bumped against solid flesh.

"Hang on, lady. We've got the Tuareg on our tail!" The driver stomped on the gas pedal. His thick black hair whipped at the corners of his grin as he glanced at her. "Grab that hand strap over the window, and don't let go."

"Take me to the United States Embassy!" Tillie demanded above the roar of the engine. She clutched the strap he had indicated as the Land Rover hurtled down a hill toward the Niger River. Anger boiled through her, but she knew enough to be afraid, too. Maybe this had something to do with Arthur's investigation of the manuscript thievery ring in Timbuktu. Or maybe it had to do with her work for PAAC.

Either way, it was far more adventure than she had bargained for, and she wanted out.

Two

"Listen, I work for the Pan-African Agriculture Committee," Tillie yelled over the rattle of the Land Rover's engine. "I want to talk to the authorities. Take me to the embassy."

"The embassy?" The driver uttered a muffled curse. "You don't know what's going on here, do you?"

"I know I just about got kidnapped by a Targui."

"Do you plant trees at the PAAC compound?"

That question again. "Yes, I plant trees. Why? What's going on?"

The man glanced back at her, his eyes narrowing. "Did the Targui give you anything? A piece of paper?"

"Paper?" Tillie suddenly recalled the child's odd action—her focus darted to the palm-sized amulet that swung from her neck. The handwrought silver locket had been threaded onto an intricate hand-beaten silver chain. Strange symbols were engraved on the tarnished metal, and they surrounded a bead of yellow amber embedded in the front. The ancient amulet was encrusted with dirt and grime and looked as though it would crack if she tried to open it. She glanced up again.

"Hey!" she exclaimed when she looked out the window. "Where are you taking me? This isn't the way to the embassy!" She tried to pull herself upright as the Land Rover bounced along a crowded street that led to the river.

She shot the driver a wary look. "Who are you? Are you in cahoots with that Targui?"

"I work alone."

Frowning at the terse reply, she shielded her actions from him as she dropped the necklace down her blouse and buttoned the top button. The locket was meant to be hers. After all, the ragged boy had given it to her . . . the tree-planting woman.

Hanging on to the strap, Tillie ventured another peek behind. The Targui was nowhere in sight, his dromedary no match for the Land Rover. And yet this maniacal driver continued his headlong race through Bamako.

"I asked you a question!" he hollered. "The Targui—did he give you anything?"

Tillie scowled. "And I asked you a question! *Two* of them, in fact. Neither of which you have deigned to answer, so I'll repeat them. Who are you, and where are you taking me?"

His eyes sparked. "I'm Graeme McLeod. Now, how about handing over that paper?"

The Land Rover barreled onto the road that ran along the brown Niger River. Tillie tightened her grip on the leather strap. "I don't have any paper."

"Look, lady, you don't know this, but your life is in danger. I'm trying to protect you, OK?" His eyes flashed with irritation. "And you're sure not making it easy. Didn't you get that Targui's message? He and his pals are after you. You're the tree-planting woman. Now give that piece of paper to me, and this will all be over. I'll take you straight to the embassy."

"Take me there right now. I'm under the protection of

the United States government. If someone is after me, they can handle it."

Graeme clenched his jaw. "Ten months . . . ," he muttered. "Ten months of searching, and I have to run into this. OK. If you won't give me the paper, you'll just have to come along for the ride."

Glaring at him, her heart in her throat, Tillie debated giving the man the amulet and being done with the whole ugly mess. She was crazy not to. But the boy had given it to her, to the tree-planting woman. She had to know why. What was in the locket—and why did this man want it so badly?

As the Land Rover rattled along the river road, a hundred thoughts raced through Tillie's mind. Hannah. Where was she, and what would she do when Tillie didn't show up at the house? Arthur. Would he really have shot and killed that Targui? The thought sickened her. And this . . . this ruffian driving her who knew where. She had no idea what kind of man he was or what he would do to get the amulet from her.

She closed her eyes for a second, trying to calm her racing heart and thoughts. How could God let this happen?

She looked at McLeod again. With his shaggy black hair and scruffy chin, the man looked the perfect pirate. His long, sunbaked nose might have made him handsome but for the obvious fact that it had been broken at least once. His strong white teeth could have lent him a dashing air, but the cynical tilt to his lips erased every trace of the debonair. His square jaw and firm chin were appealing, but his teeth were locked in a clench so tight the muscle in his cheek jumped. All the man needed was an eye patch, and he could have passed for a buccaneer.

An American pirate in Mali? Well, why not? The desert attracted all kinds of adventurers. This renegade's faded blue jeans and tan shirt clung to his tall frame, revealing a strength Tillie knew she should fear. But her outrage at the events of the afternoon overrode any wariness.

She climbed into the empty front seat and shifted her focus to the passing houses. She had no idea where he was taking her. Obviously they were traveling away from the city's center, but where were they going?

"I hope you realize this is as much a kidnapping as when that Targui grabbed me," she snapped. "You could spend a lot of time in jail, you know."

He turned to her, and for the first time she looked into his eyes. Deep blue-green, they were the color of the desert sky. One corner of his mouth turned up, softening the harsh line. "I prefer to think I rescued you. I guess you haven't thought about where you'd be if I hadn't come along when I did."

"I can take care of myself, McLeod. That Targui never would have gotten away with me."

"I did, didn't I?"

Tillie pursed her lips and looked away. They were leaving the city, and she began to worry in earnest. The houses grew farther apart. Dusty fields took their place. A glint of sunlight on the river caught her eye, and she tried to remember what Arthur had told her the night they met.

Explorers had come to find the direction in which the Niger flowed. Mungo Park was the one who discovered that the river was shaped like a huge question mark. It began far to the southwest of Bamako and wound north toward the Sahara. Then it turned southward and spilled out into the Bight of Benin.

Of course! The Niger flowed north from Bamako. Tillie scrutinized the muddy waters and saw that the Land Rover was traveling with the current. Graeme McLeod was taking her north.

Toward the desert.

Oh, Lord. Panic rising in her throat, she realized Arthur would have no idea where she was by now. The Targui must be miles behind. Who was this man—and what could he possibly want with the amulet? Her mind quickly ran through possible ways to escape.

"I need a rest stop," she announced. "A bathroom."

"Sure you do." His mouth tipped into a slight smile. "We'll stop when the sun goes down."

"Sunset!" Tillie glowered at him. "Hey, I'm expected back at my house already. People are waiting for me, and I have to go to work tomorrow. Look, McLeod, I told you I need to stop now. I mean it."

"We've got to get to the rapids before the sun sets."

Rapids! Tillie looked down at her cotton skirt and sandals. How was she ever going to escape this demon in the darkness, near rapids, and in these useless clothes? She rested an elbow on the door handle and tried to moisten her lips. It was useless. Her nostrils burned with the acrid scent of the air. The sifting dust that covered her legs and skirt in a fine powder absorbed every droplet of moisture from her body.

The sun dipped swiftly toward the flat, barren horizon, as it always did in Africa. As Tillie was beginning to abandon all hope of escape, Graeme swung the Land Rover off the track.

She craned forward. "What are you . . . where are—"

"Right here." He pulled the Land Rover to a halt in the midst of a scrubby growth of banana trees.

Sitting back, he let out a breath. "OK, now let's get you some relief and a bite to eat. You can get out of the Land Rover and take care of business in the bushes. But I wouldn't advise trying to run. The moon won't be up for hours, and you probably know there are some unpleasant critters in this part of Mali. Cheetahs, lions, leopards . . . jackals."

Giving the man a final glare, Tillie threw open the door and slid out of the Land Rover. The banana trees closed over her head, and the dry, scratchy grass crept up beneath her skirt to her thighs. One thing was for sure. She wasn't about to go any farther without finding out what was inside the locket. Maybe it held the answers to what was going on.

She crept behind a kapok tree and drew the amulet out of her blouse. Squinting in the twilight, she gingerly pried apart the silver clasp, opened the locket, and touched a tiny square of folded paper.

"OK, so there is something," she muttered.

Holding her breath, she lifted the message from its hiding place. Whatever had been written on it must explain why she'd been chosen by the ragged boy . . . why the Targui had come into Bamako on his camel . . . why Graeme McLeod had taken her out of the city—

"I'll take that," he growled from behind, locking her wrist in one hand and jerking her against him as he tried to tug the paper away. "You lied to me, lady."

"I did not!" Tillie gasped through clenched teeth. "I didn't know there was anything inside the amulet."

"Amulet?"

"Yes, and anyway, the boy gave it to *me.*"

The heat from his hand burned her stomach as they struggled over the paper, each wanting it but neither willing to risk tearing the fragile scrap. Suddenly he let go of her and she stumbled forward, the amulet's contents still in hand. Surprised, she stood staring at him in the fading light.

"Look, I want you to cooperate with me," he said, his voice softer. "If you'll come back to the clearing, we can sit down and talk this over."

"And if I don't?"

"I've spent ten months in Mali tracking down that document. Longer than that in England. I've got to have it, OK? You'll go along with me one way or another."

"Oh, really?" She refolded the paper and slid it back into the locket. Slipping the chain around her neck, she pushed past him toward the clearing. Finding the fallen branch of an old gray baobab tree, she sat on one end.

"So explain," she demanded when he hunkered down beside her.

"Are you going to let me see the paper?" He took a small flashlight from his pocket. Flicking it on, he held it out. Its weak beam cast a gentle glow on the tall yellow grass and her leather sandals.

"I want to read it first," she declared. "The boy gave it to me. It's meant to be mine."

He considered for a moment, then nodded. "You're probably more right about that than you're going to like." He held the flashlight out to her.

"Whatever that means." She slipped the chain over her head and took the flashlight from him. "Just don't grab me anymore, OK?"

"No problem."

She gently opened the ancient silver locket and lifted out the paper. As she unfolded it, she heard the man beside her draw a deep breath. She thought she detected a quiver of anticipation in his hands.

The paper was very old—yellowed and creased. A single paragraph in English had been written in a spidery hand. Tillie held up the flashlight and read silently:

25 December, 1806—

I believe it is Christmas Day somewhere, though not here. I know I will not live to see tomorrow. The Bight of Benin the blight of Benin. Ailie when I get back will you let me rest? Will you keep the Moors away? The Bight of Benin the blight of Benin. Ahmadi Fatouma has the wealth in safekeeping for me. Ailie we will buy that house on Chester Street. Mine mine mine! I have the wealth. I possess the treasure of Timbuktu. One day, one day the white man will come here. One day, one day the white woman will come here. She will plant trees and make it a garden for tea parties. She will plant trees. She will find the treasure of Timbuktu. And the curse of the Bight of Benin will be ended.

Mungo Park

Graeme lifted his chin. "So what does it say?"

"It's weird. Sounds like he's rambling."

"Who? Who's rambling?"

She looked at the document again. Mungo Park—he was

the explorer Arthur had told her about. Had he really written this? And what about the tree planting? What was the significance of that?

"Are you finished?" Graeme's deep voice broke into her reverie. "May I see it now?"

He reached out to take the paper, but Tillie whisked it away. "Wait a second!" she whispered. "First I want you to tell me something."

"What?"

She could sense his eagerness, like a leopard stalking prey—muscles coiled and ready to spring. It seemed all he could do to resist overpowering her to have his way.

"I want you to tell me who you are," she said. "Why do you want this paper so badly?"

"I told you. I'm Graeme McLeod, I'm an American, and I've been trying to find that paper for nearly two years."

"Why? What do you think it says?"

"The more you know about it, the more danger you'll be in. Just let me see it."

"First tell me why you want it."

He sighed and she could see his knotted biceps tighten further. "I believe that paper is a page from the diary of Mungo Park." He searched her eyes as if seeking confirmation.

"Mungo Park," she murmured, keeping her focus trained steadily on him, betraying nothing. "The explorer."

"Yes, the explorer. Almost two years ago, I heard rumors that the page had come to light. There's been a theory—a legend—that a secret message written by Mungo Park exists. It supposedly talks about some strange things. About a woman who plants trees, for example."

Tillie shivered and turned the paper over in her hands. "What are you going to do with it?"

"I hope I'm going to get to read it."

"I mean after that."

"I don't know. I need to read it to find out what to do next."

She looked down at the sheet of paper, then took a deep breath and placed it on his thigh. He stared at her for a moment. When he gingerly picked up the paper, she leaned over and held the flashlight at his shoulder while he read.

Tillie tried to reread the yellowed scrap with him, but she found her attention drawn away by the nearness of his shoulder and the thick mane of black hair that brushed her hand. How strange that she should be tempted to rest her head against such a man's shoulder.

Well, she was tired and disoriented. She wished Hannah were here. Hannah would know exactly what to do. Pray. That's what she would recommend. But Tillie felt she hardly had time to think, let alone formulate a prayer.

"He wants you to walk in him one day at a time." One day at a time. How about one minute at a time? Tillie flushed at the memory of Hannah's gentle reprimand. Her big plans were worth less than nothing at this moment. *"He's the vine and you're only a branch. If you remain in him and he remains in you, you will bear fruit. . . . But apart from Christ, Tillie, you cannot do a thing."*

Apart from him, nothing. Walk in him. One minute at a time.

Oh, Lord, help me.

Tillie opened her eyes and looked down at the paper. Graeme obviously had read and reread it by now.

"This is just great," he snarled suddenly. He leaned back, knocking the flashlight from her hand and extinguishing its beam. They both bent to grope for it. As Tillie found it, his hand closed around hers.

"Look . . . what's your name?" he whispered, taking the flashlight from her. "That guy in the market—did he call you *Matilda?*"

"No, please. I'm Tillie. Tillie Thornton."

"Look, Tillie. I think you'd better listen carefully to what I'm about to tell you. You're in for some rough days."

"I don't know what you're talking about."

"I'm talking about the journal. I'm talking about Mungo Park and the legend and the curse. I'm talking about you, Tillie Thornton. You're the tree-planting woman. So now, whether you like it or not, you're going to have to go in search of the treasure of Timbuktu."

Graeme explained that he didn't understand the meaning of Mungo Park's wording on the ancient document any more than Tillie did. Nor did he know the significance of the legend that had become so important to the Tuareg. But he did know one thing. For some reason the Tuareg believed the document was cursed—and so was the treasure.

"No one can handle it but the tree-planting woman," he said. He refolded the paper and slipped it into the locket. Then he opened Tillie's palm and placed the necklace in it.

She felt the hair rise on the nape of her neck. "Me. I'm the tree-planting woman in the legend."

"At least the Tuareg think you are."

"Great."

"So, are you hungry? I've got a few bananas in my bag."

"Hungry! Who can think about food? What about the curse and that Targui who's after me? What does all that mean? And the message in the amulet? Mungo Park couldn't possibly have known about me. He wrote this almost two hundred years ago."

Graeme tapped the flashlight against the fallen log. "My guess is that our friend on the camel—he's an *amenoukal,* by the way, the chieftain of a federation of Tuareg drum groups—brought the document to light because of you, the first tree-planting woman the Tuareg ever heard about."

Tillie felt sick. In the past three weeks, she'd sent a flurry of letters to various agencies in the Sahel asking if any of the tribes living there would be willing to donate a large plot of arid land for her first tree-planting experiment outside the capital. The Tuareg were nomadic, but no doubt the officials had spoken to them about her project.

"The Tuareg probably think they can get to the treasure through you," Graeme said. "I imagine the *amenoukal*'s looking for us—you—right now."

"But I don't know where it is!"

"He thinks you do. And now that you have the document, you'll find him the treasure. At least, that's how he sees it."

Tillie looked out toward the Land Rover. A half-moon was rising over the banana grove. Tillie frowned. Graeme had told her it wouldn't come up for hours. He had lied to her. Maybe he was lying about this, too. Maybe he wanted the treasure for himself. Or, more likely, maybe he was involved in some kind of illegal business and was trying to use this fantastic story about Mungo Park as a cover.

She studied the amulet in her hand. Brilliant in the silver moonlight, it fascinated her in spite of herself. What would Hannah be thinking? and Arthur? They needed her. Even her neem trees needed her. She couldn't go off on some wild treasure hunt. It didn't fit with her plans.

Your plans? She heard the echo of Hannah's voice. Maybe she did put too much faith in her own plans, but surely God had no purpose in sending her into the desert . . . with a black-haired stranger who couldn't be trusted. . . .

Tillie stiffened. What had she been telling Hannah that very afternoon in the marketplace? She wanted desperately to go into the desert. She longed to be with the Africans and learn their languages. She ached to touch lives for Christ. But . . . but not like this! It wasn't sensible.

My ways are not your ways. Neither are my paths your paths. She had learned the verse at Hannah's feet many years before. Now it echoed in her mind and heart. What if God intended to accomplish through her exactly what she'd always expected—but in a far different way than she'd ever imagined? *Remain in him . . . and you will bear much fruit.*

She shook her head in confusion. *Much fruit?* How, when she was being chased by the Tuareg and forced to travel with a renegade like Graeme McLeod?

Trust in the Lord your God.

She drew a deep, steadying breath.

Trust me.

She nodded. "OK," she whispered.

"Huh?"

"I said OK." She lifted her focus to Graeme's eyes. "So now what happens?"

"Unless you'd prefer to travel to Timbuktu by dromedary, you can hitch a ride with me."

"You realize I'm supposed to be in Bamako. If I don't go back, everyone will be looking for me."

"I thought you just said you'd go!" Frustration filled his deep voice. "Look, suit yourself. I'm going on to Timbuktu, and to tell you the truth, I'd rather go it alone."

"Something wrong with my company?"

He shot her a glance, his eyes traveling over her, taking in her dress, her mutinous expression. "You're a scientist, right? Trees and all that. Well, the desert is no laboratory, and the Tuareg won't care about your college education or your test tubes. You can't walk very well in a skirt and sandals. You won't eat three squares a day or drink soda pop, you know?"

She knew. She also knew she felt more at home in the wilderness than she ever had in a laboratory.

"I can drive you back to Bamako," he went on, "but the Tuareg will grab you in a second. Remind me to tell you about the Tuareg sometime. They have fascinating ways of dealing with those who disappoint them. Either way—it's your choice."

"Doesn't sound like much of a choice to me, McLeod." She stood up and strolled to the Land Rover. Her hands brushed the tips of the elephant grass. She picked one and chewed its sweet end. She didn't want to have to trust this guy, to put her life in his hands, but what else could she do?

Arthur would be frantic, of course. She thought of the man who wanted to make her his wife. With his blue eyes, light brown hair, and square shoulders, Arthur always drew

attention. And his circumspect behavior and air of sophistica-
tion always commanded respect. He had told her he cared for
her, and she believed him. He was a gentle, quiet person—
nothing like this character who claimed to have "rescued"
her. Tillie closed her eyes and tried to let the cool night
breeze drifting across from the river calm her.

All right, Lord, I'll go toward Timbuktu. She would go with
Graeme McLeod—at least until Arthur caught up with
them, as she was sure he would. She would pray for safety,
and she'd use whatever opportunity God brought her to do
his work.

A rustle in the grass startled her, and she turned to find
Graeme beckoning her to join him. He held a bunch of
bananas aloft like a prize and shook it lightly, a silly grin
softening his face. His expression reminded her of an
excited, endearing boy. Shaking her head at the transformation in him, she walked back to the fallen log and curled
her legs beneath her on the grass.

"Care for some dinner, *mademoiselle?*" He held out a
banana to her in both hands, as if displaying a bottle of rare
wine for her inspection. When she made a face and
snatched it from him, he laughed aloud and began peeling
his own fruit. Taking a bite, he chewed thoughtfully for a
moment. "I won't risk a fire tonight," he said. "Maybe I'll
be far enough by tomorrow to chance it."

"So, how far is Timbuktu?"

Graeme let out a breath. "You're coming with me, then?"

"As long as you keep your distance. I don't fraternize
with kidnappers."

He mused for a moment. "Well, you might be useful in
the long run."

"Useful?"

"Crocodile bait." He gave her a quick wink. "In the Land Rover we can make it to Timbuktu in a couple of days. It's rough going, but I think she'll hold up. By steamer it would take longer, and the river's not always passable."

Tillie dropped the banana peel into the grass. "Where am I supposed to sleep? Are you going to set up a tent or something?"

"There's your tent." Graeme jabbed a thumb toward the Land Rover. "Home."

Tillie stiffened. "I'm not sleeping in there with you."

"What's the matter? Wouldn't your boyfriend approve?"

"Arthur Robinson is my fiancé . . . sort of. And no, he would not approve."

"Arthur Robinson. That gray suit you were with? Well, I'd sure obey him if I were you."

Tillie bristled. He was baiting her. "I don't obey Arthur. I obey my—my moral values. And my conscience."

Angry with herself and with Graeme, she stood. Walking toward the Land Rover, she stared up at the moon. Why hadn't she told him she was a Christian? That she obeyed *Jesus?* Why couldn't she just say it?

Fuming, she climbed into the back of the vehicle, formed a pillow from a pile of clothes, and closed her eyes. She could hear Graeme moving around near the Land Rover. Lying stiffly on the hard metal, she thought of what he had said. Arthur was a fine man. He did deserve her respect, even her obedience.

"I'm not sleeping out in the grass," Graeme said, climbing into the front seat. "OK?"

"Scared?" she taunted him.

"You bet."

Tillie wedged herself against the wheel well. She felt the front seat move as he tried to get comfortable in the cramped space. For some reason, the image of the last time Arthur had kissed her popped into her head. He was always so careful. He didn't even like to hold her hand in public, and he never impetuously hugged her or gave her a peck on the cheek. Once, when she'd leaned her head on his shoulder, he had asked her to remove it. Those had been his exact words: "Please remove your head from my shoulder, Matilda darling."

She stared at the olive green wheel well. Her mother had died when she was young, and her father had never remarried. Hannah was already widowed when she had come to look after the Thornton children, so Tillie had had few role models for the proper behavior between a man and a woman. Maybe it wasn't right to show affection. But then, why did she long for it so much?

In a moment all was silent in the truck. She looked up at the stars winking down on the hidden Land Rover. Around it, a symphony of night noises swelled in intensity as the animals of Africa called to one another, challenging, seeking food and mates.

"Look . . . Tillie," Graeme said in a low voice. She went rigid as he leaned over the seat and put a warm hand on her bare arm. "I'm sorry about what I said. I'm sure your boyfriend is a nice guy. I know he'll be glad to have you back safe and sound when this is all over."

"Thank you."

"And your folks, too. I imagine they'll hear about this through the embassy."

Biting her lip, Tillie shrugged away from his touch. "My

father lives in a remote area and probably won't know about it until it's over. My mother died when I was young."

Graeme was silent for a moment. "Well, it looks like we have something in common after all."

Tillie didn't want to know anything about the man in the front seat. She didn't want to feel sympathy for him. She didn't want to like him. She didn't even want to care about him—not in any deep way. Wasn't it possible just to live out your witness and share the Lord with people without having a relationship with them?

A man like Graeme . . . who lied . . . who had grabbed her off the streets for his own purposes . . . who was probably up to something illegal. . . . She didn't know a thing about him that appealed to her. And she didn't want to.

If only this metal floor weren't so hard. After being dragged alongside a loping dromedary, pulled nearly in two, and tossed headlong into a speeding Land Rover, her entire body felt bruised and stiff. Her shoulders ached, and a knot had lodged at the back of her neck.

"Here, put this blanket under you." He tossed it over the seat. "You'll rest better."

She rolled onto her knees, spread out the blanket, and lay down again. She didn't look at him—not more than a glance. He was big and his knees jutted up toward the Land Rover's roof. This wasn't right. Not that she would ever let the man touch her. It just didn't feel right.

"Better?" he asked.

"Thanks."

"Sweet dreams."

"You, too." She shut her eyes, and though she prayed hard, sleep didn't come for hours.

Graeme stared up at the black ceiling of the Land Rover. He preferred stars. He preferred silence. He preferred being alone.

Not that the woman behind him wasn't attractive. What man in his right mind would resent the company of a long-legged blonde with bright blue eyes and a smile that could melt butter? From what he could tell, she had a keen intellect, too, and a spirit of adventure to go with it. Africa didn't beckon the timid.

He glanced over the seat back at the sleeping figure of the woman he'd thrown bodily into his vehicle that afternoon. She must be tougher than she looked. He'd expected her to burst into tears, hand him the document, and beg to be taken to safety. Instead she had argued with him, tricked him, threatened him, and bullied him.

He liked that in a woman.

His grin died as her boyfriend's image floated into his mind. Old Arthur probably liked it, too. The guy had nearly shot the Targui to save her. A stupid move like that would have gone over great with the Malian government. Graeme could see the newspapers plastered with it now. Love could do strange things to a man.

Not that Graeme would know. He lifted a hand to the open side of the Land Rover and traced the denuded silhouette of the baobab tree with a finger. Come to think of it, he couldn't remember the last time he'd been in pursuit of a female. His research had taken all his time and energy in the past few years, and he'd been more than happy to lose himself in his quest. Things with women didn't work out well for him. Never had.

Of course, when you took into account what he'd grown up with, it was no wonder. That was fine, too. He didn't need people around. Didn't like them. Especially women.

Now he had this blonde lioness tagging along. Her presence would attract the Tuareg like a swarm of bees to a frangipani tree. Any man with an ounce of sense would hand her back to her boyfriend at the first opportunity. Graeme McLeod had never had to be responsible for anyone but himself. And why should he? He'd taken care of his own needs for as long as he could remember. That was enough.

He hunkered up on one elbow and looked again over the seat at the sleeping woman. She could be trouble. Already was, in fact. He studied the long braid that curled down her arm. Moonlight painted it a pale, lustrous gold. Gold. Like the treasure of Timbuktu. He gently picked up the hank of long hair and weighed it in his palm. Soft, heavy, it was warm from the contact with her skin. He held it to his nose and shut his eyes. How long since he'd been this close to another human?

The treasure of Timbuktu. What was it? She had asked him that evening. Just as he'd asked himself a thousand times before. He didn't know.

But the scent of her golden hair tugged at him more surely than the promise of all the treasure in Timbuktu.

His eyes flew open at the realization, and he dropped her

braid as though it had stung him. Sinking back onto the Land Rover's cramped seat, he crossed his arms over his chest and stared out at the baobab tree.

THREE

A jingling sound disturbed Tillie, and she rolled over. She heard voices . . . low male voices murmuring, conferring. A branch broke. Coming fully awake, she listened to the sounds from the edge of the clearing.

"Graeme?" she whispered.

Nothing. The Land Rover was empty. As a prickle of alarm slid down her spine, she sat up. "Graeme?"

He opened the Land Rover door. "Mornin', glory."

"Where were you?" She looked into his eyes. Blue-green in the morning light, they were soft, almost gentle. "I—I thought I heard something."

"Sleep well?" He climbed into the front seat, put the key in the ignition, and turned toward her.

"Sort of."

"You wiggled."

"You snored."

He grinned. She let her focus dart from his eyes to his powerful arms and back to the mane of dark hair framing his face. How could anyone look so fresh at this hour of the morning? Brushing awkwardly at her tangled hair, she realized how dirty and stiff she felt. The blue cotton skirt she had ironed the morning before was now creased into a hundred wrinkles, and her sleeveless blouse had lost a button.

"Well," she said, coughing slightly. "I guess you didn't hear anything then? Back there—"

"I heard 'em, all right." He peered through the brush toward the road they'd driven down the day before. "Camels."

"Camels?" Tillie gasped. "Tuareg!"

"Time to catch the school bus." Graeme turned the key, put the Land Rover in gear, and sped out of the clearing onto the track just ahead of the long parade of camels. The fearsome blue-veiled figure atop the largest camel drew his sword, shouted, and spurred the caravan toward the vehicle.

"Here they come!" Tillie shouted over the rattle of the Land Rover's wheels. "Go!"

"I'm going."

"Can't you drive any faster?"

"This baby's doing good to get up to forty."

"Forty! What kind of a vehicle only goes forty?"

"This one. Get up here, and tell me what our pals are up to."

She clambered into the front seat beside him and peered past his shoulder as the gaily decorated camels slowly receded in the trailing dust. Their veiled drivers continued to shout and brandish swords that glinted pink in the early light.

"They've fallen back, but they're mad," she told him. "And they know they're on the right track."

"No doubt about that one. We'll have unwanted company all the way to Timbuktu."

Chewing at her lower lip, Tillie realized that although the Land Rover outdistanced the camels, the road had narrowed into a single rutted lane. She glanced at the gas gauge. Less than half a tank. She'd seen a gas can bolted to the rear of the Land Rover, but could they get far enough ahead of the Tuareg to have time to make use of it?

The muddy Niger also took on a new look. Its normally placid flow had churned into bubbling white rapids. The shallow water rushed over glass-smooth stones and swirled into pools dug by spinning pebbles. "Hand me a banana, Mat," Graeme shouted as he drove.

"Mat?"

"Matilda, right?"

"Tillie."

She reached over the seat, pulled two bananas from the bunch, and handed one to Graeme. Then she leaned back, peeled her breakfast, and tried to keep her thoughts as far as she could from the man beside her. It was impossible to talk over the roar, which was too bad because conversation would have distracted her. As it was, she had the dubious privilege of being able to study her companion at length—something she refused to do! She didn't want to waste any energy dwelling on an adventurer who courted danger and was probably up to no good.

Better to think about her neem trees. She was sure the small staff PAAC had employed for her could look after them. Still, it bothered her to be away.

Mat. What kind of a dumb nickname was that? Better than Matilda, anyway. She wished Arthur wouldn't call her that. Even *darling* got on her nerves. Mat. It made her sound tough. Spunky. Bold.

Never mind! she scolded herself, realizing where her thoughts had drifted again. *You have more important things to figure out.* Such as how to get word to Hannah and Arthur, what to do if the Tuareg got their hands on her, and what the writing in the amulet meant.

Mornin', glory, he'd said to her. She sort of liked that. As though she were a flower. A growing thing. She liked the way he'd smiled at her, too. Calm and assured, even though he'd already seen the camels. Even though she looked like a dust mop on a bad day.

Tillie's relentless thoughts drifted from her banana to his hands. His long fingers spread over the steering wheel, and he worked the rattling gearshift expertly. He had rolled his window down, and his hair blew away from his face, revealing the hard planes and angles. How had he broken his nose? Why did he always grit his teeth? She could see the dust settling on the ends of the long black lashes that framed his deep-set eyes.

Where had this man come from? What had brought him to Africa? The amulet, of course. The journal of Mungo Park. The treasure of Timbuktu. But why did he look so comfortable here? So much more at home than Arthur.

At the thought of her almost-fiancé, Tillie shook herself mentally. *Will you stop already? The best thing you can do about Graeme McLeod is ignore the man!* Sufficiently chastised, she settled back in her seat, determined to follow her own counsel.

They drove without speaking, and Tillie watched the rapids melt away and the river return to placid brown.

Finally, Graeme pulled the Land Rover to a stop and broke the quiet. The sun had passed its zenith and was lowering in the west, and the rays filtered through the dust settling around the vehicle. "It's time to eat and gas up," he said. He reached behind him, opened a box, and took out two more bananas.

Tillie mentally groaned in hunger, but she said nothing as he offered her one.

"Banana?"

"Thanks." She began to peel. "Graeme, I'm glad you're taking me to Timbuktu instead of . . . well, what I mean is, I'm thankful for the Land Rover. I don't think I'd do too well on a camel."

"You'd be fine on a camel." He smiled at her. "The skirt might be a little awkward."

"I guess it would."

Tillie took another bite and looked out the window, suddenly uncomfortable. Though there was nothing overly personal in the comment, the look in his eyes had held a warm awareness. All she'd intended to do was thank him, not draw his attention to herself. That was the last thing she wanted.

In fact, she told herself stubbornly, at this moment what she wanted most was a good hot meal and a warm bed. At home. With Hannah. Surrounded by security and safety.

Are you sure? a soft voice within her inquired, and she shifted uneasily in her seat. Of course she was sure! And yet . . . she couldn't deny that the escape that morning had done more than startle her. She'd felt a rush of excitement when the Land Rover roared out of the clearing and she saw that they had outmaneuvered the *amenoukal*.

"I'm glad you spotted the Tuareg this morning," she said, trying to dispel the awkwardness of the moment. "I don't know what they want with the amulet, but they're sure determined."

"What they want is the treasure."

She studied him for a moment. "What do you want, Graeme? Are you after treasure, too?"

He inclined his head. "Of a sort."

"What sort? You told me you've been tracking this down for more than a year."

"I have. And I'll get it. No matter what."

"No matter what? No matter if someone gets hurt? No matter if you have to do something illegal? No matter what happens to me?"

His profile hardened. "Those are not my primary concerns right now. I've got to get to Timbuktu before the Tuareg do."

Tillie stared at him. "So you don't care whether I'm safe or not?"

"You're safe."

"But you don't care. I don't know where the treasure is, so I'm useless to you, right?"

"You'll slow me down."

"Wait a minute." Tillie flung the banana peel to the floor. "You mean if I'd been outside the Land Rover this morning and the Tuareg had gotten too close, you would have driven off without me? You'd have left me there?"

"Hold it, now!" Graeme shot her a frowning glance. "Where'd you get that idea?"

"That's the most selfish thing I've ever heard. If I inconvenience you, you'll just go off and leave me."

"Inconvenience me? No. However, if you continue to get on my nerves . . . ," he growled.

"If I slow you down, you'll leave me in the desert. You'll let the Tuareg have me."

His scowl deepened. "Right now, I'd consider personally feeding you to a crocodile," he snapped, throwing his own banana peel into the paper sack behind him. Without another word he threw open the door and stomped outside. Turning in her seat, Tillie watched as he lifted the spare container of gasoline from its bracket and emptied it into the tank. He was blazing mad—hotter than the afternoon sun beating on her back.

Maybe she'd been wrong to question him. Maybe she'd judged him unfairly. Hannah had certainly warned her not to be judgmental if she didn't want to be judged herself.

Graeme stormed back to the Land Rover, climbed in, and turned the key in the ignition. The Land Rover sputtered to life, then coughed and died. He pumped the gas pedal several times, then tried the key again. Nothing.

As he pounded the steering wheel, Tillie decided she'd better not criticize his motives again. She had no idea where he stood in this entanglement with the Tuareg—and if Arthur was close on their heels, it wouldn't be long before she could turn the whole mess over to him and the government.

Until then, it seemed much wiser not to further antagonize the man who, for the present, held her safety in his hands.

"Great. Just great." Graeme ground his teeth. Turning the key now caused only a useless whirring under the hood.

"What's wrong with it?" Tillie asked.

"How should I know?" he snapped. "The temperamental thing has done this to me over and over. Slide over here and start it when I tell you to."

She watched as he opened the hood to pour a little gasoline into the carburetor. His faded shirt flapped open in the breeze, and he wiped a greasy finger on his jeans.

"Now!" he yelled. "Crank her up."

She turned the key, and the Land Rover whined down to nothing, like the last sobs of an exhausted, crying child. She groaned.

Disgusted, he slammed down the hood and strode to the back of the vehicle. She turned to find him stuffing blankets and bananas into an old army-green knapsack.

"What are you doing? Aren't we going to try to start the Land Rover again?"

"The Land Rover's dead." He slung the pack onto his back. "We're on foot now. I suggest you get ready to do some walking."

"But that's crazy! The *amenoukal* will catch up to us if we don't have the Land Rover." She scanned the barren countryside. "Maybe there's a village around here with a mechanic or something. . . ."

Graeme looked up and shook his head. "This is the edge of the Sahel. There's no mechanic from here to Algeria. This buggy needs a new starter, and we sure aren't going to find one out here."

Tillie swallowed the dry lump in her throat and frowned down at her wrinkled skirt. Thorny seeds in the zak grass made her leather sandals impractical. Wistfully, she thought of the white tennis shoes parked in her closet in Bamako. Worse than the sandals, though, was the fact that she didn't have a hat. Without one, she'd burn to a crisp.

She eyed the supplies in the back of the Rover. How could they carry enough water for both of them? And what if the Tuareg—

Her frantic thoughts were disturbed by the sound of stomping footsteps. She looked up in time to see Graeme disappear around a clump of bushes beside a bend in the river.

Well! He was gone. He really had left her. She could go where she wanted now. Of course, there was only one path to Timbuktu, and it followed the course of the Niger River. The *amenoukal* was on the path, certainly not far behind. And Arthur was surely on it, too. If she stayed here . . .

The image of climbing a tree and hiding until it all blew over inserted itself in her brain. Safety. Security. Escape. Why not? It was crazy to think God had sent her into this mess. A loving God wouldn't allow such a thing. Would he?

No. Of course not. There was nothing for her to hold on to out here at the edge of the desert. She had no weapon. No food. No one to guide her but a renegade who would abandon her—make that *had* abandoned her—at the first opportunity.

"Some trust in chariots and some in horses." Hannah's voice washed over Tillie like a spray of warm water. *"But we trust in the name of the Lord our God."*

Squeezing her eyes shut, Tillie swallowed at the knot in her throat. *Trust in the Lord.* She doused her doubt with the comforting words of Hannah's verse and gradually felt her heart grow calm again.

OK, Lord. No chariots, horses, or Land Rovers. I will trust in the name of the Lord my God.

Breathing a prayer for safety and guidance, she grabbed the last bunch of bananas and a ragged blanket and jogged after Graeme. As she rounded the bushes, she saw him standing on a grassy knoll a few yards away. He watched her approach, his mouth drawn into a tight line.

Surprise tumbled down her spine like spilled marbles. "I didn't expect you to wait."

"I didn't expect you to come."

She stopped to catch her breath. "I'm here." She blinked at the sweat stinging her eyes and brushed her thick braid over her shoulder. "Believe me, there are a thousand places I'd rather be right now, but I know I have no choice but to go with you."

"I'm flattered." Graeme turned and strode down the knoll.

Tillie walked beside him, her skirt picking up prickly zak seeds and her sandals catching in the tufts of grass growing along the river's edge. Curse her careless tongue! She hadn't meant to offend him. After all, he'd been nothing but civil to her. He had saved her from the *amenoukal*. He had fed her, given her a place to sleep.

And he'd called her *Mat*.

Oh, she wished this whole crazy thing would be over— God's will or not.

Graeme looked over his shoulder at the woman trying her best to match his stride on the narrow road. He knew he should slow down, but the sun was setting fast, and he needed to find shelter. One more day and the Land Rover would have gotten them to Timbuktu. Now it was impossible to know how long the trek might go on—if they could even manage to stay ahead of the Tuareg.

"You said you'd tell me more about the Tuareg," Tillie said. Her train of thought startled him with its similarity to his own. "Would you fill me in now?"

He walked on in silence a few paces before speaking. "What do you want to know?"

His tone of voice was anything but encouraging. "Everything."

"I've spent almost two years working on this case. If I told you everything I knew about the Tuareg, it would take a month."

"Case? Are you working on a case? You never told me that."

"You never asked."

"Whom do you work for?"

"I thought you wanted to know about the Tuareg."

"I want to know whom you work for!"

"I'll tell you about the Tuareg." He kept his eyes on the path. "The Tuareg are a nomadic race. They live in flat-topped tents made out of sheepskin or cowhide. They measure wealth by the number of dromedaries they own, and they increase their wealth by stealing them. *Tuareg* in Arabic means 'abandoned of God.'"

"Nobody's abandoned by God."

"I wouldn't be so sure about that."

"Maybe you're not. But I am."

"You haven't met the Tuareg."

"Oh, yes I have—the one on the white camel. It doesn't matter what people do or how they live. God's love never abandons us."

He gave her a sideways glance. "Always been this naive, Mat?"

"It's called faith. Believing even though you don't have proof."

"I'd call it chuckleheaded." He could hardly fathom that

a woman who had her feet planted in the firm soil of science and logic would give any credence to the implausible hocus-pocus of religion. He had no doubt that God had set the world spinning. However, he was equally convinced that, having done so, God had abandoned his creation to its own fate long ago.

"Let's say someone does something bad to you," he proposed, deciding to toy with her a little before his rational arguments devoured her. "I mean really bad. Are you going to stick around?"

"All right," she jumped in. "Let's imagine you're a father, and your son . . . oh, what's the worst thing you can think of? Maybe your son uses illegal drugs or robs people or . . . what? What's the worst thing a son could do?"

Graeme felt his throat tighten. "Kill someone."

She nodded. "Say your son kills someone. Are you going to abandon him? Are you going to stop loving him? Are you going to deny that he's your son?"

"Maybe."

"Of course not. Anyway, God doesn't. He loves us too much."

"You sound awfully sure of that for someone who's tramping toward the desert with a band of Targui chasing her."

He watched a smile play around her full lips. "I wondered about it, you know," she said softly. "It's not like I wasn't scared when the *amenoukal* grabbed me. But then I remembered I'm never walking alone. I will fear no evil."

So much for logic.

As they went on in silence, Graeme watched the sun go down for the second day along the Niger. Another black night was coming on, and he wondered where they could rest without the protection of the Land Rover. Tillie might fear no evil, but he knew enough to be wary. They would need a place safely away from the river but close enough that they could find their way back to the road in a hurry if the need arose. Which it just might.

Behind him, the woman trotted to keep up with his long strides. What good was reason in the face of blind trust? All the same, something about her wide-eyed gullibility drew him. To his surprise, he found himself wanting to take care of her. Protect her. Maybe he was getting soft in the head. Or maybe just being near a woman had stirred something inside him. Some buried tenderness. When he listened to her talk, her voice soft yet confident, he half wanted to believe in her version of God himself. Crazy.

Better to concentrate on things he was certain of. Like the Tuareg.

"Did you know the Tuareg call themselves 'the people of the veil'? They're Moslems, but most of them aren't very religious. They use sand rather than water for their ablutions. Timbuktu is their seasonal camp, and they don't venture much farther south. Certainly not into Bamako. They spend four months a year on the river before heading into the desert."

As he said the last words, he turned off the rutted road toward a tangle of thorny brush, tamarinds, and tall grass.

This would have to do.

Tillie followed Graeme into the brush, slapping at the mosquitoes that danced around her head and arms.

"Where are you going?" she called after him. She tried to keep up, but she was forced to stop several times to yank her skirt free of thorns. "Graeme?"

Just as she was certain she had lost him in the darkness and brush, she spotted a spark of light deeper in the tangle. She pushed through to it—and caught her breath. The heavy growth had indicated a stream—a tiny tributary just beyond the edge of a small glade. Crouched over a small fire, Graeme looked up at her.

"Ready for a banana?"

She stepped into the clearing. "Frankly, I could eat a horse right now. But a banana will do."

Graeme dragged a couple of battered bananas out of his knapsack. "If you want to wash up first, I imagine the stream's fairly clean."

Tillie looked down at her scratched and bitten legs. Her hair hadn't been combed for almost two days now, and it was tangled with small twigs and burrs. Her cotton skirt hung tattered and her sleeveless blouse gaped at the neck. "Do you have a comb I could borrow?"

He stood and stretched. The hem of his shirt lifted as he flexed his arms. Tillie tiredly watched his biceps bunch up like a pair of coconuts and then relax. He leaned over and rummaged through his sack again. "Here," he said, tossing her a small black comb.

Too thankful for the comb and the promise of water to be bothered much about clean clothes, she walked through the brush to the nearby brook. Sitting by the water, she took the pins and rubber bands out of her tangled hair. She had always worn it long because Hannah had never wanted to cut it. In fact, all three Thornton sisters had long hair in various shades of blonde and red. Hannah had taught them to braid, and from that time Tillie had never been without her thick, straw-colored plait.

Just as she did every morning, she worked her hair loose through her fingers and began to comb it—strand by tangled strand, front to back. When she had finally unknotted the last piece, she leaned over the stream and scooped a double handful of water to splash over her gritty face.

"Maybe this would help."

Graeme's voice startled her into dropping the water. Unnoticed, he had slipped up beside her to the bank. He dipped a cloth into the stream, wrung the fabric out, and spread it in his hand.

"Allow me," he whispered.

She drew back. "Really, I—"

"You always this skittish around men, Mat?"

"No, I'm . . . I'm engaged . . . sort of, and I don't think . . ." She caught her breath as his fingers brushed a wisp of hair from her forehead and he ran the cold cloth across her cheek. "I don't think—," she repeated, slightly dazed.

He smiled lazily. "I don't think it's going to matter."

Watching him as he wiped her face, Tillie became aware of her shallow breath and thudding heartbeat. His eyes were luminous, almost gentle. The rigid line had melted away from his mouth, leaving his lips pliant and compelling. This Graeme was not the hardened man who snapped at her and slammed his fist into nonfunctioning Land Rovers. Neither was this the rogue who had wheeled around the corner and rescued her from a blue-veiled Targui.

This was someone she'd never met.

"Who are you?" she murmured.

"Who do you think I am?"

"I don't know. One minute you're telling me I'm useless to you, then you're threatening to turn me into crocodile bait, then you're walking off into the desert without me. And now here you are washing my face."

"Something wrong with that?"

"I've never met anyone like you."

He was silent a moment. "I've never met anyone like you."

She pulled back from his hand as it rested against her cheek. "You don't know anything about me."

"I know you plant trees at the PAAC research station in Bamako. I know you're engaged to some English guy. Sort of."

"He asked me to marry him. So I'm engaged."

"Not unless you said yes."

"I haven't had time yet! Look, Arthur Robinson is a good man. He's moral, and he has a solid, respectable job, and he's . . . he's very . . . very . . . nice." The word sounded anemic, even to her own ears.

"Does he take care of you when you're scared?"

Her eyes flashed. "I'm not scared."

"You should be. You're in a fine mess. But you shouldn't be scared of me."

"Then why won't you tell me who you are?"

Abruptly, Graeme stood to his full height and walked back toward the fire. Following close on his heels, Tillie stared at his broad back.

"You know who I am," he said.

"No, I don't. Why are you in Africa? What do you do for a living? Why have you been chasing that document?"

A thought suddenly hit her . . . powerful and undeniably logical. "You're not one of those book thieves, are you? Stealing rare old manuscripts from the library in Timbuktu and then selling them on the European black market?"

Graeme studied the ground. "You know about those books?"

"Arthur told me." She crossed her arms, pinning him with a disgusted look. "This is great! Just great! I'm traveling across the desert with a kidnapper and a thief!"

He hunkered down beside the fire and pulled a banana from the stalk. "I'm Graeme McLeod," he said, his voice barely audible below the chorus of night insects. "I'm not a thief; I'm a writer. Freelance. I work on grants from various places, among them the British Museum, *National Geographic,* and the Smithsonian."

Her eyes narrowed in disbelief. "A writer? Where's your notebook? Your computer?"

Graeme peeled a long strip down his banana. "My stuff's in the knapsack."

Tillie didn't know whether or not to believe him. He certainly didn't look or act anything like a writer, at least by what little she knew of writers. "And you came all the way to Mali to find out about the Mungo Park rumor."

"Yes."

"Why?"

"Because the British Museum is paying me to."

"Why?"

"Because the museum and I are interested in Mungo Park."

Tillie shook her head in frustration. He was the most confusing and irritating man she had ever met. With his propensity for talking in circles, she wouldn't have been surprised to learn he was a politician.

"I'm interested in Park for a lot of reasons," Graeme explained quietly. "I grew up on stories about him. My mother was from Scotland. Mungo Park is my ancestor." He stopped speaking for a moment as Tillie absorbed this news. "My reason for being here in Mali," he went on, "is to find out what happened to him. Mungo Park disappeared without a trace. He left a wife, Ailie, and several children."

"And a journal."

"He'd written a complete journal of his journey down the Niger. He wanted to find its mouth, but he disappeared six hundred miles from his goal. So did the journal. I want to know what happened to him."

He met and held her gaze. "And I think, with the help of the clue in your amulet, I'm going to find out."

FOUR

In the low light of the dying fire, Tillie could make out little more than the solid bulk of Graeme's shoulders, the glint of a twisted copper-and-brass bracelet on his wrist, and the unwavering focus of his blue-green eyes. A writer? A journalist?

She conjured pale fingers pecking away at a computer keyboard. A sterile office. Rows of books. Framed university degrees on the walls. Not this hard-muscled pirate! Graeme was an adventurer, an explorer, a daredevil. Something menacing clung to him, something that announced that he could not be pushed around, while at the same time daring people to try. She had come to realize he gave away only very small pieces of himself, unwilling to let anyone know him too quickly or too well. He made her nervous . . . edgy. Chilled, she rubbed her bare arms.

"Cold?"

When she nodded, he stirred the fire with a stick. Sparks burst upward, a shower of orange stars. A tiny flame came to life and licked the edges of the charred wood. The heat warmed her, even though she knew the light would beckon more mosquitoes.

"Tired?" Graeme asked, his deep voice even.

"My feet hurt."

"Tomorrow won't be any better."

"I know."

She watched him run a hand behind his collar as if to unknot the kinks in his neck. He raked his fingers through his hair and gave his head a shake. "I'm bushed. Time to sack out."

Bending to unbuckle a sandal, Tillie let out a deep breath. There was so much more about this man she wanted to know, but his terse sentences were devoid of all but basic information. Eat. Drink. Walk. Sleep. His questions were no better. Hot? Cold? Tired? The message was always the same. Don't ask about me, and I won't ask about you.

Well, so what? Why should she care if the high-and-mighty Graeme McLeod was aloof and uncommunicative? She didn't need to know anything from the man but the direction to Timbuktu. And tonight she was too tired to concentrate on anything but her aching feet. The chilly desert breeze on her bare arms made her shiver.

She studied him as he pulled a threadbare blanket from the knapsack and spread it on the stubbly ground. Close quarters again. She shut her eyes. *Just don't let him touch me, Lord, because I'm afraid of what I'd do—*

What you're afraid of, that mocking inner voice spoke up, *is that you'd like it.*

The thought stiffened her tired spine, and her eyes widened a fraction. Ridiculous. Absurd. Totally impossible. There was nothing about this man that she liked or respected.

Liar.

She didn't dignify the accusation with a response. Instead, she continued her study of her companion, watching as he stretched out full length, cocked his hands behind his head, and shut his eyes. When she heard his breathing deepen and felt sure he was asleep, she left the fire and sat down on her half of the blanket. Listening to the growing sounds of night, she threaded her fingers through her hair and began to braid it. Silky and thick, the familiar waves comforted her. The rhythmic motion of twisting the three hanks together began to calm her. This ritual she knew. She could braid anywhere, even at the edge of the desert in a night as dark as onyx. She could relax, let the tension ebb, bathe herself in the peace of one thing that would not change.

Behind her, a warm hand circled the plait. "Leave it down."

She stopped, her heart racing. "I sleep with it braided."

"Don't. Leave it down."

She dropped her hands and turned to him. He wore that look again—the one she had seen only once or twice since they'd met. Tender. Searching. Almost accessible. It was the look of a man who had chipped a small opening in the stony barricade around his heart.

His eyes beckoned. She looked away. She had no desire to know this man. She didn't want to see inside his soul. She belonged to Arthur . . . to her work . . . to God. Graeme wasn't a believer. The hard fact firmed her resolve to stay distant. She couldn't let her feelings get in the way of what she knew was important and right.

"I always sleep with my hair braided," she repeated quietly. She finished the plait, wrapped a rubber band around the end, and tossed it behind her. Willing herself not to think about the man beside her, she lay down with her back to him. Closing her eyes, she concentrated on Arthur. He liked her hair, and he never once mentioned the braid. It didn't seem to bother him the way it bothered Graeme. Arthur was definitely better suited to her.

Arthur's face swam before her eyes as exhaustion made its inroads. Pale blue eyes. Light brown hair. She could hear his voice now, so proper and British. All his plans. All his goals. *Darling, Matilda. Darling.* He thought she was charming, lovely. He wanted to marry her. Marry her . . .

"Sweet dreams," someone murmured beside her.

It wasn't Arthur's voice. Nor was it his face that carried her into sleep.

Tillie woke with a start. A hard hand gripped her arm, and she felt a heavy breath on her neck.

"Be quiet!" Graeme hissed. "Don't move."

She swallowed and lifted her head, peering into the early morning mist that had rolled off the river. "What? What is it?"

"I hear someone out there." He listened. "Great. Don't those guys ever sleep?"

Adrenaline coursed through her. "Graeme?" She sat up. At first she could hear nothing. Then she began to distinguish a distant jingle, a low grunt, human voices. The Tuareg caravan.

Her breath hung as she leaned back into Graeme, instinctively seeking his protection. The *amenoukal* would find her. Her footprints were obvious in the dry dust of the road. What would happen? What would he do to her when he got his hands on her?

"I don't know where the treasure is." The words

tumbled out. "I don't know where it is, Graeme. I don't know what Mungo Park meant—"

"Calm down." Crouching behind her, he pulled her against his chest and wrapped his arms around her shoulders. "Listen," he whispered in her ear, "if we let them pass, they'll think we're still ahead."

"Our footprints are all over the road. They'll know where we stopped."

"We'll have to count on the fog. It's thick this morning. They'll have found the Land Rover, so they know we're on foot. Nothing we can do about that. Just be still. When we're sure they've gone on past, we'll take off behind them."

"I can't stop shaking," she whispered hoarsely.

He rubbed his hand down her arm. "Fear no evil. Remember?"

Chagrined, she let out a groan. "I'm a jellyfish."

She could feel his chuckle through her back. "Don't be so hard on yourself. If God's looking down on this little spot of Africa at all, he's got to be wearing a smile. Matilda Thornton: pillar of faith."

Tillie shut her eyes. She was weak, and Graeme knew it. When put to the test, her faith didn't hold up. She couldn't keep from trembling and wishing for escape. As for trusting in the promises of God . . . well, she was trying. That was the best she could do right now.

As the sounds of the caravan grew louder, Graeme tensed behind her, his iron arms still around her. Tillie waited, barely daring to breathe as she listened to the occasional cluck of the Tuareg camel drivers and the steady tinkling of saddle bells.

She fought against the lump in her throat. Graeme had

every right to mock. Where was her faith? She closed her eyes. *Fear no evil . . . Thy rod and thy staff . . . valley of the shadow . . .*

The sounds of the caravan stopped. A shout of discovery rang out from one of the Tuareg, and the air suddenly filled with excited cries.

"Game's up," Graeme growled against her ear. "They've pegged us. We're going to have to make a run for it. Follow me."

He grabbed the knapsack, leapt to his feet, and started through the brush in a line parallel with the river. Tillie scrambled after him, her heart in her throat. A few yards away, she could hear the shouts of the Tuareg as they plunged into the thicket on their camels.

"Can you swim?" Graeme called over his shoulder.

"Yes," she huffed. But a river filled with hippos . . . crocodiles . . . snakes. *No, Lord. Please, not that.*

Sucking in deep breaths of crisp morning air, she ran, heedless of the soft earth giving way beneath her feet. *Run!* she told herself. *Run, Tillie!* She hurdled a fallen branch, skidded down a stony escarpment, splashed through a stream. Climbing the bank on the far side, she tripped over a root and sprawled to the ground. Mud smeared the side of her cheek. The taste of metal filled her mouth. Blood.

Crashing sounds of the Tuareg camels closed in. Bells. Shouts. She pushed onto her elbows. *Got to run, Tillie! Get up! Get away!*

"Come on, Tillie-girl." Graeme was there, pulling her upright, dragging her behind him.

"You go," she puffed, her lungs bursting. "They want me.

They'll keep me alive for the treasure. But you . . . you . . . just go on."

"Move your feet, lady! We're not stopping now!"

They burst through the underbrush and out onto the sandy bank of the Niger. Fifty yards away, the Tuareg *amenoukal,* who had waited for his prey to be flushed out, swung around on his saddle.

"Oh, no!" Tillie swallowed a gulp of air. "Graeme, look!"

Tall, regal beneath his blue veil, the chieftain narrowed his dark hooded eyes. *"Enta da!"* he bellowed, lifting a scrap of pale blue cloth like a battle banner. *"Eglir! Tek! Tek!"*

"My skirt," she mouthed. "Graeme, he's got a piece of my skirt." It must have torn off as she waded through the thorny brush into the clearing the night before.

"We couldn't have left a better calling card." Graeme raked his fingers through his hair. "Come on; let's head downriver until we can find a place to cross."

"Io! Io!" At the beckoning of their leader, the Tuareg warriors swung back through the brush toward the river. The *amenoukal* spurred his dromedary full tilt down the road.

"Run!" Graeme shouted. "Run!"

Tillie sprinted behind him down the road. "O Lord, O Lord," she chanted with every breath. "Help, help, please help!"

They followed the road around a bend in the river. Graeme began to outpace her, and she knew she didn't have much left. In a minute he'd head into the river. She could hear the camels closing in. *Go, Tillie, go!* Her thighs ached. A sharp pain knotted her side. *Help, Lord, help!* She was slowing.

"Hey!" Graeme shouted a few feet ahead.

Swiping at her eyes, Tillie slogged toward him in a slow-motion nightmare. Her sandals weighed two tons. Her mouth was a dry crack in her face. What was Graeme shouting about? He ran toward her, pulled her toward the river, forced her legs to run.

A putrid, musky smell engulfed her. She couldn't breathe. Mere paces behind her, the mounted Targui lunged. His hand latched onto her collar. He jerked. Buttons flew. Tillie screamed.

Her feet flew out from under her, and she hit her head on something hard. As her vision swam, she realized she hadn't been lifted up—she'd been thrown down. Down into something. And that something was sliding into the current of the muddy Niger.

Tillie rolled to her knees, aware that the dromedaries were charging into the river after them. Graeme thrust a short pole into her arms. "Push!" he shouted, plunging an oar into the water. "Push out into the river!"

She jammed the pole into the river bottom. The tiny boat inched toward midstream. On the bank, two native fishermen shouted curses at the white-skinned thieves who were making off with their dugout. But the danger lay with the lead camel—the *amenoukal*'s white camel—which continued making its way in the powerful river. The veiled Targui snarled at Tillie and unsheathed his gleaming broad-sword.

"Graeme," she uttered in rigid disbelief. His back to the

shore, he was frantically pulling the rope that held the anchor. "Graeme . . ."

The *amenoukal* raised his weapon and let it fall in an arc aimed at Graeme's neck.

"Graeme!" she screamed. "Watch out!"

Tillie heaved her pole out of the water and swung it over her head to block the attack. The shock of the broadsword smacking into the pole reverberated down her arms. The wood broke in two and hurtled through the air as she fell backward to the floor of the boat and breath whooshed from her lungs.

Graeme dropped the stone anchor beside her, and the boat swung free. Using the broken pole, he maneuvered it toward midriver. Caught by the current, the dugout drifted away from the *amenoukal*'s floundering dromedary.

"Hey!" Graeme laughed out loud. "We did it!" He reached down, grabbed her around the shoulders, and pulled her toward him, planting a kiss on her cheek. "We did it!"

"Did we?" She grabbed the side of the boat, as stunned by his kiss as by their escape. "Are you sure?"

"Take a look."

The *amenoukal,* a demonic vision brandishing a broad-sword, faded from view in the river mist. She let out a breath. "We got away."

"Darn right we did."

"Thank God." Relief coursed through her. She hugged her knees to her chest and buried her head, fighting unex-pected tears.

"Mat—you all right?"

Unable to speak, she squeezed her eyes shut. She felt the

boat wobble as he moved to crouch in front of her. He unfolded her arms and lifted her chin.

"What's the matter?"

She shook her head. "I was so scared. I'm still scared."

"Come here." He ran his hands up her arms, pulling her closer to him. "You were a champ. You saved my life back there, you know."

Dismayed at the unexpected flood of warmth she felt for a man she shouldn't trust, she shrugged away. "He would have killed you! It's not worth it. Whatever the treasure is, it's not worth a human life."

"Nobody got hurt."

"Not this time." She met his eyes. "Look, we both know he's not going to give up. We're in this leaky little boat. A boat we stole—"

"We'll get it back to the fishermen."

"Maybe so. But how far can we go? The river may be deep enough for a boat right here, but Arthur told me it's been so dry there are places you can just about wade across the Niger. And we're moving at a snail's pace. He's going to catch up, Graeme, and I'm not about to sit by and watch him behead you. It's all a misunderstanding, anyway. The treasure, the tree-planting woman, all of it. Once I explain that I don't know anything about any treasure—"

"Explain? Was that a man you can explain things to?" The corner of his mouth tipped up. "Come on, Mat, cheer up. We won this round."

She let her focus drift to the shore. Every time she looked at Graeme, she saw that sword swinging toward his neck. Her stomach turned over. She didn't want him to die. Not on her account. Not on any account. She glanced at him again.

"Mat," he said, taking her hand between both of his. "Tillie . . . there's nothing wrong with feeling scared when the situation fits. It doesn't mean you're weak. It doesn't mean you've failed. You've got a strength, something inside you. It's something I've never seen. Back on the road yesterday you told me you didn't believe God ever abandons us. So this morning in the brush and on the river . . . did he?"

"No. His love never leaves us." Pulling her hand away from his, she stared out at the swirling brown river. "But that doesn't mean we live under some lucky charm, some guarantee of safety or protection. We can be victimized by circumstances like illness or accidents . . . or by human evil. It's just that during those times we know he's there, loving us, helping us endure. All our lives, in whatever we face, he loves us and stays with us."

Graeme studied her face for more than a minute, his eyes searching hers as if he could read answers in them. "If you honestly believe the God of the entire universe is with you through every problem, and he's always there to love you no matter what, that's something. That's really something."

"I'm sure of it." She managed a smile. "And maybe because of it, I don't want to see you get hurt."

"Aw, I thought your worries had something to do with the prospect of never seeing my handsome face again." He sat back and regarded her with a lazy grin. "Now I find out you just want to make sure I don't die before you can save my sinful soul. Baptize me in the waters of the Jordan.

Pluck me from the fires of hell. Rescue me from eternal damnation. Wash my transgressions in the crystal—"

"Enough!" Tillie had to smile. "In the first place, *I* can't save your sinful soul. That's between you and Christ. In the second place, I'm beginning to like you better than I should. And third, if you've never felt the peace—"

"Whoa, let's go back to the second place."

She stared at him, nonplussed. Why had she let *that* come out? "Let's don't."

"Let's do." His voice was quiet as he spoke. "Look, Tillie, the truth is, I didn't plan on you any more than you planned on me. I didn't count on . . . ." He paused, searching for words. "I didn't expect to . . . it's just that I'm a basic kind of guy, you know? Happy, sad, mad—that's about the range of my emotional makeup. I like to eat, sleep, take a hot shower when I can get one. I figure you live and then you die, and that's about it. But while I'm here, I like to do things that make me feel good." He bent and brushed a kiss on her lips. "Like kiss a beautiful woman."

As he drew back, she covered her mouth with her fingers. His kiss, even though it had been feather light, burned in a way Arthur's never had. Confused, she stared into his eyes as if he could explain why. He shouldn't have done it. She shouldn't have wanted him to. But he had, and she had. And now her heart hammered in her ears, and her lungs couldn't seem to take in enough air.

"Looks like we made off with a mess of fish," he said, turning away. "No wonder those two fellows were so mad. We stole their boat *and* their dinner."

"Mmm," she murmured, barely hearing him. She had

wanted him to kiss her. She couldn't deny it. She looked down into the boat. The minute Graeme had grabbed her off the street, she had felt them moving toward this moment. Now it was done, and she had betrayed the good, Christian man who loved her.

"It's really more a dugout than a boat," he said. "No seats."

She stared blankly at the rough fishing net, a length of damp rope, and the fish. A dozen or more perch lay squirming wide-eyed in a waterproof basket filled with water.

She couldn't let it happen again. She wouldn't. Graeme was not the right kind of man for her, no matter how attractive she found him. Come to think of it, maybe that was why she found him so attractive. Because he was dangerous, risky, all wrong.

You don't even know who he really is, she chastised her heart. *You've seen so many sides of him you don't know which is the real Graeme McLeod.*

What about his quest for the document and the treasure? Was he a treasure seeker like the Tuareg? Or had she guessed right about him being part of the rare-book smuggling ring? If not that, then probably some other illegal venture. Whatever he was, Graeme was not for her. She couldn't fall victim to his rugged looks and his air of adventure when she knew his heart wasn't right.

Be strong in the Lord, she told herself. *Be of good courage.*

"Did you notice that village we passed a few minutes ago?" he was saying. "I bet those fishermen live there. We'll send their boat back to them once we hit Segou."

Tillie had not seen the village. In fact, she had done

nothing but think of the escape. And then the kiss. Biting her lip, she hugged herself against the chill morning air. She had to get past it and move on toward her goal of handing her problems with the Tuareg to the authorities. Once she could get away from Graeme, the turbulent feelings he aroused inside her would ebb. Everything would be the same again. Normal. Comfortable. Predictable.

Graeme was handling the oar, expertly steering them midcurrent around floating driftwood and an occasional jutting boulder. She watched him, telling herself to recognize the truth. He was just an ordinary man; his kiss had been nothing more than a gut response to their escape; her inner turmoil was merely lack of sleep and a good meal.

"You've been on a boat before," she said, making conversation.

"Haven't you?"

"Sure. But you're good at rowing. Last time I tried it, I went in circles."

He smiled, his eyes crinkling a little at the corners. "I guess in my line of work I've learned to run just about anything that moves. Boats. Motorcycles. Hot-air balloons. I ran a train once. Kabul, Afghanistan. Great place."

"Can you fly a plane?"

"Never actually done it, but I've watched the procedures often enough. I reckon I could."

She lifted an eyebrow. "A plane is pretty complicated."

He shrugged. "You do what you have to do. I bet you never thought you'd be able to knock away a broadsword in full swing."

She fell silent. "They'll be following us down the river, won't they?"

"Yes."

"What's the next town on the river?"

"Segou."

"There'll be a phone there. Police." She met his eyes. "I'm going to the authorities, Graeme. I want this thing over."

He leaned back in the boat and stretched out his legs. Regarding her with a look she couldn't fail to read, he laid down the oar and let the current take them.

"Funny you should feel that way," he said. "I'm just starting to enjoy myself."

The sun scorched the little boat from midmorning on. Graeme forced himself to concentrate on the pied kingfishers soaring overhead and the occasional hippopotamus that surfaced to stare at them. Hunger gnawed at his stomach— growing almost unbearable as night began to fall. Mosquitoes and flies buzzed and stung them.

He knew Tillie had to be miserable, her bare arms exposed to the mosquitoes and her skin slowly flushing from pink to dusky rose. They had eaten the last of the bananas the night before, and the little river water they let themselves drink was muddy and foul.

She didn't utter a word of complaint. Turning into herself, she fell completely silent. She bailed water. Rowed. Poled over sandbars. Slapped at mosquitoes.

Graeme found he didn't have much to say either. Not only were the hunger, insects, and heat making him miserable, concern about their pursuers nagged at him.

Often, when the boat swung around a bend in the river, he caught a glimpse of the Tuareg caravan keeping pace overland with the sluggish river. The Niger was so wide Graeme knew they were relatively safe. But they couldn't go on much longer before they would be forced to dock, and there were too many places where the water was shallow enough to let even a sand-loving camel across.

When the sun dipped behind the treetops, Graeme pulled in the oar. "Tillie, we've got to stop."

She lifted her head, her blue eyes bright in the waning sunlight. "I want to go on."

He searched her face, wishing he could read her better. Was she afraid—as she ought to be—or was she so focused on her goal of getting help in Segou that she wanted to continue? Or could it be that what made this righteous, upright young woman so determined to continue was the prospect of being alone with him one more night?

His eyes scanned her face, and another possibility presented itself. Maybe she wanted to go on because the quest intrigued and compelled her—as though she were becoming a partner with him in adventure.

Her face radiated some of the same burning intensity he had felt within himself so often. Go. Grab life by the tail. Hang on. Maybe she *did* want the challenge.

Or maybe you're just imagining things, he told himself cynically, *because you want to believe you've found someone with a similar urge to court danger, a similar drive to see what's waiting around the next corner.*

"We don't have a choice," he said. "We've got to stop. If we get hung up on a sandbar in the dark, the Tuareg will take us like candy from a jar."

"They'll take us no matter where we stop. The caravan is on the bank just over there. I've seen them following us."

"I know. Look, we'll wait until it's so dark we're sure they can't see us. Then we'll find a bushy place on the other bank to land. We can eat a bite and get some sleep."

"A nap before the moon comes up," she clarified. "Then we'll take off again. All right?"

"You're the tree-planting woman. Whatever you want."

She gave him a slight frown before taking up the oar. When darkness truly had set in, she paddled the boat to the shore opposite the Tuareg, and Graeme tied it up in a stand of thorny brake and tall reeds. Grabbing his knapsack and the basket of fish, he climbed out of the rocking boat.

"Where are you going?" Tillie whispered.

"Don't you want some dinner?"

"They'll see us if we light a fire."

"Too bad. I'm hungry."

He could hear her splashing after him, gasping as the sharp reeds jabbed at her already tender legs. If he could have picked her up and carried her, he would have. But he was sure she wouldn't let him. He'd gone too far already with the kiss.

Finding a dry spot, he stopped and flattened some reeds with his boot. "You want to watch out for crocs and hippos around here." He dropped his knapsack on the ground. "Hippos come ashore to feed at night, you know. Crocodiles sleep on the bank."

"Crocodiles? I thought you were kidding about that earlier."

"No joke." He set down the fish. "We're just now

coming into croc country. You'll probably see some tomorrow."

Her focus darted to the shoulder-high reeds, and he knew she was imagining jaws ready to clamp. Edging through the grass toward Graeme, she sat down quickly.

"I wouldn't worry about it. They really only like to eat one thing." He paused. "Blondes in skirts," he said and gave her calf a squeeze.

She nearly jumped out of her skin. "Graeme! Don't do that!"

He couldn't hold back a laugh.

"It's not funny." As though the reality of their situation finally caved in on her, Tillie dropped her head to stare at her tattered skirt. "I'm burned to a crisp, my skin is on fire from these stupid mosquito bites, I'm starving and thirsty, and I wish you would just stop irritating me."

Graeme studied the top of her head . . . her wavy hair stuck with leaves and grass seeds, the once-neat part down the center now helter-skelter, her thick braid a frayed rope. He'd asked a lot of her. After all, she was a scientist, a gardener, a lady in a skirt and sandals—not a wanderer like him on a quest for hidden treasure. He sighed. It had been such a long time since he had shared even part of his life with another human being. He'd almost forgotten what it meant to look out for anyone but himself.

What he ought to do was leave her in Segou tomorrow and finish his work alone. It would be best that way. Unfortunately, he had begun to enjoy her company a little. More than a little. She had spunk. She had chosen to take on the challenge of the trip when it would have been easier to wither in defeat. He liked that. But then, she'd made it clear that what he liked didn't matter a whole lot.

He reached into the basket beside him and pulled out two fish. Tillie Thornton would be out of the picture soon. Her boyfriend would come along and send the government after the *amenoukal*. The authorities would whisk her to safety. Without the tree-planting woman, the Tuareg would be forced to abandon their search. Then what would become of the amulet?

Graeme knew he had better plan what he'd do if someone went off with the scrap of Mungo Park's journal. He knew the basics now, but he wanted to examine the wording more closely. Something in those strange, rambling sentences had captured the imagination of the blue-veiled nomads.

Well, until he had a chance to examine the paper more closely, Tillie was just going to have to put up with sticking with him. Gutting and scaling the fish, he turned his attention to the job at hand, all the while telling himself that he wanted Tillie with him because of the journal, not because he might miss her.

Before long, Graeme had built a small fire and spitted the filets on two green sticks. A savory aroma filled the night air, and Tillie's stomach turned over in hunger. When the fish were done, he handed her a stick.

"Better than bananas," he said. "Eat up."

She took a bite and savored the mouthful. Nothing had ever tasted so good.

"Hannah never cooked fish for us," she commented. "I guess it's the Kikuyu in her. She's into beans and corn. Maybe a little goat meat."

"Hannah?"

"The woman who took care of my brother and sisters and me after our mother died. She's been living with me in Bamako."

"She'll be worried about you."

"Not Hannah. Prays too hard to worry." A smile crossed her face as she thought of the old woman's stiff curved fingers tracing over the crinkly pages of the little Kikuyu Bible she'd been given as a child. "'Do not seek what you shall eat, and what you shall drink, and do not keep worrying.'" The simple repetition of the Scripture Hannah had quoted so often comforted Tillie. "'Your Father knows that you need these things.'"

"Your father?"

She nodded. "God the Father. It's a verse out of Luke. Hannah filled our heads with Scripture for so many years that none of us can go half an hour without remembering some little scrap of a verse that fits whatever situation we're in. It's probably Hannah's greatest gift to us. I doubt a real mother could have done better."

"God the father and Hannah the mother," Graeme said, his voice tight. "Not a bad family tree."

Tillie glanced over at him. As she took another bite of fish, she wondered again at his strangeness. He was so withdrawn about himself. All she knew was that he had no mother. What had happened to her? And what had been his relationship with his father?

Her own father had been emotionally distant after his

wife's death. A lost man. Until Hannah had explained God's loving role as parent to her, Tillie had felt empty and alone. Then "God the Father" and "Hannah the mother" had been enough. More than enough.

Studying Graeme, she thought of Arthur. Arthur had no bitter edge. No buried anger. He had not been driven to hardness the way Graeme had. On the other hand, Arthur had never allowed Tillie close enough to see into his heart. He kept her distant—not out of pain as Graeme tried to do, but out of propriety. In Arthur's world, it wasn't mannerly to share deep feelings, to scream in anger, to rail at the world, to cry or laugh or shout.

With Graeme, emotion seemed torn out of him in brusque, bitter tones that sliced and hurt. Or deep belly laughs. Or the slamming of a Land Rover hood. His way was unsettling—difficult maybe—but it was real. And honest.

"What was your father like?" Tillie asked.

He looked up in surprise. "My father?"

"You haven't told me much about yourself. I thought you might tell me about your father."

Graeme scowled. "He's dead."

"I'm sorry."

"Don't waste your tears."

Tillie shrank from the venom in his voice. "You're not sorry?"

"He's dead. That's all there is to it. What good would it do to be sorry?"

She stared at him. Clearly, he wanted no part of this conversation. But tomorrow they'd reach Segou, and he'd be gone. Not two days ago she couldn't wait to be away from him; now she found she wasn't ready for their separation.

She lifted her chin. "So, how did your father die?"

"What is this—twenty questions?"

"Just one."

He hurled his stick into the air as far as he could. "Killed. Somebody killed him. No great loss."

"You hate him."

He hooked his elbows over his knees and looked up at the black sky. "Hate a dead man? Not much point in that."

"Hannah says hate and love are two rivers that rise from the same spring. She would say you hate your father so deeply because you wanted to love him deeply."

"Maybe Hannah doesn't know as much as you think."

"Maybe Hannah knows more than you're willing to admit." Tillie set aside the stick and rummaged in the knapsack until she found the comb. She unbraided her hair and began tugging the comb through the tangles. She had started to rebraid when his warm hand covered hers.

"Look at me, Tillie," Graeme said. "See this nose? He broke it twice. Drunk, of course, but I never thought that was much of an excuse for rearranging your own kid's face."

She could feel his hand tremble as it tightened on hers. He moved her fingers from her braid to the bridge of his nose and traced their tips over the lump that marred its perfect line.

"This mouth." He trailed her hand over his lips. "Busted. I was twenty-three before I saved enough money to get my teeth fixed. Jaw's still out of whack, but I'm used to it."

"Oh, Graeme." She thought of the way he gritted his

teeth, working his jaw as though pain and anger were knot-ted inside it.

"I'm not telling you this to get sympathy. You said I hate him, and I'm showing you why." He unbuttoned the first two buttons on his shirt and drew her hand to his chest. Beneath the crisp hair, she could feel a long ridge of flesh, a curved snake reminding him of the pain and evil with which he had lived.

"Knife," he explained. "My father's weapon of choice."

Her eyes met his as she struggled against a wave of grief. "Graeme, I'm sorry."

"Look, I'm not the only kid in the world who ever had a mean dad."

"But a knife? A knife goes beyond mean. It's wicked. How could a father use a knife on his own son?"

"That night . . ." His voice grew husky as he spoke. "That night, he'd been drinking as usual. He was beating on my mom, also as usual, and I stepped in. That was not usual. I'd never been big enough to stand up to him. But that night he was . . . his eyes . . . I'll never forget his eyes. Red rage. But desperation, too. And agony . . . some kind of agony. He turned on me and took out the knife. My mom screamed at him, but he never heard her. That's when he . . . when . . ."

He stopped speaking and bent over his knee. His cocked arm covered his face. Tillie laid her hand on his shoulder. What did she know about horrors like these? Drunkenness, beatings, knives. Dear God! How could any child survive such brutality?

Her eyes rested on Graeme. It was as though he were a child again, caught in the pain of remembrance, his walls down and his pain open for her to see. What could she say? How could she help?

God, can anything heal scars like these?

She touched his hair, ran her fingers through the ends of it as she imagined his mother might have done. At her touch, he looked up briefly, his face stony, then turned his eyes toward the moon. The muscle in his jaw jumped, and she reached out to stroke it, wanting to erase the clenching, wanting to comfort. But he pulled away and stood up.

"We'd better get to the boat. We need some sleep, and I don't want to sack out here with the hippos."

"Graeme, I—"

"Forget it, OK?"

Hurt washed over her at his curt dismissal. Standing stiffly, Tillie picked up the knapsack as Graeme stamped out the ashes of the fire. Taking the bag from her, he strode off toward the boat. She worked on her braid as she followed, trying to will her mind away from his words, from his emotion-choked voice. She couldn't let his pain draw her sympathies too far. She couldn't save him. Couldn't fix him. Couldn't risk that close a tie with this man.

Tomorrow, Graeme McLeod would be out of her life. She would go on with her own plans. *God's* plans. She forced her thoughts to the present . . . to tramping through the brush and finding the boat and getting some rest.

They climbed into the bobbing dugout. Tillie sighed at the cramped space. She was getting used to sleeping with no room to spare. On the damp floor, she pressed herself against the boat's hard wooden side. Graeme wedged his large frame into the tiny space at her feet.

"Are you going to sleep like that? Sitting up?"

He lifted his head. "There's not much room."

"Here, we'll sit side by side. I'll sleep with my head on your shoulder. Arthur will just have to understand."

"Arthur won't understand, but I'm not going to worry about that if you don't."

When he settled beside her, she tucked her head into the curve of his neck, and he slipped his arm around her shoulders. His cheek drifted onto her forehead. Closing her eyes, Tillie tried to sleep, but thoughts of the man beside her flowed into her mind . . . the way his hair blew back from his face, his arms bunched with muscle as he steered the boat. . . .

Squeezing her eyes tightly, she fought the desire that welled through her, a sudden urge to turn in the boat, to feel his arms caress her and let his lips find hers again.

The midnight air was filled with cries and shrieks and the quick whirring of insect wings as they flitted overhead. But all Tillie could hear was the sound of her heart thudding against the side of Graeme's chest.

And then he moved, tightened his arm around her, turned her into him. She lifted her focus to his eyes.

"Something you said earlier," she whispered. "It's not true. You're not just a basic kind of guy with no range of emotion. I don't think you truly believe we live and then we die and that's it. I think that's all a mask you wear. Under it, there's another man." She watched shadows form and vanish in his eyes. "I'm glad God saw fit to put my safety into the hands of the man behind that mask."

He was silent a moment, as if absorbing her words. "Good night, Tillie-girl," he murmured at last, his gaze on her lips.

She shivered.

FIVE

"Tillie! Tillie!" An urgent voice.

"What . . . what is it?" She opened her eyes, her chest heaving with the struggle to take in air. "Where is . . . ? Don't let them . . ." Wincing against the unseen, she peered up into the shadowed face of the man bending over her.

"It's OK, Tillie." Graeme's words soothed her. "You're here in the boat. You're safe."

"I saw the sword . . . the broadsword. Blood. Blood dripping . . ."

"It was a dream. The Tuareg aren't going to get you. Look."

She followed the line of his pointing finger across the river. On the opposite shore, pinpricks of light gleamed like the eyes of tiny devils. The caravan camp.

"Let's get out of here, Graeme," she whispered.

"You all right?"

"I'll be better when we can't see them anymore."

He nodded and looked up at the moon. "OK. We'll give it a shot."

He untied the boat, handed Tillie the oar, and poled out into the channel. The current caught the dugout, and it glided along, erasing the sight of Tuareg fires. After they rounded a bend, Tillie permitted herself to relax. She looked at Graeme as he steered, his concentration on the task. Their conversation of the evening slipped into her mind, and she studied his broken face.

How long had it been since his father had done that to him? How long since his father had died? And his mother? When had she died? What had Graeme done before she met him? For that matter, what did he really do now?

She thought about how right it felt to be with him, to trust him. When the Tuareg had been so close, she'd leaned on his strength and trusted him to keep her safe. When the *amenoukal* had raised his sword, the drive to protect Graeme had been immediate, instinctive.

Warning flags flew. *You can't save him from his past, Tillie. And you can't change his rejection of God. Don't confuse missionary zeal with affection.* She had seen too many friends—good Christian women—marry men they thought they could save or heal or fix. They ended up with marriages filled with pain and confusion. Every action has a reaction. This truth was borne out in her friends' lives as most of them ended up going to church without husbands, raising children with uncertain loyalties, and turning to friends for the spiritual communion they should have shared with their spouses.

God was there with them, but he did not prevent their poor decisions—decisions that went directly against his guidelines in Scripture—from affecting their lives.

Tillie had no desire to fall into that trap. She would put her emotions aside and remember the truth about Graeme. The only truth that really mattered: he did not share her belief in Christ. Nothing more.

Please, God, nothing more.

They floated for what seemed like hours before the sun finally showed its pale yellow head. Small villages came and went, children wading in the shallows, women fetching water, men mending nets.

Tillie dreaded spending another day under the burning rays, fighting the insects and hugging her groaning stomach. Graeme looked better than she felt. His shaggy hair blew softly back from his face, softening the hard lines of his chin and the slope of his nose. Even when relaxed, his arms and legs maintained their powerful coils, giving him physical reserves Tillie knew she lacked.

"Are you sure we'll make it to that town today?"

"Segou?" He glanced at her over his shoulder. "If we keep up this pace and don't have any more run-ins, we might get there tonight."

"What then? I mean, even after I go to the police, the Tuareg will still be hunting me. I don't know where their treasure is."

"The *amenoukal* thinks you do. You're the tree-planting woman. You're the only one who can get at the treasure."

She knotted her fingers. "But it's ridiculous. Mungo Park didn't know anything about me. The Tuareg must realize that."

"There's something about you that mesmerizes them." He laid the paddle beside him and let the current take the boat. "Still have that document?"

Tillie pulled the silver amulet from inside her blouse and took out the folded paper. Opening it across her knees, she reread the message. "'Twenty-five December, 1806.' Does that mean anything to you?"

"The last time Mungo Park was heard from was in

November of 1805. So if the document is really a piece of his journal, it means he lived many months longer. It means he could not have been killed at Bussa like everyone thought."

"Bussa? Where's that? Tell me everything you know."

Graeme leaned back in the boat. "Mungo was an adventurer. He was born in Scotland, the son of a farmer. There were thirteen children in the family. His father wanted him to become a Presbyterian minister."

Graeme spoke as if he had known Mungo Park personally—as if he were a beloved friend. Tillie felt drawn in, as she did when Hannah spun the old Kikuyu tales her father had told his children around the village fire. "Did your father tell you about Mungo Park?" she asked.

"My mother was the storyteller." He fell silent for a moment, lost in the past. When he spoke again, his voice was harder, free of emotion, as though he had wrapped up his memories and stashed them far away. "Park wanted to be a doctor, not a minister. He studied medicine at Edinburgh University, and then he worked as an apprentice for a Doctor Thomas Anderson. Anderson had a beautiful daughter, Ailie."

Tillie glanced at the paper on her lap. *"Ailie when I get back will you let me rest? Will you keep the Moors away? . . . Ailie we will buy that house on Chester Street."* She lifted her head. "Did Mungo marry Ailie?"

"Not at first. The African Association, based in London, asked him to go to Africa to gather information on the rise, the course, and the termination of the Niger River. This river—" he glanced at the water— "was a great mystery to the English, but they knew they wanted in on the gold and other treasures that had been rumored for centuries. In 1795, Park left England on the brig *Endeavour*. His first journey into Africa was a nightmare. As he traveled overland toward the Niger, he had to pay a tribute to every king along the way. Moors captured him and held him captive for more than two months. They threatened and tortured him. Finally, in July 1796, he made it to Segou."

"Segou? Where we're going!"

"That's the place."

Tillie studied the brown river with greater interest. Mungo Park could well have traveled this very spot. "What happened in Segou?"

"Mansong, the king of Segou, gave him a bag of five thousand cowrie shells. They're little rounded seashells— worth nothing now but used as currency back then. The king basically paid Park to get rid of him. Park left Segou, but nine days later he was so sick and hungry he was forced to turn back. When he got to Bamako, he was robbed again. In December 1797, he finally made it back to England."

"I'll bet he was ready to hang it up."

"Wrong. He had fulfilled only part of the African Association's request. He had determined that the Niger flowed south to north. Every previous report had insisted it flowed the other way. No one could believe it. A river that flowed away from the ocean and into a desert? Park insisted he was right. More important to him, he had not found the mouth of the river, and he was really bothered by that."

Tillie fingered the fragile document. "What about Ailie?"

"After he wrote a book, *Travels in the Interior of Africa,* he moved back to Scotland and fell in love with Ailie. They married in 1799. He set up practice as a country doctor."

"So that was it?"

"Africa called him back. He had recurring nightmares about it. He had to return. So in 1805 he took off again, leaving Ailie and their three children. This time he had a military escort. Again he had problems. His troops were undisciplined. They battled dysentery, bees, kidnapping, tornadoes, rain, vomiting, and fever. When he reached the Niger, three-fourths of his men had died and all his pack animals were either dead or stolen."

Tillie searched the paper for clues as Graeme spoke. "Did he know any of the rulers in the area? Couldn't any of them have helped him?"

"Park finally arrived at Segou again and sold the rest of his goods. But he made the mistake of telling the king, his pal Mansong, his plans for the coming of white traders and the end of Moorish domination."

"Why was that a mistake?"

"Most sources believe word of that conversation got to the Moors, who controlled trade on the Niger. Anyway, Mansong gave Park two half-rotten canoes, again eager to get rid of him. On November 16, 1805, Park wrote the last entry in his journal and sent it to England. That was the last anyone heard from him."

The sun was high in the sky now, and Tillie wiped at the perspiration on her brow. After folding the paper carefully, she slipped it back into the amulet.

When she looked up, Graeme had fastened his gaze on her. "Keep the amulet safe, Tillie. It may protect you if the *amenoukal* gets his hands on you. They're superstitious people, and they think it's charmed."

She swallowed. "I figured you would want it. It's the clue to the treasure."

"Is that what you think? That I'm after the treasure?"

"I don't know what you're after. The treasure or the story you're writing . . . or the journal itself. It would be valuable, wouldn't it?"

"The journal would be valuable to me for my book. Research." He picked up the oar and examined it. "So what are you after, Tillie? A lifetime of planting neem trees in the desert? A cushy job as a professor somewhere? Or a businessman husband, a couple of kids, and a town house in Soho?"

"Did you say 'neem trees'?" She couldn't hide her surprise. "How did you know I've been working with *Azadirachta indica?* Even Arthur doesn't know which species I've been working with."

"Arthur should pay closer attention to the woman he thinks he's going to marry. I learned that the Tuareg were on your tail, so I spent a few days finding out about the mysterious tree-planting woman. You've been in Mali almost a year. You live in a tiny three-room house with an African woman." He paused. "That would be Hannah?"

"Yes."

He nodded. "Your house has no air conditioner and only one fan. You work for PAAC, which has given you a little office and a compound that you've planted with neem saplings. You've been experimenting with species from Mexico and China. Your staff has planted sorghum and corn seedlings around the trees. Why is that, by the way?"

"Protection from the desert wind. It works very well."

"Good. You've tested the use of the neem tree for fire-wood and fence poles. You've been experimenting with the leaves and seeds. For?"

"They contain a natural pesticide. Farmers can extract it and use it against yellow-fever mosquitoes, cockroaches, beetles, worms, and other pests. It even cures stomachache."

"You've sent letters to PAAC requesting transfer into the Sahel, but they won't let you go north yet. You've also written the Malian government for donations of land in the Sahel." He lifted his dark brows. "Have I missed anything?"

Tillie turned away and looked out at the river. She loved the little compound, loved the two acres that were hers to manage. She loved the saplings, the struggling corn plants, the smell of moist, rich earth.

"You've missed a lot," she said. "I want to plant 250 miles of windbreaks across the Sahel. I want to try growing a species of leguminous tree that's been planted successfully in East Africa to help stabilize atmospheric nitrogen in the soil. I want to try using leaves and branches from my trees as fertilizer. I want to work with Malian women, educating them, and . . . and there's a lot more. A lot." She shrugged at her own grandiosity. "I have big dreams."

"And Arthur? I guess you know your sort-of fiancé's being transferred to London."

Incredulous, she stared at him. "You checked out Arthur, too?"

"I'm thorough."

Irritation swept over her. "It's really not your business, Graeme. Our future plans are between Arthur and me." But for all her protestations, she couldn't help reflecting on the truth in what Graeme said about a man paying attention to his fiancée. Arthur didn't even know the species of her trees. He'd never asked. He had been inside her compound only twice, and then it was for a quick look-see before heading off to a meeting.

What was even more important, though, was that Arthur had never asked about her dreams. He had no clue they didn't have anything to do with a flat in London or a television or life in upper-crust British society.

Sighing, Tillie gazed across at the bank. The river was deep here and more than two miles wide, so they kept the dugout no more than fifty yards from the bank. Its edges were lined with reeds, and—she caught her breath. Crocodiles. A dozen gray crocodiles were sunning themselves on the bank.

"What's wrong?" Graeme lifted his head.

She pointed.

"I figured we were about here." His voice was even. "They should thin out farther down. We'll be out of the worst of them by dark."

Along with the crocodiles, the hippo numbers had increased. It was a fertile area of the river. Dense green forest choked the west bank. The east side had been cleared for the road, which provided the crocodiles with a perfect basking place for their cold blood. Tall reeds rose from sandy peninsulas that hosted lines of white herons and sandpipers. The ever-present kingfishers swooped and plummeted into the river.

"It's going to be harder navigating here," Graeme said. "I did the Nile in Uganda once, and the hippos were a nuisance. Keep your eye on the—whoa!" He jerked the oar from the water. "Hang on, Tillie!"

She whirled around as a huge head surfaced inches from the boat. A beast with piggy eyes and round rubbery ears blew a spray of water into the air. Shouting at Tillie to use the pole, Graeme plunged the paddle into the river. The hippo easily matched their speed and opened its enormous mouth in rage at the invasion of its territory.

Tillie thrust the pole into the river, but it failed to hit bottom. The hippo's huge maw opened like a pink cave with wide flat teeth and sharp incisors instead of stalactites. The creature was so close she could see the hairs on its gray chin, the remnants of grass stuck to its tongue, the purple veins inside its cheeks. A deafening bellow rolled across the water before the hippo snapped its mouth shut and plunged under the water.

"Where is it?" Graeme demanded. "Don't lose it!"

"To your left," she shot back. "There." She watched the animal glide along beneath them. "It's following us, Graeme."

He leaned over the edge of the boat. "Whatever happens, hang on to the boat. Don't go into the water."

"What's it going to do? Why won't it leave?"

"We're in its territory." He tried to steer the boat toward the swiftest current. "I've heard of them biting canoes in half. And they'll take the head off a calf."

"But they're herbivores, aren't they?"

"Mean herbivores."

Tillie prayed in earnest as the hippo followed the tiny boat. Suddenly it surfaced again, trumpeting in anger and spewing water over Graeme through its flexible nostrils.

Graeme let out a roar of disgust, grabbed the hem of her skirt, and began to wipe his face.

"Not with my skirt!"

"Where's the hippo?"

Tillie scanned the water, but the beast had vanished.

For a moment all was calm. "Did it leave?" she whispered.

"Don't know. Let's hope so."

He leaned over. River water sloshed against the side of the boat with a gentle, slapping sound. A kingfisher cried overhead. A leaf drifted by.

"I think he's gone." Graeme let out a breath. "I bet he—"

The hippo surfaced directly under the boat. Tillie grabbed the dripping sides of the tiny craft as it lifted into the air. Graeme tried to reach out to her.

"Hang on!" he shouted as he slid along the bottom. "Don't let go!"

She clung until her white hands ached as the boat rose and fell, tipped and turned like some carnival ride gone amok. Graeme grabbed for her arm just as the boat capsized with a loud splash. Tillie tumbled into the muddy river, briefly conscious of blue sky above before she went under.

She floundered for heart-hammering seconds before flailing to the surface as she sputtered for air. Graeme shouted at her from ten yards away. He had somehow stayed with the boat. "Tillie, swim! Swim to shore."

No. She wanted to go to him, but he was floating away fast. Too fast. Her leaden legs drifted out from under her. She went under a second time. *They'll take the head off a calf.* Her thoughts reeled with images of hippo jaws ready to snap at her bare legs . . . of water snakes disturbed from their nests . . . of crocodiles eager for an easy dinner.

She fought back to the surface, choking on muddy water. Painfully aware that Graeme was struggling for his own life, her mind cried out to their only defense. *God! Help us!* She swallowed fear, breathed the prayer again, and willed her limbs into motion.

Terror threatened to overtake her. She knew with every stroke that her legs might disappear between the teeth of some animal; with every splash her life could be snuffed out. She was a moving target to the crocodiles, no different than a struggling antelope or drowning gazelle. Lunch.

Fighting heaving sickness in her stomach, she struggled on. Toward the bank. It was too far. She couldn't see Graeme at all. She'd lost him. Hannah's voice drifted like a river current into her head: *"He will give his angels charge concerning you, to guard you in all your ways. They will bear you up in their hands, lest you strike your foot against a stone."*

Or a crocodile, Lord. Or a hippo.

And then her feet touched the sandy bottom of the river. She struggled to stand and saw that she had made it to a clear spot, a grassy inlet sheltering two white-feathered cormorants.

They stared at the gasping creature rising from the river like some incarnation of the Swamp Thing, then flew off in alarm.

Stumbling up onto the grass, Tillie heard a swishing sound behind her. She swung around to see a huge gray crocodile staring at her from the shallows. Its powerful tail whipped back and forth. Then it surged forward on squat legs.

Choking back a scream, Tillie scrambled toward the nearest

tree. She nearly tripped over a surprised baby crocodile . . . grabbed a low limb . . . pulled her legs up at the last instant.

Trees! Thank God for beloved, beautiful trees! She hauled herself to the top branches. Below, the crocodile snapped at the tree trunk twice in frustration before waddling off.

Dear Lord, where is Graeme? She pushed through a veil of leaves and scanned the river. At first she saw nothing. Then far down the bank she spotted the hazy outline of the tiny boat. It was upright and bobbing close to the shore. Graeme had righted it! But where was he?

Fear prickled down her spine. Graeme had stayed with the boat. The hippo would have gone after him.

"Graeme!" she shouted, coughing up a mouthful of water. "Graeme, where are you?"

Listening for a response, she stiffened at what she heard. Behind her on the bank came the soft jingling of camel bells. She leaned back on the thick branch and closed her eyes. The Tuareg had caught up.

Their chieftain would see the boat. He would know she was here. Her first thought was to crouch in the tree. She could wait forever. Trees were her second home. Maybe the *amenoukal* would think she had drowned or been eaten. She peered through the leaves.

The white camel led the caravan. Its rider's slate blue turban and veil covered all but his black eyes. His broadsword glinted in the sunlight. Tied to his spear, the rag from her skirt fluttered in the breeze. The battle banner of his crusade, his quest for the grail.

There could be no doubt the man would find the boat and would order every tree searched, every hillock explored, every inlet examined. He would not rest until he was certain she was gone. And she would be, she decided suddenly. If she ran, if she kept hidden, she could reach the boat before they saw her. She had to.

Arms and legs aching, she broke a dead branch from the tree. Not much protection, but better than nothing. Checking to confirm that the crocodile was gone, she climbed down the tree and crouched beside a root. The caravan was close already, and she would be exposed as she ran, but she had to take the chance.

She had lost her sandals in the swim. Could she do it barefoot? "No snakes," she murmured. "Please, Father, no snakes." She gathered her dripping skirt around her hips and took off through the stubbly grass toward the boat. Behind her, she heard a shout. They had seen her.

The camels loped down the track behind her. She focused on her goal. *The boat. The boat. The boat.* The words pounded in her brain. Her pursuers were gaining. She ran around a sleeping crocodile. She leaped over a tangle of thorny brake. Camels snorted behind her. Warriors chucked and whipped at their beasts. The *amenoukal* shouted. Closer. Closer.

The boat. The boat. She was almost there when something rushed out of the forest, hit her full force, and knocked the ragged breath from her chest. She reeled, stumbled, plummeted. Her head exploded. White stars flared like fireworks. Night fell.

Tillie jerked awake. A hazy aqua sky canopied her. Where was she? What had happened? She struggled to sit up and couldn't. Her head felt like a squashed papaya.

"Mornin', glory." Graeme's voice drifted out of nowhere.

"Graeme? Where are you?"

"I'm here, Tillie-girl." His hand covered her forehead, brushed the hair that blew in the soft breeze. "We're back in the boat."

He lifted her slowly to a sitting position. It was true. They were floating along in their little boat as though nothing had happened.

"Where's the *amenoukal?* Are there crocodiles?"

"You've been out for a while. I was looking for you in the woods when I heard the Tuareg coming down the track. That's when I spotted you. The *amenoukal* almost had you, and then we sort of knocked heads. I barely got you into the boat in time."

"You nearly killed me." She rubbed the back of her neck. "But thanks."

"Better me than that Targui . . . or a croc."

"I thought you'd planned to use me for crocodile bait all along."

The corner of his mouth turned up. He reached out to her and ran the side of his finger down her cheek. "Changed my mind."

She shivered. "Graeme, he's going to get me next time."

"There won't be a next time. Not if I can help it." He looked away, the muscle in his jaw twitching. "When I couldn't find you in the river . . . couldn't hear you . . . I went crazy or something." He gave a low chuckle. "You'll get a kick out of this. I prayed."

"Really? What's the world coming to these days?"

He smiled at her, his face gentling. Deeply moved by his

confession, she laid her hand over his. "Thanks, Graeme. It helped."

Her head throbbing, she slid down into the boat and shut her eyes. Knowing he was there was enough. She was so tired. She felt more drained than she'd ever felt in her life. She was sore and bruised, her skin was torn and scraped. Every finger ached; every joint felt wrenched from its socket. Her mouth tasted brackish, her eyes stung, her ears rang. Breathing was an effort. She coughed every time she inhaled.

And there was something else about the experience. Something more significant. For the first time in her life, she had relied totally on God. She hadn't been able to trust in her own plans—there were no plans, no schedule, no checklist. No one had been there to rescue her. No one had told her what to do.

Trust me, he had whispered in her heart that day in the Bamako market. One day at a time. One minute at a time. And she had.

Wrapped in the warm damp arms of the little boat, rocked by the river, she felt God's peace fill her. In Bamako, where she had everything planned and organized, she hadn't been able to hear his voice. But in the middle of a crocodile-infested river, he had spoken to her heart. Through prayer, through impossible circumstances, even through Graeme and his concern, the Holy Spirit was showing her his ways. His plans. Himself.

"Trust me. Trust me alone."

Letting out a breath, she ran her fingers over her damp cotton skirt. She could feel the amulet beneath her blouse.

It was safe. She almost wished she'd lost it in the river. Mungo Park's beloved Niger.

Though she wanted to sleep, hunger scratched at her stomach with its gnarled fingers. She hauled herself up on her elbows, folded her legs under her, and ran her fingers through the damp tangles of her braid. The comb would have been lost in the river with the knapsack. And Graeme's notes for his story on Mungo Park were lost, too. If there really were any notes.

It bothered her how easily she trusted this man in the boat. An uncomfortable pattern was developing. Something would remind her of his suspect character—that he had kidnapped her, that he was hunting the amulet and the treasure, that he claimed to do and be things he had never proven. But then she would fall under his spell, and all her uncertainties would fade. She would laugh with him, share food with him, tell him her ideas and listen to his, and pretty soon she would begin to rely on him again. She would trust him.

She'd heard about kidnapping victims who developed relationships with—even obsessive dependencies on—their abductors. Weren't there stories of lawyers who fell in love with convicts they were defending? Who even went so far as to help them escape? Even the Bible related the story of David, who joined up with the Philistines for a while when he was running from Saul.

Tillie mentally shook herself. She wasn't falling in love with Graeme. And she wouldn't trust him too far. She couldn't afford to.

Pulling the wet rubber band from her hair, she watched the sun begin its familiar descent in the African sky. From the pale gold hue of a frangipani blossom, the sun would transform into the bright yellow of ripe bananas and then to the brilliant orange of mango juice. She loved Africa. It was impossible to imagine true happiness anywhere else.

"Are we going to make it to Segou tonight?" Her bobby pins were knotted with twigs and leaves, and it was all she could do to work them out.

Graeme's glance took in her struggle with her hair, and the corners of his eyes crinkled in silent amusement. "I don't know. The river's moving at a snail's pace, and that spill we took slowed us down. I think we ought to just drift tonight. If we snag, we snag. It's better than camping out with the crocodiles."

"I agree." Working to separate her hair into three hanks, she decided she might cut the braid off when she got home. In all her years roaming the wild Kenya brush, her skin had never felt so dirty, her hair so tangled, her mouth so brackish. As she began the rebraiding, Graeme's hand closed over her own for the third time.

"Leave it down."

His dark hair caught red glints from the fading sunlight. She read the expression on his face, one she was coming to know intimately. For a moment she hesitated; then she lowered her hands. He took her hair and combed his fingers through it, working out the start of the damp braid.

"You have beautiful hair, Tillie."

That word again . . . *beautiful*. He had called her a beautiful woman the night before. With a sigh, she leaned back against the edge of the boat. She could sense him looking at her. Just the color of the man's eyes made her heart pound against her ribs. Suddenly she sat up, unable to bear the tension between them.

"Graeme," she began, meaning to tell him the truth about everything. About Arthur and how he and she were meant for each other. About the way God had brought them together and surely wanted them together for life. But as she tried to formulate the words, she realized that they would never come. They weren't the truth at all.

Silently, she reached out to Graeme and touched his cheek. She ran her gaze over the knotted line of his jaw, its hardness in angular contrast to his silken hair. She could see the craggy slope of his nose, his father's legacy. Gently, she traced her fingertips over the planes of his face, as if her caress could somehow smooth away every mar, her touch erase each memory.

"Graeme," she whispered.

He covered the bridge of his nose with his hand, a child-hood instinct of trying to hide it. Then he dropped his hands to his knees. "Beauty and the beast," he said with a derisive laugh.

"I had Prince Charming in mind." She put her index finger on the arch of his nose and ran it slowly down. "'Man looks at the outward appearance, but the Lord looks at the heart.'"

"More Bible verses, Cinderella?"

She smiled. "Blame Hannah. She says our looks don't matter. If any man is in Christ, he's a new creature; the old things pass away, and new things are created."

"New things." He ran his fingers through her long hair and pulled a strand of it over one shoulder. "That's for sure."

Tillie closed her eyes and lay down. Graeme eased himself into position beside her, ready for sleep. She rested her head on his chest. Like a jewel-studded bowl turning slowly overhead, the sky faded from sapphire to amethyst and then to ruby and topaz before melting into the utter blackness of onyx. Sleep came swiftly.

Tillie did not wake up until well after sunrise. Graeme sat in the prow, trying to steer with the branch she had used as a club and watching her sleeping face. By the time Tillie opened her eyes, the sun was beating down, intensifying the queasiness in the pit of his stomach.

He studied the little morning ritual that had become so familiar to him. Tillie . . . soft morning Tillie . . . wiping her eyes, running her fingers through her hair, stretching with both arms open wide as though she could hug the whole world. A little yawn. A little sigh. She folded her arms over her knees and blinked sleepily like a kitten just stirring from a nap.

As she looked around at the muddy river, he could read her surprise at the increase in river traffic. The day before, they had passed several small villages and had seen a few boats. Now the river was crowded with canoes and dugouts.

"What's going on?" she wondered aloud.

"Segou. We're almost there."

"Can you see the town?"

"It must be just ahead. But Tillie . . . we have company."

Her hand tightening on the edge of the boat, Tillie

followed the line of his gaze. Far on the east bank, the caravan of Tuareg camels wove along the busy road. The
amenoukal rode in the lead, the banner of her torn skirt
whipping in the breeze.

"After all that," she murmured, "we didn't escape."

He tried to read the expression in her blue eyes. Fear?
Worry? No, it was something else. A kind of peaceful resignation had settled around her like a shawl. It was as though
all her apprehensions about the Tuareg had been wrapped
in some kind of certainty that everything was going to work
out.

As they drifted helplessly toward the main pier of the
picturesque little town, Graeme realized he felt a strange
sense of comfort himself. With the Tuareg still in pursuit,
Tillie would need him. Even if he wanted to, he couldn't
abandon her in Segou. It would be natural for him in this
situation to stay close to her, to watch over her. For some
reason, that sounded like the best job description in the
world.

She turned to him, her hair long and loose, like a golden
cape. "What are we going to do?"

"What do you want to do?"

"Could we bypass Segou and take the boat on to
Timbuktu?"

"We haven't eaten for almost two days, Tillie. And we
need an oar."

"I know." Her eyes searched his, as though she could
read answers in them. He'd never been looked to for guidance, never been needed, rarely been wanted.

"I think we ought to chance a stop." His voice sounded
lower, more gentle than she'd ever heard it. "Once we hit

the pier, we can make a run for safety. We can lose ourselves in these crowds pretty easily. And there are a lot of ways to get out of Segou. There's a river steamer, tourist buses. . . . I may even be able to round up a vehicle—" He broke off. "Tillie . . . what are you staring at?"

She had paled to the color of dry ivory. Her fingers knotted together in her lap. He twisted around. Toward the pier marched the Tuareg caravan—camels and warriors, women, children, pots and pans, bells and folded tents, a modern vision of the army of Israelites on the march. Like the Red Sea, the crowds parted to let them pass. Fishermen shouted at the clumsy camels. A little boy leapt into the water. Someone threw a coconut. At the end of the pier stood a stiff Moses in a pale khaki suit and a straw hat.

Tillie swallowed. "It's Arthur."

Six

Arthur had come to save her, and she should be thankful. God had provided. God had blessed her with Arthur. She should be grateful, aching to fall into his arms, dizzy with joy.

"Matilda!" he shouted, lifting his rifle in a sort of salute. She hesitated, then waved. "Matilda, darling!"

Tillie turned to Graeme. He met her eyes, a small wry smile on his lips. *Don't make me leave him, Lord,* she heard her traitorous heart whisper. *Not yet.*

It wasn't dreading London or losing her neem trees that made her want to be near Graeme. It was the man himself. Something about him. The way he smelled of sunshine and Africa. The reflection of the blue-green sky in his eyes. The rhythm of his heart in her ear, and the solid fortress of his chest against her cheek. The touch of his fingers in her hair, and the sound of his voice when he said her name. *Hey, Tillie-girl. Mornin', glory.*

No, not yet. Please, Lord, not yet.

"Guess this is it," he said.

"Yes." She meant no. *Please, no.*

"You'd better tell your boyfriend to watch his backside. Those Tuareg aren't likely to be intimidated by that popgun of his."

Tillie had no choice but to turn from him. The *amenoukal* was lashing a vendor away from his dromedary as Graeme spoke. She knew the man would not stop at the mere presence of a British authority. In 1990, the Tuareg in northeast Mali had rebelled against the government. They'd gained a degree of autonomy, but unrest continued. Their lack of respect for leaders other than their own was well documented, and Arthur would be a mere irritant in the path of their pursuit.

"Arthur," she shouted at him. "The Tuareg! Behind you!"

He turned in the direction she was pointing, stiffened, and raised his gun. The *amenoukal* continued to advance.

"He knows he won't be shot," Graeme said quietly as they drifted to the pier. "British and French soldiers won't shoot without provocation."

He tossed a rope to a youth and pulled the boat until it bumped against a piling. Tillie laid her hand on his arm. "Graeme, we can't use our plan of escape now. Arthur will try to stop the Tuareg. He could be killed."

Graeme nodded. "I know." He concentrated on tying the boat.

"Then, I guess . . . thank you for bringing me to Segou," she said.

"No problem." He looped the end of the rope into a coil. "So long, adios, and all that."

"OK, then . . . 'bye."

He kept fiddling with the rope, not looking at her. The Tuareg headed down the pier. Arthur brandished his rifle. Her heart aching, she knew Graeme was pushing her out of his life. She swallowed the hurt, brushed past him, and lifted her hands to the waiting dockworker.

"I represent the British government," Arthur shouted in his perfect Eton accent. As Tillie stepped onto the pier and walked to his side, she had no doubt that his words were unintelligible to the *amenoukal*. Arthur grabbed Tillie's arm and pushed her behind himself. "I give you fair warning, sir. Should you come one step farther, I shall be forced to shoot."

The *amenoukal* slowed his dromedary and gestured behind himself with his broadsword. From the back of the caravan, a small white camel ambled forward bearing a beautiful woman on a tooled leather saddle. She wore a flowing white burnous, heavily embroidered in silver at the neck. Her light skin, fine nose, and almond eyes revealed a patrician ancestry. She held her head high, her swan neck straight in the haughty posture of royalty.

The *amenoukal* spoke a few words to her, and she nodded. Then she turned her kohl-rimmed eyes to Tillie. "Ahodu Ag Amastane, *amenoukal* of Tuareg people," she said in careful English, "will take Tree-Planting Woman now."

Arthur glanced at Tillie.

"It's me," she whispered. "I'm the tree-planting woman."

He scowled at the *amenoukal*. "You may not have her, sir. She belongs to the American government. She belongs to me."

The *amenoukal* fired a series of questions at the regal woman. She listened, answered gracefully, then bowed on her camel and turned it back into the caravan. By now a huge, jostling crowd had gathered on the pier, everyone gaping at the dromedaries and the white-skinned strangers.

The *amenoukal* raised his spear, his coffee-bean eyes locked on Tillie. *"Tek!"* he bawled out. *"Tek! Tek!"*

Lowering his spear, the *amenoukal* spurred his dromedary down the plank boardwalk. The caravan filed after him. The rickety pier shuddered beneath the camels' splayed feet. Children screamed. A cart rolled into the water. Dogs howled. Arthur took aim.

"Don't shoot him!" Tillie cried out.

"Robinson, give me that thing," Graeme barked behind them.

Arthur whirled around. "Who is this, Matilda?"

"Give me the gun," Graeme commanded. "I'll hold them off. Get Tillie out of here."

She flinched at the anger in the Targui's dark eyes. "Arthur, give him the gun."

The camels loped toward them. Onlookers shouted and scurried for cover.

"Now!" Graeme growled. He jerked the rifle from the Englishman and pushed Tillie off the pier. For the second time she went under the Niger's muddy water. She bobbed to the surface in time to see Arthur leap into the river beside her.

"Follow me," he sputtered.

They swam between docked boats and past floating trash. A tattered basket. A coconut. A sandal. Behind them, Tillie could hear the angry yells of the Tuareg, the shrieks of the crowd, and then gunshots.

"No!" Turning, she started back toward the pier.

Arthur grabbed Tillie's arm and pulled her up beside him. "Come on, darling! Let's get out of here."

She wrenched her arm from his grip and turned to the pier. Tuareg dromedaries had overrun the spot where Graeme had been standing. Two of the camels had splashed into the river and were roaring and spitting as their owners fought to right them.

Arthur took her arm. "Come on, love. Don't waste your breath."

"He brought me all this way, Arthur. The least I can do—"

"It's you they want. We'll check on him later. Now, come."

She had no choice but to stumble out of the river and follow him as he pushed through the throng of marketgoers. They raced down narrow streets crowded with brown mud houses and whitewashed mosques. Her bare feet ached, but she scarcely noticed. All she could think about was Graeme.

Arthur turned onto a flight of stone steps. They ran up and around a corner, through a brass-studded wood door, and into unexpected cool air. Refrigerated air. Chilled marble floors. The scent of sandalwood. The lobby of a hotel.

Tillie stopped. Stared. She could hear her skirt dripping on the floor. The room was filled with mottled shadows, philodendrons in ceramic pots, arrangements of fresh orange-and-blue bird-of-paradise flowers. Low wooden coffee tables stood among sturdy linen-upholstered armchairs. A rack of magazines occupied one corner beside a cart of petit fours and tiny cucumber sandwiches.

She turned to Arthur. "Where are we?"

"My hotel, of course." He wrung out the tail of his suit coat. "I must see if they've laundry service. Wretched business, swimming in the Niger. We'll have dysentery, no doubt. I suppose they'll have to check us for parasites before we can catch our flight to England. Come along, then, darling. I've a bit of a surprise for you upstairs."

"Arthur, I can't stay here," she said in a low voice. "The Tuareg want me. I'm the tree-planting woman."

"I don't know anything about that, but I do know you look half-dead, and we both smell like the very devil himself. Now, not another word. I'm taking you upstairs to have a good bath and a hot meal. After that, you can tell me everything that's happened."

Without waiting for her response, he started up the narrow flight of stairs. Tillie glanced at the hotel manager, who was clearly displeased at the puddle of Niger River water forming on his marble floor. Broken Land Rover, boat, crocodiles, hippo . . . marble floor, air-conditioning, Persian carpets. She felt like she had entered some sort of time warp.

"Matilda, darling." Arthur's voice filtered down the stairs.

She started up, her bare feet moving as though they were directed by someone other than herself. She walked down a carpeted hall, following Arthur's trail of droplets until she came to him. At a heavy wooden door, he pulled out a key and inserted it. As he pushed inward, she caught her breath.

"Hannah!"

"Ndimi. Njoni kwangu." Beckoning with familiar Swahili endearments, the old woman folded her close, heedless of the younger woman's wet clothes and river smell.

Tillie found she couldn't stop her tears. *"Kuja kwako*

kumenifurahisha sana," she murmured, thankful that Hannah had come.

"*Bas, bas,*" Hannah soothed. "*Habari gani, katoto?*"

"I'm OK."

"*Nitupende.*"

"I love you, too. Oh, Hannah, are you all right?"

"Of course, my child." Dark fingers cupped her face. "Let me see my Tillie. Ehh, your eyes are sad. Tell Mama Hannah. Where have you been all these days alone?"

"I haven't been alone. God was with me, Mama Hannah. And so was Graeme."

"Graeme who? The chap on the boat?" Arthur locked the door behind them. Stepping to the table, he flipped open his suitcase. She saw that it held his pistol and a supply of ammunition. He snapped the bag shut and turned to her. "Perhaps you'd better tell me right now what's been going on."

"I'm tired." She rubbed a hand over her eyes and leaned on Hannah. The room was dark and cold. In its center stood a carved bed covered with heavy blankets and white pillows. "I need to sleep. I've been in that boat . . . three days . . . or was it four?"

She wandered across the room and pushed back the door that led into a modern bathroom with gleaming fixtures and a claw-footed white tub. "I need a bath. I've been in the river. . . . There was a hippo. . . ."

"Food first," Hannah announced, snapping to life and marching to the bed. Wrapping Tillie's chilled, wet body in a warm bathrobe, the old woman gave her a tender kiss on the forehead and settled her on the covers. "*Bwana* Robinson, please call to the hotel kitchen for hot soup, a bit of meat, and some fresh bread."

Arthur picked up the phone and began to order. As Tillie sank against the mattress, she smiled at the way Hannah could make anyone obey. She took the old woman's hand and closed her eyes. Graeme's face materialized. Black hair blowing in the breeze. That look in his blue-green eyes. She sat up in bed and reached to grab Arthur's wet coat sleeve.

"You have to find Graeme," she told him. "Graeme McLeod, the man in the boat. They'll think he has the document. They'll kill him to find me, Arthur. You have to do something."

"Document?" He frowned as he eased her back onto the bed. "He'll be all right, darling. You must rest. I'm taking care of you."

Tillie wanted to tell him she didn't need protecting. God had seen her past a crocodile and a hippo, for heaven's sake! She had lived on bananas and slept on a tiny boat in a swarm of mosquitoes. She had swum across the Niger and learned to trust the Lord one moment at a time. But the words ricocheted in her head and refused to form on her tongue.

In moments a knock sounded at the door, and Arthur brought in a tray piled with food. Sitting beside Tillie, Hannah ladled soup down her throat and forced her to eat the bread and stringy beef. Just when Tillie thought she had enough energy to explain about Graeme again, she closed her eyes and tumbled into exhausted sleep.

Tillie woke in the night. At first she was lost, groping for the sides of the boat, seeking out Graeme's warmth. Then she recognized Arthur asleep in the chair beside her bed, his suit crumpled and his light brown hair spilling over his forehead. Hannah lay next to her in the bed, her skirt tucked modestly around her feet. Tillie sat up, painfully aware of what her body had gone through in the days on the river.

Careful not to disturb Hannah, she slipped out of bed and hobbled across the cool floor to the window. She parted the heavy cotton curtains and peered out into the African night. A wrought-iron balcony jutted from the window ledge. The hotel was probably a relic of French occupation, no doubt used only by a few tourists now. Below, the lights of the small town fanned out from the line of the river.

Somewhere out there Graeme slept. She whispered a prayer for his safety as she thought back on their strange days together. He was not at all the man she had taken him for at first. She remembered him throwing her into the Land Rover, slamming down the hood, grabbing the amulet from her hand.

She marveled again at the change in him as the days on the river drifted by. She had seen into his heart and had shared with him a part of hers. Where was he now? Was he safe? She pressed her palm against the chilled windowpane and leaned her head on her fingers.

"Darling, are you all right?" Arthur laid his hand on the back of her neck. "I heard you get up."

Startled at his unexpected touch, she let out a breath. "I was . . . I'm worried about Graeme McLeod. Have you heard anything?"

His mouth hardened. "Nothing. Matilda, I realize the man helped you get to Segou, but how much do you really know about him? You must be careful of that sort of bloke out here in the bush country. People have all kinds of motives for what they do."

"Graeme saved me from the *amenoukal*. He fed me and kept me safe. I owe him the courtesy of making sure he's safe, too."

"Forgive me for contradicting you, Matilda, but the man kidnapped you!" His voice was tight. "Darling, you must open your eyes. That man is no better than those camel-riders who were after you. He's involved in . . . wrong-doing."

Tillie stared at him. "What are you saying?"

"This McLeod fellow has been making a bother of himself around Bamako for several months. When I was frantically trying to find out who he was and what he might have done with you, I learned that he's been poking around in the military and embassy libraries, asking strange questions at the museums, trying to get into Tuareg camps, and making a general nuisance of himself. Someone told me they'd seen him heading north in his Land Rover. Darling, I've been mad with worry."

"Oh, Arthur, I'm so sorry."

"I've taken all this time away from my work when I should have been wrapping up my projects. Hannah insisted on searching for you, and I certainly couldn't object to that. I booked us on the first flight to Timbuktu, though you know how I feel about those little planes. I spoke with the authorities there, but of course no one had heard a thing. Then the British embassy got word that McLeod's Land Rover had been discovered broken down at the edge of the Niger, so we flew back to Bamako and drove up here searching the river all the way. We passed the Tuareg caravan, but they refused to speak to us. Finally, this morning in Segou, a bellman here at the hotel told me a white woman and man were floating in on a small boat."

Dear Arthur, Tillie thought. He'd been so worried. She took his hand and pressed her lips to it. "I'm sorry. I know it must have been awful for you."

"Did he touch you, Matilda?"

"No, Arthur, not like you mean. He was good to me. We became friends." She wondered why her well-meant words sounded so much like a lie. "Graeme is a writer. That's why he was poking around the museums and libraries in Bamako. He's doing some kind of an article."

A look of irritation crossed Arthur's face. "A writer? Is that what he told you? Look, you'd better give me all the details. I ought to know."

But she suddenly felt too tired to talk. "I want to take a bath, Arthur. Please, just let me do that."

She wandered wearily into the white-tiled room and bent over the tub. He followed her in and took over the running of the water. Tillie lifted her attention to the mirror.

Shock spread through her at the face in the glass. The washed and pressed and carefully braided Tillie had vanished. The days on the river had brought such changes she scarcely recognized herself. Her hair, bleached by hours in the sun, billowed around her face in untamed waves and curls that fell well past her shoulders. Her face had lost every girlish curve and become the lean, sunburned face of a woman. Her blue eyes swallowed up every other feature with their luminosity.

Arthur stood staring at her. "You've changed."

"I know." She smiled as she walked back to the tub. "I've been through a lot."

The tub was nearly filled with clear, steaming water, and she ached physically for it. But as she bent to turn off the faucet, she felt Arthur's hands slide around her waist. She held her breath, closing her eyes as he began to kiss her cheek.

"Arthur," she whispered. "Please, Arthur. Not now."

He stepped away from her. "For heaven's sake, you've been sleeping with another man for days! I'd like some confirmation that you're still mine."

Stung by his harshness, she searched his eyes. "What's happened to you?"

"Are you denying you slept with him?"

"I slept *beside* him. I had no choice, Arthur. We were in a tiny boat. What would you expect?"

"I would expect you to be faithful to me. You're mine."

She was too tired for patience. "I'm not yours, Arthur. I'm not anyone's! I care about you. I thank God for you. But I'm not *yours*. Now, if you don't mind, I would like some privacy."

Hurt wrote itself across his pale blue eyes, and he backed away. They had never exchanged harsh words, but Tillie found she couldn't make herself care. She wanted to be left alone.

"If that's how you feel," he snapped, shutting the door behind him.

Slowly she slipped the robe off her shoulders; she unbuttoned her tattered cotton skirt and let it drop from her hips. She pulled away the dirty blouse and ruined underwear. After unhooking the necklace, she lifted the amulet and turned it over in her hands. Still holding it, she stepped into the tub and sank to her chin in the steaming hot water.

She was angry with Arthur for the first time. Why had he been rude about Graeme? Why had he acted so possessive? Was that the nature of his love?

The amulet dangled from her fingers, its silver glinting in the light. She wondered if the document had survived the river. Gingerly she pulled it out and saw that it was dry. The locket had been lined with wax to protect it. Someone had intended the page to be preserved many years. Mungo Park?

Again she wondered how she fit into the legend of the treasure. She scanned the page from the journal. Christmas Day . . . Graeme said that date meant Park had lived longer than everyone believed. His deep voice filtered into her heart as she tried to sift the words for any possible clue. Ailie was Mungo's wife, and the journal had been written to her, almost like a letter.

The Bight of Benin the blight of Benin . . .

What could that mean? And who was this Ahmadi Fatouma? Mungo had written that this man had the treasure in safekeeping. Was he the one who had taken the page from the journal? Had he hidden it in the wax-lined amulet?

The treasure of Timbuktu. Those words had to mean something, but what? Tillie tried to remember what she had read about the fabled city. Hadn't it been a trading post for salt caravans hundreds of years ago? There had been libraries with wonderful books. Surely all kinds of gold and other riches had found their way into the city.

She looked at the paper again. *"One day, one day the white man will come here. One day, one day the white woman will come here. She will plant trees and make it a garden for tea parties. She will plant trees. She will find the treasure of Timbuktu. And the curse of the Bight of Benin will be ended."*

What was it Graeme had told her? Mungo Park had informed the king of Segou that white traders would come to the area, ending Moorish domination. Was that the white man of whom he wrote in his journal? Then who was the white woman? Surely not her. He could have had no idea she would come. Yet the Tuareg had held the document for years, waiting for a tree-planting woman.

Shaking her head, she refolded the paper and wished for Graeme. Maybe in the security of the hotel room they could sort out what the journal meant. She set the amulet on the cushion of her clothes and slipped her head under the water. Where was Graeme now? Could Arthur have found out more information about him than she knew? Something unwholesome? She couldn't deny that Graeme was in pursuit with as much determination as the *amenoukal*. And she had seen no proof that he was a writer.

She let the clean water lap over her face. She wanted to erase it all, erase Graeme, his kiss, his gentle touch, that look in his eyes. For that matter, she wanted to erase Arthur, too. Arthur with his rifle and his possessiveness and his certainty that she would spend the rest of her life with him in London.

Lord, what now? What's the plan? As she scrubbed the river from her body, she asked him for guidance. *Just tell me what to do. Make me love Arthur. Take Graeme out of my brain. Explain this treasure business to me. I have to know. I have to understand. How am I going to take the right path unless you show me?*

She climbed out of the tub and toweled off. *Father, I don't love Arthur. That's all there is to it. I don't love him, and I can't marry him.* The story of the biblical Jacob popped into her head. Jacob hadn't loved Leah. He was in love with her sister, Rachel. But when their father tricked him into marrying Leah, Jacob did what was right. He stayed with her, gave her children, cared for her. Love had nothing to do with it.

Standing in front of the mirror, she combed out her hair. *But I can't. I just can't marry Arthur, Lord. Not when I love Graeme.* She frowned at her reflection. Where had *that* come from? How could she love a man she'd known only five days? And she certainly couldn't be thinking about spending the rest of her life with him. *Do not be bound together with unbelievers. . . . What has a believer in common with an unbeliever?*

They shared a love for Africa. That had to be it. They both liked adventure; they'd both lost their mothers; their fathers had hurt them. She and Graeme were survivors. They could eat bananas for three days and float down the Niger and . . . and . . .

She turned from the mirror. And that wasn't enough.

She slipped into a clean robe and tied it at her waist. Hands in her pockets, she stared down at the tile floor. *So, what am I supposed to do, Lord? Aren't you going to tell me the plan?*

"*Trust me.*"

With a sigh of frustration, she stepped back into the bedroom. Hannah lifted her head and patted the sheet beside her. "*Okahaha,*" she whispered, beckoning in Kikuyu, the language of her youth. Tillie curled onto the bed, and Hannah drew the blankets over her shoulders.

"'Trust in the Lord with all your heart,'" she whispered, reciting perhaps her favorite lines from the Proverbs of Solomon, "'and do not lean on your own understanding. In all your ways acknowledge him, and he will make your paths straight.'"

"But, Mama Hannah," Tillie began. "The trouble is—"

"'When you lie down, you will not be afraid.'" The older woman ran stiff fingers over pale gold hair. "'When you lie down, your sleep will be sweet. Do not be afraid of sudden fear, nor of the onslaught of the wicked when it comes; for the Lord will be your confidence, and will keep your foot from being caught.'"

The words of comfort washed over Tillie, and she closed her eyes, resting once again in the arms of the one who loved her unceasingly.

The smells of crisp bacon, golden eggs, and hot buttered toast drifted around Tillie, tantalizing her, drawing her from her dreams. When she lifted her head, she saw a bamboo tray, white plates, a small pink rose in a silver vase, and what surely must be manna from heaven. And she saw Arthur's loving smile.

"Good morning, my darling Matilda," he said softly.

"Mornin', glory," she heard someone else whisper.

"Arthur, this is incredible," she said to drown out the voice. She elbowed herself up into a sitting position. "I've been living on bananas."

"I'm here to take care of you now, and I don't intend my fiancée to survive on bananas." He drew out the white napkin and spread it across her lap. "There you are. First-class service."

She lifted the silver fork and knife, cut the egg, and speared a triangle. "Where's Hannah?"

"She's gone down to the market to buy you some new clothes. You lost your sandals, didn't you? I could hardly believe the condition of your things when I threw them into the dustbin this morning."

Tillie lifted her head. "Dustbin?" His words registered. Her blood dropped to her knees. She set the tray aside, threw back the covers, and jumped out of bed. "Arthur, where are my clothes? What have you done with them?"

She raced into the bathroom and stared at the bare tile floor. Arthur dashed in behind her. "Matilda, what in heaven's name are you ranting about? What's the matter?"

"My clothes. There was something with them. A necklace on a silver chain. An amulet." She turned to him. "Where are my clothes? Where did you put them?"

He grabbed her shoulders. "Stop raving, Matilda."

"My life depends on that amulet. I need it."

"Your life does not depend on a necklace. Your life is in my hands, and I mean to keep it safe. Now, is this what you're going on about?"

He reached into his shirt pocket and pulled out the amulet. Tillie snatched it and pressed it to her chest. "Oh, thank God! Arthur, you don't know how important this is. Look, we have to find Graeme."

"Find Graeme? We've no need for that renegade. He's done his part."

Tillie stood still, trying to calm her thundering heart. How could Arthur be so callous? But of course he didn't understand what she and Graeme had been through. He didn't know about the treasure. About the legend. About the *amenoukal*.

"It's just that Graeme and I—"

"No, Matilda. There is no Graeme and you any longer. It's us now. The two of us." He lifted her chin. "What does he need with you?"

He was right, of course. Graeme had seen the document. He knew as much as, if not more than, she did. He didn't need her. He'd told her more than once that she would slow him down. Hinder his quest.

"He doesn't need me," she said in a low voice. "I'm just worried he may have been hurt on the pier yesterday."

"Matilda." Arthur placed a hand on her arm. "I'm sure he's fine."

"Maybe. But as soon as Hannah comes back with my clothes, I'm going out to the market to look for him." She met his frown with pleading eyes. "Try to understand. Graeme is my friend. He took care of me. I have to find out if he's OK."

"That man you call your friend obviously dragged you through hell to get to Segou. Think of your condition when I found you."

"It wasn't his fault. We went the only way we could go. With the *amenoukal* on our trail the whole time, we did well to get this far. You don't know what I've been through."

"And I don't want to know. I simply want you to stop this fantasy and return to being the woman I intend to marry. I want you beside me when we step off that plane at Heathrow. I want you on my arm at my welcoming bash at the club. I want everyone to see you. You're my prize, darling."

She stared at him, then shook her head. "No, Arthur, I'm not. That prize is your fantasy. I'm sorry, but I just don't have the luxury of thinking about the future right now. The *amenoukal* is going to come after me for the treasure. He can't get the treasure without me, and if he finds out I've gone back to Bamako, he'll follow me there again. I've seen the look in his eyes, and right now that's a lot more important to me than any bash or club."

"Treasure?" His voice was toneless. "You never said anything about a treasure."

"It's all here." She held up the wrought-silver locket. "Inside this amulet is a page from Mungo Park's journal. He talks about a woman coming to Mali to plant trees, and he rambles on and on about a treasure. The treasure of Timbuktu. That's what the Tuareg want, and since I plant trees, they think I can help them get it."

Arthur sat down on the bed. "Can you?"

"Of course not! I don't know anything about it. Graeme and I studied the journal entry, but it doesn't make much sense to either of us."

"The Tuareg want the treasure. Graeme McLeod wants it, and he's done the research. Then there must be a treasure."

"I guess so, but I sure don't know where it is. It was probably in Timbuktu originally, although that was nearly two hundred years ago. Some man other than Mungo Park was in charge of it. For all we know, he may have taken it out of Timbuktu. The point is, the *amenoukal* thinks I can get the treasure for him, and he's not going to stop until I do."

"What sort of treasure is it? Does the journal say?"

Tillie fingered the amulet. "Park talks about buying his wife a house with it. I imagine it's money or something. Anyway, the treasure is all tied up with some legend and a curse. The Tuareg seem to think I can break the curse. Arthur, I really don't know what it's all about. I just know Graeme says the *amenoukal* will not stop until he has me. He tried to kill Graeme once already to get at me, and then yesterday at the pier, Graeme faced that Targui again to protect me. The man has a broadsword, Arthur, and he won't hesitate to use it."

He wasn't listening. "Gold. It has to be gold." He stood and took her shoulders in his hands. "Haven't you read about Timbuktu? The mysterious Queen of the Sands. It used to be a fabulous trading town with universities and libraries. It had trade routes to Venice and Cairo. Every imaginable luxury passed through Timbuktu—fabrics, spices, copper, ivory, slaves. And gold."

Tillie shrugged away. "What difference does it make? I don't care about the treasure. I care about Graeme's life. And my own. Can you imagine what the *amenoukal* will do when he finds out I can't show him where his treasure is?"

"Forget the *amenoukal*—don't you see what that money could mean to us? All my life I've struggled. I've lived in dingy flats and taken the Tube to work. I've worn rags and cooked my own dinners and existed hand-to-mouth. I want more than that. More for us. I want us to live well, darling. I want a house, a car, holidays on the Continent. I should like to build a savings portfolio—stocks, bonds, even properties."

She stared at him in total disbelief. "Are you nuts? Some guy is trying to kidnap me, and you're talking about stocks and bonds? That's disgusting, Arthur! What about the fact that I nearly lost my life over that stupid treasure? And Graeme? I've got to make sure he's all right—"

"Graeme again?" he exploded. He grabbed the edges of her robe in his fists. His eyes flamed. "Graeme this and Graeme that! What is it with the two of you?"

She stared up at him, her breath caught in the back of her throat. When his blazing eyes met hers, she held his gaze for a moment, then wordlessly looked to where his hands gripped her robe.

He let out a breath, dropped his hands, and stepped away. "I'm sorry, Matilda. Sorry we've been arguing so much. You must try to understand how I feel when you speak about that man. I cannot bear the thought of anyone taking you from me."

"No one can take me from you," she said quietly. *But I can leave.* The thought was clear and firm. *I can walk away from you if I have to.*

"I'm glad to hear it. And forget what I said about that ridiculous treasure. You're my treasure. All I care about is getting you as far away from here—from danger—as possible."

"That would be fine, Arthur." She slipped the amulet over her neck and dropped it inside the bathrobe. "But it's hard to think beyond all this right now."

"I'm sure that's true. All the same, you must try to put it behind you." He gave her a warm smile. "If you'll be all right, I'm going to pop down and speak to the hotel manager about my suit and perhaps make a telephone call or two. In the meantime, why don't you do something with your hair—plait it up or something. You look rather wild with it down, Matilda darling."

He squeezed her arm and headed for the door.

As he opened the door to leave, Hannah slipped into the room. Her bright yellow scarf sat slightly askew on her head. Arms full of clothes, she stared at Tillie.

"I believe it would be wise to dress quickly, *toto*," she said. "Outside the hotel I have seen a gathering of camels."

SEVEN

Hannah's crooked fingers dropped a white dress over Tillie's head. "Quickly now, *toto*," she muttered as she tugged a flowing blue-and-white striped robe over the dress. "Take this turban, too. It will cover your hair."

Tillie stepped into a pair of leather thongs and began winding the turban around her hair. "Does the Targui know I'm here?"

"I believe he does."

"Mama Hannah, he wants something from me, and I don't have it. I don't know what to do. And then there's Arthur. I can't go to London with him. It's not right! But Graeme's not right either. If you could just meet Graeme . . ." Her confused rambling trailed off, and she looked at Hannah, fighting sudden tears. "I don't know, Mama Hannah. I don't know."

"Immanuel," she whispered. "God is with us."

"They've found us!" Arthur burst into the room, ran to his suitcase, and took out the small handgun.

Hannah locked the door behind him, then backed against it, arms outstretched, as though her small, birdlike body could keep out the horde. Heart beating like a Tuareg war drum, Tillie dashed to the window. Down in the street, the warriors were dismounting from their drome-daries. A youth held the *amenoukal*'s white camel.

"Arthur, we have to leave right now," she whispered.

He turned to her, his gun on the half cock. "They won't get near us if I have this. Except for those ridiculous medieval weapons, they're all unarmed. We're going to stay right here until this thing is settled."

"You don't understand. I have to get out of this place. If I'm here, they'll hurt you and Hannah."

Before he could reply, a thud shook the door. Hannah let out a squeak and leapt forward.

"It's him," Tillie hissed, grabbing her *ayah*'s arm. "Come on, Mama Hannah. Arthur, follow me."

She unlatched the glass door and stepped out onto the balcony. The hammering increased behind her, and the bedroom door shivered on its hinges. Arthur hesitated a moment before jumping to the table and stuffing his pockets with ammunition. Then he joined the two women, helped them over the rusty iron rail, and clambered out beside them onto the narrow ledge that surrounded the hotel.

"Watch your step," he whispered.

Her heart leaden, Tillie clutched the rough mud bricks behind her back as she looked down at the dromedaries on the street. "Hold on to Hannah, Arthur. Don't let her fall."

A shout sounded below.

"They've seen us," Arthur growled. "If you'd let me—"

"Wait, I have an idea." Tillie took Hannah's shoulders and helped her back onto the balcony. "Stay here with Arthur," she told the old woman. "They'll hurt you if you're with me. Please, Mama Hannah, pray for me."

"Matilda!" Arthur snapped. "What do you think you're doing?"

"I'm going down alone. See that alley beside the hotel? It's too narrow for a camel. If I can get to it, I'll run to the market. Look for me there. If we can't find each other, I'll meet you in Timbuktu."

"No, darling! Don't be ridiculous."

She turned to the wall, pushed one toe in the space between two bricks, found a handhold, and began climbing down. "Take care of Hannah for me, Arthur. I'm counting on you."

She heard the first of the Tuareg breaking through the door into the hotel room. The men on the street shouted encouragement to their comrades. Still on the ledge, Arthur pulled out his gun and leveled it at the intruders.

"No!" Tillie cried.

A Targui fell screaming in agony past Tillie to the ground two floors below. His broadsword tumbled from his hand and landed beside him with a clatter.

"Tillie! Tillie-girl!"

The voice grabbed her attention away from the wounded Targui. A dark-haired man waved from a flimsy-looking three-wheeled motor scooter. As the scooter sped up a narrow street toward the hotel, a wash of relief flooded through her.

"It's Graeme," she shouted to Arthur. "Bring Hannah! Hurry up. He's got a scooter."

"Run, Matilda. I'll meet you in the market."

"Arthur, this is our chance. Bring Hannah!"

"I mean to put a stop to this nonsense." He took aim at a second Targui.

"Not like that, Arthur!" she screamed. "Hannah, please come—"

"*Nenda, toto!*" With a flutter of her fingers, Hannah urged Tillie to flee. The old woman crouched in the corner of the balcony, her eyes closed and her palms cupped over the top of her yellow head scarf. "*Mungu akubariki. Tutaonana.*"

Even at this moment, the *ayah* wished God's blessing on her *toto*. As Arthur squeezed the trigger, Tillie turned away and gritted her teeth, unwilling to hear the awful *whang* of the bullet.

"Arthur!" she yelled again, fury raising the pitch of her voice. Another wounded Targui slumped onto the balcony rail.

It was no use waiting any longer. She could hear the scooter approaching. Taking a deep breath, she scrambled down. Her aching legs carried her onto another balcony. The popping sound of Arthur's gun barely registered. Below her, the *amenoukal* strode from the hotel and began to mount his dromedary.

Graeme tooted the horn as he threaded his scooter between the skittish camels. It sounded like a bullfrog with bronchitis. He revved the engine and churned up spirals of dust. Chaos broke out in the caravan as camels spat and swung their heads. Warriors shouted. The acrid scent of engine smoke filled the air.

For no longer than a heartbeat, the scooter slowed under the balcony. Tillie dropped onto the backseat like a monkey dropping from a coconut tree. Throwing her arms around Graeme's chest, she held on as he gunned it down the alley.

"What about your pal?" he shouted over the motor's whine.

She glanced back to see Arthur leap to the street himself, fire off two rounds, and dash for the narrow alley beside the hotel. "Oh, no—he's left Hannah on the balcony!"

"I'll take you back." Graeme turned a corner and slowed the scooter.

"Wait! They don't want her. They'll follow us." She squeezed her eyes shut and rested her cheek on his back. "Lead them away from her. Go to the market."

Past the end of her flapping turban she saw the *amenoukal* and his men pursuing them rather than Arthur or Hannah. The Tuareg dromedaries loped along in the dusty wake of the little machine.

"Those camels can make twenty miles an hour for at least six miles at a dead run, and I can barely do better than thirty on this scooter. We'll be sitting ducks in the market," Graeme called over his shoulder. "We've got to get out of this town."

"I can't leave Hannah here."

"Won't Arthur go back for her?"

Doubt twisted inside Tillie. "I don't know."

"We'll call the hotel from Djenne. It's the next town upriver." The scooter whipped down the street, scattering people left and right. "We'll make sure she's all right."

As the camels struggled to keep up, the *amenoukal* raised his spear and drew back his arm. Graeme spun the scooter around another corner and sped down a slope toward the river. It bounced onto the pier, lifting Tillie from the seat momentarily as they rattled down the loose old boards to the water's edge.

Graeme slammed the scooter to a stop, jumped off, and grabbed Tillie. Hand in hand, they raced to the edge of the landing and leapt into a tiny fishing boat. He picked up a paddle, tossed her another, and started rowing like crazy.

God, what I wouldn't give for an outboard motor, Tillie thought, sucking air into her lungs. But such things were rare. She looked out across the wide expanse of brown water. A huge old boat was pulling out toward the midstream current, puffing thick black smoke as it moved. The river steamer.

She turned back to the pier. Snorting, bellowing camels lined up at the water's edge. The *amenoukal* brandished his lance. His dromedary, so right for the desert, had failed him again on city streets. The Tuareg leader raised a hand, and the group of warriors gathering on the pier bristled with spears.

"Graeme!" Tillie called out a warning.

The *amenoukal* dropped his hand. Spears like long silver rockets hurtled through the air. Graeme flung himself across Tillie and flattened her to the wet floor, crushing the air from her chest. Five spears splashed into the water around them. Another stuck with a thud, vibrating on the wooden floor near her head. She winced.

In the time it took to draw a breath, the barrage was over. She opened her eyes and lifted her head. One spear had buried its point in the hull of the boat, another hung askew from the side, the rest floated lazily in the brown water.

Graeme sat up and pulled her into his arms. "OK?" His breath warmed her hair.

She nodded. The scent of his clean shirt mingled with

something spicy on his skin. She pressed her cheek against his chest and closed her eyes. "Are we safe?"

"For now."

"I feel sick about leaving Hannah on that balcony."

His hand molded over her shoulder. "I'll take you back right now if you want."

"I'd never get to her." She pictured the old woman, so strong despite her fragile appearance. "If the Tuareg leave her alone, she'll be OK."

"I suspect they've got someone else on their minds."

She lifted her head. Like the return of a bad dream, the whole caravan—warriors, women, children with pots clanking, bells jingling, tents wobbling—was filing down the riverbank, keeping pace with the little boat.

"Last thing I did was shove you back into the Niger. Not exactly a grand farewell," Graeme said, handing her the oar again. "I was worried about you."

She studied his eyes and saw the truth written in them. "I'm OK. But I heard gunfire as I swam away. How did you escape from them yesterday? And how on earth did you find me?"

"I had motivation." He slipped the oar into the water and resumed paddling.

Tillie shook her head as they rowed toward the steamer. What did that mean? The treasure, the journal . . . or her? As usual, she couldn't quite read him. She hardly cared. Just the sight of his dark hair blowing away from his face, his blue-green eyes searching the shoreline, his little half-smile . . . the essence of Graeme tugged at her heart, warmed her, thrilled her. They were together again. That was enough for the moment.

"Graeme—," she began, but her thought was cut short, and she looked around. "What's that noise?"

His head jerked up. A soft gurgling, gushing sound came from behind them. "Trouble."

The spearhead had split the bottom of the boat, and water was seeping through. Graeme grimaced and began paddling like a demon, guiding the boat toward the steamer. Tillie grabbed a half-gourd dipper and began bailing.

She could see the steamer's passengers gathering at the rail as the tiny fishing boat plowed through the water toward them. It was a race she was afraid she and Graeme couldn't win. Either the boat would sink, or the steamer would pull into the current before they could reach it.

Graeme propelled the tiny craft, his arms pumping in a steady rhythm. Tillie bailed as fast as she could, but she was losing the battle. The boat settled deeper and deeper. The farther it sank, the slower it went.

"Tillie!" Graeme shouted above the din of the steamer engines. "We've got to jump, or we'll never make it. Swim like that croc was after you."

She glanced down at the muddy water swirling around her ankles. Lifting her head in time to see Graeme dive off the edge, she sent up a prayer, peeled off the robe, and plunged in after him. The current sucked her under, surprising her with its strength.

Graeme swam to her side and matched his strokes with hers. They cut through the water, pulling closer and closer to the steamer. The wake lifted and slapped at them, trying to churn them under. Tillie could feel her arms tiring, her legs slowing, her spirit weakening.

Just ahead of her, Graeme shouted something in French.

A heavy rope smacked into the water ahead. "Grab it. They'll pull us up."

She snatched the raveled end. He wrapped one arm around her waist, took hold of the rope, and signaled to the steamer's crew. The rope began to rise, lifting them out of the water like a Christmas ornament caught on a string of tinsel. They bumped against the rusty orange side of the ship, then dangled outward again. As they inched toward the deck, they twirled and spun, sending a shower of silver droplets into the river below.

"I've been on a lot of wild rides," Graeme said, "but this beats 'em all. The Niger Express."

Tillie turned her head, saw the sparkle in his eyes, and couldn't hold back a grin. "I can't believe I ended up in that water again." She let her head drop back and laughed out loud. "One bath, one meal, and one set of clean clothes, and then I'm right back in the river. It's unbelievable!"

"Aw, admit it. You're having a ball."

I wouldn't go that far, Tillie thought. But she realized that the tension-filled hours with Arthur had worn on her more than all the days on the Niger.

"I'm just glad you're OK," she whispered.

"Partners again?"

She searched his eyes. Water had made damp spikes of his eyelashes. A tiny rivulet ran from his sideburn down his jaw and dripped off the end of his chin. Partners? *Do not be bound together with unbelievers. . . .* She cut off the voice in her heart as his lips found hers.

Just for a moment, Lord. . . . Her plea dissolved as she drank him in, wanting only to be with him in spite of all she had been taught was right.

"Tillie," he whispered, his ragged breath on her hair, "the things I'm feeling right now scare me more than all the crocodiles on the Niger River."

For the remaining moments of their ascent, she closed her eyes and allowed herself to enjoy the echo of his words and to soak in his warm presence. His chest was firm under her hands, and his arms encircled her like a vise. She couldn't have fallen back into the river if she'd wanted to.

When they again bumped into the side of the old steamer, she looked up to find eager hands reaching down for her. Like a wayward piece of cargo, she was hoisted through the air and deposited on the deck.

"Bonjour, madame." A handsome African man spoke in polite, well-formed French. "On behalf of the Compagnie Malienne de Navigation, I welcome you aboard the *Soumar.* You arrived just in time."

"En retard." Tillie turned to the ogling crowd and held out her hands to those who had rescued her. *"Merci beaucoup."*

Graeme scrambled onto the steamer and in fluent French began arranging to book passage to Djenne. Tillie surveyed the old boat in wonder. Though it was dirty, rusty, and damp, it clearly hailed from a time of elegance. Everywhere she looked, signs of the ship's glory days were evident. Like a grand wedding cake that had sat too long in the bakery, the steamer was frosted with pink iron garlands and baroque curlicues. Tall pillars were hung with metal ivy and faded roses. The banisters had been carved of cherry and polished to a high sheen by the innumerable hands that slid over them each day. Remnants of ruby velvet curtains hung in several cabin windows, and a few tatters of oriental carpeting still clung to the stairs.

Feeling as though she had walked into an old fairy tale book filled with faded lithographs and bound in shabby covers, Tillie leaned against the railing that circled the lower deck. This deck was taken up by two large cabins with bunk beds for the third- and fourth-class passengers. From the throng of curious passengers pressing for a closer look to the crystal chandelier hanging askew in the passageway ahead, it was a strange, dizzying fantasy.

She had to marvel at herself. One moment she had been running from the *amenoukal*—cornered, almost certain to be captured, half-paralyzed with fear—and now . . . now she felt almost exhilarated. If only she could be certain Hannah was safe.

Immanuel. God is with us.

The reassurance swept over her. One day at a time. One minute at a time. The Lord was not a security blanket, not a good-luck charm, but he was with her. Always with her. In the river, out of the river, in Land Rovers and boats, on scooters or steamships.

And he had sent Graeme. She looked at the man who had come for her. His eyes animated, he conversed comfortably in French with the African steward. His wet blue shirt clung to his chest as he coiled the long rope. In the few hours they were apart, Tillie had missed him more than she thought she could miss anyone.

He intrigued and fascinated her. He made her laugh, made her think, made her search. He was strong and honorable and kind and good.

Do not be bound together—

Enough! She cut off the thought again. Turning to the shore, she pictured Hannah in the little hotel room. Her old *ayah* would be searching the Scriptures, praying for Tillie. Her *toto*.

Tillie closed her eyes, struggling with her confusion and a niggling guilt. Was she ignoring God? Relying on her emotions rather than the truth? *Oh, Mama Hannah,* she thought, wishing her *ayah* were there beside her, ready to offer wise cousel. *God wouldn't have allowed Graeme into my life if he were going to hurt me. My Father wouldn't let me stumble down a wrong path. What I feel for Graeme can't be bad. God wouldn't do that to me. Would he?*

She could almost hear Hannah's response: *"Do not seek your answers from me,* toto. *'If any of you lacks wisdom, let him ask of God.' You know the source of truth, Tillie. Remember what Christ taught, and let his words enrich your life and make you wise."*

For once, the thought of the Scriptures and Christ's words didn't bring her a sense of comfort. Instead, the doubt and guilt she'd been trying to ignore went from niggling to irritating. With a sigh, she turned away from the rail—just in time to take in Graeme's appreciative stare.

I can handle this, she thought stubbornly. *I can enjoy him without getting tangled, and then I can go on with the rest of my life the way I always have.*

"You are fortunate, sir," the steward was saying to Graeme as she walked toward them. "The steamer is on its way now to Djenne. The boat usually cannot travel this part of the Niger except in the rainy season. You will find Djenne a safe harbor from the Tuareg. The city is only accessible by boat. A car, airplane, or camel cannot go into Djenne."

"That's a stroke of luck. Looks like our shadows will

have to leave us alone for a few days." Graeme winked at Tillie.

"On the upper deck are our luxury, first- and second-class cabins," the steward said with a bow. "Shall I show you to a room?"

"Two rooms." Tillie tugged a small silver ring from her finger and dropped it into the man's hand. "It's all I have to pay you with."

He glanced at Graeme, one eyebrow raised in inquiry. "Monsieur?"

"Two rooms," Graeme affirmed.

"Honnête homme. We do not often see such honor among Christians."

Tillie followed the two men down the deck. She knew most Malians practiced Islam and thought of all white people as Christians. How many unmarried tourists had this man watched take a room together on his rusty steamer? Because of her white skin, every action would be attributed to Christians, every word and encounter would be a witness to those who watched with critical eyes.

She swallowed hard, hoping she wouldn't simply give the Malians more reason to hold Christians in disdain.

As she followed Graeme and the steward, she noted how passengers gawked and elbowed each other, commenting in an array of dialects about the newcomers who had been lifted from the Niger. A little girl tried to sell Graeme a bunch of bananas. He glanced at Tillie, made a face, and shook his head. She laughed. An old woman pressed forward to display a handful of bracelets and a tray of rings. Graeme stopped, pulled a beaded ring from the tray, and handed the woman a few damp coins.

Taking Tillie's left hand, he slipped the ring over her ring finger. "A promise from a man of honor."

She lifted her head, startled, but the steward bustled away, Graeme beside him asking questions about Djenne and the path to Timbuktu.

Tillie looked down at the muddy Niger. *You strange and mysterious river,* she thought. *How many more changes will you bring into my life?*

Tillie's luxury cabin was a seven-by-eight-foot reflection of the ornate, slightly garish steamer. Though cramped, the room contained a small window, a sink, and a bidet. A bed with a straw-filled mattress, red blankets, and fluffy pillows stood beside a gilded dresser. Bleached white towels were stacked at the end of the bed. The ceiling, dripping with plaster roses and ivy, had been painted in shades of neon pink and green.

Wanting nothing more than a hot shower, Tillie had sent Graeme off to find his own room, clean up, and then buy her something to wear. The bathroom was shared by eight cabins, but it was cleaner than she had expected. Someone had left a bar of soap on the porcelain sink and a small bottle of shampoo in the shower. She slipped the amulet over her neck and set it on the sink. The water was warm and the soap fragrant as she lathered herself.

As she poured a palmful of shampoo and worked it through her hair, she heard someone walk past the bathroom door. "First-class delivery service," Graeme called. "Package on your bed."

"Thanks."

"Meet you on deck."

As she heard the door close, Tillie let herself dwell on that moment dangling over the river when Graeme had kissed her. That had been one perfect kiss. The ring on her finger twisted around as she rinsed the shampoo from her hair. *A promise from a man of honor.*

Arthur would be outraged if he ever found out. She studied the beaded ring under the cascade of water. Tiny nuggets of raw glass—red, amber, cobalt, emerald—strung on a thin silver wire. It didn't matter whether Arthur knew or not. She'd never agreed to marry him, and she had no intention of ever doing so. Not even if he followed her all the way to Timbuktu.

All her life she had been wanting the kind of magic she felt around Graeme McLeod. She had suspected there must be more to love and marriage than the tender feeling she had when Hannah patted her cheek or the warmth of her brother, Grant's, quick hug or even the mildly pleasant intimacy of Arthur's kisses. She had seen such passion in movies, read about it in books. A racing pulse, a flush of the cheeks, those longing glances. Now that she had tasted such things for herself, she wasn't about to settle for a congenial, platonic life with Arthur Robinson.

She picked up her white dress from the bathroom floor and rinsed it out under the warm water. The image of Hannah's knobby fingers washing dishes flashed into her mind. Hannah would like Graeme. There was no question about that. Hannah liked people with spunk, people who walked straight into the headwinds of life as she did. Hannah admired bravery and honesty. She would respect a man who put human beings ahead of schedules. She would like Graeme, respect him, admire him. But she wouldn't want her *toto* to marry him.

"I'm not marrying him," Tillie said out loud as she wrapped her wet burnous around her and tiptoed back across the hall to her cabin. "I'm just going to Timbuktu with him. That's all."

After toweling off, she lifted the twine-tied bundle and picked apart the knot. A pale pink dress tumbled onto the bed along with a plastic comb, a toothbrush, even some underwear. The tunic was simple, straight, and clean-cut, yet it was also delicate and feminine. Tiny rosebuds had been embroidered around its scooped neck and along the short sleeves. She wouldn't have chosen it for herself, but when she tried it on, she realized it suited her. She felt beautiful. Truly, wildly, wonderfully beautiful—and it was his doing.

She slipped into her sandals as she ran the comb through her hair, then opened the cabin door and stepped out into the hall.

You'd better watch yourself, Graeme McLeod, she thought with a smile. *Your rosebud is blossoming.*

Lunch in the luxury dining room was a grandiose affair. Graeme decided it must be a custom left over from French colonialism. There were fresh tropical fruits, mango juice, papaya juice, a leg of lamb, slabs of goat cheese, and mountains of fresh-baked bread. It was enough to make a hungry man weep. But when Tillie walked down the stairs, resplendent in that pink dress, her golden hair floating all around her shoulders, he forgot all about food.

She thanked him for the dress, and he followed her to the buffet line, tagging behind her like a little wag-tailed puppy. Something about the way she smiled at him, her cheeks flushed and her blue eyes heavy-lidded, sent a weight to the pit of his stomach. *This* was the woman he'd thrown into his Land Rover? Had he really pushed this enchantress headlong into the Niger River? If she wanted to murder him, he wouldn't blame her.

But she talked and laughed and ate her way through lunch, her eyes saying a lot more than her words. Somewhere between the oxtail soup and the vanilla custard, it occurred to him that she had climbed out of that hotel room and dropped right back into his arms, leaving her boyfriend behind. Now, there was an interesting thought, one he wanted to turn over and examine like that scrap of paper in the amulet around her neck.

After lunch they wandered to the upper deck and stood side by side at the railing. Fishing boats plied the shallows. Egrets and pied kingfishers turned and wheeled overhead, while the occasional hippo surfaced to blow a stream of water.

"Remember that hippo circling us?" Tillie leaned on the rail, her shoulder inches from Graeme's.

"I'll never forget your face when he came up under us, and we were riding around on his back like a couple of kids on a Tilt-A-Whirl at the fair."

She laughed at the memory, and he slipped his arm around her. Without a moment's hesitation, she leaned into him and nestled her head against his chest. He swallowed. What was happening?

From the minute he'd pushed her into the water and watched her swim away with her boyfriend, he'd wanted her back. He had escaped the Tuareg with a few gunshots in the air to scatter them, rented a room for the night, and arranged to send the fishing boat back upriver to the village where they'd taken it. Then he'd booked himself a spot on the CMN steamer to Djenne.

But he couldn't go.

Instead, he had spent the night combing the streets and alleys of Segou asking people if they'd seen a white woman with golden hair. When he found the hotel, he made up his mind to go talk to her. And then he couldn't do that, either. After all, she was where she'd wanted to be all along. Safe, secure. With another man.

That morning, when Graeme saw the Tuareg gathering around the hotel, he'd almost blessed them. They'd given him a chance to see Tillie again. Like a man possessed, he had rented the scooter and raced to her rescue, half expecting her boyfriend to plug him with that pistol of his. Instead, she had dropped back into his life, gone with him eagerly, responded to his impulsive kiss, and was now snuggled up to him like he was the best thing to come along in years.

"It's been fun," she murmured, "all this running around. I can't deny I'm thankful to take a break from it, though. Even Arthur got treasure fever the minute I told him what was going on."

"You told him?"

"A little."

Graeme studied the shoreline a moment. "Listen, Tillie, about this Arthur guy—"

"I don't want to talk about him. Or the treasure. I don't want to hear the words *tree-planting woman* ever again."

He couldn't blame her. At the same time, he wanted to keep her talking. He wanted to know as much about her as he could. Her thoughts. Her feelings.

"About that tree-planting business," he said, tossing out bait. "I think I've figured out what Mungo Park meant when he wrote those words."

He could see that she was torn. Wanting to know, wanting to leave it all behind. "The tree-planting part? Really?"

"Let me see the document."

She opened the amulet and slipped out the roll of paper.

He scanned it. "Right here at the end, I think Park was looking into the future. I think he foresaw a time when the Niger would be as it is today—fully explored and inhabited. He knew white men and women would live here. He had warned the king of Segou about it. He could envision the land looking like a little piece of Scotland, white women planting trees and gardens, and having tea parties to boot."

In spite of herself, she looked at the paper in his hand. "But why does he write, 'She will plant trees. She will find the treasure of Timbuktu'? Like they're connected."

"I think he believed that when white people moved onto the land, they'd find the real treasure of Timbuktu. To him, the real treasure must have been the land itself."

"And the river." She lifted her eyes. "Graeme, I think you're right! I think he was looking to the future. The tree-planting woman isn't me after all. It's civilization. Englishmen and their women coming to tame the land."

He folded the page and put it in the amulet. "That's my theory. Let's take that concept and see where it goes. How do you think the Tuareg interpreted it? What do you think they plan to do?"

She gave a low laugh. "You never give up, do you? I don't want to think about why we're here or what happened to bring us here, remember? I don't even want to speculate about what's going to happen. I just want to be here and rest. For today, I just want to be with you, and I don't want to think about yesterday or tomorrow."

He brushed a kiss on the top of her head. "OK, then. No past, no future."

She fell silent a moment. Then she repeated his words in an almost inaudible whisper. "No future."

The lead weight that had settled in Graeme's chest the minute Tillie echoed those words sank lower as the day wore on. He knew what she meant. They didn't have a future together. Couldn't. Two people thrown together like that—one of them practically engaged and the other alone and determined to stay that way—didn't just toss their old lives off the deck of a steamer.

So they spent the afternoon wandering the decks, talking about nothing in particular, watching the shoreline slide by. The other passengers at first stared at the white man and woman who strolled among them. But after a while they tired of gawking and went on about their selling and bartering and chatting in the sunshine.

Graeme and Tillie chatted about mundane things. About the steamer and how it negotiated the sandbars. How many of the passengers probably made their homes aboard it.

How trade had changed in Mali from salt, gold, ivory, and slaves to cloth printed in Hong Kong, beads made in Taiwan, and battered tinned goods brought in from France and England. They talked about the color of the river, the species of trees on the shore, the numbers of fish being pulled up in nets. But they didn't talk about what the next day would bring. Or the next week.

Tillie floated beside Graeme all that afternoon, a cloud of pink and gold, just out of his reach. And the more he thought about losing her again, the deeper that lead weight in his chest sank. He decided to take all she would give. He held her hand, wove his thick brown fingers through her slender ones as though he could somehow absorb their softness into his own body. He memorized the melody of her laughter, the rhythm of her voice, the silly words she invented when fussing over children or puppies. Like an addict, he was drawn to drink in the smell of her hair—spice and herbs and flowers. And the more he drank, the more he wanted.

That evening a steward brought their dinner to a small, private, first-class sitting room. A table set with candles stood in the center of the room. A sofa with plush pillows sat near a bookcase. They feasted on fresh fish broiled in butter, steaming bread, and plump black dates. The air was warm, and the slight breeze that filtered through the porthole did no more than make the golden candlelight waver.

As they ate, he searched her face, willing her to give him something to take away the heaviness inside him. "We'll get to Djenne tomorrow," he said, trying again to point her toward the future.

She lowered her eyes. "What time?"

"Around midmorning, I imagine. Maybe noon. So . . .

have you given much thought to Timbuktu? Are you going to—"

"Please don't talk about it, Graeme."

"Look, Tillie—I'd like to know what's going to happen between us."

"I don't know what's going to happen. I don't know." She twisted the cloth napkin in her lap. "I don't know what to do, Graeme. I'm not impulsive like you. I have to think."

She rose and turned away from him. He tossed his napkin onto the table. He hadn't meant to snuff that light in her eyes. The dispirited droop to her shoulders troubled him more than he cared to admit. He longed for the sparkling Tillie, the adventurer who could race a hippo to shore and outrun a crocodile.

"You're not impulsive like me, huh?" he asked, forcing a lightness to his voice. "Are you sure?"

She glanced back at him in confusion, and as she did, he flicked water at her from his glass. "Oh! Graeme, stop that."

She lifted her hand to smack him on the shoulder, but as she did so he poked a finger into her ribs.

"Impulsive, am I?" He grinned as she took a step backward and stumbled onto the couch. But when he tried to tackle her, she grabbed a pillow and clobbered him over the head.

Fending off a rain of blows, he trailed her around the tiny room like a hungry lion. Lobbing pillows back and forth at each other, they scrambled around the little table and edged across the floor. Tillie laughed until tears ran down her cheeks.

"Graeme, the candles!" she shrieked as he dived for her

and dropped her onto the sofa amid a shower of feathers from a burst pillow. "OK, OK. I give up. I quit."

He smiled and kissed her lightly. "Never give up, Tillie," he whispered. "Never quit."

Her lower lip trembled, and she bit it. "All day I've told myself I could do this. That I could just be your friend. Be light and easy about us."

"Nothing's light and easy right now. You've got a Targui, fully equipped with a broadsword, who thinks you're going to find him a stash of gold. And you don't have Arthur Robinson. You've got me."

"Oh, Graeme." She sat up and stared down at the floor. "I'm walking a tightrope."

"I'll catch you if you fall."

"It's you who's going to make me fall."

"You know I wouldn't do that."

"Not on purpose. But you're here . . . and you're all these things I like . . . things I want. Things I can't have."

"Look, if it's Arthur—"

"It's not Arthur." She jumped up and walked to the cabin door. "It's not Arthur. It's you and me. We're different."

"So?"

"So, it's not right. You're your own boss, Graeme, but I'm not in control of my life. I don't make my own choices, not like you do. And I'm happy about that. A long time ago, I surrendered who I am and what I want to Christ. That puts you and me poles apart. It makes us fundamentally opposite. That's all." She opened the door, and he could see she was crying. "That's all, OK? Just leave it."

He watched the door close, listened to the latch click, and he wanted nothing more than to walk out onto the deck, grab her, and kiss her. He wanted to wipe those tears of confusion off her face. He wanted to tell her he'd never hurt her, swear he'd protect her, promise anything it would take to keep her.

Instead, he lay back on the sofa and cocked his hands behind his head. Matilda Thornton was a woman unafraid to live in Africa, to jump into the Niger River, to outwit a crocodile, to knock a broadsword away from a Targui. But something was holding her back where he was concerned.

There was something in her life that was more important than anything else. Something strong enough to seal her heart away from his. Something so potent she would stifle every emotion she so clearly felt for him. Something so powerful she would give up everything she wanted just to keep it. Could it really be this business about her faith in God? Surely rational people like Tillie didn't give control of their lives to some unknown, unseen spirit. Did they? Faith as strong as Tillie's required a basis that was solid, concrete.

No. This wasn't about God. The barrier that kept Tillie from him had to be human. Maybe her old friend Hannah had warned her away. Or maybe it was Arthur Robinson. Graeme studied the curls of plaster dripping from the ceiling. What was it that held Tillie's soul?

Eight

"Father. Lord. Savior."

Tillie murmured the words as she showered before dressing in the white dress Hannah had bought her. Early morning sunlight slanted into the cabin. Lifting her face to its warmth, she dropped the amulet down her neckline. For all its delicate design, the pendant was proving to be a heavy yoke. She let out a deep breath.

The thing is, Father, Graeme cares about me. Cares enough to give me his promise of honor. Not every man would do that.

She twisted the ring as she stepped into her sandals. *I care about him, too. I like him. I want to be with him. Would you really send a man like Graeme into my life, put him before me like a sugar cube held out to a horse? A man who's everything I've dreamed about. Just the kind of man who could share my strange, unconventional lifestyle. Handsome and kind and honorable. A good man.*

She struggled with tears of confusion. *And because he's not a Christian, I'm supposed to reject him? Why are you testing me like this, Lord? This is not fun. This hurts.*

She walked out of her cabin, down the narrow hall, and up the flight of steps to the deck. Graeme was standing at the iron railing, his dark hair ruffling in the breeze as he huddled over a map. She knew it was a map of Djenne.

Boxed in. That's what I am, Father. I need to get away from this river so I can think. But it's here, all around me. Inescapable. And what could I escape to? Arthur? I want to know the future, but you won't tell me. Not even a clue. The only thing you've made clear is that no matter how much I want to be with Graeme, I can't.

As she walked across the creaking boards, Tillie saw the city nestled in the middle of the river like an island. She stopped at Graeme's side, and he looked up. His face was drawn, as though he hadn't slept any more than she had.

"Mornin', glory." His voice was hoarse. He took her hand and slid his fingers between hers. Then he went back to his map.

As the steamer puffed into port and the anchors dropped, she scanned the town. Djenne was an island located eighteen miles off the main Bamako-to-Mopti road at the southern end of an inland delta. Surrounded by a natural moat and latticed with waterways, the town was made up of clay houses and mosques boasting facades decorated with porches, all lined in pointed crenellations. Old men on mats rested their bent backs against the clay walls. Across the sun-dappled river a fisherman gripped a net between one hand and his outstretched feet. In the other hand he held a bobbin that he dipped in and out across the net.

"It's like something from a different age," she whispered.

"What is?"

"The town. Look at the dugouts. They're filled with dried fish. They have canopies. It's hard to believe no one can get here except by boat. Like Shangri-La. I wonder if the old men have ever seen cars or airplanes."

He glanced up from his map. "Hmm? Seen what?"

She pursed her lips. "What are you doing?"

He folded the map and slipped it into his jeans pocket. "I've made a decision. Come on."

"What about our stuff? My pink dress—"

"We're taking the steamer on to Mopti this afternoon." He pulled her through the crowd toward the row of dugouts waiting to ferry people ashore. "I want to go into Djenne and find the police station. We'll call the hotel in Segou, check on Hannah, and find out if Robinson is here yet. Then we'll get this thing between you and him settled once and for all."

"Between me and Arthur?"

Instead of answering, he began to dicker in French with the pilot of a dugout, haggling over the price of the trip. Shoving two bills into the man's waiting palm, he looked back at Tillie. "This guy says he can take us to the police station. We can go the whole way by boat."

She followed him down the rope ladder into the bobbing canoe. "I told you this is not about Arthur." She squatted on a splintery board beside a pile of flopping fish.

Graeme thinks I love Arthur. He thinks that's what is holding me back. Arthur. Oh, Lord, I can't even think about Arthur.

If I keep insisting it's you, Father—it's my relationship with you that matters most—he'll resent that. Why would he worship you when he sees you as a barrier to me, and not as the Way to a new life? Maybe he would turn to you, but would it be honest?

The dugout slipped into one of the canals between two rows of clay houses. It was an eerie feeling, floating along when reason said a person should be walking or driving. Djenne was filled with busy traders hauling baskets of fish, dates, millet, and yams to the town market. As in Bamako, children scampered along the wooden boardwalks beside the white-skinned visitors. Some giggled and danced around like silly marionettes. Others tried to sell poorly woven blankets or fly-encrusted food as the dugout skimmed past.

The fisherman was a skilled pilot who navigated his boat as if it were a precision race car. They whipped around corners, sliced the water beneath crude bridges, and zipped past piers of docked dugouts. Graeme sat in the prow of the slender boat and drummed his fingers on the smooth wood. Through the sheer turban fabric that blew around her face, Tillie studied him. His lean legs were tensed for action, as though he might leap off the boat at any moment. His arms were roped with the strain of his clenched fists. The tiny muscle in his jaw beat a regular rhythm, and his focus darted back and forth, missing nothing.

The dugout bumped into a whitewashed clay building beside the bustling marketplace. Graeme scrambled to the boardwalk. He gave rapid instructions to the fisherman as he helped Tillie out of the boat.

"This is the police station," he told her. "This guy's going to wait for us here."

"You think they'll have a phone?"

"They have one. Whether it's working or not is another matter."

As they walked into the sleepy little office, Tillie's heart hammered against her ribs. What if Arthur was here in Djenne? Could she tell him it was over between them? Tell him just like that in the middle of this mixed-up mess when she could hardly think straight?

Spotting them, an official stood and walked around his

sagging desk to greet Graeme like an old friend. "Monsieur McLeod! *Bonjour!*"

Confused, Tillie watched the men shake hands and slap each other on the back. *"Tout à vous,* Mohammed," Graeme said. *"Ma compagnon de voyage,* Matilda Thornton."

"Mademoiselle Thornton." He kissed the back of her hand. *"La belle dame. Bonjour, bonjour."*

Graeme rattled off a long monologue that had something to do with the steamer, the Tuareg, Bamako, and Djenne. Tillie spoke Swahili, Kikuyu, Kikamba, a little Maasai, and some German. But she could barely get by in French. It frustrated her to no end. All she could tell was that Mohammed was welcoming Graeme back to the town. When had Graeme ever been to Djenne?

"What's he telling you?" She touched Graeme's arm. "Have they seen Arthur and Hannah?"

"Says he can't remember. He's going to go through his files. They make every tourist sign some documents when they pass through." Graeme leaned over the sheaf of tattered papers to watch as the official began riffling through them.

Tillie strolled around the dull, gray room. Through fly-speckled windowpanes she could see the busy, colorful open-air marketplace next door. Inside, two bored-looking clerks sat at their desks sorting through stacks of yellow papers. The thought of seeing Arthur again sent a curl of discomfort through her stomach. And Hannah. What would Hannah say if she knew how deeply her *toto* had come to care for the black-haired stranger? And she would know the minute she saw them together. Hannah's warm brown eyes didn't miss a thing.

Trust me, God had said. Trusting was harder now than it had been when the hippo dumped her into the Niger. Strange to prefer terror to an aching heart. She wandered across the room and stepped out into the blinding sunlight. *Trust me.* She meandered down the red-painted concrete stairs and sat beside a clay newel near the market.

She couldn't plan. Couldn't decide. Couldn't act. She had walked into a box. A blind alley. She felt trapped by walls that were squeezing her in, tighter and tighter.

She stood up and followed the wall along the water's edge. The fisherman in his little dugout waved at her. She tried to smile and failed miserably. Was there any way out? Pressed by the crowds of marketgoers, unable to move ahead and unable to turn back, she leaned against the clay wall and slid to a crouch.

What am I supposed to do, Lord? Her dress bunched around her ankles in folds of soft white fabric. She dipped her head and studied her hands.

"He who belongs to God hears what God says." The words from John's Gospel were as certain as the beaded ring of honor on Tillie's finger. So were the passages from Luke: *"Whoever is ashamed of me and my words, of him will the Son of Man be ashamed. . . . No one of you can be my disciple who does not give up all his own possessions."*

Give it up. Give him up, Tillie.

That was her answer, then. Give Graeme up. Walk back to that police station. Turn in the amulet. Say good-bye to him and go home to Bamako. She belonged to God. She was his disciple. She had chosen that a long time ago, and she still wanted to serve him more than she wanted anything—or anybody—else.

The truth was difficult, painful. And yet, as she stood, peace drifted around Tillie's heart like a warm blanket. She turned back in the direction of the whitewashed building, lifted her chin, and stepped into the street.

A sharp blow slammed into her back, knocking the breath from her lungs and buckling her knees. Before she hit the street, she was whisked into the air and flung across a blue-robed shoulder.

"Tree-Planting Woman," a deep voice said as everything went black, "you belong to me now."

Slowly Tillie became aware of her surroundings. She was bouncing along, upside down, slung over the *amenoukal*'s shoulder. Disoriented, it took her a moment to realize the chieftain was running on foot in the middle of a thick force of his Tuareg companions. Broadswords, spears, flowing black robes, and leather sandals were all she could see. Her turban unwound from her head and trickled down the street like a rivulet of melting vanilla ice cream.

"Graeme!" she screamed. "Graeme, help!"

She lifted her head from the *amenoukal*'s broad back to see Graeme hurtle through the police station doorway and stop in shock.

"Tillie! What in—" He ran down the stairs and disappeared in the jostling crowd.

She had no choice but to lower her head. Their broadswords drawn, the Tuareg pounded down the sidewalk and around a corner. The crowd scattered in panic before the phalanx.

Blood throbbing in her head, Tillie pummeled the *amenoukal*'s muscular back as hard as she could. He didn't pause, didn't even flinch. In fact, his gait was exhilarated, triumphant. Again, she tried to lift her head to see where Graeme was. The excited throng blocked her view.

"Put me down!" she yelled. "I don't know where the treasure is! I don't know anything. Put me down!"

The *amenoukal* chuckled low in his throat and ran on. The Tuareg battalion jogged across a bridge and down a narrow alley. As they moved out onto another sidewalk, they slowed to a trot.

Tillie's head reeled. Dizzy, sure she was going to be sick, she couldn't think what to do beyond shouting. And then the *amenoukal*'s wiry hands grasped her waist, lifted her into the air, tossed her. She saw spinning blue sky, minarets of a mosque, someone's wash hanging on a line. Headfirst, she tumbled onto the hard deck of a boat.

For a moment she couldn't breathe, couldn't see. Then her lungs sucked in a huge breath of air, and her vision cleared. The *amenoukal* seated himself regally before her, a sneer of victory lighting his eyes above the blue veil. His slippered foot rested on her stomach. His broadsword pinned her burnous to the bottom of the boat.

"Look, *monsieur,* this is all a mistake. Error. *Comprennez-vous?*" As she spoke, she scanned the large boat's green-and-white canopy flapping in the breeze that blew along the canal. Six rowers—none of them Tuareg—paddled as fast as they could. Their shiny black backs tensed and relaxed over and over with their work.

"*Parlez-vous français?*" she tried again. "How about English? Do you speak English? Monsieur, you are making a mistake. I'm not the woman you want. The police are coming after you. You'll never get away."

The *amenoukal's* eyebrows lifted slightly, and he gave a shrug. *"Maktoub,"* he said. "You understand? *Inshallah."*

As Allah wills. So the Targui thought Allah was behind the whole thing. Great. What could be worse than a broad-sword-brandishing treasure hunter who believed he was on a divine mission?

She took a deep breath. The smell of fish flooded her nostrils and jerked her back to attention. Allah, was it? She'd see about that. Raising her fist, she slammed it into the man's calf. "Get your foot off me!" she shouted.

He drew back in surprise, and she scrambled to her knees. Tearing her burnous from the sword, she jumped up and grabbed the bamboo support of the canopy.

"Graeme!" she hollered.

The *amenoukal* knocked her back to the floor—but not before she caught a glimpse that lifted her heart. Just behind the *amenoukal's* dugout knifed the little fishing boat she and Graeme had taken to the police station. Graeme sat at the prow, rowing like a fiend. In the stern, the fisherman matched Graeme stroke for stroke.

Tillie closed her eyes. She had to think. Had to get away. The *amenoukal's* boat, for all its six rowers, was nearly three times as large as Graeme's. It had to be slower. Graeme would catch up. She had to trust that. And she wanted to be ready when he did.

Opening her eyes to narrow slits, she watched the *amenoukal* shout directions at his oarsmen. Boats filled with the other Tuareg would be ahead of the one that carried her. If she could somehow . . .

A weapon. She needed some kind of weapon. She glanced left and right. Her eyes fell on a dead fish—some sort of large dried-out carp with no eyeballs and a gaping mouth. It looked as hard as a rock.

"Batter up," she shouted. Grabbing the fish by its tail, she leapt to her feet and cocked it over her shoulder in her best Mickey Mantle pose. Then she unleashed her home-run swing.

The *amenoukal* stiffened in shock, eyes hardening to black points as the fish smacked into the side of his head and sent him sprawling to the floor of the boat. *"Ai! Ai!"* he screeched.

"Out of my way!" Tillie flung herself to starboard and pushed between two rowers. The *amenoukal*'s enraged roar rang out behind her as she dived into the canal.

An oar struck her shoulder. Pain shooting down her arm, she sank into the depths of the murky water. When she touched the slimy causeway with bare toes, she propelled herself forward. One-armed, she swam as fast and as far as her breath would allow before surfacing.

Blinking drops of water, she realized she had eluded the *amenoukal*. Barely. His boat had slowed and was circling back to retrieve her.

"Tillie!" The hoarse shout drew her attention. Graeme's boat was closing fast. She kicked forward and lifted her arm to him. Eyes narrowed in concentration, he bent and hauled her out of the canal. "Are you all right?"

"Barely," she gasped, collapsing on the floor of the boat. "Graeme, get me out of here."

"Keep your head down. This guy means business."

As Graeme spoke, the *amenoukal*'s boat pulled alongside

the dugout. Graeme shouted at the fisherman and pointed to their escape route.

Tillie grabbed Graeme's arm. "You can't go that way. The rest of the Tuareg are ahead of us."

"We can't go back."

"Monsieur, monsieur! Le Targui!" The fisherman stared in horror at the *amenoukal's* boat. The Targui had climbed to a platform on the prow of the boat. He threw back his sleeve, uncovering his arm to the shoulder.

"De mal en pis! Tout est perdu," the fisherman wailed before throwing himself over the side.

"What's going on?" Tillie clutched the side of the boat. "What's he doing?"

"Giving us a Tuareg threat. I can't turn this boat around. We're trapped."

Four boats circled the little dugout in the narrow channel. The *amenoukal's* boat came at them again. Rage glittering in his coffee-bean eyes, he drew his broadsword. Tillie froze. He would kill Graeme to get her back. She knew it beyond the shadow of a doubt.

The boat bumped into the dugout. The *amenoukal* raised his sword. Graeme gave Tillie a push. "Jump, Tillie! Jump!"

Acting on instinct, Tillie screamed, "You jump!" She scrambled to her feet in the wobbly dugout and slammed a shoulder into Graeme, knocking him over the side. Regaining her balance, she leapt onto the *amenoukal's* boat, threw herself to the floor, and covered her head with her hands. "Stop, *s'il vous plaît!* You have me now. Don't hurt him!"

The Targui jumped down to the deck beside Tillie, again pinned her tunic to the floor with his sword, and grabbed a length of rope. As he bound her arms and legs, he shouted orders to the other boats. Then he dragged her to one of the bamboo masts and lashed her to it.

"Tree-Planting Woman," he snarled. "You stay with Ahodu Ag Amastane, *amenoukal* of Tuareg people. You find treasure of Timbuktu."

"That's what you think," she muttered, turning her head to one side and refusing to look at him.

Where was Graeme? All she could see was the little boat bobbing empty in the canal. The train of canopied dugouts slid along the canals of Djenne, under bridges, past rows of fishing boats, between clay houses and mosques. Farther from the police. Farther from Graeme.

The Tuareg had her now, and she didn't have a clue where their stupid treasure was.

She watched the town of Djenne slip by. As the boats swept out of the canal into the river, she struggled to loosen her hands. It was useless. She was trapped.

The *amenoukal* sat on a small stool in front of her, squinting in the afternoon sunlight. His eyes, deep-set and as penetrating as arrows, were set off by two thick brows. If his eyes reflected a man of war and greed, his clothing revealed a man of vanity.

His blue turban swooped and billowed above his head, curled down into a huge bow at his neck, and fell gracefully over his shoulders. Despite the sweltering African heat, he wore at least three layers of clothing. The outer layer was a fantastically embroidered dark blue burnous lined in silk and belted with a heavy silver girdle. Beneath the burnous he wore a white wool gown with wide sleeves. Its breast was ornamented with row after row of pinned or hanging silver amulets, some nearly as ancient as the one Tillie wore.

Under that, he wore a blue shirt and a pair of bloused blue trousers. At least ten silk cords had been knotted over the burnous. Finally, the *amenoukal*'s feet were graced by the most ornately embroidered slippers Tillie had ever seen.

As she looked down at her own bare feet and wet white burnous, her thoughts flew back to Graeme. Where was he now? Would he come for her before it was too late? She closed her eyes and leaned her head back against the bamboo pole. How could she expect him to risk his life for her again and again? It would mean death if he tried it.

She knew the *amenoukal* would not let her go. She would have to try to find the treasure. Which, of course, she couldn't do. So that would mean her death, too.

Her stomach knotted with tension, Tillie turned the situation over so many times she was sure she had examined it from every angle. She tried to pray, but no words formed. She didn't even know how to begin seeking God's guidance in this predicament. There was no solution. She was so absorbed in her misery, she barely noticed when the dugout bumped ashore.

The *amenoukal* knelt to untie her bonds. "Tree-Planting Woman. You come."

"Do I have a choice?" she snapped back.

The chieftain loosened the ropes, and Tillie rubbed her sore wrists and ankles. She didn't want to follow the man, but there wasn't a thing she could do about it. Standing stiffly, she grasped the bamboo pole that had held her prisoner and looked out into the purple twilight.

Flat, sheepskin or cowhide tents clustered along the riverbank. Each had a fire burning brightly in front of it, where one or two dark-robed women tended the evening meal.

After living in Bamako among so many Muslims, it felt strange to see men veiled and women unveiled, as was the Tuareg custom. Children scampered to the shore and pointed excitedly at the newly arrived dugouts. Tillie wondered vaguely if one of them was the boy who had fastened the amulet around her neck to begin this nightmare.

She tried to ignore her cramped and sore muscles as she followed the *amenoukal* to the edge of the dugout and climbed down into the chilly water. When he tried to assist her, she shoved his hand aside. "Don't try the knight-in-shining-armor routine now," she mumbled. "Just leave me alone."

He laughed, picked her up, and set her in the water. "Come," he ordered.

Wading barefoot through the shallows, she turned back to see the dugouts slipping away into the river. The Djenne fishermen would have nothing to do with this Tuareg camp and its foreign ways. Would one of them return to Djenne and tell the police where she was? *Please, Lord.*

As the *amenoukal* and his hostage walked up the sloping bank, the sea of children parted respectfully before them. Tillie noticed that these children did not clamor to touch her white skin and golden hair. They kept their distance. Already they were assuming the proud independence of their people.

When the Tuareg group reached the first tent, Tillie spotted the woman who had spoken English on the pier in Segou. She had emerged from inside the dwelling and now stood outlined in the fire's glow. The *amenoukal* jerked Tillie to his side, held her arm in a viselike grip, and gave some sort of instructions to the woman. Tillie listened carefully, trying to pick out any word she might understand, but their language bore no resemblance to the native Bambara she had heard in the compound at Bamako.

Finally the woman nodded and turned to Tillie. "Come, Tree-Planting Woman," she said in a clear, high voice. "You come with me."

The *amenoukal* grunted and let go of Tillie's arm. He turned away without a backward look and marched off with his men. Tillie moved forward to follow the woman, her heart heavy. What would happen to her this night? and the next? She knew she had time, a few precious days, before the *amenoukal* and his caravan would arrive in Timbuktu. In those few days she had to come up with a way to save herself.

Following the Tuareg woman beneath the large camel-hair awning that jutted from the tent, she tried to pray. Again, nothing. She was too tired, too wet, too angry. Nothing came.

When she slipped under the flap of the tent, it was as though she entered another world, a virtual sea of stunning opulence. Layer upon layer of thick rugs carpeted the large floor. Rich silk pillows—red, blue, gold—lay in heaps around the perimeter of the room. Along one wall stood a low, wood-framed bed. It, too, was blanketed in thick coverings against the chill night air of the desert. A brass lantern hung from a center pole, its flame shining through a hundred pierced holes to give the room an eerie mingling of dappled shadows and lights.

"This is tent of Ahodu Ag Amastane, *amenoukal* of Tuareg people," the woman announced as she swept into the center of the chamber, her white burnous billowing behind her. "Here you see saddle of *amenoukal*'s camel. Gazelle leather. Beautiful, yes?"

Like an obedient schoolgirl on a museum field trip, Tillie looked at the enormous leather saddle with its three-pronged horn and elaborately embroidered fittings. "Yes, it's beautiful."

"Here are weapons of *amenoukal*. Broadswords, which we call *takouba*. Spear. Shield. Tuareg, people of veil—we do not use arms of treachery like white men. No guns or pistols."

The woman's dark eyes flashed as she spoke. Against her will, Tillie fell captivated by the hypnotic gaze and lilting voice of the Targui. "The mirror of *amenoukal*." She held up a small framed mirror that reflected the spinning light of the brass lantern. Then she picked up a small, one-string violin. *"Imzad,* we call this. Is beautiful, yes?"

"Yes," Tillie agreed softly. "It's beautiful . . . but listen, please, who are you? What is your name?"

"I am Khatty, beloved wife of Ahodu Ag Amastane." She gave Tillie a small smile. "Now, Tree-Planting Woman, you come with me."

They walked across the thick carpet to a second flap in the tent. As they pushed through, Tillie found herself in another dimly lit chamber, equally opulent, if not more so. Pillows lay scattered around the room, and the brass center light tilted and swung in a gentle breeze from an opening in the tent, making the shadows whirl fantastically across the walls.

"My room," Khatty announced. She swooped a ringed and braceleted hand outward and gestured theatrically around the interior. "My cushions. My rugs. My mirror. My cookery pots. The bags of my clothing."

"Very nice," Tillie murmured, sure she was supposed to be impressed—which she was. Though the items in the room were simple, somehow in the tent they had been transformed into objects fit for a princess, a role for which this lovely Khatty was perfectly suited. Her kohl-lined eyes gleamed with high intelligence. The shape of her long nose added to an air of nobility. Her lips, darkened with dye, were full and sensual.

"You are hungry," Khatty stated. "You will eat now."

She clapped her hands, and a timid girl hurried into the room through a hidden entrance. The *amenoukal*'s wife fired off a round of instructions and then snapped a curt dismissal that sent the child scurrying away.

"She is *amrid*—servant class," Khatty explained. *"Amrid* are as slaves to us. *Kel ulli* are people of goats. They tend our flocks. And *ineden* are our blacksmiths. Outcasts, of course."

"Of course."

Tillie watched in fascination as the woman peeled away her heavy burnous and stood preening before her mirror. She wore a long white gown heavily embroidered in a bold red design. Gold loop earrings hung to her shoulders, and a band of red ribbon ran through her elaborately braided hair.

"So . . . what are you going to do with me?" Tillie asked in a low voice. "You've worked pretty hard to catch me. What happens now?"

"You go with us to Timbuktu, of course. There you find treasure. Then you return to man with black hair. Do you love him?"

The unexpected question hovered in the air. Tillie

looked away, as though the answer were hidden somewhere in Khatty's collection of pillows.

"You love him, yes?" the woman repeated.

"I do care about him. He's very . . . Graeme is . . ." She wanted to explain, but how could she detail everything that had happened between herself and Graeme?

"Tuareg are great lovers," Khatty was saying. "Very skilled. You learn about love from us—how to love your man from example of our people."

Tillie swallowed. "I can't stay here, Khatty. You must understand. I need to go back to Bamako."

"You stay until you find treasure of amulet. Treasure belongs to *amenoukal*. He is displeased with you now, Tree-Planting Woman. He is angry you try to escape him."

"My name is Tillie. I'm not the tree-planting woman in the amulet."

Khatty's dark brows arched in scorn. "You are that woman, of course."

"You are mistaken."

"You are woman of great honor to us, people of veil. You come to break curse—to bring us great treasure. Once we were kings of desert! Tuareg people pillaged salt caravans that went across sands. Pillage was our work. But now caravans are no more. We wait for Tree-Planting Woman to bring us treasure. And you come. *Maktoub,* as God wills it."

Tillie bit her lower lip and looked down at the beaded ring on her hand. How could she explain that she was just a scientist who wanted to help people like the Tuareg hold the desert sands away? She was just a plain and simple woman with no special powers to break curses or find treasures. But how to convince this majestic creature of something so mundane?

"Now, our dinner!" Khatty dragged two heavy pillows to the center of the room as the serving maid edged into the tent and placed a loaded tray on the floor between the pillows. Seating herself with much ado, Khatty patted the accompanying pillow as a sign for her guest to join her. *"Io,"* she said. "It means 'come.'"

Though she hadn't eaten for hours, Tillie felt reluctant to be absorbed so easily into the woman's command. She needed time to think, to sort out a plan of action, some way to escape.

"I'm very tired," she began.

"Eat first. Sleep later. Sit, Tree-Planting Woman."

"OK, OK." Tillie sank onto the pillow before the Tuareg woman. The silver tray between them held two bowls of milk, a small flat cake, a plate of dried dates arranged around a white cheese, and a bowl of steaming rice.

"This you drink," Khatty announced, lifting the bowl of milk to Tillie's lips.

"What is it?"

"Drink."

She took a sip of the pungent liquid and tried not to grimace at its musky flavor. "Milk?"

"Camel's milk, of course," Khatty said with a laugh. "Now a wheat cake. Eat it. You like?"

Tillie nodded, relieved to have the camel's milk behind her. But Khatty was pressing her on. "This is *tikomarin,* our cheese. Made of goat's milk. Here, dates. Rice. Beautiful?"

"Beautiful. Khatty, where did you learn to speak such good English? I'm impressed."

"Hmph!" Khatty sniffed as she picked at her cheese. "We Tuareg women are well educated. We read and write, just as you. But I am more educated than most. *Amenoukal* sent me to mission school in Mopti before we married. He wanted me to learn foreign tongues. I speak English, French, some Arabic. You?"

"Very little."

"I thought as much. Americans are proud people, thinking no other tongue as fine as theirs. They are wrong."

Tillie's head began to clear as the food warmed her stomach. "When will we get to Timbuktu?"

"Two days or more. A dromedary can walk one hundred miles in a day, but now we have to watch for police and government. We do not like. *Amenoukal*, my husband, has made decree before Tuareg people. We sleep tomorrow near Mopti. After that we go to Timbuktu. Then you find treasure." Khatty stretched out her long legs, leaned back on her arms, and returned to her favorite subject. "*Amenoukal* says I am most beautiful of all his wives."

"I'm sure you are. How many wives does he have?"

"Five. And many children. I am newest wife. No children yet. Soon I bear him many sons."

So that was her weak link, Tillie thought. Khatty was a new wife with no children. And she seemed to care deeply about her husband. All of those things made her vulnerable. It was imperative to win this woman's trust. Tillie needed an ally if she was going to survive the coming days.

"You must love your husband very much," she said softly.

"Oh, very much. I make poems of love for him each

night when he comes to my arms. You make poems to your lover with black hair?"

"I don't make poems very well."

"No? Come then, we make English poem for your man." Khatty threw back her head and closed her eyes. She began singing in a high-pitched voice. "Come, oh desert lion, son of waran, man of strength and great wisdom. Your hair blows like ropes of sand in black night. Song of *djenoun* blows your sand-dune locks. Oh, man of black hair, man who sees heart of Tree-Planting Woman, come. Take her heart, tie it to your spear, fight to win her love. Oh, son of waran, son of waran, come with your love spear and pierce heart of Tree-Planting Woman."

When Khatty finished her song, she slowly opened her dark liquid eyes and looked at her guest with a sly smile. "Beautiful?"

"Beautiful," Tillie affirmed. The haunting melody and lilting words had moved her almost to tears. "You do know about love, don't you?"

"Of course."

"Why do you call Graeme the son of waran?"

"Waran is giant lizard of desert. We call waran grand-father of Tuareg people."

"Lizard? You mean like a monitor lizard?"

"Yes, Egyptian monitor. Very big. As long as a man." Khatty closed her eyes and took in a breath. "Waran is very powerful. Like your black-haired man who tries to protect you."

"And you think I'll see this man again?"

"You find treasure for *amenoukal*, and you will be highly

honored woman of Tuareg. Then you have your lover and any other man you need."

"The treasure." Tillie shook her head. "Can you tell me why the treasure is so important to you and your people?"

"Not to me!" Khatty snorted. "To me, treasure means nothing. But to *amenoukal*, it is everything. To me it is no more than a tale, like tales of long ago we women tell in darkness. But to *amenoukal* treasure is hope. We have lost our caravans. Our camels die with drought. And government tells us to become farmers!" She spat on the ground. "Farmers!"

Tillie took another bite of her wheat cake. This clearly wasn't the time to tell Khatty her own dreams of helping hungry people like the Tuareg learn to plant crops and farm the desert.

"I'm tired and dirty," she said to her hostess. "Is there a place I can get some water to wash myself?"

Khatty frowned. "Water to wash? Water is made for cooking and drinking only, Tree-Planting Woman. Water does not agree with skin. You will surely fall ill if you wash!"

"I will surely not fall ill. I wash myself every day, and I would like to do so now."

"I cannot allow Tree-Planting Woman to become sick. You are in my charge. *Amenoukal* would never forgive. No water for washing." She reached out and patted Tillie's hand. "You want good sleep and clean burnous. Here, look what Khatty has for you!"

The tall woman rose and swept over to her bags of clothing. After sorting through piles of silk and wool garments, she pulled out a heavy blue burnous and an eggshell blue gown. She carried them to Tillie and laid them in her arms.

"For Tree-Planting Woman."

"Thank you, Khatty, but I really must bathe first. I've been in the river water today. The canal. Please let me have a bath before I put on your beautiful clothes."

"No bath. You put on burnous. I tell servant to prepare your bed."

Tillie stared after her in exasperation. She wanted to be furious with the pompous princess, but she couldn't bring herself to dislike Khatty. For all her arrogance, the woman seemed to have a good heart. More important, Tillie realized she could make the most of their relationship if she kept it amiable. Khatty was her only chance.

She slipped out of the stiff white dress. Could it have been just this morning that she showered on the steamer? Could it have been just last night that she and Graeme had shared their dinner and their laughter? Where was he now?

She tugged on the clean gown and wrapped her arms around herself. She had to believe Graeme was trying to find her. He had made it clear how much she meant to him. She had to trust that.

Why? a voice from within whispered contrarily. *Why should you trust him at all? You're basing your confidence in him on the passions of your heart, not the rationale in your head.*

She wanted to deny it, but she couldn't. Even after all this time with him, she knew very little about Graeme McLeod. What about his relationship with the Djenne police? How had he known that policeman, Mohammed? And why hadn't she ever seen a notebook, pencils, or research? Surely a real writer would jot something down once in a while! Nothing about Graeme seemed to substantiate his claims about who and what he was.

What if Graeme had found Arthur? Her stomach turned over at the thought. There was no telling what Graeme would tell Arthur about her. And Arthur. She pictured him firing that pistol, his eyes a translucent blue. If those two men ran into each other . . .

"You are nearly as beautiful as I." Khatty's voice carried softly across the tented room.

Tillie lifted her gaze and watched the woman glide to her side. "That's quite a compliment."

"Of course. Now you come with me, Tree-Planting Woman." She took Tillie's arm and led her out of the tent into the starlit sky. The low wooden bed piled with blankets had been taken outside and set up in front of the tent. "You sleep here. All Tuareg sleep outside. It is our custom."

Grateful for the promise of rest, Tillie sat down on the edge of the bed. Other members of the clan were lugging their beds to the front of their tents and climbing beneath the layers of bedding. In a moment, Khatty's bed was carried out by her servants and placed a few feet from her guest's.

Tillie adjusted the folds of her gown and slipped beneath the covers. "Where's your husband? Is he going to sleep outside, too?"

"Of course. But now he talks with other men of our drum group. They make plans for treasure of Timbuktu."

NINE

Tillie slept, but only after she had counted every star in the desert sky, listened to the grunts of the camels, and made a hundred plans of escape—none of which would work.

She was awakened at first light by a rough shake on her shoulder.

"Tree-Planting Woman, *io*. Come."

Opening her eyes wide, she looked up into the veiled face of the *amenoukal*. She struggled onto her elbows, blinking back sleep and the nightmares that had seemed so real. "What do you want from me?"

"We will put you on your camel, of course." Khatty's voice behind the *amenoukal* was light with suppressed laughter. She said a few words to the tall man, and he chuckled deeply.

"Ah, Tree-Planting Woman." The *amenoukal* reached out and touched Tillie's cheek with a gentle stroke.

Recoiling, she looked up in time to see a flash of jealousy cross Khatty's face. Unaware of his wife's reaction, the *amenoukal* spoke to her briefly before striding away, his sandals kicking up puffs of dust.

"He says you are beautiful when you sleep," Khatty reported. Her lips were tight. *"Io, enkar.* Come, get up, get up. Your dromedary is waiting."

Tillie took a deep breath and slid out of bed. She had no desire to provoke ill will in the Tuareg woman, but there wasn't time to reassure her. After allowing Tillie a moment to relieve herself, Khatty led her to the line of kneeling camels and questioned one of the men in attendance.

"This one is for you," Khatty explained. "You ride dromedary before this day?"

"Never."

"Of course not. *Maktoub,* then. God's will be done."

Tillie stared after her as Khatty sauntered away, her hips swaying like a belly dancer's in the pink sunrise. She turned to her camel, which sat in the sand chewing contentedly, surveying the landscape beneath two-inch-long eyelashes and looking like it hadn't the least intention of getting up.

Her dromedary was scrawny, its yellow hide patchy and its knees nothing but wrinkled black leather, but the century-old saddle trappings were impressive. Several layers of heavily embroidered blankets, some tasseled and fringed, formed the base for a huge leather saddle. Its seat and backrest were worked in mystic designs meant to protect the rider. The three-pronged saddle horn, which had been tipped in silver, took on a fiery sheen as the sun rose.

Most members of the Tuareg clan had mounted their dromedaries already and were watching her with undisguised interest. As their white-skinned hostage started to climb on, the *amenoukal* appeared at her side. He slipped his long fingers around her waist, boosted her into the air, and gestured for her to pull herself onto the saddle. She flung one leg over the camel and struggled to sort out the gown and burnous that had tangled between her legs. Just when she thought she had herself balanced and arranged, the *amenoukal* pulled a whip from his belt and tapped the camel, which lifted onto its knees in one jerky motion.

"Whoa! Hold on a second now!" Tillie threw her arms around the saddle horn as the camel slowly straightened its hind legs.

Its rear rose like the light end of a teeter-totter, and the ground dipped crazily in front of Tillie. She slid forward, certain she was about to tumble onto the animal's neck. Then the camel pushed up on its forelegs. Flung backward, she grabbed the saddle horn again just in time to keep herself from sliding down its back to the ground.

Laughter rippled across the spectators, men chuckling behind their blue veils, women tittering openly. One little boy rolled on the ground, convulsed in giggles. Trying to maintain a shred of dignity, Tillie pulled her burnous over her shoulders, continued to hug the saddle horn, and dug in her knees for dear life.

A moment later, the *amenoukal* grandly mounted his white dromedary and called for the caravan to set off. On the ground—which seemed far below to Tillie—the encampment of tents had been dismantled and loaded on camels and donkeys. Not a sign remained that the Tuareg caravan had slept there. Every campfire had been buried, every trace of their passing erased.

Her camel plodded forward with a deep swaying motion, and Tillie clutched the saddle horn and prayed for safety. For all her experience on horses, nothing had prepared her for this stomach-sloshing journey. The Tuareg looked more at home on their dromedaries than they did on the ground; she felt like a kid on a carnival ride.

As the sun rose in a periwinkle sky, she worked at matching her body to the wavelike rhythm of the camel's gait. The day grew blistering hot, and Tillie thanked the Lord for the burnous, in spite of its heavy weight. Though she sweltered inside it, she knew she would suffer a good deal more without its protection from the sun's burning rays. Before long her throat felt parched and scratchy, but the caravan riders drank almost nothing during the day—just a little camel's milk and a few dates to sustain them.

Khatty's jealousy faded in the glow of her fascination with the tree-planting woman. She rode her dromedary beside Tillie's for the greater part of the day and peppered the American with questions. Tillie did her best to answer everything. In the process, she learned as much about the Tuareg as she could.

"Tonight we'll sleep near Mopti?" she asked.

Khatty sucked on a date. "Yes, near Mopti. Big market is there, of course. Beautiful things to buy. But we do not go into city. *Amenoukal* does not trust men who want to take treasure from him. Your black-haired lover. And that man of the British government who shot two of our people. A very bad man."

"But Graeme and Arthur don't want the treasure. They're following the caravan because they're afraid the *amenoukal* will kill me."

"Kill you? Why? You will give him treasure. You are Tree-Planting Woman."

Tillie twisted the beaded ring on her finger. Dare she tell Khatty she had no idea where the treasure was—or even what it was?

"Why does the *amenoukal* think I'm the tree-planting woman?" she asked.

Khatty gave her a look of scorn. "Necklace you wear, of course. Paper inside speaks of you. You read it? It is powerful charm. Words say Tree-Planting Woman will find treasure."

"How do you know about the amulet?"

"It is with Tuareg people many years. Two hundred years."

"Do you know where the paper inside came from? Do you know who wrote the charm?"

"White man. We have legend of long ago. Legend says white man came to river with great treasure. He wrote many words. A book."

A chill skittered down Tillie's spine like cold marbles. The journal. The Tuareg knew about the journal. "Where is this book?" Tillie asked.

Khatty shrugged. "We look for treasure, not book. White man died and left treasure hidden until Tree-Planting Woman comes. Now you come and you find treasure for *amenoukal*."

So there was a journal. Or had been at one time. Tillie wished she could see Graeme. Just a glimpse of him might give her the courage to go on. Knowing he hadn't abandoned her would give her strength.

She fanned her face with the end of the veil Khatty had given her earlier that morning. If only she could get away . . . but she knew there was no way of escape. She had thought of every possibility. All day she had been surrounded by armed men. Even if she eluded them, she had no idea how to convince this stubborn camel to take her to safety. She could barely make the beast go at all. It spat, growled, and twisted its head, more ornery than any mule she'd ever encountered. At night she would be encircled by the same armed men. Escape was out of the question.

She felt alone. Abandoned by everyone.

God never abandons us.

The words she had spoken to Graeme with such confidence slapped her in the face. *God never abandons us,* they mocked. *Na-na na-na na-naah. Silly Tillie. Silly Tillie.*

Graeme believed God had set up the natural laws and then abandoned the universe to function on its own. She certainly felt on her own now. Maybe Graeme was right. Maybe God wasn't the least bit interested in some anonymous little bundle of molecules and DNA wandering the edge of the Sahara on a camel.

Or worse. Maybe God was toying with her—playing this gigantic trick as some kind of a test to see how long she would last. Hadn't he done that very thing to Job?

She felt abandoned. Alone. Afraid. And angry.

"Lo, I am with you always, even to the end of the age."

The words Christ had spoken welled up inside her, as familiar as her own name. For the first time in her life, she sneered at them. *Sure,* she thought. *Always. Unless you feel like tossing me out here to a pack of hungry Tuareg.*

"I will be with you; I will not fail you or forsake you."

In the middle of the desert?

"Be strong and courageous! Do not tremble or be dismayed, for the Lord your God is with you wherever you go."

Tillie closed her eyes and gave herself to the swaying rhythm of her camel. Throughout her life the Lord had spoken to her through his Scriptures. She had memorized verses by the hundreds at Hannah's feet. Were they true? Could she trust the promises of God's faithfulness even when she was heading farther and farther into the valley of the shadow of death?

The Lord is the one who goes ahead of you; he will be with you. He will not fail you or forsake you. Do not fear, or be dismayed.

She drew a deep breath. *Do not fear, Tillie. God is with you. Even here. Even now.* She brushed a finger over her damp cheek. *OK, Father. I'm trusting you for now. For this minute. For this hour.*

"Tonight you wear different gown," Khatty was saying. "I paint your face yellow, white, and red of unmarried woman, and—"

"Wait a minute. You want to paint my face?"

"You do not listen to me, Tree-Planting Woman? That is bad. Be careful to listen to what I say, or *djenoun* will take your heart."

"Djenoun?"

"People of empty places . . . people of night. Spirits. Sometimes we call them *effri,* wicked spirits. You hear them wailing when moon is high and full. Tonight we camp near Mopti. *Amenoukal,* my beloved husband, has declared night of celebration. *Ahal.*"

"Ahal?" Tillie's heart began to sink. "What's an *ahal?*"

"Feast of love. Singing and poem-making. And when night is late, men gather around one woman they wish to love that night. She tells them stories and listens to their courting. Then she makes a sign to man she chooses for her lovemaking."

As Tillie watched Khatty arrange her skirts on the dromedary's back, fingers of apprehension traveled up her spine. She didn't like the sound of this feast at all. "I imagine I'll be tired after all this riding," she said. "I guess I'll skip the *ahal.*"

"You are Tree-Planting Woman," Khatty said softly. "Honored one. Many men will gather to seek your sign." She sighed in resignation. "Ahodu Ag Amastane, my husband, already declares he will sit before you tonight. Of course, you must choose him, great *amenoukal* of Tuareg people, to become your lover."

As Tillie stared out at the sandy Sahel landscape, she knew she had never been in such a terrible predicament. She lifted the amulet in her hands and ran her fingers over the surface of the locket, feeling the twists of spun silver and the cool lump of golden amber. Graeme had told her this locket contained the hope for her safety, but she had no idea how to use it.

Graeme. Was he somewhere near? Even if he had followed her, what could he do? Tillie's fingers tightened on the amulet.

Maybe Mungo Park *had* possessed a treasure. Maybe he had buried it somewhere near Timbuktu two hundred years ago. Could she find it? Maybe a historian somewhere would know something. But who? Where?

As evening fell, the sweltering air grew strangely chill, and she smelled rain in the far distance. She squeezed the amulet as though she could somehow press out the answers. What was the significance of Mungo Park's cryptic message? Did those strange rambling words really mean anything? She tried to recall everything Graeme had told her about the man. Bits and pieces. None of it locked together into a complete picture in her mind.

She thought of the amulet itself, recalling the rows of ancient silver charms pinned to the *amenoukal*'s chest. He certainly believed her amulet was charmed. In fact, the whole quest for the treasure must be some kind of mystical religious experience for him. The silver necklace was charmed, its message was magical, and she was the honored tree-planting woman.

But so what? She still didn't know where the treasure was!

As the sun dropped behind a craggy stone, her stomach pulled with hunger from the meager ration of food she had eaten that day. Every rib felt bruised; every vertebra seemed slipped from its niche; every muscle was knotted and sore. Her hair was full of sand, and her eyes burned from scanning the sun-blasted dunes all day.

When the shadows were long, the caravan made its way toward the river's edge. Following the narrow track, it wound like a snake until the *amenoukal* raised his hand to halt the line. With a sigh of relief, Tillie clung to her camel as it knelt to the ground, and she slid off.

The Tuareg bustled to work assembling their tents and lighting fires in the secluded area. Tillie took the opportunity to look around. Maybe this was her chance to run. The *amenoukal* stood in the middle of a throng of arguing men. Khatty sauntered over to her guest, favoring the men with a doe-eyed glance along the way.

"Talk, talk, talk," she said with a chuckle. "It is all they do."

"What are they discussing?" Tillie asked.

"*Ahal,* of course. They want to put tents in perfect place, but no one can agree. It is this way each time we have *ahal.*

Men are so eager to please women during *ahal.*" She shimmied her hands down her hips. "I go now to prepare myself. You come?"

"In a minute. I need to stretch."

As Khatty sashayed off, Tillie turned her thoughts back to escape. She had to get away—and it had to be done before dark. This was her last chance before Timbuktu, and there was no way she would submit to the disgrace of the *ahal* unless she was forced. Tree-planting woman or not, she was not about to become the *amenoukal's* lover.

Hoping anyone who spotted her would think she was taking a bathroom break, she strolled toward the river. It flowed deep on the side of the encampment. A thick grove of trees and brush grew up around the bank. The road was narrow but clear, and she knew the *amenoukal's* dromedary would have no trouble following her there. It would have to be a dash into the brush then.

She would try to slip away unnoticed and hide until they gave up searching. Then she would work her way downriver toward the lights of Mopti. Once in the city, she was certain to find someone who could help her.

Trying her best to look casual, Tillie sauntered through the collection of rising tents. Tired but elated, the children played games of tag around the dromedaries. Women bustled to build fires and finish setting up the tents. Men conferred, pacing this way and that, occasionally raising their voices in argument. No one seemed to see her.

She tugged her veil over her face and slipped toward the trees. The grass grew thicker here. She passed a low bush, and another. A tree. She crept around it.

Heart thudding, she licked her dry lips. Another tree. Past

it. A trickle of sweat slid down her back. Two more trees and she would be into the thicket. She lifted the skirt of her gown. One more tree.

A hand clamped down on her arm.

"Tree-Planting Woman!" the voice was all too familiar.

"Let me go," she hissed.

"You stay."

Swinging around, Tillie looked up into the *amenoukal*'s dark, bloodshot eyes. Fear clutched her throat. She wanted to fly at him and tear away that turban and arrogant leer. But she was trapped. Again.

"I said, let go," she repeated through clenched teeth. With a fierce shrug, she freed her arm.

"You mine." He pointed at his chest. "Mine. You find treasure."

"That's what you think."

"You find treasure."

"Listen, buster, you've got the whole thing wrong."

His chest swelled. "Ahodu Ag Amastane—"

"Yeah, yeah, yeah, I know who you are. And I'd like you a lot better if you'd just leave me alone." She turned quickly and strode back into the encampment, anger born of fear coursing through her veins like lava. "Khatty!" she yelled. "Where are you?"

"Ma imous?" Eyes wide, the young woman hurried out of the tent. "What is wrong, Tree-Planting Woman? *Io!* Come inside!" Khatty took Tillie's hand and pulled her into the tent. "No anger, please. This is night of celebration. You enjoy Tuareg feasting. You become part of us. You are honored woman."

"Honored woman? All right then. By the power of my

position as honored Tree-Planting Woman—by the power of this amulet—I want a bath! And I want it now!"

Khatty fell to the floor of the tent and covered her eyes with her hands. "Yes, yes! Please, do not be angry! I send for water at once." She turned and yelled at her cowering maid. "Give me water! *Ekfid aman! Ekfid aman!*"

A little astonished at the effect of her own words, Tillie watched Khatty scramble to her feet and run out of the tent. She continued shouting at her servants, who raced shrieking toward the river.

"Good grief," Tillie whispered. Graeme had been right. There was power in the amulet. Power from the fact that these people were superstitiously afraid of its force. Could she use their fears to her advantage? Why not? They were using her.

Before she had time to figure out a plan, a flock of anxious servants sidled into the tent carrying pot after pot of water. Time to put Drama 101 to use. Playing her role to the hilt, she strode around the chamber, inspecting the water, examining the servants, quibbling over this and that as she'd seen Khatty do.

When fifteen clay pots had been set on the floor, she clapped her hands. "That will do. Enough."

Khatty peered between the flaps of curtain as the servants scurried out. Tillie beckoned her. *"Io!* Come on in; I won't bite." Seeing the young woman's blanched expression, she relented. "Look, I'm not angry, Khatty. I'm just glad to have the water. You could do with a bath yourself."

"Ai! Ai!"

"Oh, never mind. I wouldn't force that on you."

"Please, Tree-Planting Woman, do not be displeased

with me. Ahodu Ag Amastane, great *amenoukal* of Tuareg people, commands me to stay with you. He fears you escape and give treasure to your friends."

She let out a breath. "But I don't even know—" She caught herself and shook her head. "Never mind."

Kneeling, Tillie dipped her hands into the cool water and rinsed the grit and dirt from her face. Then she disrobed and washed her arms, legs, body, and finally, her hair. Khatty was more than solicitous about the event taking place in her tent. She was downright curious. After drying off with a linen cloth and wrapping it around herself, Tillie followed the Targui to the pile of bagged garments lying in one corner.

"Will you wear another blue burnous?" Khatty asked. "We wear finest clothing to *ahal*. Perhaps white is better? Or golden one will look lovely with your hair."

"I'm not going to the *ahal*, Khatty. I'm very tired tonight."

"Oh, Tree-Planting Woman, *amenoukal* commands you go to *ahal*. You sit with me for singing and stories."

Tillie squared her shoulders. "I am the tree-planting woman. And by the power of the amulet, I will not—"

"You go to *ahal*."

The voice behind her made Tillie swing around in fear. She grabbed a wad of clothing and held it up to her chin.

The *amenoukal* stepped closer. "You go to *ahal*, Tree-Planting Woman."

Tillie swallowed as he slid his lamplit broadsword from its scabbard. Directing a flood of invective at Khatty, the *amenoukal* never took his eyes from Tillie's face. Then, with a final thrust of his sword into the air, he turned on his heel and strode from the chamber.

"Allah save us!" Khatty fell to her knees.

"What? What did he tell you?"

"Oh, Tree-Planting Woman, you must go to *ahal*! *Amenoukal* commands it. You must go, or he will . . . he will . . ." The young woman's voice choked with sobs. "You do not know this man. He is very powerful. . . . He will . . ."

"OK, OK. Calm down, Khatty." Tillie let out a sigh and lifted the young woman to her feet. "I'll go to the *ahal*. But you'd better understand right now, I'm not going to be his lover."

"*Ai!*"

"Don't start yipping again." Tillie stood and met the woman's eyes. "In my religion it's forbidden to sleep with a man unless you are married. I won't go against the law of God."

Khatty blinked. "You are Christian?"

"Yes, I am. You know about my faith?"

"But of course." She smiled proudly. "I go to mission school at Mopti, remember? I tell you that already. I know about Jesus Christ, born of virgin, die on cross, come to life again. I know it!"

Tillie let out a laugh that mingled amazement and relief. "I guess you do."

"Islam teaches Jesus was great prophet like Mohammed. A wise teacher sent by God. But Christians say he is God's son."

"Who do you say he is, Khatty?"

"Mmm. Very difficult for me to say." She pulled a deep purple burnous and a navy gown from her bags of clothing and shook them to smooth their wrinkles. The candle in its brass lantern wavered but did not go out. "Who do you say he is, Tree-Planting Woman?"

"I believe Jesus Christ is the Son of God."

"Easy for you. Here I must live Muslim ways. I am fifth wife of my husband. No choice. Islam is in every part of my life. Holidays, prayers, laws, marriages, births, even food and drink. Very hard not to live Muslim ways in Tuareg caravan."

Tillie stood for a moment watching the whirling shadows. Feeling more than ever as if she were lost in some fantastic nightmare, she slipped off the linen towel and put on the clean garments. "I'm sure it would be hard for you. Sometimes it's hard for me to be a Christian. It's hard for me to have faith."

"No."

"Yes, it is. When your husband captured me, I felt afraid. It's been hard for me to trust that God is with me. And even when my faith is strong, sometimes I want to break God's laws." She smoothed down the fabric with her hands as the image of Graeme's face formed in the lamplight. "If I love a man, I may be tempted to sleep with him, Khatty. But I've made a promise to my Lord not to do that, not to break his command. That's why I will not spend the night with your husband."

"You are strong."

Tillie glanced out at the starlit sky. She didn't feel strong. She felt weak and frightened. In spite of her bold words, she feared that her trust in God was tenuous. Christ would always be faithful to her . . . but could she be faithful to him?

Khatty gathered up her combs and began to work on the snarls and knots in Tillie's hair. "I believe Jesus Christ is son of God," she said softly. "But I cannot be Christian. Impossible for me in Tuareg caravan."

Tillie turned and laid a hand on the young woman's arm. "It's not impossible."

Khatty shrugged. "No? We see about that. Now you live in Tuareg caravan. Tonight you go to *ahal,* and my husband try to make love to you. I watch you, Tree-Planting Woman. I watch you be Christian tonight in Tuareg caravan."

Tillie closed her eyes as the Targui braided her hair into a score of tiny plaits and wound them through with ribbons and silver chains. *As if it weren't hard enough just to survive, Lord,* she mused. *Tonight I'll have one Targui trying to force me to break your commandment and another watching to see how I live out my faith.*

Her frustrated words to Hannah echoed in her mind. *"I've been here almost a year, and I'm sure I haven't touched a single life."* Was it only a few days ago that she'd been with Hannah in the Bamako marketplace? At that time the ache in her heart had been palpable. She had wanted to share Christ with the people of Mali. Wanted to help, to make a difference. She had envisioned doing so by handing out pamphlets or starting a little Sunday school.

But not this! God apparently expected her to live out her faith when she was pushed to the extreme . . . stretched to her limits . . . afraid for her life. It was too hard. Too much.

"Beautiful," Khatty murmured. "Now I paint you."

"This is enough. The hair is great. Really."

"No, no. Paint is very beautiful. *Amenoukal* like paint on his women."

"Terrific."

As the serving maids bustled around the room setting up

pots of paints, Khatty propped a large mirror in front of Tillie. Murmuring admiration, she began to paint her guest's face in dramatic shades of red, yellow, and white.

"Now!" Khatty's face was lit with a fiery glow of triumph as she sat back and surveyed her handiwork. "Now you are ready for *ahal*. Now you are ready for Tuareg feast of love."

TEN

The two women walked out of the tent into the darkness. Khatty had dressed herself in a heavily embroidered indigo burnous. Decked with silver rings, earrings, necklaces, amulets, and armbands, she had painted her face, too, but not in the bold shades of Tillie's. Instead, she had deepened the alluring lines of kohl around her eyes and had stained her lips a dark claret.

Stopping in front of another tent, Tillie and Khatty joined other women of the Tuareg drum group who sat before an older woman. In her arms the woman bore a one-stringed musical instrument. Its bowl and neck were carved and painted, and the old woman stroked it with a curved bow.

"Assou plays *imzad*," Khatty whispered. "Music of Tuareg people is made with *imzad*."

As Khatty finished speaking, Assou began a high-pitched song. Tillie twisted her beaded ring and looked around her. The men were nowhere to be seen, and again she wondered if she could use this chance to get away. But when she rose to her knees, she saw them approaching in groups of two and three.

Like a cluster of debutantes, the Tuareg men had dressed in their finest clothing. Turbans adorned with sweeping bows and silver pins wound around their heads in fantastic shapes, covering all but their eyes. They sported burnouses embroidered in gold, silver, red, and white threads. Ornate charms and amulets hung around their necks as they swept into the group of women and took their places.

Tillie sensed the *amenoukal* beside her as he lowered himself to the ground, sinking into his burnous like the Wicked Witch of the West. She wished she could dump a bucket of water on him and make him evaporate completely. His eyes, blacker than lumps of coal, stared at her. Unwilling to kowtow to him, she stared back.

He wore a dark indigo turban knotted at his neck and pinned with a gold and amethyst brooch. His black burnous had been sewn with golden threads that took the shape of monitor lizards—the beloved *waran* of the Tuareg. His black veil was fringed in gold, and his long fingers sported golden rings set with fiery jewels. His slippers, made of dusky blue embroidered silk, bore golden tassels on each toe.

Tillie tried to pray, but no words would come. She swallowed hard and tore her attention from the man who now clutched her mind as if he possessed that, too. She slid closer to Khatty, drawing her knees up to her chest.

Women began to wail their love songs. Men replied in deeper tones. Hours slipped by. Khatty tried to explain the meanings of the songs, but Tillie could hardly listen. Instead, she watched the younger woman. It was clear by the way she murmured and flirted with her husband that Khatty was in love with the man. But the way the *amenoukal* looked at Tillie left her no doubt that he had set his sights on the tree-planting woman. Her heart broke for Khatty . . . and quaked for herself.

When the moon was high and the feasters had sated themselves on songs, camels' milk, and date wine, Khatty leaned over and whispered in Tillie's ear. "It is time. Now you go away to a place near trees. Men who wish to admire you follow."

Her blood hammering, Tillie shook her head. "No, Khatty, I—"

"Yes! It is custom. If not, *amenoukal* will—"

"What happens under the tree?"

"You tell men a story or make poems. All men who wish to be your love-partner will make sign in your hand. They draw circle with finger, then touch center of circle. After that, you make sign to each man. If you do not choose man, you draw line from wrist to fingers. But if you choose man, you draw line from wrist to fingers, then follow it back. Men will all leave; then man you have chosen returns. You go to my tent with him for courting."

Khatty finished speaking and sat in silence for a moment, her dark eyes searching Tillie's face. Then she heaved a heavy sigh. "*Amenoukal* of the Tuareg goes with you, I am certain," she whispered. "You must choose him."

"No."

"*Enkar!* Get up! Go, Tree-Planting Woman!"

Khatty shoved an elbow into Tillie's ribs and prodded her to her feet. Stumbling out into the darkness, Tillie watched the other small groups of men and women making their way into the cover of night. She grasped the edges of her burnous to her chest and glanced behind her. Already three men followed. Their leader was the *amenoukal*.

Help me, Father. Please help.

Wiping the sweat from her forehead, she tried to think as

she made her way through the cluster of tents out into the low shrubs. She could hear the plaintive wailing of the old woman and her *imzad* as she spotted a tall palm tree. Sinking to her knees at its base, she crossed her arms over her chest.

"Tree-Planting Woman," the *amenoukal's* voice was low. "Tell story."

Tillie glanced at the row of five veiled and turbaned men seated around her. The *amenoukal* had placed himself in front of her and was waiting, his eyes hidden in shadow.

Clearing her throat, Tillie looked up at the stars. "Tell story," she repeated, trying to think of the longest possible tale she knew. *War and Peace?* Too Russian. *Moby Dick?* Too wet. Maybe if she ran together every single one of Grimm's fairy tales, it would be sunrise before she finished.

"OK, let's see. Once upon a time, there was a poor but beautiful girl named Cinderella. She had three wicked step-sisters and an evil stepmother, who always wore a blue turban and liked to go around slashing people's heads off."

The *amenoukal* gazed at her in fascination. Tillie launched into the story Hannah had told her and her sisters a hundred times. Aware that the men would hardly understand a word she said, she embellished the tale with every tidbit that came into her mind. She couldn't bring herself to look into the men's faces, so she stared out at the moonlit river and the gleaming dunes beyond it.

"And so the handsome prince fell in love with the beautiful Cinderella in her silk gown and glass slippers," she went on. "They danced and danced all the night long until the clock began to strike twelve. Of course, you fellows probably don't know what a clock is. Suffice it to say, it was way past Cindy's bedtime."

She drew out the story as long as she could, unconsciously knotting and unknotting her fingers as she spoke. "And, of course, the glass slipper fit, and the prince knew right away that this poor little housemaid was his beautiful Cinderella. He asked her to marry him then and there. She said yes, of course, so he put her on the back of his white stallion, and they rode off to the castle to live happily ever after. And that's the end of that one. Now, um . . . Snow White. Let's see . . ."

In the moment she was silent, the *amenoukal* reached out and clamped his hand over Tillie's. "Enough story, Tree-Planting Woman."

He forced open her palm, drew a wide circle, and pressed its center with his forefinger. She jerked her hand away, but it was grabbed by a second man who made the same motion on her palm. When the third man repeated the gesture, Tillie yanked her hand from his grasp and pushed it deep into the folds of her burnous.

"That's enough." Shaking, she turned away from the men and looked at the swaying grass. "I'm not doing it, and I don't—"

"Tree-Planting Woman." A man at the far end of the row snatched her wrist.

"No," Tillie snapped. "Leave me alone. I get the idea, OK?"

The man opened Tillie's palm and took the third finger of her left hand. Grasping the beaded ring, he pulled hard and twisted so that she yelped in pain.

"Ouch! Listen, buster—!" Tillie drew back to clobber

him when her focus crystallized on the man's face. She narrowed her eyes and looked under the indigo turban that swooped over the man's forehead and mouth and wound into a wide knot at his neck. She could see a few strands of black hair, a pair of dark eyebrows, a long nose. A broken nose. And then his right eye—a deep blue-green eye— winked.

She stifled a cry, turned to the other men, and took their palms one by one. As Khatty had instructed, she drew a line from wrist to fingers, signifying her refusal of each man's attentions.

When she held the *amenoukal*'s hand, she felt the heat of his desire against her own cold fingers. She traced a hard line from his wrist to his fingers, then folded his hand and shoved it away. He sat bolt upright, rage darkening his features as she traced and retraced the palm of the man who sat at the end of the row.

Grunting in acknowledgment, all the men rose and ambled away. But the *amenoukal* turned back to Tillie and looked at her with hatred in his eyes. She picked up the amulet and held it out in front of her like a shield.

"*Ssst,*" she hissed. "Don't take another step. The Tree-Planting Woman has chosen. Go away."

The chieftain glared at her for a moment longer, then whirled on his heel and stomped off. Alone, she rose to her knees and searched the clearing. Could she have imagined it? No, there he was now. The man in the indigo turban slipped out of the shadows and ran to her through the tall grass. She jerked off her veil and held out her arms.

"Graeme!" she whispered as he caught her up and swung her around and around. "Is it you?"

"You scared me half out of my mind with that stunt back in the canal, Tillie-girl. It feels good to hold you again."

She slipped her arms around him and laid her cheek on his dark burnous. "Graeme, your life's in danger here. The *amenoukal* will kill you if he finds out who you are."

He tilted her chin and brushed her lips with a quick kiss. "Let's get out of here. It's a short hop to Mopti, and I've got an old truck waiting for us in town. Come on."

He nestled her against his side and led her across the clearing toward a copse of tall banyan trees. But when they reached the first tree, someone moved out of the shadows.

"Tree-Planting Woman!" It was a woman's voice, filled with whispered terror. She beckoned across the clearing.

"It's Khatty," Tillie told Graeme. "She's seen us."

"It's OK, she knows about me. She's the one who rigged me up in this outfit."

"Tree-Planting Woman, come to my tent!" Khatty took Tillie's hand. "Bring black-haired man. Ahodu Ag Amastane is there. He waits for you. He cannot believe you choose another. You must show him you do not escape, or he comes after you now. Already he thinks you trick him. Come, come quickly!"

"We can't afford to let him catch on yet," Graeme's voice was low. "If he's after us, we'll never make it to Mopti. Come on, we'd better do what she says."

"No, Graeme! You don't know the man like I do. I can't go back."

Khatty stood wringing her hands. "Tree-Planting Woman, Khatty protect you. You see. Come! Come!"

Graeme gave Tillie's shoulder a reassuring squeeze and

prodded her forward through the brush. Khatty breathed a huge sigh of relief and faded into the night.

Approaching the lighted tent, Tillie could see the *amenoukal* standing before the open flap, his fists planted on his hips. His black burnous fluttered and whipped behind him, its golden waran lizard flashing in the firelight. She tried to breathe normally as she led Graeme up to the fire, knowing the *amenoukal* was now close enough to unleash a death swing with his broadsword.

As they took the final steps toward the awning, Khatty materialized beside the *amenoukal* and grasped his arm. Pulling him to her side, she began singing a high-pitched love song and stroking his hand. Tillie avoided the man's gaze and slipped into the tent.

Graeme followed her through the dusky room and into Khatty's chambers behind it. "Come here, Tillie," he whispered, pulling her close. "Scared?"

"Not anymore."

Holding her tight, he stroked her hair and kissed her forehead. She rested her head on his chest and listened to Khatty's song. Tillie watched the *amenoukal*'s shadow as he paced back and forth. He muttered angrily, resisting his wife's advances.

"Tillie." Graeme's whisper sent chills down her back. "Have you seen any weapons in this room? Knives or anything?"

She shook her head. "They're all in there. With him."

"Then we'd better lay low until he settles down. Come on, let's get a couple of those pillows."

Still numb with disbelief that Graeme had found the caravan, wooed Khatty into giving him a disguise, and then rescued her from the *ahal,* Tillie watched him drag a heavy pillow to the center of the room. He sank onto it and propped his elbows on his knees.

She looked down into the face of the man she had thought she might never see again and couldn't hold back a smile. Graeme looked completely out of place in the sweeping turban and jeweled burnous. She could see his jacket discarded on the carpeted floor. Out of one skin and into another. He was a man who fit wherever he found himself. Thank God.

Thank you, God!

Reaching up, he took her hand and pulled her down onto his lap. They sat in silence, listening to Khatty make up soothing poems to placate her angry husband. Her practiced charms soon began to take effect, and the man at last stood still to let his wife work her loving ministrations upon him.

"She loves him, you know," Tillie whispered. "I can't understand it, but she really does love him."

"I know. That's why she helped me tonight."

Tillie drew her head from the curve of Graeme's neck and looked at him. "Why?"

"She didn't want him to have you. She believes in love more than she believes in the power of the amulet. She cares about him more than she cares about the treasure. And I'm pretty sure she wanted to see the two of us together, too."

Tillie nodded. That she could believe. Khatty had been enamored with the idea of Tillie and her black-haired man from the very beginning. Her feelings for their relationship had shown in the poem she had composed for Graeme.

"I think, too, she wanted my God to win out over her

husband's," she said. "She learned about Christ at a mission school, and she believes he is God's Son."

Her heart softening even more toward her Targui ally, Tillie watched the shadows as Khatty seduced her husband away from his anger and toward her love. She was a good woman. But she was correct—it would be hard to live as a Christian in a Tuareg caravan.

"Tillie," Graeme whispered. "Khatty was right, you know. We do belong together."

She studied his face and saw he meant what he said. *Lord,* her heart cried yet again. *What do you want me to do? You know how I feel about Graeme . . . and how he feels about you. . . .* Despair welled up within her. *Father, why does it have to be so hard?* She wanted to share her confusion, her struggle, but she couldn't. Not yet. Instead, she met his eyes and shook her head. "I just wonder how long. This amulet keeps tearing us apart."

"It brought us together."

She looked down at her beaded ring. "I didn't think I'd see you again."

He covered her hand with his. "You're with me from now on. No more heroics, OK?"

"I'll do what I have to do."

"Tillie." He bent over her and let his mouth meet hers in soft kisses, promises of commitment. His lips moved across her cheek, down her neck, then up to the curve of her ear. "Tillie, when you jumped onto the *amenoukal's* boat the other day . . ."

"He would have killed you."

"You saved my life." His voice was a husky whisper no

louder than the desert wind blowing outside the tent. "I've never known a woman with your strength."

"Just keep your promise of honor. . . . Always tell me the truth. Be who you said you were."

"Tillie, I can't—" He stopped speaking and let out a hot breath. "You can't know the whole truth about me. I have to—"

A guttural noise nearby stopped his words, and he looked across to the shadows of Khatty and the *amenoukal*. They had moved inside the other chamber and were speaking in low voices.

"I honor you, Tillie." Graeme lifted Tillie from his lap and stood. "I won't betray your trust. I swear that."

He took the brass lantern by its finial and blew out the light. The room fell into nearly total darkness, and he dropped back to his knees, listening for a sign that their absence wouldn't be noticed.

Tillie sat alone, chilled. She couldn't know the whole truth about him? What had he meant by that? They were together again, but her heart felt heavier than stone.

Graeme's hands found the back of her neck, and his fingers slipped through the tangle of braids and silver chains. "We've got to get out of this place and head for the truck in Mopti. Come on."

He stood up and pulled her to her feet. She motioned toward the curtain through which the servants always entered and exited. Together they slipped across the room. Graeme lifted the heavy flap and stepped out to scout the area. In a moment his head popped back inside. "It's clear. Let's go."

Tillie stood in the darkness for a moment, remembering

her hours in the tent with Khatty. The Targui woman had become a real friend. Almost like a sister. "Thank you, Khatty," she whispered into the blackened chamber. "Thank you for believing in love."

The Tuareg fires were no more than glowing embers when Graeme and Tillie slipped past them and scrambled down the stony embankment to the river. Running hand in hand, they stumbled through reeds and over stubby bushes that caught at their flowing burnouses.

Graeme's billowing gown impeded his run. But his exhilaration at freeing Tillie and having her beside him again outweighed any concerns.

"Why don't we take the road?" Tillie whispered. She lost her footing and splashed into the river.

He hauled her back onto the bank. "You'll see."

"But what about crocs and hippos?"

"Stick with me. You'll be all right." Before long, he pulled her to a stop, waded into the water, and pushed back a thicket of brush that hung over the river. "Here we go. The finest transportation in these here parts."

"A boat." Surprised, she watched the tiny dugout drift out into the shallows. "It's the fisherman's boat from Djenne. How did you get it here?"

"The guy sold it to me, and I rowed it up the river. That's how I found the Tuareg camp."

"You spotted the camp from the river? I don't see how. The Tuareg made a huge effort to hide their tents and erase every trace of where they'd been."

"I know. For a while I thought I'd lost you for good. Then this afternoon, after I'd wandered around in Mopti a while, I decided to backtrack the river. That's when I spotted the glimmer of a fire. It was a miracle."

"A miracle?" She cocked her head. "Like you had divine help or something? Like the God of the entire universe is with you through every problem, and he's always there to love you no matter what? That's something, Graeme. That's really something."

At her recitation of his own statements of doubt, he couldn't hold back a grin. "Hey, it's making a believer out of me. Ready for a boat ride?"

"It'll feel like home."

He reached out to help her into the bobbing dugout. Once she'd settled herself at one end, he pushed them out into the river and then climbed aboard. He paddled hard until he found the midstream current. As the drift took them, he settled back and stretched out his legs with a contented sigh. "Huck and Jim on the river again."

He watched the emotions play over her features. "How far is Mopti?"

"We'll see the lights in a few minutes. It's just around a bend or two."

"I still can't believe I got away."

"Hey, where's your faith?"

"I almost lost it."

No. The unspoken plea rose up inside him. *Don't let her lose her faith.* Her words from a previous conversation jumped into his mind. *"It's called faith,"* she had said. *"Believing even though you don't have proof."* Tillie had more faith than anyone Graeme had ever met. Her confidence in God had stunned him at first. Then it had moved him. Now it beckoned him.

Keep her strong in her faith. Help her keep on believing. Make her heart strong. Who was he talking to? God? Strange how comfortable it felt. How right. *Give me faith, God. Help me know how to believe.*

He fell silent, watching the water and thinking about the changes in his life. He knew Tillie had been elated to see him. The way her eyes had lit up had been clear evidence of that. But now that they were alone and safe, he noted that her smile had faded. She smoothed the gown over her legs and looked out at the river. "Any word about Hannah and Arthur?"

"No." He searched her eyes. "You've had a lot of time to think in the past couple of days. Still planning to marry Arthur and move to London?"

She twisted the ring on her finger. "To tell you the truth, I don't know what I'm going to do about anything. Ever since that little boy hung the amulet around my neck, I've just been trying to survive. Back in Bamako, I thought I knew who I was and what I wanted."

"And now?"

"Now I'm not sure."

He knew it was a risk, but he leaned forward to take her hand. "Well, I know who I am, Tillie-girl. I know what I want. And if it's OK, I plan to stick with you 'til you get things figured out."

Her warm eyes and smile were more than enough reward. "I'd like that," she said.

He leaned back again, unwound the turban from his

head, and dropped it into his lap. Taking one end, he dipped it into the river. "Now, Miss Tree-Planting Woman, let's get you back to your normal shade."

She laughed, and the sound warmed him. "I forgot what Khatty had done. How did you ever recognize me?"

"You were the only blonde Targui in the vicinity." He lifted her chin and dabbed off the garish paint, while she untangled chains and ribbons from her braids.

"I don't know how you kept a straight face through that whole charade. Did you hear me mumbling along, trying to think what to say?"

"Cinderella. It was the best version I'd ever heard. I thought it kind of fit. The poor tree-planting woman taken in hand by Khatty, the Targui fairy godmother. Transported in the richest finery to the grand *ahal*."

"And then swept away by a handsome prince."

Graeme grimaced and shook his head. "I don't know about that part." Their glances met, and the look in her eyes sent his pulse pounding.

"I do. You're my handsome prince." The light in her eyes flickered, and it was as though a cloud descended. She looked away, and he had to strain to hear her say in a small voice, "I'm just not sure I'm in the right fairy tale."

When the lights of Mopti swung into view, Tillie saw that the three small islands that comprised the town were clearly visible. The cement bridges connecting them glowed with bright electric lamps.

"I've got a friend in Mopti," Graeme said. "The truck's

at his house. He told me to call from the marketplace, and he'll come get us."

"You know a lot of people along this river."

"Been here awhile." He lifted his paddle into the boat. "Research."

She studied his expression in the moonlight. Was he telling the truth this time? Research. Somehow the word sounded artificial.

"Look," he said, his voice rough. "I need to tell you something. There's an airfield in Mopti. My friend tells me there'll be a plane out to Bamako in the afternoon. I can get you on it."

"A plane?" The idea of leaving the river seemed stranger than the thought of swimming with crocodiles again. This was her chance. She could fly back to the city and be in her PAAC compound by afternoon. She could tell the police about everything. Hand over the amulet. Be done with the whole thing. And then . . . what?

She thought of Arthur. Hannah. Khatty. Graeme.

"Just get us to Mopti," she told him. "I'll decide after I've put something in my stomach and slept on a decent bed."

"Better think it over good. We wouldn't want you to be impulsive now."

She lifted her head to find a crooked smile softening his features. His dark hair was a little mussed from the turban, and she wanted to run her fingers through it. She longed to touch him, feel his arms around her, know he was real. Could she leave this man? Fly away back to her old life? Go on as though nothing had happened between them?

Now *that* would take a miracle.

The dugout glided toward the lighted pier, and Graeme

maneuvered it into a berth. The sloping cobbled expanse of the deserted marketplace on the main island rose from the riverbank. They docked, tied up the boat, and climbed onto the pier.

Two ancient telephones, wires exposed, hung from a pole at the edge of the market. Graeme lifted a receiver. "This one's dead." He picked up the other phone and jiggled the wires. "I've got a dial tone. OK, Robert ol' pal, where's your number?"

He reached into the pocket of his blue shirt and pulled out a small leather box the size of a cigarette pack. With one finger he flipped open the lid and riffled through a stack of cards.

"What's that?" Tillie asked as he found the one he'd been hunting and began to dial. "Your little box. What's in there?"

"I keep my cards in it. It's waterproof."

"What cards?"

"Business cards, notes for my book. I told you about that."

"You said you kept them in that bag we lost in the river. I thought you were just—"

"Making it up? You don't believe I'm a writer? I told you Mungo Park is my ancestor, and I'm working on his biography. You didn't believe me?" He turned to the phone as his call was answered. "Hey, Robert. Graeme. We pulled into town a couple of minutes ago. . . . Yeah, I found her."

He gave Tillie a thumbs-up. While he talked, she scanned the town, half expecting a camel caravan to parade over the bridge. The place was silent. Graeme hung up the receiver.

"He's coming down to get us. Did you know it's four in the morning?"

"He must be a good friend."

"Robert's with a mission here in Mopti. Comes from Scotland near Mungo Park's birthplace. I met him in Bamako. We both hung out at the library."

"Are you really writing a book about all this? Or are you looking for the treasure like everybody else?"

"I told you what I do."

"There's a lot you haven't told me."

"This hasn't been a leisure cruise, Tillie. I need you to have faith in me."

"Faith."

"You're good at that, remember? Believing in something you can't quite put your finger on. Trusting someone who can't tell you everything past, present, and future."

She wanted to respond, but a pair of bright lights swung around and stopped in the center of the marketplace. "That's Robert." Graeme beckoned her toward the Land Rover, where a gray-haired man waited behind the wheel.

"Hey, Robert, sorry to get you up in the middle of the night."

"No trouble," he replied in a thick Scottish accent. "Mary's waitin' up at the mission. And this must be your young lady."

"Robert McHugh, I'd like you to meet Matilda Thornton," Graeme said as he climbed into the back of the Land Rover. "Tillie, this is Robert."

"Pleased to meet you, Mr. McHugh." Warming to the softness in his blue eyes, she guessed the man to be in his sixties. She sat down beside him. "Please, call me Tillie."

"And I'm Robert to you." He drove the rattling Land Rover out of the market area and into Mopti. It was a short distance to the mission, an old whitewashed building.

"The truck's in the garage," Robert told Graeme as they climbed back out into the night air. "But you must come inside and relax a bit."

The door to the mission house flew open, and a tiny white-haired woman bustled down the steps. "Robert? Are you back already? Graeme, you found her! I'm so pleased. And is this your young lady, then? I'm Mrs. McHugh, dear, but you must call me Mary."

"I'm Tillie Thornton."

"Such a lovely name. My goodness you are thin. Have you had anything to eat lately? You look as though you've been through quite an ordeal. Do come inside and warm yourself. I've made some tea, and I just baked a cake this morning—yesterday morning. Oh, who knows which day it is? Come in, come in!"

Tillie couldn't help but smile as she followed Robert's wife into a warm living room. Four overstuffed chintz-covered chairs congregated around a newly built fire. A tray of teacups with tiny roses painted around their rims sat on a table nearby. A wolfhound rose from the carpet and greeted his master with a wet-nosed nudge.

"Your home is lovely," Tillie said with a laugh of disbelief. "I feel like I'm in Scotland somewhere. Like I could look out the window and see gorse and heather instead of sand."

"I know just what you mean. I've been into the desert myself, and home does seem a dream when I get back to it. Now sit yourselves down, both of you. I can hear the kettle whistling. I'll just pop into the kitchen and bring out my teapot. We'll have a bit of tea before we trundle you off to bed."

Tillie sank into one of the chairs and shut her eyes. An hour ago she would have sworn she would be spending this night fending off the *amenoukal*. Now she was waiting for a cup of hot tea served by a Scottish missionary.

What next, Lord? What next?

"So, you found her with the Tuareg, did you?" Robert McHugh was asking Graeme. "They can be a difficult lot, can't they? Mary, did you hear that? Tillie's just spent some time with a band of Tuareg."

The little woman bustled into the room bearing a pot of tea and a large raisin cake. "With the Tuareg, did you say? My goodness, how did that happen? You must tell us all about it."

As the four sipped milk-and-sugar-sweetened tea and devoured thick slabs of raisin cake with marzipan icing, Graeme and Tillie related the adventures of their journey.

"Now what about this Arthur Robinson chap?" Mary asked. "The Englishman. How does he fit in?"

"Good question." Graeme glanced at Tillie.

Tillie stirred her tea. "Arthur's on his way to Timbuktu. I'm supposed to meet him there."

"Won't you be taking the plane back to Bamako this afternoon?"

"I'm not sure."

"But you'll be going on to Timbuktu, won't you, Graeme?" Robert asked. "You can't give up your project. Finding that journal will add an important chapter to the history of the Niger. You mustn't abandon it."

"Sometimes I think I'm on a wild-goose chase," Graeme said. "Maybe Mungo Park just scribbled down a few thoughts and stuck the paper in a necklace. For all I know there never was a journal."

"There's a journal," Tillie said quietly. "Khatty told me about it. A book, she called it. She said it was very old, and that the paper in the amulet came from the book."

Robert slapped Graeme on the back. "Then you must go on looking, my dear man! You can't give up your search until you've exhausted every possibility. Tillie is welcome to stay here with us if she'd rather not go anywhere. She'll be perfectly safe until you get back from Timbuktu, won't she, Mary? Really, old man, I cannot tell you how important I believe this is."

"Yes, Graeme. Do go on." Mary beamed at Tillie. "We should love to have you here with us, dear."

Graeme sat up and placed his hands on his knees. "I don't know what Tillie wants to do, but I'm sure I'll think better after a little sleep."

"Of course! Here we are chattering away, Robert, and they're nearly dead on their feet. What time is it? Half past five! It's almost time to get up. I have the guest room all ready. Graeme, show Tillie to it, and you can sleep in Robert's study."

Mary bounced to her feet and scurried around the room tidying up the tea things. Graeme showed Tillie down a long hall lined with oak-framed portraits of the McHugh children. At the far end of the house was the tiny guest room. He pushed open the door.

"Mary brought the linens and rugs from Scotland years ago," he said. "They were in the old manor house out on the moors where she grew up. The rocking chair was her mother's. You'll feel like you're home."

"You've visited a lot?"

"They're good friends." He shrugged off his burnous and draped it on a blue chintz sofa. After stepping out of his boots, he padded over to the fireplace, lifted the poker, and stirred the glowing coals.

Tillie curled onto a chair and rested her cheek on its padded wing. Strange to step from a world of tents and camels to one of tea and cake and blue chintz. Disoriented, she looked up when Graeme walked to her side and draped himself onto the neighboring chair. His physical presence seemed to fill the little room.

"Good shower in the bathroom next door. Water's always hot."

"I'm beat."

"We've been up all night. It's dawn outside."

She ran her fingers through the tangles in her hair. "I feel a little slaphappy. Kind of like when I was eight years old and had been to a slumber party and stayed up all night with my friends giggling and trying on makeup."

He acknowledged the image with a sleepy grin. "Too tired to talk?"

"I don't know if I'll make sense." She looked into his eyes and knew there was no escape this time. "OK, talk."

"Those two days we were separated. You thought things over. The amulet. Your boyfriend. Me. So what's the verdict?"

She brushed her hand over her eyes. "I missed you, Graeme."

"Arthur?"

"Worried about him . . . that's all." She paused. "Listen, Graeme, out there in the desert, I had good memories of our days together. I wanted to see you again. At the same time . . . I'm confused."

"You don't know who I really am. The whole writing thing. The police in Djenne. The journal." He hooked one leg over the arm of the chair. "What's your heart telling you?"

"I'm trying to listen to my head."

"And?"

When she didn't answer right away, he jumped out of the chair and knelt to stir the fire again. "I'm trying to be rational, too, but something's happening. Something I didn't count on. Here's the deal. I came to Africa to do what I needed to do. I had a goal. . . ."

His voice drifted in a circle around her head. Desperate to understand who this man was and what he could mean to her, she shifted in her chair to keep awake. "OK," she mumbled. "You had a goal."

"Right. I did the things I needed to do to get where I wanted to be. Research. Contacts. Travel. Set everything up."

Her eyelids drifted down. She could listen with her eyes closed. "Mmm, you set everything up."

"Came to Mali. Library . . . Tuareg . . . you in the marketplace. You know?"

She swirled up to consciousness. "The marketplace."

"But then we started traveling together . . . the Land Rover . . . that night by the river . . . lost you . . . missed you . . . wanted you . . ."

His voice went around and around like bathwater down a drain, and there was nothing she could do to hold it.

When she opened her eyes, Tillie realized Graeme hadn't moved from his chair, either. Tousled black hair had fallen over his closed eyes, and his breathing was deep and easy. He had sprouted a thick growth of whiskers in the days of travel, and she couldn't resist reaching over to brush her fingers against his chin. She traced the curve of his cheek and stroked her fingers up into his hair. When she pushed aside a dark curl, his eyelids slid open. She dropped her hand.

He caught it. "Don't stop."

As he wove their fingers together, she let out a sigh. "Graeme . . . about last night. I'm sorry. I fell asleep while you were talking."

"So did I." He smiled. "Mornin', glory. You're beautiful."

She touched her hair, remembering the tangles and paint and dirt. "You're a better storyteller than I was at the *ahal.*"

"I never lie."

Propping her chin on her hand, she regarded him. "But you don't tell the whole truth, either. You're exasperating."

"Likewise." He ran the side of his finger up her cheek. "Well then, what's the plan, Cinderella? What are you going to do today?"

She looked beyond him to the open window. Late morning sunlight streamed through the branches of a frangipani tree. Outside on the street, horns honked. Someone rang a bicycle bell. The sweet perfume of tropical blossoms filled the room.

Images drifted through her mind: Hannah and their little house in Bamako, an airplane tracing the course of the Niger River southward, Arthur in his gray suit and striped tie, Khatty swirling past her tent, a brass lamp swinging in the desert breeze . . .

What should she do? Go back to the familiar, to safety? Or go on into the unknown?

Some trust in chariots and some in horses . . . or Land Rovers . . . or airplanes . . . *but we trust in the name of the Lord our God.*

"Trust me."

"Let's see about that truck," she said. "It's high time I found the treasure of Timbuktu."

ELEVEN

When Graeme stepped out of the bathroom, he spotted Tillie riffling through a basket she had found beside her door. She had showered before he did, and her hair hung in damp, dark gold tendrils almost to her waist. One of Mary McHugh's terry-cloth bathrobes, pink with little white-ribbon roses, clung to her skin.

"Mary's left us some things," she told him, unaware how long he'd been watching her. "Her note says she and Robert will be back at three. They've gone to the market."

"Anything to wear in there?" He had wrapped a towel around his waist. The thought of pulling on the same jeans he'd worn for five days was enough to make him consider a pink terry-cloth bathrobe himself.

Tillie lifted out a man's white shirt, though it would be small on Graeme. Then she unloaded two pairs of khaki slacks, a few pairs of socks, three khaki shirts in various sizes, and a pair of well-worn suede boots. At the bottom of the basket lay a thick chocolate bar and two small oranges.

She stood and tossed him the white shirt. "It has a pocket for your notes."

"Still doubting I'm a writer?"

"You don't act like a writer."

"What does a writer act like?"

"A writer writes things down now and then."

He grinned. "I'll try to do better. Now how about those pants?"

She handed them to him. "I kind of like the towel."

Facing her, he could read a reflection of his own thoughts in her eyes. They were a pair. A matched pair. They shared more than common interests—they knew their own hearts.

Her drying hair floated around her face in wild, honeyed waves. Her eyes spoke conviction and passion. She had been tested; she would be tested again. He knew she would hold strong.

As Tillie turned into the guest room and shut the door behind her, it came to him that he loved this woman. All his life he had been aware that he'd never known love. Never felt it. Was convinced he wouldn't know it if he saw it. Couldn't feel it if he tried.

In the hallway of the little mission in Mopti, his uncertainty evaporated like a drop of dew on a Sahara morning. He loved Tillie Thornton. Heart and soul.

He could go on without her, but he wouldn't want to. He would do all in his power to protect her. Please her. Honor her. Fulfill her. And if the time came, he would lay down his own life to save hers.

Graeme slid his arm around Tillie's waist as they walked down the hall. They had just entered the living room when the front door opened and Mary scurried into the room. "Oh, la, you're up!" she sang out. "Had your lunch?"

"Not yet," Tillie said.

"It's half-past three already, did you know? Time for tea. Robert's out in the garage working on the truck with the chaps. It's looking very good, he thinks. Graeme, will you just pop out there and call him in to tea? Tillie and I shall set the table. We'll make it a high tea. Come along, dear!"

Tillie watched Graeme walk out the door; then she turned to follow Mary. The little woman bustled here and there, picking up this, exclaiming over that, taking a random path through the house. Tillie thought it was sort of like tagging after a pink helium balloon that has lost most of its air and wants to bounce along the ground just out of reach.

The kitchen was a medium-sized room with a gas refrigerator and stove. The two women gathered the tea things from the pantry and set them on a wheeled bamboo cart. Tillie carried armloads of cold meats, breads, scones, butter, jams, and cakes into the dining room. Mary whipped up two large omelettes filled with cheese and mushrooms.

When the tea was ready and everyone had assembled in the dining room, Robert blessed the food. The meal tasted better than any Tillie could ever remember eating. Graeme gave her an amused look from time to time as she devoured three scones dripping in honey and butter, her entire omelette, and two slabs of cold roast gazelle, while washing the food down with cup after cup of hot tea laced with milk and sugar.

"Have you made your plans yet?" Robert wanted to know. "The truck's running rather well at the moment. I think it should get you to Timbuktu, if that's where you're going."

"It is," Tillie said. "I'll be going on with Graeme. You know, Robert, I've resisted my part in this mess with the *amenoukal* ever since that child threw the amulet around my neck. But this morning I finally realized I want to know what the blasted treasure is myself."

Mary hooted. "A girl after my own heart! When I was your age, lass, I was ready for any adventure. Why do you think I married this roving minister? Not for the money, I can assure you of that!"

"Now, Mary." Robert patted her hand. "It's not been a bad life, has it? We've had enough to live on."

"More than enough. My life's been all the richer for having married this man and followed him round the globe on his mad whims."

"Mad whims?" Robert echoed.

"Your callings, then. 'The Lord has called me to India, Mary,' he announces. 'The Lord has called me to Peru. The Lord has called me to the Sahara.' Your callings have made for a full and rewarding life. The Lord has blessed us richly, as he always does when we follow his will."

"I admire you, Mary," Tillie said. "It must take a lot of strength to keep leaving your home behind all the time."

"My home is with Robert, just as yours will be with the man you choose to marry. You'll never need another, lass."

Mary looked from Tillie to Graeme, as if expecting one of them to say something revealing about their relationship. When neither did, she went on unfazed.

"Now, what can we get you for your trip? I shall fill that basket with food. You'll find precious little to eat between here and Timbuktu, you know. And I'm glad to see the clothing fits. We keep a supply of old army things in the church. You never would believe who shows up needing something to wear! Robert, haven't we a few old blankets we could spare? And sheets—you'll need sheets to put up as a buffer against the wind. You'll have to spend the night in the desert. It can be dreadfully cold, as you know."

Robert nodded. "One can't be too careful in the desert. I shall get the blankets and whatever else looks handy while Mary sees to the food. Graeme, you and Tillie had better go out to the garage and get the feel of the old truck. She's rather temperamental, I'm afraid."

Gradually the canvas-covered truck bed was loaded with supplies, including several spare cans of gasoline and water. Before long, Graeme and Tillie climbed into the huge, rusty vehicle and said their good-byes. Graeme fired up the engine, a sound like a tank battalion coming to life, and they headed down the road to Timbuktu.

The late afternoon had gone gray and windy. As the truck rattled along the rough track beside the river, the sun dipped lower and lower.

"When will we get to Timbuktu?" Tillie shouted over the racket from the unmuffled exhaust.

"Tomorrow afternoon, I expect. The road veers away from the river pretty soon. We'll be in the desert in a few minutes."

"Why doesn't the road follow the river?"

"There's an internal delta up ahead. Gets pretty swampy. No one can be sure where the Niger will go when the rains come."

"Feels like there's a storm coming now."

"Sky looked pretty clear from Mopti, but I've never seen the desert this color."

Tillie wanted to talk to him about the amulet. She had made up her mind to find the treasure—if there was one—and now she wanted to hear his thoughts. But her throat would never hold out over the din of the truck, so she sat back in her seat and lifted the amulet from beneath her shirt.

Opening it carefully, she took out the old document and unfolded it. She had a strange feeling that there were clues in the wording itself. Mungo Park certainly had not intended to sound like he was writing out a charm or an ominous portent, but the Tuareg had interpreted his words to have deep significance for their future.

Robert had said Graeme was hunting Park's journal. Behind the cover of the sunglasses Mary had given her, Tillie studied him for a long time. His face, chiseled by hard living and the sun, seemed relaxed; his intent eyes were fixed on the road ahead. His neck and arms were deeply tanned, making his crisp, white cotton shirt fairly gleam. She could see the bulge of his notecase in his pocket. Why hadn't she ever noticed that before? She couldn't help wondering if there were other things she should be seeing and wasn't.

Looking down at the document again, she read the words.

25 December, 1806—

I believe it is Christmas Day somewhere, though not here. I know I will not live to see tomorrow. The Bight of Benin the blight of Benin. . . . Ahmadi Fatouma has the wealth in safekeeping for

me. . . . Mine mine mine! I have the wealth. I possess the treasure
of Timbuktu. One day, one day the white man will come here.
One day, one day the white woman will come here. . . . She will
plant trees. She will find the treasure of Timbuktu. . . .

What on earth had he meant? More important, what did
the Tuareg think he meant? She reread the page. She knew
the Bight of Benin was the name of the gulf at the mouth of
the Niger River. But what was the blight of Benin? The
treasure of Timbuktu? The tree-planting woman? Once
again, she folded the paper and reinserted it in the locket.
None of it made sense.

She put the amulet back under her shirt, dropped her
hands to her lap, and let out a deep sigh. The sky had
turned to violet, and thin clouds lay across the distant horizon. The truck left the riverbank to rumble down the rutted
track in the midst of low brush, sand dunes, and a few
scrubby trees.

The sun was a huge orange gumdrop in the sky when
Graeme pulled the truck to a stop beside an outcropping of
rock. He set the parking brake and turned off the ignition.

"Time to eat," he said.

"Let's keep going. I'm not hungry yet."

"I'm not surprised, the way you scarfed down those
biscuits and eggs."

She took off her sunglasses and looked at him through
lowered lashes. "I didn't notice you holding back."

"I never hold back. Let's see what Mary put together for
us in that basket." He threw open the squeaky door and
climbed out of the truck.

Tillie sat for a moment, wondering how he could possibly think of eating. Resigned, she looked around the side to see if he had found the basket. Graeme was nowhere in sight. She slid out of the seat and jumped to the ground. At the back of the truck, the canvas flap was still in place.

"Graeme? Where are you?"

"Up here. On the rocks."

He had scaled the outcropping and was scanning the horizon with a pair of binoculars. Her heart jolted. "Do you see the Tuareg caravan?"

"Not a trace." He clambered down the rock. "No camels in sight."

He unzipped the canvas flap and sorted through the provisions in the back of the truck. "Lantern, candles, blankets, water, sheets. Good for Mary. Listen, I want to keep going as long as we can see the road tonight."

"Sure. Anything wrong?"

He had told her he never lied. But if their pursuers were in sight, she deserved to know.

"The sooner we get to Timbuktu, the better off we'll be."

Graeme hauled the heavy basket from the truck and carried it to the rock. He spread a checkered cloth, then dug around inside the basket and pulled out a package of sandwiches and a block of cheese. Suddenly Tillie realized she was hungrier than she thought.

"I'm glad you decided to go to Timbuktu," he said around a mouthful. "Seems the real Tillie is coming out of hiding."

"The real Tillie?"

"A woman who loves life, who takes risks. Most people would call it quits after the stuff you've gone through. But not only are you still here, you're champing at the bit to find out what that treasure is."

"Got me all figured out, huh?"

"Hardly."

"You know, I looked over the document again. I don't want to wait until the *amenoukal* catches me again before I figure it out."

"He's not getting his hands on you."

Tillie looked up from her sandwich, surprised at the vehemence in his voice. He tossed his half-eaten sandwich back in the bag and slid off the rock.

"Do you think we can decipher where the treasure is?" she asked.

His back was to her as he leaned against the rock. "If we put our heads together we might. I have some ideas, but I can't make all the pieces fit."

"Give me a few of those pieces. We know who Mungo Park was and what he was trying to accomplish. His goal was to follow the course of the Niger to its mouth."

Graeme nodded and went on, "We think we know what he meant by using the words *tree-planting woman*. He was probably referring to his vision of the future of Mali when white men and women would settle here to farm the Niger valley."

"We know the Tuareg got their hands on the amulet about two hundred years ago. Their legends say the writing in the amulet comes from a book. And we think the book may be Mungo Park's last journal."

"So we've got a man, a goal, a journal. We know the Tuareg have been reading the inscription in the amulet to mean one thing, when Park may have meant something else."

"Could the treasure have been one thing to Park and something else to the Tuareg?"

Graeme shrugged. "Park thought he could use the treasure to build a house for Ailie on Chester Street. It must have been something he thought he could barter."

"Was there gold in Timbuktu two hundred years ago, Graeme? Do we even know what the city was like?"

He dug his notecase out of his pocket. "We know what the Englishmen who backed Park's African expeditions believed about Timbuktu. They based their hopes for gold and riches on a description by a guy named Leo Africanus." He flipped through his cards. "This is from *Leo the African's History and Description of Africa and the Notable Things Contained Therein,* written in 1526. I took these notes from the English version, which was published in 1600. 'The rich king of Tombuto, hath many plates and sceptres of gold, some whereof weigh 1,300 pounds. And he keeps a magnificent and well-furnished court. . . . He hath always three thousand horsemen, and a great number of footmen that shoot poisoned arrows. . . . Here are a great store of doctors, judges, priests, and other learned men, that are bountifully maintained at the king's expense.'"

The ancient words brought the fabulous city of Timbuktu in its glory days to brilliant, colorful life. Tillie felt like Dorothy stepping out of black-and-white Kansas into Technicolor Oz. She shut her eyes as Graeme continued reading.

"'And hither are brought diverse manuscripts or written books out of Barbarie, which are sold for more money than any other merchandise. The coin of Tombuto is of gold without any stamp or superscription; but in matters of small value they use certain shells brought hither out of the kingdom of Persia' . . . and it goes on."

"Gold plates and sceptres. Gold coins." Tillie shook her head. "Graeme, do you realize Mungo Park really may have hidden treasure somewhere in Timbuktu? What would you do with it if you found it?"

"I'm not hunting the treasure, Tillie. I told you that."

"But what if we find it?" Somehow she had to make him tell her the truth about his own goals.

"I want Mungo Park's journal. If we found some kind of treasure, it would belong to the Malian government." He crossed his arms over his chest. "I don't think there is any treasure. All we have is a scrap of the journal. That page is authentic, and the rest of it must be somewhere. That's what I want."

"It means a lot to you."

"I want to know what happened to Mungo Park before he died. I want to know what he was like at the end of his life." He gave a low chuckle. "My mom used to tell me stories about him when I was a kid. I always wanted to be like him—the adventurer, the bold explorer."

"You are like him."

"Not really." He straightened and turned around. "You get enough to eat?"

Her eyes flashed. "Graeme, you *are* like Mungo Park. If I'm that woman who loves life and isn't afraid to take risks, you're no different. We're in this together."

"You had the adventurer in you all along, Tillie. I knew

it the minute I tossed you into my Land Rover. You're a fighter."

"We did have our moments in the beginning, didn't we?"

"The first thing you did was yell at me. Fought me like a honey badger."

"You always bring out the beast, um, best in me," she quipped.

He laughed.

She paused thoughtfully. "You know, I've never yelled at Arthur in my life."

"Too bad for Arthur." With a wink, he grabbed the basket and walked back to the truck.

The night turned black, and the stars were hidden from view by a thick haze that spread across the sky like spilled honey. As the truck rattled along, Graeme tried to focus on the topography, but he could make out very little. It was like traveling in a vacuum.

Hours passed, and the road ahead began to whip into a whirling sea of grass, twigs, and sand. He fought the steering wheel to keep the truck on track. Tillie sat beside him, as stiff as a windup doll. The wind picked up; the truck swayed. Sand peppered the windshield like pellets from a BB gun. Graeme finally braked to a stop, cut the ignition, and leaned back in the seat.

Even with the engine off, Tillie had to shout over the wind. "What's going on?"

"Gotta stop."

"I thought you wanted to go on to Timbuktu."

"It's getting bad outside." He turned the headlights back on.

Tillie stared out the windshield. The inky sky had crept down close, and now it seemed threatening. Whole bushes whipped across the road. There was a strange pall, an eerie half-glow to the landscape.

He switched off the headlights. "Sandstorm's coming."

"Are you sure?"

"Only one thing looks like a sandstorm."

"It's going to catch us head-on, isn't it?"

"Reckon so."

Her eyes narrowed. "You spotted the storm from the outcrop back there where we ate. Why didn't you tell me?"

"I thought I might be able to outrun it." He put his hand over his eyes and rubbed his temples. "Look, I didn't want to worry you. You've been through a lot."

"Should I worry?"

"A little." He brushed back his hair and sat forward. "I guess we'd better try to make the best of it. We'll weather it better in the back of the truck. The sand is starting to sift into the cab. I suspect it's going to get uncomfortable in a few minutes. Come on."

He pushed open the door. Blowing sand and grit hit him in the face. He threw his arm across his eyes and covered his nose with his hand. Tillie slid across the seat. Holding her close, he pushed her head into his shoulder and jumped with her from the cab to the desert floor. Sand bit into his cheeks and flew into his ears. It cut through the fabric of his khaki pants and stung his legs like biting ants.

Sheltering Tillie, he stumbled through ankle-deep sand to

the back of the truck and flung down the tailgate. They clambered onto the corrugated steel bed; then he caught the metal gate and pulled it closed. As he tucked down the flapping canvas, Tillie fell onto the pile of blankets in a fit of coughing. He tied a handkerchief over his face.

"Tillie!" he shouted above the wind. "Put this over your nose and mouth. Breathe through it."

He tore off his shirt and threw it to her. She clutched it to her face, breathing into it like an oxygen mask. Even in the relative sanctuary of the covered truck bed, the grit found easy entry. Sand piled up in the corners and seeped through the tiny seams of the canvas covering. Graeme rooted around in the supplies until he found a box of matches. When he struck one, their haven lit up like Ali Baba's cave. Tillie crawled to his side and held the glass globe of the lantern while he fumbled with the wick. At last the tiny spark wobbled into flame, and she lowered the globe to keep it from blowing out.

"Hand me a blanket," he called over the moan of the wind shuddering around and through the truck.

She helped him tie the blanket by its four corners to the steel frame over the truck bed. They worked around the inside of their shelter, layering sheets and blankets like a baklava pastry. With the insulation the sand lost most of its sting, and the wind had fewer cracks to penetrate. They stuffed bits of torn fabric into every opening.

By the time the lantern's wick had burned to a low flame, the truck had become almost comfortable. Graeme untied the handkerchief from his face and looked around. Like some fantastic crazy-quilt tent, the inside of the truck had walls of bedding tied helter-skelter in a riot of daisies, rosebuds, tulips, and daffodils. Pink blankets, blue blankets, white sheets, and yellow-striped sheets muffled the wind and kept out the sand.

"Thank God for Mary McHugh and her sheets," he said.

Tillie glanced up. "God again? You think maybe he took time out from ignoring his universe to provide us with some sheets?"

He smiled, glad she was still percolating. "I think maybe both of us are going to end up on our knees before this storm runs out. I should know better than to try to outguess the desert."

"We'll be OK. You have a Bible on you?" She read the answer in his face. "There's something in Deuteronomy . . . something like . . . 'In the howling waste of a wilderness, he encircled him, he cared for him, he guarded him as the pupil of his eye.'"

"Hannah taught you that?"

Her eyes softened, and he knew the African woman was never far from Tillie's thoughts. "The Scriptures are God's Word, she used to tell us. If you want to know him, listen to his words. We listened a lot."

"'The howling waste.'" He sank onto a remaining blanket beside her and tugged off his boots. He tilted one, and sand poured out. "I can't quote the Bible, and I can't guarantee you're going to come out of this one OK. Sandstorms are unpredictable. I'd have made you stay in Mopti with Robert and Mary if I'd known it was coming."

"*Made* me stay?" Her eyebrows rose imperiously.

He struggled with a grin. "*Suggested* you stay."

"I wanted to come," she said, reaching out to touch his

arm. "Even knowing about the sandstorm wouldn't have stopped me."

He stretched out his legs and crossed his ankles. At least it was a chance to be alone with Tillie. Kind of nice actually. Enclosed, secure. Sort of a cocoon from which something beautiful might emerge.

"Mungo Park was in a sandstorm once," he said, draping his arm around her shoulders. "He'd been held captive by the Moors for more than two months. Finally, they let him go, and a sandstorm blew up. I don't think it lasted long, but it exhausted his supplies. He wrote that rain fell for more than an hour after the storm. He quenched his thirst by wringing out and sucking on his clothes."

She stiffened slightly. "We have enough water, don't we?"

He reached beside him and jostled the heavy can. "We'll be OK for a few days."

"A few days? Graeme, are you serious?"

"This might last a while." He listened for a moment to the sounds outside the truck. "To tell you the truth, I don't think the storm's hit us yet."

She fell back against the pile of blankets. "So what's *this?* Fairy dust?"

He grinned. "Come on, Tinkerbell. We might as well get this place as comfy as we can. I'll check out the food supply. Why don't you see what's in those boxes Robert packed? I'm not going to worry yet. Only trouble is, I've heard these storms can really change the landscape. The dunes move, and they can bury stationary objects like—"

He caught himself too late.

"Like trucks." Her voice was dull.

"We'll check outside now and then to see how she's holding up."

"And if the sand is starting to bury us alive, we'll just take our handy-dandy shovels and dig ourselves out."

"If we had any handy-dandy shovels."

Muttering something, she began digging through the wooden boxes stacked against one wall of the truck bed. As she counted screwdrivers, socket wrenches, and rolls of electrical wiring, Graeme opened the baskets of food Mary had packed. There were salted crackers, hard-boiled eggs, oranges, papayas, candy bars, cans of beans, and . . .

"Bananas." He held up a bunch, his grin broad. "We'll live, Tillie! Manna in the wilderness."

She groaned.

They spent at least an hour sorting through and arranging things. Tillie hung the lantern from one of the metal ribs over the truck. Then she improvised a miniature table out of an upended box and put two pillows around it for seats. She covered the box with a pillowcase decorated with sprays of roses, put the bananas in the center, and set plates and tin cups around them.

Then she turned four empty crates on their sides to make shelves, and she stacked the cans and packets of food in neat rows, everything visible and handy. She created two pallets out of the remaining blankets and pillows. She used an old rag to sweep all the sand into the corners of the truck. Then she dusted off her hands and sat back on her heels.

"Home," she said.

"Sweet home," he finished.

Graeme had never seen anything like it. In fact, he'd been watching her work as he checked the supply of kerosene for the lantern and rigged a couple of air vents out of some tightly woven netting he'd found. Nesting, he'd heard it called. But he had never actually seen such a transformation. The truck could now claim a dining room, kitchen, and bedroom. It was downright cozy.

Again his heart turned over in his chest. Mary McHugh had said Tillie would make her home with the man she chose. He was starting to see that "home" could be anywhere, as long as things were right between the woman and the man. Did he want to be that man in Tillie's life? Her one love? Her home? Well, something was making his chest ache and his eyes burn.

"Now what?" she asked. She sat against the side of the truck bed, her legs folded and her hands in her lap. "We wait it out?"

"Pretend you're stuck in an elevator."

He hunkered down beside her. If he was ever going to work things out with this woman, if he had any hope of finding out what made her tick, he had to use this time. This chance.

"Tell me everything I need to know about Tillie Thornton," he said.

"We already did that on the steamer."

"There's a lot I still don't know."

"Anything you don't know, I probably don't want to talk about."

"How about Arthur?" He jumped into the middle of it with both feet. "You planning to marry him? You're a loyal woman. I imagine he promised you home, security, children. A future you can count on."

"I'm not going to marry Arthur."

Relief washed through him like rain on desert soil.

"When I threw you into the Land Rover, you thought you would. What changed your mind?"

She stretched out her legs and stared at the toes of her boots for a long time. "You," she said finally.

"You don't sound very happy about that."

"I'm not sure how happy I *can* be over all this. I know Arthur isn't right for me. You said some things that helped me see that."

"So, what is right?"

"If I knew that I'd tell you."

"What about me and you?"

She looked up at the swaying oil lantern with its wobbly flame. "I feel like that lamp sometimes. Like I'm just a tiny flame, a flicker of spirit in a great big desert. In spite of my concerns, I've loved the thrills of this adventure up the Niger. But I know I'm not strong enough to go on waging a crusade the way you do."

"I'm on a crusade?"

Her eyes clouded. "We're not on the same team."

"I didn't know you saw this as a game."

"It's not that. I'm talking about bigger things." She ran her fingers through the sand that had sifted into the corner of the truck. "When I have a chance to stop running and I look at my life, I realize it's not the Tuareg or the amulet or the treasure that matter. They're insignificant."

"What matters, Tillie?" he asked, but he already knew her answer.

"Our hearts. What we believe in. What we're devoted to." He could tell as she spoke the words what they cost her. Her voice was low, heavy, as though weighed down with an enormous weight. She raised her eyes to meet his, and the pain he saw there startled him. "You're not a believer, Graeme. I am. That makes us as different as sand and water. Even when you mix those two, very little can grow. Believe me, I've tried. It's barren and miserable. When the sun beats down, the water evaporates just like that. When the wind hits, the sand blows everywhere. In the end, there's nothing left."

He sat back, looking away from her, staring at the side of the truck. "Sounds desolate."

"It would be. Eventually."

He could feel her looking at him. Waiting.

He had nothing to say.

If he did what he wanted—took her in his arms, held her, kissed her—he might make her believe anything was possible. He might even convince her she was wrong. Paint dreams of a future she couldn't resist. Teach her to betray her heart.

But he had lived too long in the desert she'd described. He was sand. Empty. Barren. If she came to him, he would drink her dry. Use her up. Leave her nothing but a mist. He wouldn't do it on purpose. It would just happen because of who he was. And who she was.

She was a believer. She had faith in an almighty God. Hope. Love. She bathed in these things. Everything in her life was washed in the water of her beliefs. And she held that living water out to him like the Holy Grail. Beckoning, beckoning. Just one taste. Just a sip and he'd be washed, too. Clean of his past. A new man.

He closed his eyes, regret sharp and bitter. Could he believe it? He had done so many things. So much wrong.

He was sand. Could that possibly change? "I guess you think I'm a lost cause."

"Anyone who's lost can be found. Anyone who's blind can see. Anyone who's willing to let his old self die can be born again. All it takes is surrender."

"It takes faith. I've never believed in anything I couldn't see or touch, Tillie. Even if God didn't abandon the world, he's still just some ephemeral spirit floating around."

"A spirit who was made human in the body of Jesus Christ."

"A guy who died on a cross." He shook his head. "Even if you buy the idea that Jesus came to life again, you're still dealing with a spirit—not with somebody you can touch."

"He touches *me,* Graeme. His Spirit lives inside me. Even when I'm struggling—and believe me, I do—I have no doubt his power is real. I can feel that. I can rely on it. My faith is based on what I see and feel in my own life."

"I see it in you, Tillie." His chest felt tight. "But I don't see it in me."

She brushed a finger under her eye. "Sand and water. They don't belong together."

"I guess you're right."

"Bedtime, then?" Her voice sounded small, trembling. Had his stoniness made her cry?

She was crawling over to her pallet. It was all he could do to keep from stopping her and taking her in his arms. Did she hurt the way he did? Did she care more than she could admit?

He slid onto his own bed. "If I could change things, I would," he said into the darkness. "But I can't change my past. I can't change who I am."

"Graeme . . ." Her voice cracked, as though her throat were dry from overuse. "Graeme, you—"

Before she could finish what she'd started to say, a blast of wind slammed the truck like an iron fist. The lantern rocked and its tiny flame blew out, plunging them into darkness. The truck shivered, rocked, swayed.

"Graeme!"

Clearly disoriented, Tillie flailed out. He caught her hand and pulled her across the gap between them.

"It's OK, Tillie," he whispered. "I've got you."

TWELVE

Sand and wind continued to buffet the truck, making it rock like a toy boat in a bathtub. Tillie lay stiff in Graeme's arms. The storm was more frightening to her than the *amenoukal* and his broadsword, she realized. In that arena she had been a player; now she was nothing but a prop. She felt vulnerable. Fragile. Anything could happen to her.

Dear Lord . . .

Her prayer ran out of words. Instead her heart groaned its message. Fear. Turmoil. The storm. Graeme. Graeme more than anything. Why did she have to reject him? She wanted him. Lord, she wanted him.

"Tillie, can you hear me?" His voice in her ear was low.

"Yes," she whispered. She looked over her shoulder at the smooth line of his bare shoulder.

"I'm going to try to light the lantern."

The muscles moved under his skin as he rose to a crouch. She sat up and watched the outline of his hand move out across the darkness and strike a match. Turning his back to her, he lifted the glass chimney and lit the wick. She let her focus wander over his tousled mane of hair as it fell down his neck and lay softly forward over the curve of his ear. His profile was lit by the gentle yellow glow that cast deep shadows in the hollow of his cheek and beneath the razor-straight line of his jaw.

He adjusted the wick to a low, steady flame. She studied his broad back with its long ridge that ran into the curved waist of his khaki trousers. She traced the lean, hard lines of his legs that tapered into the leather boots he always wore. Her eyes felt full of him.

This man, this Graeme, was the man she loved. He was the one she wanted forever.

She loved him for his strength, his bravery, his sense of adventure. She loved him for that silly grin, and those flashing blue-green eyes, and that ready tease. She loved him for his quick mind, his gentle nature, his easy laughter. And she loved him for the pain he had known, pain that had given him sensitivity and depth. He was impulsive, unpredictable. She felt that these few days with Graeme had been packed with more excitement than she'd known in her whole life.

Graeme knelt beside Tillie again and slipped his arm around her shoulders. She saw that his eyes had gone deep and soft.

"You can relax," he said. "We'll be all right."

"It sounds so angry."

"Be glad you're not a Targui. They're weathering this thing in their tents." The air inside the truck was close, but their insulation held. "It's good to hold you, Tillie. I've missed you. When I'm with you, my life feels complete. And that scares me. I don't have a lot of security to offer you. My life's not stable. I doubt it ever will be. I don't want it to be. I want the life I'm living right now. The adventure, the peaks of excitement, are what make life worthwhile."

"The Mungo Park life."

"That's right."

"Mungo Park left Ailie back in Scotland."

"I never thought a woman would be a part of my life. When you grow up like I did, with the kind of father I had, you doubt your ability to build a family."

"Even though it's what you want most in the world."

He was silent a long time. She imagined him taking her words, weighing them.

"Even *if* it's what I want most in the world." He shook his head. "I know I'm not a prize catch, but these days I can't imagine myself going on without having you around."

"Partners in adventure."

"More than that." He turned her to face him and gripped her shoulders. "The only security I can promise is myself. I'll be with you, Tillie. As long as you'll have me, I won't leave you."

She closed her eyes. His commitment had not come easily; his vow was no idle promise. This was a man who had distanced himself from people for many years. His pledge to her would not be broken.

Graeme opened his eyes and stared into the blackness. Breathing hard, his hands clammy, he fought away his dream of the Tuareg *amenoukal*. The man had been dragging Tillie behind him across a dune, her limp feet making two parallel lines like Land Rover tracks. He had run after them, following the tracks, but the sand had begun to billow and blow and erase the path faster than he could run. He was losing her. Losing her.

He raked his fingers through his damp hair. Never had he seen such total absence of light. Was he awake or asleep? Still dreaming? Tillie's arm lay curled on her lap, her fingers resting against his hand. He touched their tips—soft, warm, real.

His movement stirred her. "Graeme?" She reached up and laid her hand on his face. "Oh, it's you. Thank goodness."

He held her to his chest, buried his face in her hair, tangled his fingers in its waves. "I dreamed you were gone. Tillie, I swear if I'd known there was going to be this much danger . . . I never would have . . ."

"You didn't know what was going to happen to us any more than I did." She brushed the hair from his cheek. "Don't worry about me. I'm going to be OK."

"We've got to figure some way to get the *amenoukal* off our backs. We've got to get this treasure thing out of our lives. I never wanted it to become so threatening."

"Shh. It's OK."

It wasn't OK. Nothing would be OK until she was safe. He pressed her head against his chest. Outside, the sandstorm raged on like a lion trapped in a cage.

"Do you hear that sound?" Tillie's voice was low.

"What sound?"

"That wailing noise. I wonder if it's the *djenoun*."

"The what?"

"The *djenoun*. Khatty told me the *djenoun* are the people of the empty places. The people of the night. She said they make that strange droning noise. The Tuareg are afraid of the *djenoun*."

He relaxed a little. "Sounds like your basic bogeyman story to me."

"I guess so. Did I tell you Khatty made up a beautiful poem about you? She called you the son of a waran."

"Doesn't sound like much of a compliment."

She laughed. "The waran is the Egyptian monitor lizard. For some reason, the Tuareg honor it. I think Khatty meant it as a term of praise. She says you're a terribly brave man for going up against the *amenoukal* on my behalf."

"It's a toss-up as to which of us has rescued the other more often." As the memory of his dream faded, he felt his muscles unknot. "Khatty's special to you, isn't she?"

"In a strange way. If we'd been born in the same culture, we might have been friends. Maybe even good friends. We understand each other's minds. In spite of Khatty's haughtiness, she's easy to like. She's intense. She cares. But you should have seen her bossing her servants around. And the food. Ever tasted camel's milk?"

"Sure. Right now that sounds almost good. Are you hungry?"

"Thirsty."

"It's the lack of moisture in the air. My eyes feel like they're full of sand. Probably are. Come on, let's see what we can find to eat."

Graeme fumbled around in the darkness until he found the matches and lantern. Their cave filled with soft light as the tiny lamp came to life. He filled two small plastic cups with water and handed one to Tillie. The water was cool as it ran down his parched throat and settled in his empty stomach.

Tillie looked around their makeshift home. A smile lifted the corners of her mouth. "It's holding up pretty well."

There were growing piles of sand in each corner and

along the perimeter of the truck bed. Occasionally more sand would sift down from the ceiling and scatter across the blankets.

"Maybe it's good we're here in the middle of the desert," she said. "At least we're safe and we can rest." She looked into his eyes. "Are we safe, Graeme?"

"From the *amenoukal?* He'd never find us in this."

"From the storm. Do you think it's burying us?"

He reached out and thumped the canvas with his fist. There was a dull thud. "It gives a little. I don't think we're in too deep. I'm a little concerned about the roof, though."

"If it caves in—" She stopped abruptly. Listened. Sudden silence settled over the truck. "What's going on?"

"Storm's over."

"Just like that?"

The wind had gone all at once, as though a giant hand had covered its source. The truck stopped shuddering, and Graeme realized it was resting at an odd angle in the sand. Muted light filtered through the patchwork of sheets and blankets. A gentle glow settled on the piles of sand along the metal floor.

"I'm scared to move," Tillie whispered. "Like if I do, the wind will start up again."

Instead, a new sound took the place of the wind. A rushing, splattering noise. Water.

"It's raining, Graeme."

"Come on, Tillie-girl. Let's get out of this sandbox."

They pulled down the sheets covering the canvas flap, brushed back mounds of sand, and wrenched open the gritty tailgate catch. Graeme gave the gate a shove, and it fell with a clang.

"Graeme, look!" Tillie's voice was hushed.

He straightened beside her. Their world had completely changed. From a dry, barren plain with scrub grass and low bushes, the landscape had become nothing but desert as far as the eye could see. Dunes rolled to the horizon. Rain cascaded like buckets dumped from heaven. And the smell . . . clean, fresh, wet.

He bounded out of the truck and slogged to the top of the nearest dune. Warm rain washed over him. He shook his head and sand flew out of his hair. His dry, parched skin soaked up the moisture. He closed his eyes, opened his mouth, and tasted the raindrops.

"Graeme!" Tillie waved from the top of another dune. Her hair streamed down her shoulders, her shirt and trousers stuck to her skin, her feet sank into the sand. She started to laugh. "I feel like a sponge."

"You look like a sponge."

In answer, she sprinted toward him and threw her arms around him. "I love this crazy place!" She threw back her head and gave a gurgling chuckle as the rain ran down her throat.

Graeme lifted her into his arms and swung her around and around until they fell dizzily onto the sand. Rolling down the dune, they tumbled over until they lay gasping with laughter. When he reached for her, she rolled away and sprang to her feet. She raced up another dune and waved her arms like a cheerleader gone mad.

"Come back here!" he shouted, trotting after her.

"Catch me!" She shrieked as he lunged, missed, and rolled back down the dune. Holding her stomach with laughter at the sight of him lying spread-eagled on the sand,

Tillie turned and ran to the top of another dune. "Hey, lazybones! You can do better than that."

Graeme was on his feet and halfway up the hill before she could move. She took off like a gazelle, all arms and legs, dashing down the dune.

"No, no, no!" she cried.

It was too late. His arms went around her waist. She struggled, but he held her tight.

"Yes, yes, yes." His mouth covered hers. "Always say yes to me, Tillie-girl."

For a moment he believed she was his, completely and wholly. But then she drew back and lifted her eyes to the sky. "It's clearing already."

"I'd stay here forever with you. Just like this."

She grinned. "We'd be mummies by this afternoon if we did that. The sun is after me already."

The moment was over. Her shield of resistance was back in place. She wouldn't come closer; her heart held her back.

"Let's see if we can get that monster of a truck going again." When he relaxed his arms, she moved away. He watched in fascination as she brushed the sand from her clothes. "You keep that up, and we'll never get to Timbuktu."

She blushed from her neck to the roots of her hair. "I'll get to Timbuktu with or without you." Turning, she started back toward the truck. "The secret is in my amulet, and I'm going to figure it out."

"Sure you want to?"

"Positive."

Graeme stepped over to the truck and kicked at a tire half-buried in sand.

"Can we get it out?" she asked.

"Maybe. The sand is wet enough to give us some traction if we hurry. But that's not the real problem." He looked up and scanned the horizon. "The road is gone."

She frowned. Here and there a sign of what might be the rutted track emerged from the sand, but it looked impossible to follow. "Any ideas?"

Graeme shrugged and began digging the loose sand away from the tires. Tillie slammed the tailgate and helped him dig. When they walked around to the cab, Graeme opened the door to a shower of sand and slid onto the seat. Tillie climbed in beside him.

"There's a compass on the dashboard," he told her. "Robert assured me it works. I know we're going north, and I expect the storm has wiped out the road only part of the way. If we can get over these dunes, we'll find it again somewhere ahead. But this truck wasn't made to go over sand. That's what dromedaries are for."

Tillie reflected for a moment. "Do you suppose the *amenoukal* is near?"

"No idea. Let's go."

He turned the key in the ignition, and the engine ground over. He could hear Tillie breathing in prayer, "Come on. Come on, start."

As if in answer, the engine coughed to life and began its familiar rattle. She let out her breath and leaned back as he put the truck in gear. It lurched forward as though eager to leave the desert, spun for a moment, then climbed out of its ruts and rolled across the sand.

"Doing good, babe," he whispered as the truck crept over the uneven surface.

Keeping a close eye on the compass, he worked the gears, edging forward, careful not to stall. The truck wailed like a banshee. Over one dune. Down the steep side. Into a ravine. Up a slanted scree. After what seemed like hours, the truck suddenly crested a hill, and they spotted the road a hundred yards to the west. The desert faded, and the landscape returned to typical Sahel terrain.

Tillie reached over and kneaded Graeme's taut back. He let out a breath. "It's getting dark, but I want to keep going."

"I'll drive."

"She's all yours." He pulled the truck to a stop but left the engine running. They traded places, and he watched her take the wheel, throw the engine into gear, and maneuver the truck back onto the road. Amazing woman.

The night closed in quickly, and Tillie flipped on the headlights. The landscape altered little during mile after mile of bumpy road. Stars winked on one by one in the rain-washed sky. She rubbed her eyes. Yawned.

Graeme felt tired enough to sleep again. He shut his eyes. Memories of Tillie dancing across the dunes played inside his eyelids. Rain streamed down her hair. She laughed.

"Graeme!" The truck bounced to a stop.

He lifted his head. "What's the matter?"

"Look at that light." A faint glow lit the horizon just ahead. "What is it?"

He took her hand and wrapped it in his. "It's Timbuktu."

THIRTEEN

The mysterious Queen of the Sands rose out of the desert like an ageless, shimmering jewel. Tillie and Graeme sat in the old truck and gazed at the city that meant the end of their quest. For a long time they could neither move nor speak, each thinking private thoughts of what might occur in Timbuktu and what their future would be once they left her.

"She's beautiful," Tillie whispered.

Graeme turned his head and studied the woman beside him. "Are you ready for what may happen here?"

"I can face anything. Do you have a plan?"

"We'll go into the town and find the Sankore Mosque. I know a guy who works in the library there. I think he can help us."

"You know about that library?" Doubt drifted up inside her like oil on a clear pond. Arthur had told her the hidden library held volumes of great antiquity and value. And someone was stealing them and smuggling them out of Mali. "Who is this man you know? How do you know him?"

"Mahamane Samouda. He helped me with some of my research on Mungo Park. He speaks English. We corresponded in it. He's prominent in Timbuktu, and he's aware of just about everything that goes on. He'll know if Arthur and Hannah are here. And he'll have word on the Tuareg if they're in town."

At the mention of Arthur, Tillie's fears joined her doubts. "Graeme, about Arthur—"

"He said he'd meet you in Timbuktu, right? I'm sure he's waiting."

Twisting the beaded band on her finger, she searched the darkness. "He was upset the last time we were together. I don't know how he'll react when he sees me again."

"He didn't want you traipsing up the Niger?"

"Not with you."

"Ah."

"When I told Arthur about the amulet and the treasure, he got very interested in finding it. He said it could give us financial security after we married."

Graeme's brows drew together. "Is that why you decided to look for the treasure? Are you thinking about life with Arthur again?"

"I'm thinking Arthur may be more interested in the treasure than in me these days." Her mind reached back for something he had said. "Arthur's worried about having money. He said we should find the journal. He said it would . . . it would be worth a lot."

Graeme leaned forward. "Mungo Park's journal?"

"He said it would have immeasurable value of its own."

"If he values his life, he'll forget that idea."

"Graeme! How could you say such a thing?"

He hesitated, weighing his words. "As far as I'm concerned, I'm not looking for the treasure. I want that journal. If Arthur tries to get in my way—"

She stared at him. "I can't believe I'm hearing this! The

journal is just a book, Graeme. And I don't care if Arthur does find the treasure."

"The *amenoukal* will make sure that never happens. I imagine the Malian government will make sure, too. Look, let's leave Arthur out of this until we've talked with my friend at the mosque. If we can pool the information we already have with anything Mahamane Samouda can tell us, we may be able to head in the right direction. Are you with me?"

"What does it look like?"

His smile was mirthless. "Partners."

Tillie wished she could shake off her discomfort and return to the easy camaraderie they had shared during the sandstorm. She threw the truck into gear, stepped on the gas, and sent them rattling toward Timbuktu. "All right. Let's go find Mahamane Samouda."

The moon was high, and Tillie's watch told her it was nearly ten o'clock when she turned onto Timbuktu's only paved street. It ran between rows of boxlike clay houses, relics of antiquity suffering the indignity of a tarmac road. Beehive ovens perched at the street corners, and minarets rose high over the town.

Finding the Sankore Mosque wasn't hard. It was the oldest and largest of the three mosques in Timbuktu. Studded with long wooden spikes, its tall, slope-sided minarets pointed skyward. A wall of stone and clay, buttressed and topped with rounded crenellations like a Muslim version of a medieval castle, surrounded the mosque. Except for strange, thin Arabic melodies floating from latticework windows, a deathlike silence shrouded the town. Tillie parked the truck, and she and Graeme climbed out.

"I'm not allowed inside, am I?" she whispered as they walked up the steps of the mosque. "I don't think women are permitted."

"We'll see." Graeme knocked on the heavy door. A cockeyed old man in a white cap and caftan opened it. Graeme asked him a question in French. One of the man's wandering eyes looked at Tillie, and the other studied Graeme—then he scowled and started to shut the door.

"Mahamane Samouda?" Graeme asked.

The doorkeeper hesitated, then signaled the couple to wait. Fifteen minutes dragged by until finally a middle-aged man appeared at the door. He looked outside. Skin the color of latte, eyes sharp and black, he adjusted a pair of gold-rimmed spectacles perched on his nose.

"Oui?"

"Mahamane Samouda?" Graeme repeated.

"Oui. C'est moi."

"I'm Graeme McLeod. I wrote to you from the United States and from Scotland."

"Ah, Monsieur McLeod." The man nodded. "Graeme McLeod from United States. You are here in Timbuktu? Have they sent you—"

"Yes," Graeme cut in. "This is Matilda Thornton. She's with me."

Tillie held out her hand, unsure of the Muslim man's reaction to an unveiled white woman. But Mahamane grasped her hand firmly. "Welcome. You like coffee? Something to eat? Come inside."

Graeme put his arm around Tillie's shoulders as they walked through the front door. They slipped out of their shoes as Mahamane indicated and followed him down a long hall away from the inner holy areas.

"I am in the library tonight preparing a lecture. You are fortunate to find me. Usually I am at my home at this late hour, Monsieur McLeod."

He opened a door and led them into a cavernous room. A small brass lamp hanging on a long chain from the ceiling provided the only light, but it was enough to reveal a hint of the splendor the mosque must once have contained. Threadbare carpets in shades of indigo and burgundy had been strewn haphazardly across the floors. Chairs studded with brass nails were clumped in groups, as though scholars had just abandoned them. Like a maze with no defined entrance or exit, row upon row of carved shelves rose to the ceiling. Each shelf was crammed with scrolls and large books with leather bindings. A musty smell permeated the room, the scent of mildew mingled with old leather, incense, and wood smoke.

Mahamane led Tillie and Graeme to a darkened corner of the room and motioned them to sit beside him on two faded red brocade pillows trimmed in raveled gold fringe.

"Now, Graeme McLeod," he said in a library whisper, "what do you need of me?"

Graeme opened his mouth to speak, but a door opened. The cockeyed doorman entered, carrying a tray with a silver pot of steaming coffee and a plate of dried dates. Mahamane dismissed the man, then filled three tiny cups with thick black Arab coffee. Tillie accepted hers and took a sip.

"As you know, we've come from Bamako to search for Mungo Park's journal," Graeme began.

"There is such a document?"

"We think so. The Tuareg told Tillie about it."

"Ah, the Tuareg." The man's expression told Graeme he doubted the Tuareg would tell the truth about anything.

Graeme went on. "We feel pretty sure the journal—if it still exists—was stored near Timbuktu."

"Or inside Timbuktu?"

"Possibly. We need to know more about the town. Can you tell us what Timbuktu was like when Mungo Park was here? Which buildings were in the town. How the economy worked. Do you have any books on that?"

"Ah, Timbuktu was very different in those days. But wait one moment, please. Permit me to find the sources." He gave a slight bow, then stood and vanished into the maze.

"Is there any way the journal could be in the library somewhere?" Tillie whispered. She could see Mahamane Samouda climbing around on ladders and stools. "This place is incredible."

"I asked him to check when I wrote to him. The journal's not here."

Mahamane carried three thin volumes back to his visitors. He arranged himself on a cushion and opened the first book.

"We do not have any record of Mungo Park's visit to Timbuktu." He began flipping through the pages. "Of course, such information presumably could be found in the journal you seek. But here I have a letter from a man named Laing to another man named Warrington. It was written on September 21, 1826, some years after Mungo Park's death."

Tillie leaned forward, trying to see the words inscribed in the old volume. "What does the letter say?"

"Many things. Mr. Laing tells Mr. Warrington that he has no time to give a full account of the city of Timbuktu because he is saving the details for his journal. But he does say . . . let me see . . . ah, yes. 'In every respect except in size (which does not exceed four miles in circumference), it has completely met my expectations.'"

"But what were his expectations?" Tillie asked. "Had Mr. Laing heard of Timbuktu from someone else? From Mungo Park?"

Graeme took the packet of notes from his pocket and began leafing through them. "Remember Leo the African? Laing had heard the same tales of Timbuktu that Mungo Park knew."

"You have done your research. Indeed, the only recorded description of Timbuktu available in the days of both Laing and Park was this—" he lowered the second book and opened it— "the writings of Leo Africanus. He speaks of this mosque, the Sankore Mosque. He tells of the palace erected in the time of King Mansa Musa. That was between 1312 and 1337. He speaks more of the king of Timbuktu in the time of his visit. At that time, the king was Muhammad Toure. Here Leo mentions the trade in fabrics, spices, copper, gold, ivory, ostrich feathers, and slaves. He tells of the fertile farming from the Niger River overflow. He says that the people of Timbuktu are hospitable and hold many celebrations. And here he speaks of the trade routes from Timbuktu to Venice, Genoa, and Cairo."

Mahamane stopped reading and leaned back against the wall. Graeme had been taking notes as the scholar spoke, and he now began sorting his cards into small piles. Tillie watched as he worked.

It felt strange to see him doing something he had claimed to do from the start, but something she had never quite believed. Now she saw for herself that Graeme was indeed a writer. He was researching Mungo Park. He wanted to find the journal, not the treasure. Or rather, the journal was the treasure he sought.

But what was Mungo Park's treasure? Something from the town of Timbuktu? Had Timbuktu in the Scottish explorer's time looked the way Leo Africanus described it? Though two hundred years had gone by, it must have been nearly the same. Laing had come to Timbuktu after Mungo Park and had written that the city lived up to his expectations in all but size.

So what was the treasure? Could it be gold, as the *amenoukal* and Arthur hoped? Might it be ivory or silver or copper? Maybe Mungo Park had been given some treasures from the king's palace. After all, the explorer had known the kings of the Niger.

Graeme looked up from his sorting and spoke to Mahamane. "Now what about Mungo Park himself? Do you have any information about what might have happened to him after he left Timbuktu?"

"Permit me also to find it here in my book." He lifted the last volume from the stack and ran his fingers down one page after another. "You see, the Englishmen who had sponsored Mungo Park were upset when he did not return from his second journey to Africa. They made every attempt to find out what had happened to him. In 1810, a man named Isaaco volunteered to go and find out. He reached Sansanding. You passed it between Segou and Djenne, though you probably did not see it. There he found Mungo Park's guide Ahmadi Fatouma."

"What did the guide say?" Tillie asked.

"He told Isaaco the story of what happened to Park. He said that the Scotsman decided to stay on board his little boat and never land, so he would not have to pay ransom to the kings of the Niger. He made enemies everywhere. The boat was under constant attack. At Timbuktu, Park and his crew were attacked by three canoes, but they held them off and finally killed the attackers. When they got to Yauri, Mungo Park sent gifts ashore for the king."

"What gifts?"

Mahamane smiled at Tillie's riveted attention and thumbed through his book. "Ah yes, five silver rings, powder, and flints. But the king of Yauri was displeased. He put the guide, Ahmadi Fatouma, in irons."

Tillie looked at Graeme. "Maybe Ahmadi Fatouma never gave the king any gifts. Maybe he hid them for himself."

Graeme cocked an eyebrow. "Maybe. What happened next?"

Mahamane went back to his book. "Later Ahmadi Fatouma was freed, but when the boat reached Bussa, it was ambushed. Now here is what Ahmadi Fatouma told Isaaco about that attack: 'They threw everything they had in the canoe into the river and kept firing. . . . Mr. Park took hold of one of the white men and jumped into the water; Martyn did the same, and they were drowned in the stream in attempting to escape.'"

"But how did Ahmadi Fatouma escape?" Tillie asked.

"Good question," Graeme said. "There's another problem with the guide's story. Mungo Park knew how to swim."

"I don't believe that guide was telling the truth," Tillie said. "He must have made the whole thing up to absolve himself of guilt—and to keep the treasure a secret."

"Treasure?" Mahamane leaned forward.

Graeme placed a hand on Tillie's arm. "The treasure in some of the Tuareg legends. I've been looking into their stories for clues to finding the journal."

Tillie glanced at Graeme. It was obvious he didn't want Mahamane Samouda to know about the treasure or the document in the amulet. But why not? The African's mind was a library of resource material. With all the information at hand, couldn't Mahamane help them find the journal? She fingered the silver chain around her neck.

"You've been very helpful," Graeme was saying. "This information has added a lot to my understanding of events."

Mahamane folded his arms in contentment. "It is my pleasure to assist you, Mr. McLeod. To know that I speak to a descendant of Mungo Park is an honor."

Graeme grinned and stood up. "One last thing, Mahamane. Have you heard any news of an Englishman here in Timbuktu, a fellow from the British embassy?"

The Malian's dark eyes narrowed. "Many tourists come to Timbuktu from many lands."

Tillie spoke up. "His name is Arthur Robinson."

Mahamane nodded slowly. "I have heard this man has come to our city from Bamako. An old African woman is with him. Small, like a bird. She does not wear a burkah. They say she is a Christian."

"That's Hannah." Tillie let out a breath of relief.

"I do not know where they are staying."

"We'll find them." Graeme turned to Tillie. "Why don't you go have a look at the rest of the mosque while I get some details about present-day Timbuktu from Mahamane? I'll see about a hotel and a gas station."

She frowned for a moment. Why did he want to send her off now, when they were ready to go? Did he want private information from the librarian? Or did he expect her to scout around and turn up another clue to the missing journal?

"I'll see what the doorkeeper can show me," she said. "Mr. Samouda, I'm privileged to have been allowed in the library of the Sankore Mosque. Thank you."

"No, no, not at all."

"Excuse me, then." Tillie glanced at Graeme again and padded across the soft carpeting to the door. As she walked out into the darkened hallway, she could hear Graeme's voice—low and urgent—as he spoke to the librarian.

Leaning back against the wall, she peered through the crack of light that filtered from the open door. She could see the two men standing between the bookshelves. Graeme's forefinger jabbed as he spoke, as if making a point Mahamane Samouda must not miss. The other man's head began to nod in agreement. Then Graeme stuck his thumb out toward the door behind which she hid.

She swallowed and shrank back into the shadows. Something moved behind her. She glanced down the hallway. Was someone watching her? She'd had this feeling once before, at the market in Bamako.

Chills prickling down her arms, she peeked back into the dimly lit library. What was Graeme up to?

Mahamane knelt to the floor and lifted the three books he

had shown them. Her heart faltered as Graeme unbuttoned his shirt. The librarian handed him the slender volumes one by one, and Graeme slipped them into his clothing.

As he began to fasten the buttons, Tillie turned away. *Oh no, Lord! Dear God, this can't be.* She felt sick. Nauseous. She had to get away from the door. He mustn't find her.

She ran down the hallway toward the silhouette of an arched niche. An alcove. Dark. Quiet. She could think. She darted into it and collided full force with the wiry old door-keeper. Gnarled hands grasped her arms. An angry voice sputtered in French.

"Let me go." She pushed at his hands. "Let go!"

"What's going on?" Graeme's voice rang down the hall. "Tillie?"

The old man released Tillie's arms and evaporated into the darkness. She sagged. "Graeme. I'm here."

He rounded the corner. "Tillie, what happened? I heard you cry out."

"It was that . . . that . . ." She put her hands on Graeme's chest and felt the hard outline of one of the books hidden under his shirt. Her lip trembled. "I brushed up against something. Never mind."

His breath escaped in a hiss. "I thought the Tuareg had you again. Let's find a hotel and get some rest."

"I want to talk to Hannah."

"We will." He led her through the mosque toward their shoes. "This place is amazing. If I could spend a few months in here, I'd be in paradise. You interested in coming back to Timbuktu after everything blows over?"

She looked up as she tied the laces on her suede boots. "Me?"

"Partners." His tone was light, relaxed. "Remember?"

"Maybe."

"Maybe Timbuktu or maybe partners?"

"Just maybe."

She tried to shift her thoughts from the scene she had just witnessed—from the undeniable proof that Graeme was involved in the book thievery ring Arthur had told her about. She would have to tell Arthur what she'd seen. She would have to admit what a fool she'd been. Graeme was no writer. He was a thief.

"Now what kind of an answer is that?" He draped his arm over her shoulders. "Didn't Leo the African's description of Timbuktu fire you up? And all that stuff about Ahmadi Fatouma, the guide. There's no telling what's hidden in that library. I'd be back in a flash if I could get my hands on those old books."

I'll bet you would. Tillie shook her head, dismay and disbelief eating at her stomach. Graeme took her hand as though nothing had happened, but everything felt different now. Frighteningly different.

She noticed that the doorkeeper was absent from his post as they passed through the gate. Had he been spying on her while she spied on Graeme? If so, why? Did he suspect Graeme and Mahamane Samouda of their crime? Or was the doorkeeper a partner with them in the thievery?

She could do nothing to stop the assault of questions and doubts as she walked beside Graeme down the stairs and out into the silent street.

"We've got to talk about all this," he said. "After listening to Mahamane Samouda, I've come up with some new theories to add to our collection. I'd like to sound you out on them."

"Sure," she said. The thought of spending one more minute with Graeme was torment. She wanted nothing more than to escape, to find the quiet—and the time—to put it all in place. To understand.

It didn't take long to find the Azalai, a dingy but air-conditioned hotel, the kind of place where Arthur would be likely to stay. Graeme and Tillie walked across the cool lobby to the front desk. The clerk, a sleepy-looking young man, assured them they could have two rooms.

"Do you have other guests?" Tillie asked.

"We have thirty-nine rooms, but only three are occupied, madame. With the famine and the end of Air Mali, we have few tourists these days. You have come from Bamako? Would you like for me to arrange a tour of Timbuktu in the morning? A camel ride?"

"No," Tillie cut in. "No camel rides, thanks. Do you have a guest named Arthur Robinson? An Englishman from the British embassy?"

The young man studied his register. "No Robinson here. He may stay at the government rest house. Shall I ring it for you?"

"I'll call from my room."

She could hardly wait to shut the door on Graeme, call Hannah, and pour out everything. Just the sound of the old woman's voice would ease her heart. The walk was a short one, down a narrow hall and up a flight of stairs. The room was small but comfortably furnished with a bed, a small table, a couple of chairs. Tillie dropped into one of the chairs.

"I'm pooped," she said.

Please, Lord, let him leave. Send him away so I can think.

Graeme tossed his bag to the floor and flopped into the other chair. "I can't get over this—air-conditioning. All the comforts of home. Man, I'm famished. Are you? The lobby clock said twelve-thirty. We'll get something to eat as soon as things start to stir around here in the morning."

Fighting for control, Tillie studied him. That familiar dark hair she knew so well. Those honest blue-green eyes. His smile. How could this man be a thief? He was a writer. She had seen the note cards.

She also had seen him stealing books.

"Graeme—," she began and couldn't go on. What could she say to the man she had thought she loved? A man she now felt she didn't even know?

His mouth melted into a smile. "I planned a brainstorming session and a few winks of sleep. But now I look at you." He sat up and leaned forward, elbows on his knees. "I'd like to spend time with you, Tillie. Alone and safe. But we're never going to have time to ourselves if we don't get this thing worked out."

She brushed a strand of hair out of her eyes. "I want to find answers as much as you do."

Maybe more. She tried to read his face and saw nothing but openness. Honesty. Concern.

"Then let's get to work. Give me just a second, OK?" He picked up his bag. As he walked toward the bathroom, he began unbuttoning his shirt. "Why don't you call the government rest house? You'll feel better once you've talked to Hannah."

He shut and locked the bathroom door. As Tillie waited, she knew he was removing the books from his shirt. Putting them in his bag. Would he pass them to someone else? *Lord, Lord.*

She reached for the phone. In spite of the primitive surroundings—clay mosques, a single paved road, thatched roofs—she had the rest house on the line in less than a minute. A servant answered; then he went to summon Hannah to the lobby.

The familiar voice was soft, gentle, comforting. *"Habari gani, toto?"*

"I'm OK, Mama Hannah. It's been . . . it's been a long trip."

"Mbona unasitasita?"

Tillie smiled. Hannah wanted to know why she was hesitating. She had read her *toto* in an instant. Switching to Swahili meant they could speak in private.

"Arthur Yuko wapi?" Tillie whispered.

"Anasimama pale mlangoni pake. Simameni kiaskari."

Arthur was standing beside his door. Like a soldier. Tillie let out a breath. That sounded like the Arthur she knew. It would be almost a relief to see him. She might not love him, certainly didn't intend to marry him, but at least she could count on him to look out for her.

"Habari, Mama?" she asked, just to make sure Hannah was all right.

Instead of giving the expected "ehh" of reassurance, the old woman fell silent. Finally, she whispered into the phone, *"Mgomba una maembe."*

The banana plant has mangoes. Tillie frowned. What did that mean?

"Hannah—"

"Sst. *Sikiliza, toto! Kikulacho ki nguoni mwako."*

Another of Hannah's favorite Swahili sayings: That which bites you is in your clothes.

"Hannah, please don't start with the proverbs. Tell me—"

"Usije, toto. Usije. Tutaonana."

The phone went dead. Chilled, Tillie looked up as Graeme walked back into the room. Hannah had instructed her not to come to the rest house. *Don't come, toto. Don't come.*

She'd never known Hannah to be anything but calm. The eye of the storm. *Father, what do I do?* She had to protect Hannah. But from whom? And what had she meant by all that business about mangoes and banana plants and having ants in your clothes?

Surely Hannah was OK. Arthur was standing guard over her. What could she be afraid of?

A thought hit her with undeniable certainty. The Tuareg had found the rest house. They were waiting for the arrival of Tillie and Graeme. If the Tuareg were camped nearby, Hannah would want to make sure Tillie didn't show up.

Should she tell Graeme? Could she trust him with anything now? She rubbed her temples.

"Time to get to work." He set his bag by the small table and pulled the note cards from his pocket. He sifted through them, sorted them into piles, and placed them on the tabletop. "I think I've got this in order. Here are the notes about Mungo Park's first trip to the Niger." He looked up. "Tillie?"

She shook her head. "Go on. What do we need to remember about that trip?"

"I think the most important thing is that Mungo had established a relationship with Mansong, the king of Segou. Not necessarily a great relationship, but they did know each other. Mansong was the guy who gave Mungo five thousand cowrie shells. Right after that Mungo turned back, even though he was still a long way from Timbuktu."

Tillie stared down at the cards. "What's in the next pile?"

"This is Mungo's second trip. I've got information taken from his letters and the journal he sent to England just before he disappeared. And this pile is the information Mahamane gave us tonight, the guide Ahmadi Fatouma's report of Mungo's death."

"And those?"

"The description of Timbuktu given by Leo Africanus. Now the thing we need to do is have another look at the document in the amulet. Then I'll tell you my theory."

Her thoughts consumed with Hannah, Tillie unfastened the necklace and laid it on the table. He gestured for her to open it, so she removed the fragile document and unfolded it.

"Read it out loud," he said.

"25 December, 1806—

I believe it is Christmas Day somewhere, though not here. I know I will not live to see tomorrow. The Bight of Benin the blight of Benin. Ailie when I get back will you let me rest? Will you keep the Moors away? The Bight of Benin the blight of Benin. Ahmadi Fatouma has the wealth in safekeeping for me. Ailie we will buy that house on Chester Street. Mine mine mine! I have the wealth. I possess the treasure of Timbuktu. One day, one day the white man will come here. One day, one day the white woman will come here. She will plant trees and make it a garden for tea parties. She will plant trees. She will find the treasure of Timbuktu. And the curse of the Bight of Benin will be ended.

Mungo Park"

She placed the paper on the table. "Every time I read this, I get the same feeling. He's not making sense. He's raving."

Graeme swallowed. "What did you say?"

"His thoughts ramble all over the place. I think he's gone mad."

"That's it!" He grabbed the document. "It's so simple I missed it completely. He *was* going mad—that's the blight of Benin. Look, Tillie, he keeps saying 'The Bight of Benin the blight of Benin.'"

"Right. But—?"

"He knew he was losing his sanity. If he had reached the Bight of Benin—the mouth of the Niger River—by the time he wrote this, he had met his goal. From the time my mother told me about Mungo Park, I wanted to believe he had succeeded in tracing the course of the river all the way to its mouth. I think this page of the journal proves it. But the wording leads me to think he got sick once he arrived there. He was going mad with fever and delirium."

"Was that the curse he said white people would end? Do you suppose he was thinking of medicines and doctors that would be here one day?"

Graeme pored over the document. "You may be onto something. Let's read the document in light of the idea that he was mentally unstable. He was lucid enough to write and to want to convey his last thoughts, but he wasn't together enough to get it down in a rational way. OK, the first part of the page, the date, tells us Park did live longer than Ahmadi Fatouma claimed."

"That means the guide was lying about Park's death." She went to stand behind him and look over his shoulder.

"There's something else that proves it. A book that had belonged to Mungo Park was found in Bussa several years after his death. I've seen it in the Royal Geographic Society Museum. It has no sign of water damage."

"And the guide said everything was thrown into the river."

"Exactly. I'm sure he was lying about Mungo Park's death."

"And 'Will you keep the Moors away?' could refer to the nightmares he had suffered after his first trip. You told me about that a long time ago."

"Right. OK, let's make a couple of assumptions. Mungo Park did not drown in the river like the guide said. He was at the Bight of Benin on Christmas 1806. But he was delirious with a fever that was ravaging his mind. He believed he was going to die."

"Then what do you make of this part? 'Ahmadi Fatouma has the wealth in safekeeping for me. Ailie we will buy that house on Chester Street. Mine mine mine! I have the wealth. I possess the treasure of Timbuktu.'"

"It means his guide was with him to the end, all the way to the Bight of Benin. It also means that whatever treasure Mungo Park had, he put Ahmadi Fatouma in charge of it. He trusted this guy who later lied to the authorities. Now why would a person who had been a trusted leader and guide lie?"

Tillie searched his face. "You tell me, Graeme. Why would a man lie?"

"Because he had something important he wanted to safeguard. Something that meant more to him than anything else."

Tillie wondered what it was Graeme would lie to protect. A chance at treasure? A smuggling operation? What could mean so much to this man that he would risk his freedom at the hands of the Malian government . . . or his life at the hands of the Tuareg?

"Whatever it was that Ahmadi Fatouma had in safekeeping," Graeme was saying, "he intended to protect it at all cost."

"Gold?" she asked.

"Maybe. It was something Mungo believed he could use to buy Ailie a house on Chester Street."

"I still don't see how the Tuareg fit into this picture." She thought about her conversation with Hannah. It could be merely a matter of hours before the *amenoukal* had her again. She needed to understand as much of Mungo Park's story as she could. "How do you suppose the Tuareg got their hands on the amulet?"

Pacing the room, Graeme rubbed his forehead in thought. He walked to the window and peered outside. Then he turned and wandered back to the table. At last he looked at Tillie.

"The rest of the story is all conjecture. We don't have any clues from the document as to what happened after it was written. That's when the journal disappeared."

"And so did the treasure." Tillie watched Graeme resume his pacing. "Review what we know so far."

"Second expedition to find the mouth of the Niger River. Mungo Park was with Ahmadi Fatouma when they left Timbuktu. They had some kind of gifts or treasure in the boat. We know they made it past Bussa, because a book of Mungo's was found there. It had no water damage—so

Ahmadi probably was lying about Mungo drowning in Bussa. They went on down the river and made it to the Bight of Benin."

"You *think* they made it to the mouth of the Niger."

"Like I said, it's all a guess. By the time they arrived at the Bight of Benin, Mungo was delirious with fever—the blight of Benin, as he put it. He had given Ahmadi Fatouma charge of the treasure. He wrote the last page of his journal, and then he must have died. That's all we've got."

"Let's say Mungo did die the day he wrote the page in my amulet—or soon after. Ahmadi Fatouma must have taken the treasure and the journal. Where would he have gone?"

"Back to his home, I assume."

"Which was where?"

"Segou? I don't know." Graeme raked his fingers through his hair in frustration. "The point is that he separated this page from the rest of the journal because . . . why? Why did he do that?"

Tillie closed her eyes. She tried to picture the guide returning up the river with the journal and his canoe full of treasure. An image of the *amenoukal* came to mind, as though he were some strange reincarnation of Ahmadi Fatouma. Then her mind wandered to Khatty, and she thought of the way the young woman had fallen to the floor in superstitious awe of the amulet's power.

Tillie opened her eyes. "Ahmadi Fatouma separated this page from the rest because he had read it. He knew what it said, and he thought it was cursed—and he thought the treasure was cursed, too."

Graeme stared at her. "But how would he have known

what it said? He couldn't read English—wait a minute. He would have passed through Timbuktu on his way back to Segou. He could have had someone read it to him here."

"Sure. There were all kinds of scholars living in Timbuktu at that time, remember? I bet the guide wanted to know what the book said, and when he heard the ramblings about the treasure and his own name and the tree-planting woman and the curse, he decided the whole thing was cursed, and he ditched it."

"If he did, it may have happened in Timbuktu. I think we're onto something. Ahmadi Fatouma thought the curse would be ended one day when the tree-planting woman came. That's why he preserved the document in the amulet. So people would know that when she came, the curse would end."

"And she would find the treasure. That's what Mungo wrote—literally. A white woman would come and plant trees, end the curse, and find the treasure of Timbuktu. So how did the Tuareg get the amulet?"

"They're raiders. Maybe they stole it."

"Where do you suppose Ahmadi Fatouma hid the treasure and the rest of the journal?"

"You seem to be into his frame of mind. If you had been the guide and had just learned that the treasure was cursed, what would you do with it?"

She closed her eyes again. It was easy to slip back into the thought patterns of Khatty and her mystic view of life. What would Khatty have done? Tillie envisioned the girl and her large, liquid, wondering eyes.

"Ahmadi would have put the treasure where he thought Mungo Park meant for it to be until the curse was ended," she whispered. "And he would have known where that was from the document. From reading Mungo's words."

Graeme pounced on the page of the journal and looked at it carefully. "Here, read it as if you were Ahmadi Fatouma. Where would you think Mungo had told you to put it?"

She stared down at the familiar words in a new light. Trying to understand them as a frightened, superstitious man would. She read silently. *"Ahmadi Fatouma has the wealth in safekeeping for me. Ailie we will buy that house on Chester Street."*

"Is there anything around here with the name Chester?" she asked Graeme. "A place, a building? Anything?"

He shook his head. "I've never heard of anything."

She went on reading. *"Mine mine mine! I have the wealth. I possess the treasure of Timbuktu."*

None of that led her to any clues. She looked at the words again and said them aloud: "'Mine mine mine!' Wait a second. . . . Graeme, is there a mine around here? Like a gold mine or a salt mine?"

He stopped pacing. "Sure there's a mine around here. There's the old Timbuktu mine. You don't think—"

"Yes! I think Ahmadi believed he was supposed to hide the treasure in the mine." She tried to make herself breathe. "Graeme, the treasure is in the mine. And so is the journal."

He grinned. "Well, Tree-Planting Woman. It looks as though Mungo Park was right. You have found the treasure of Timbuktu."

FOURTEEN

Tillie woke to a key turning in the door. She sat up and jerked the sheet to her chin. Images of the night before raced through her mind. The library. Hannah. The Tuareg. The revelation about the mine. Graeme had left the room just after that. To make some phone calls, he had told her. And she had fallen asleep, so tired she didn't even care that she was still dressed.

The door swung open, and Graeme sauntered into the room. Showered, shaved, dressed all in khaki, he looked like he had the world by the tail.

"Mornin', glory." His voice was cheerful, light.

The three books he took from the mosque must be in safekeeping somewhere, she realized. Or had he disposed of them already? Made a rendezvous with someone while she slept? She moved to get up; then she saw that Graeme was carrying a tray of food to the bed.

"Sorry to wake you. You were sleeping so soundly."

"Did you get some rest?"

"Couldn't sleep. I kept thinking about the document and our talk last night. I think the journal really may be in the mine. At least it was. If it's still there, it'll be a miracle."

Tillie bit into a soft roll. "Why shouldn't it be there?"

"For one thing, it's been two hundred years since someone hid it. Mines aren't the best storage places. I found out last night that the Timbuktu mine is partially flooded."

"What kind of mine was it? Salt?"

"Gold." He stuck up a thumb. "How's that for a connection? Anyhow, if the journal's there, I'm going to find it."

"Even if it's not, you have the last page in the amulet. That's enough to indicate that Mungo Park made it to the Bight of Benin."

"It's enough for me, but I doubt it would be enough for the experts. I need the whole journal to prove my case." He downed a demitasse of steaming Arab coffee in one swallow. "That journal has been my goal for a long time. I can't believe we're this close."

She stirred her tea. Should she tell him about the trouble he may not have taken into account? Yes. She could be honest, even if he wasn't.

"Graeme, I think the Tuareg may have found Hannah and Arthur." She watched his body language alter from easy to tense. "Last night on the phone Hannah wouldn't talk to me in English. She kept giving me Swahili proverbs of warning and caution."

"Did she sound frightened? Do you want to try to get her out of there?"

"She told me not to come."

"What about Robinson? Did you talk to him?"

"Arthur was standing guard. He didn't know I called. I think Hannah will be OK. The Tuareg won't want her except as bait to draw me out of hiding."

Graeme went to the window and checked the street. "They haven't found you yet, but they will. Look, Tillie,

I intended to leave you in town while I went after the journal. That old mine could be tricky."

She slid out of bed and brushed at the wrinkles in her trousers. She would play out this game to the end. She couldn't deny that she cared deeply about Graeme. She loved him. Loved the man she had thought he was. But she had to know everything.

"I'm getting used to 'tricky,'" she said.

The afternoon was hot, the concrete steps blinding as Tillie and Graeme headed out of the hotel and into the center of Timbuktu. They had sent a bellboy to buy a couple of burnouses and turbans, and they wore them over their khakis in a more or less futile attempt to blend.

In the daytime, the town had lost its mysterious, glimmering light and had become brazen and tawdry. A group of overweight, pink-skinned tourists in plaid golf shorts and beach hats surveyed postcards. Another group haggled over prices of cheap jewelry.

"You buy this sword," a young man shouted as he ran across the street toward the tourists. "Tuareg sword. Genuine. I sell you very cheap."

Tillie blanched at the shoddy imitation of the *amenoukal's* sword. It probably had been made in Taiwan and wouldn't even cut butter. All the same, it gave her the creeps. Graeme pushed through the crowded narrow streets and edged back toward the Sankore Mosque.

Their truck was parked beside the mosque, where they had left it the night before. The old doorkeeper had been replaced by two brawny young men who stared in open curiosity at the burnous-clad man and woman climbing into the vehicle.

Graeme started the engine and pulled out onto the street. He rolled down his window against the stifling heat. "I don't doubt the *amenoukal* is near or inside Timbuktu right now," he said. "He'll have a bead on us within the hour."

Tillie glanced down narrow, crooked streets. "He won't know about the mine. You think he can track us?"

"He's done it before." Graeme kept his focus on the road. "We'll have to move fast."

Leaving the town to its noisy commerce, the truck roared north along a stretch of barren track. Half-disintegrated into a dusty stretch of desert, the road meandered past strange outcroppings of rock and nearly vanished between sand dunes.

Tillie studied Graeme's profile. Golden light bronzed his skin. In the breeze, his hair ruffled like a nighttime sea. *Dear Lord.* The prayer welled up in her heart. *Dear Lord, I love this man so much. I've seen a goodness in him that nothing can deny. He's brave, gentle, intelligent, kind. He was ready to give up this trip to the mine to pluck Hannah from the clutches of the* amenoukal. *I'm sure of it.*

Tillie knew Graeme cared about the old woman because he cared about her. She had seen too much evidence to doubt it. More than once he had rescued her when it would have been much easier to abandon her. And he had honored her as he promised. Though she responded to his kisses, he never pushed her beyond the limit she had set.

She looked down at the beaded ring. A man of honor.

A thief.

She'd seen it for herself in the library. He took those books. Rare old books stolen from the Sankore Mosque, just as Arthur had told her. She shouldn't be so surprised, so disappointed. Darkness characterized the unrepentant heart. The father of lies could overcome any amount of human effort at goodness.

Hadn't Hannah warned her? *"Do not be bound together with unbelievers."* Tillie leaned her head against the window's metal frame. *Lord, I'm sorry. Forgive me. Forgive my disobedience.*

"Tillie?" Graeme said over the rattle of the truck. "You look a thousand miles away."

"Remembering some things Hannah taught me a long time ago."

"I've been thinking about the future. Once I get my hands on that journal, things are going to fall into place." He gave her a lopsided grin. "What would you say to a celebration in Bamako? Just the two of us."

She fought her rebel heart. "I'll have to get back to work. My neem trees—"

"Hey, the trees can wait." He took her hand, laced his fingers through hers. "Tillie, we've been through a lot together. I think we know each other about as well as two people can. You've brought a light into my life I thought I'd never see. You've taught me how to have hope. Happiness. I never want that to slip away."

"Graeme, please. I can't . . . I can't . . ."

"Don't tell me you're having second thoughts about Arthur."

"It's not Arthur!" She let out a hot breath. "It's you. I have to let you go."

"Let me go? What's *that* supposed to mean? I'm not going anywhere without you. We belong together."

"No, Graeme, we don't. We can't." She turned to the window, fighting tears. "I made a mistake. I shouldn't have let this go beyond friendship."

"It's way beyond friendship. I love you, Tillie."

"Graeme, please. Please don't say that."

"I'll say it a hundred times. I love you, Tillie. I love you—"

"It can't work. I've tried to make it clear to you. On the surface we're alike. But inside, where it really matters, we're worlds apart." She swallowed at the gritty lump in her throat. "Don't you see? I've committed my life to God's will, not my own. I can't follow him if I'm with someone who isn't. It's like those camels in the Tuareg caravan. If you tie two of them together and each tries to go down a different path, the whole caravan breaks down. It's chaos. No one goes anywhere; everyone suffers. We would suffer. We're on different paths, Graeme. I can't be with you no matter how much I love you."

His stunned eyes scanned her face. "You . . . love me? And yet you're rejecting me because of your faith?"

Her voice was no more than a whisper. "Yes."

"You're a strong woman."

She brushed a tear from her cheek. *O God, I'm not strong. I'm weak. I'm weak and foolish. And, Lord, I love him so much!* Scrunched into the corner of the seat, she stared blankly at the passing desert. She felt as barren and empty as that sand. Graeme loved her, and she had turned him away. Given him up.

He let go of her hand and shifted gears. She couldn't

make herself look at him, but she knew him so well she
could picture him in her mind. The muscle in his jaw
would be jumping, his knuckles would be white on the
steering wheel.

"You're right," he said finally. "My soul is black."

She glanced at him, surprised at the vehemence in his
voice. "I didn't say that."

"You meant it. You're a daughter of the light, right? I'm
a son of darkness." A bitter smile creased the corner of his
mouth. "Abandoned by God. Remember that argument we
had on the road out of Bamako? You said nobody's abandoned by God. You said God's like a father. You asked me
the worst thing a son could do. Kill someone, I said.
Remember?"

"Yes."

"I killed my father." He turned on her, his eyes red-
rimmed. "Killed my own father. Try to work that into your
little analogy."

Sorrow, regret, compassion all flowed through her at the
bleak expression in his eyes. "How did it happ—"

"There's more." He cut her off. "I don't regret it.
There's not an iota of repentance in my black heart. I'm
glad I killed him. I'd kill him again."

"Graeme—"

"Forget it. I got your message loud and clear." He shifted
again. "This must be the turnoff."

"Graeme, why didn't you tell me about your father
before now?"

"What difference would it make? You're right. You and
I are different. Day and night. Heaven and hell. Drop it,

OK?" He gave her a mirthless smile. "Let's finish this thing so you can get back to your trees."

The rutted track led toward a wadi—a stone formation that held a little water during the rains. The old truck bounced to a halt in front of a jagged crag. There was no sign of a mine entrance.

Tillie shivered. She felt sick. Sick with fear and confusion. Graeme was a murderer and a thief. He'd admitted killing his own father. So why did her heart ache for him? Why was his pain so raw and fresh she could feel it in her own soul?

Father. She breathed a plea to the Lord of her life. *Father, show him your truth. You can wash him. You can heal him. Father, please. Not for me, Lord, but for him. He's dying inside. You can see it in his eyes. For all his claims of being unaffected, he's being eaten up inside by grief or guilt or something, Lord. Something dark. Please, help him.*

Graeme climbed out of the truck and tossed his burnous and turban on the seat. He dug a kerosene lamp from the back of the truck. "You want to wait in the truck?"

"You know me better than that."

"Let's go then."

She followed him to the wadi and clambered up its steep slopes to help him search the rock for signs of an entrance. The sun was vertical when he gave a shout and waved her toward a craggy fissure. She crossed the crumbling stone.

He went down on his knees to peer inside. "There's scaffolding." He held the lamp inside the opening. "I can see some rough steps. The floor looks dry. I'd say this is it. We've found the shaft."

"Then let's head down."

Graeme raised an eyebrow. "Sure you want to go down into the jaws of death with a murderer?"

"'Even though I walk through the valley of the shadow of death—'"

"'I will fear no evil,'" he finished.

"You're not evil, Graeme. And I'm not afraid of you." She said the words before she realized how true they were. She was afraid of the *amenoukal* and his broadsword. Afraid of the crocodiles in the Niger. Afraid of the doorman at the Sankore Mosque. But she wasn't afraid of Graeme McLeod.

"Maybe you should be," he said. "I'm after your heart."

He turned his back on her and edged down into the hole. For a moment he was swallowed up in the darkness, but the lamplight flickered again. She dropped to her knees at the edge of the hole.

"Easy." He took her hand and guided her into the mine. "Your eyes will adjust in a minute."

The walls of the mine shaft were steep and rutted with scars made by the axes and picks of miners centuries before. The original opening had been enlarged to permit the traffic of gold-bearing dirt. Tillie tried to calm her thudding heart as she followed Graeme down the sloping floor toward a bend in the tunnel.

"What do you think the journal will look like?" she asked. "Should we start searching for it now?"

"I imagine it's hidden farther in, but it can't hurt to keep your eyes open. The other journals of Mungo Park are small. Leather bound. I'd look for a bag of some sort. Or a box. I imagine the guide Ahmadi Fatouma would have put it into somethi—"

Graeme caught his breath and stepped back, instinctively

throwing out his arm to stop Tillie. A hideous monster slithered around the bend into the circle of lamplight. A mixture of lizard and crocodile, the five-foot-long reptile moved toward them on squat legs tipped in sharp, curved claws. Its tail swept from side to side across the stone floor, its long forked tongue flicked in and out. With a hiss like a steam locomotive, its jaws parted to reveal rows of sharp teeth.

"Graeme!" Tillie choked out as she backed up toward the stone wall. "What is that thing?"

"Stay behind me," he ordered, handing her the lamp and drawing a knife from his boot. "It's some kind of monitor lizard."

"A waran," she whispered. "An Egyptian monitor."

"Whatever he is, he's steaming mad. Back up."

The creature stopped, assessing the intruders with eyes like amber beads. Tillie took a step backward. Graeme crouched, knife ready.

Claws skittered on the rock. Hissing filled the narrow chamber. The lizard charged and slammed into Graeme's legs. Its whirling tail bashed the walls. Teeth snapped. Graeme's arm swung in an arc toward its head.

Tillie shoved the lamp into a crevice. Hands clammy, she worked a heavy chunk of rock loose and raised it over her head with both hands. The reptile clamped onto Graeme's shirt. Pulling, tearing, it struggled to knock him down. He bent over the lizard's head and stabbed. Stabbed again. The knife glanced off the armorlike skin.

Tillie moved closer, looking for an opening. The monitor snapped at Graeme's leg. He bellowed in pain and tried to jerk away. Lunging forward, Tillie slammed the rock down on the animal's back.

The thud echoed down the chamber. Hissing rose to a fevered pitch. The monitor squirmed, flopped over, lay writhing on the stone floor. Graeme sprang on it, driving his knife into the creature to the hilt between his front legs.

The tunnel fell silent. Graeme slumped to the ground.

Tillie fell to her knees beside him. "Are you all right? Did he hurt you?"

He pulled his knife out of the lizard and leaned back on his elbows. "My leg. He's still got it."

She moved across to Graeme's twisted leg clenched in the dead lizard's mouth. She placed the heel of her boot against its upper jaw and pushed as Graeme gingerly freed his torn limb.

"I think a hunk of it's gone," he said.

She pulled apart the shreds of trouser. "You're bleeding a lot. He's ripped part of your calf. You need a doctor, Graeme. Let's get out of here."

"Whoa! No way. We came here to find the journal."

"You're crazy. If we don't get you back to Timbuktu soon, you're going to be too weak to go anywhere."

He leaned forward and studied his leg. "Mincemeat, but I don't think anything major's been severed. Here, help me out of this shirt, and we'll make a bandage. If we wrap it tight enough, it'll stop bleeding."

As he struggled out of his shirt, she stared at the prehistoric-looking creature. The lizard's purple tongue hung limp from its mouth. Its bloody teeth gleamed pink-red in the lamplight.

"It's awful," she whispered.

Graeme was tearing his shirt into strips. "Poor guy was just protecting his territory." He paused and looked directly at Tillie. "If you hadn't clobbered him, that could be me lying there."

"Maybe he's protecting the treasure. He is the grand-father of the Tuareg, remember?"

"And I'm Dumbo the elephant. Can you tie these ends into a knot, or are we going to sit here all night swapping ghost stories about the *amenoukal* and his reptilian ancestors?"

She tied the bandage around Graeme's torn leg and tried to dismiss the chill that the incident had cast over her. As she tucked the ends of the fabric into the makeshift dressing, Graeme's hand closed over hers.

"Are you OK to go on?"

Tillie nodded. "Sure. Can you walk?"

"I can do anything with the right motivation. Come on." He struggled to his feet and leaned against the wall.

She stood and took the lamp from the crevice. "What if the waran had a mate?"

"I don't think lizards are communal types, but we'll have to take our chances." He held out a hand. "Feel like being a crutch till I get my sea legs back?"

"Sure."

She slipped one arm around his waist. He draped his arm over her shoulders, and they headed down the stony slope and around the bend. At the bottom of the shaft, the lamp revealed a narrow passageway filled with water.

"I guess we're going in?" she asked.

"Guess so."

As they edged down the ramp, they searched the pockets and ledges in the stone. Tillie felt the tepid water soak through her shoes, socks, pant legs. Its warmth meant that it flowed from a source near the desert surface. Strange to think of a stream running beneath the desert.

"'Because,'" she whispered. "'I have given waters in the wilderness and rivers in the desert, to give drink to my chosen people.'"

"Waters in the wilderness." Graeme pulled her closer. "You're the water in my wilderness, Tillie," he whispered. "I love you."

She paused, and he removed his arm from her shoulders. He cupped her face in his wet hands and tenderly kissed her lips. His mouth was warm and pliant, and in spite of her best intentions, she leaned longingly into the kiss.

Never mind about the waran and the *amenoukal,* about the gold and the journal. As wrong as she and Graeme surely were together, this love was the treasure she had been looking for all her life.

The treasure she would have to give up.

He drew back and looked into her eyes. "Ah, Tillie-girl." Letting out a breath, he tilted his head back and let his eyes wander to the stone roof. "Tillie, I just want you to know . . . to know . . ." He paused, frowning.

This must be so hard for him, she thought sadly.

"There it is." His voice was hushed, filled with wonder.

"You want me to know what?"

"There it is." His voice was tight with sudden excitement. "There it is! The journal!"

She looked up. Nearly hidden in a high niche in the rocky roof sat a small wooden box. It was studded with points of dull gray metal. Strange carvings covered its surface.

She held the lamp high. "Can you reach it?"

He limped through the water and raised his hand. Every muscle strained to its limit as he reached to touch the box with his fingertips. Slowly, very slowly, sand trickling into his upturned face, he eased the box from the ledge.

"I have it," he whispered. He lowered the chest into his arms. "This is it."

She brushed the sand from the carved lid. "Look," she whispered. "Someone carved a message—"

Graeme's hand clamped on her arm. She glanced at the water. A succession of ripples slapped the walls. Something had entered the water near them.

A shadow edged into the circle of light. A tall figure emerged.

"*Attini,*" the *amenoukal* said. Broadsword unsheathed, eyes hidden in the shadows of his blue turban, he held out one hand. "*Attini,* Tree-Planting Woman. Give me treasure of Timbuktu."

Fifteen

The *amenoukal* stood less than ten yards away. Graeme
tucked the carved box under his arm and grabbed Tillie's
wrist. "Run!" he said, pushing her away. "Around that
corner."

Unwilling to let him try to make his own way with a bad
leg, she wrapped her arm around his waist. "Let's go!"

They slogged through the murky water of the tunnel,
the angry shouts of the *amenoukal* driving them forward.
Around the bend the water was deeper, the going slower.
Another curve ahead led to a fork and two divergent
tunnels.

"Go left," Graeme growled. "We've got to buy time. If
I can get the journal out, we can give him the chest and
whatever else is in it."

They pushed through the thigh-deep water. The lamplight revealed a small alcove. It wouldn't hide them well,
but it would have to do. Tillie clambered up onto a ledge,
and she helped Graeme up beside her.

"Take the knife while I work on this clasp." He shoved
the hunting knife at Tillie. She held the lamp above her
head as they examined the box. Its brass clasp, encrusted
with sand and grit, wouldn't budge. Graeme took the knife
back and shoved it under the clasp's nail-studded base.

"Attini." The *amenoukal's* voice echoed down the tunnel. "Give treasure!"

Water splashed against the walls. Broadswords clanged on stone. The shouts grew closer as Graeme struggled to break the clasp.

"He's getting close," Tillie whispered. "He's coming down our tunnel."

"I've almost got it. Hold the light right there." He grabbed her hand and moved the lamp directly over the brass clasp. "It's locked. The nails in this thing—"

The clasp snapped and the ancient box popped open a crack. Graeme gingerly lifted the lid. Lamplight washed over an old hat sitting on a bed of dried, crumbling grass. The hat was not a pith helmet, as Tillie imagined Mungo Park must have worn. It was a gentleman's felt hat. A dark green color, it had a dusty leather band stuck with bits of yellowing paper.

"The hat," Graeme exclaimed, his voice hushed. "It's the hat."

"What hat? You never told me about a hat."

"I didn't think it was important."

The sound of splashing grew louder. She shook his arm. "What'll we do? Is this the treasure? We've got to tell the *amenoukal* something. Graeme, he'll kill us."

"This is Mungo Park's hat." Graeme might have been giving a university lecture. "Park talks about it in one of the journals we have in England. The people were scared to death of this hat because he used to tuck scraps of paper with notes on them into the band. They thought the hat was bewitched."

"What did he write on the notes?"

"Thoughts, observations. Things he later transcribed into

his journals." He lifted the hat and handed it to Tillie. In the bottom of the chest lay two pens, a bottle of dried ink, a folded shirt, and three thin books.

"His journal!" she cried.

"No, these are his personal library. Look, no water stains. The guide was definitely lying about how he died. These are invaluable, Tillie."

"Graeme, for crying out loud, the *amenoukal's* almost here!"

"This isn't the treasure. And the journal's not here. Ahmadi Fatouma hid them somewhere else, Tillie. The journal's with the treasure."

"But where? In the mine?"

"The hat. The papers in the hat tell where the guide hid the treasure and the journal."

"Are you sure? Maybe this is all there is. Maybe we can just give these things to the—"

A clang of steel reverberated down the wall, and the blue-veiled Tuareg chieftain surged into view. Spotting them, he gave a cry of victory. More veiled warriors filled the tiny tunnel, closing in on Tillie and Graeme.

"The hat. Give it to me!" Graeme shouted.

She shoved the hat into his hand. He set it in the box and slammed the lid shut.

"Graeme, give him the chest."

"Never." He raised the knife and brandished the blade.

Silent now, the *amenoukal* waded toward them. *"Attini."*

"Ahodu Ag Amastane." Tillie took a step forward. "We have found the box. There is no treasure. Show him, Graeme. Show him the hat and the books."

The *amenoukal* jabbed the butt end of his spear into the

water and stopped. His retinue fell into place behind him. His dark eyes flicked from Graeme to the chest and back to Tillie. Graeme opened the lid and took out the green felt hat.

"You see," Tillie said. "No treasure. Graeme, show him the books."

The *amenoukal* scowled. "Give treasure of Timbuktu."

"I don't have treasure. There is no treasure."

"Legend say Tree-Planting Woman find treasure. You find."

"No, I can't. There is no treasure."

The *amenoukal's* eyes turned from deep purple to black. Without a word, he raised his spear. The Tuareg swarmed through the water. The cavern erupted into a sea of writhing, howling bodies.

Someone rammed into Tillie. Her feet went out from under her. The lamp splashed into the water and went out.

"Graeme!" she screamed. She couldn't find him.

Her head went under the murky water. A crushing weight on her chest drove the air from her lungs, and she sucked in a gulp of fetid liquid.

Before she could cough, iron hands lifted her from the water and hurled her into the air. The tunnel's dry roof flashed overhead. Fingers dug into her flesh. She fell over the shoulder of a Tuareg warrior. The musky smell of old cloth and sweaty male skin flooded her nostrils. Bright pinpoints of light swam before her eyes.

"Graeme!" she spluttered.

In the dim light, she spotted a circle of Tuareg men. Graeme crouched among them, his knife hand empty and the old chest gone. Above him, suspended in the dank air, the *amenoukal's* broadsword poised for the downstroke.

She screamed. Writhed. Slithered off the man's shoulder. "Graeme!" The sword began its deadly arc. Tillie's Tuareg captor slammed her against the wall; her head exploded, and she slumped.

A strange smell, oddly familiar, brought Tillie's eyes open. She tried to think where she had smelled it before. It was a sweet, cloying scent that worked its way down through her subconscious and into her conscious mind. Then it filled the arid crevices of her mouth and slipped into the hollows of her lungs. When it curled into her stomach, she gagged, rolled onto her side, and retched.

When she opened her eyes again, she saw a stretch of wine-and-blue carpeting. She could make out each hand-knotted tuft of silk, each golden twirl and sapphire curlicue that ran over the deep background. Her vision clearing, she traced a path across the carpet to a pair of embroidered leather slippers. Their geometric shapes wound from the heel to the pointed toe.

Her eyes drooped in tiredness, but when one of the slippers moved, she snapped awake.

"Tree-Planting Woman."

She craned her swollen neck. Her focus wandered up billowing blue trousers and a thick indigo burnous to the wide shoulders and veil of the *amenoukal*.

His black eyes flashed. "Tree-Planting Woman. You find treasure."

Bile welled up in her throat. She swallowed. Overhead, a hanging brass lantern swayed as the cloying incense she had smelled wafted from it. She was in the *amenoukal*'s tent. Khatty's tent.

Dear God! The last thing she remembered, she and Graeme were in the tunnel together. They had the chest. And the hat. And then . . . "Graeme?" The word was a croak. Struggling to her elbows, she searched the tent. "Where is he? What have you done with him?"

The *amenoukal*'s gaze was impassive. *"Attini."*

"Attini yourself, you creep." With supreme effort, she hauled herself to her feet. "Where's Graeme McLeod? What have you done with him? Bring Khatty to me. She'll understand. Where's Khatty?"

The *amenoukal* crossed his arms and turned his head regally to one side. "Khatty die."

A cold wave of disbelief washed down Tillie's back. "She died? How? What happened?"

"Khatty die."

She grabbed a tent pole for support. "You did it, didn't you? You killed her, just like you killed—"

"Khatty disobey. Let Tree-Planting Woman go."

Tillie closed her eyes. Her head throbbed, and she felt her knees start to buckle. It was impossible. Khatty had loved this man, loved him deeply.

"Khatty was your wife! How could you—"

"Tree-Planting Woman, give treasure."

"I don't have your stupid treasure! I don't know where it is. The box in the mine is all there was."

"You know. Legend say."

"Tell me what you did to Graeme. Tell me or you'll never see your treasure."

The *amenoukal*'s eyes deepened, and he clapped his hands

twice. A young boy scampered into the room, bearing the *amenoukal*'s spear. Tillie recognized him as the child who had first placed the amulet around her neck in Bamako. She realized he must be the Targui's son.

"Tree-Planting Woman." The tattered strip of her skirt still hung from the spearhead. And now something else hung with it. A bloodstained khaki shirt. Graeme's shirt.

"O dear Lord!" She sank onto the floor in a crouch and buried her face in her hands. Graeme was gone. Tears ran between her fingers and down her cheeks. Her mouth opened in a silent scream as sobs wracked her.

Graeme, Graeme . . . O God, let it not be true. Please, please, Father. She tipped forward onto her knees and covered her head with her arms. Her shoulders heaved.

"No!" she shrieked as rage poured over the pain. Every ounce of her being longed to spring on the *amenoukal,* sink her teeth into his arm, claw his blue veil away, rake her nails across his cheeks, slash his thin lips, and yank at his long black hair. She clenched her fists, struggling to submit her will, forcing down her hunger for revenge.

"God!" she screamed, the plea for his help torn from her heart. "God, please! Please!"

"Matilda, is that you?" someone called out . . . a tall, thin man in the tent opening. A Targui stood guard at either side of him.

"Arthur?"

"Matilda!" Hands bound behind him, he squirmed as his guards shoved him forward and held him by his hair.

"Arthur, what are you doing here?" Tillie wiped a hand across her wet cheek.

"They captured me in Timbuktu."

"Where's Hannah?"

"At the rest house. She's fine. Darling, what's happened to you?"

"No talk!" The *amenoukal* crossed his arms over his chest. "Tree-Planting Woman find treasure."

He gestured to his men. They hauled Arthur to their chief and threw him to the ground. The *amenoukal* lifted his spear and buried it in the tent floor an inch from Arthur's neck. "Tree-Planting Woman find treasure."

He turned on his heel and strode out of the tent. After he left, the Tuareg moved into action, grabbing Tillie's arms and legs and tying them tightly together with heavy cords. They carried Arthur to a tent pole, dropped him, and tied him to it. A few feet away, another pole became Tillie's prison. Then, as quickly as the tent had filled, it emptied, leaving Arthur and Tillie alone.

She closed her eyes and sucked in a deep breath. Her head throbbed. A blinding pain seared behind her eyes. Her mouth felt as dry as the sun-baked desert air, and she licked a drop of blood from her lip.

"Are you all right, darling?" Arthur whispered. "You look as if you've been through hell."

"Yes."

She sank into herself. Graeme was gone. Dead. Khatty, too. Her heart felt torn in two, emptied of all life and joy and hope.

"Darling, please talk to me." Arthur's pale blue eyes had sunk into his face and were rimmed with dark circles of exhaustion. A shock of thin brown hair hung over his forehead. His clothes were splattered with blood.

"What happened to you, Arthur?"

"I was staying at the government rest house in Timbuktu and waiting for you to arrive. The Tuareg found me one morning when I went into town to search for you."

"In town? But I thought they were at the rest house. When I phoned Hannah, she said you were standing guard."

"You spoke with Hannah? Odd. She didn't mention it. No, nothing happened at the rest house. In fact, I practically bumped straight into the *amenoukal* on a street in Timbuktu two days ago. He kidnapped me and brought me out here to their camp. I've had no idea where you were or what was happening. They haven't told me a thing until just now when my guards brought me in here. I take it you didn't find the treasure."

"Graeme and I figured out where it was," she told him. "Mungo Park's box. We went to the mine, but the *amenoukal* attacked us there."

"Did you find the treasure in the box? Did you find the journal?"

She blinked without comprehension. "The treasure?"

"The treasure of Timbuktu. Did you find it?"

"It was only a hat and a few books. There was no treasure, no journal."

"But that's impossible!" His voice grew hard. "Matilda, look at me. You must find the journal and the treasure. That Targui's going to kill us both if you can't come up with something."

"Graeme's dead."

He was silent a moment. "Are you sure?"

"Yes."

"All the more reason to find the treasure. If the *amenoukal* killed McLeod for the treasure, he won't hesitate to do the same to us."

"And Khatty, too. The *amenoukal's* wife. She's dead."

"Look, darling, I'm sorry about McLeod. But he's dead, and it's time to think about us. We have our future ahead of us. Nothing has changed. I mean for us to have a good life."

She twisted the beaded ring on her finger. Arthur was wrong. Everything had changed.

"I'm tired." She leaned her head back against the tent pole and closed her eyes. Her head throbbed. Her heart ached.

The aroma of hot black coffee drifted into the tent. She lifted her head in time to see the shy serving maid who had once belonged to Khatty hurry out of the tent after leaving a tray of food and drink on a table nearby. A Targui walked into the tent and untied the captives' wrists and ankles.

"They've brought a meal," Arthur said quietly. "Can you eat, darling?"

She shook her head. Her neck felt twice its normal size, and her eyes were swollen nearly shut. She reached out, found the demitasse, and poured strong, hot coffee down her throat.

"The box we found," she managed. "Mungo Park's box. The one with the hat and the books. Tell that Targui to bring it."

Arthur glanced at the guard. "But you said—"

"Tell him the tree-planting woman is going to find the treasure of Timbuktu."

Arthur spoke to the man, who then ran to the door of the tent and shouted. Cries erupted in the camp.

"Darling." Arthur leaned across and took her hand. "Are you thinking clearly?"

"I'm going to find it." She pulled her hand away and reached for another cup of coffee. "I'm going to bring it to an end."

"Do you honestly think you can?"

"I know how to look. Graeme taught me."

"Matilda, for heaven's sake, what happened between you and McLeod? I have the right to an explanation."

She let the hot liquid spill down her throat. Was Arthur so concerned about her and Graeme because he loved her? Or was it because he wanted her as his wife, an essential part of his plan for a secure, comfortable future?

"I loved Graeme," she said softly. "I still love him."

Arthur clambered to his feet and hurled his cup to the floor. "Matilda, listen to you! You're behaving like some other woman. Someone I don't even know. What about me? What about our future? What happened to that?"

She rested her forehead on her knees and wrapped her arms around her legs. It was as black as night inside her heart. How could she think? How could she talk? Tears welled.

"Darling, talk to me." Arthur was standing in front of her. She could see his black leather shoes. "Matilda, you must be reason—"

His words stopped, and Tillie lifted her head. The *amenoukal* swept into the tent. Robed and veiled in deep blue once again, he strode to her side and pushed Arthur to his knees. One of his men bound the Englishman's wrists and ankles and tied him to the tent pole again.

"Tree-Planting Woman." The *amenoukal* held out the small carved chest.

Tillie took the box and gave him a nod. "The tree-planting woman will find the treasure."

When the *amenoukal* turned to go, Tillie caught his burnous. "Tree-Planting Woman needs one thing." She pointed to his spear and touched Graeme's khaki shirt. "I want that."

The man's eyes narrowed. He gave a curt nod, untied the shirt, and tossed it to the floor at her feet.

"When I find the treasure, you will let me go back to Bamako?" she asked. "With this man, Arthur Robinson?"

A short man in an indigo turban leaned forward and whispered to the Tuareg leader. The *amenoukal* nodded again.

"Bamako," he said. "Tree-Planting Woman. Englishman."

"Untie him, then," she commanded. "No more ropes."

The *amenoukal* spoke to another of his men. As the Targui worked open the knots in Arthur's bindings, she knelt to the carpet. The remaining Tuareg made their way back outside, leaving one man as a guard at the door to the tent.

Tillie picked up Graeme's shirt and crushed it to her chest. She tried to imagine him lifeless and still, but she couldn't do it. Instead he moved across her memory like a slow-motion film. Graeme driving the Land Rover, wind whipping his black hair. His tanned fingers slipping the beaded ring into her hand. A broad smile lighting his features as he paddled the fishing boat out into the Niger's current.

Stifling a sob, she slipped his bloodied shirt over her own. She held the fabric under her nose and drank in the scent of his skin. She buttoned it, imagining his fingers touching where she touched. Unable to pray, unable even to speak, she lifted the box onto her lap.

"Matilda." Arthur's voice was low. "You've been through a terrible ordeal, but we're going to come out all right in the end. I can feel it, darling."

She opened the lid and took Mungo Park's possessions out one by one. His hat. His books. His pen and ink. His shirt.

She spread the threadbare shirt onto the carpet and gazed at the tattered collar and worn elbows. "He loved to travel," she whispered. "He was an adventurer at heart, you know. He lived for the peaks of excitement. That was how he wanted his life to be."

Arthur stared at her. "Matilda, are you speaking of Mungo Park?"

She shrugged and picked up the worn green hat with its tiny slips of yellowed paper stuck in the band. Mungo Park had put them there two hundred years ago. Only one person had removed them since. The guide, Ahmadi Fatouma.

He had taken them to the man who had read the last page of the journal. He had had these notes translated. And from their directives—from half-understood meanings—he had germinated the legend of the treasure.

She slipped the first of the three notes from the hatband and opened it. As she had done with Graeme, she willed her mind into the simple, fearful outlook of Ahmadi Fatouma. How would the superstitious guide have interpreted the message written here? What would he have believed these words were telling him to do?

The paper cracked when she unfolded it; its ink was faded and barely legible. She read the inscription in silence. *"Mad Mungo,"* it said. *"Ailie they will call me Mad Mungo. Will you still love me, Mad Mungo?"*

"What does it say?" Arthur asked. "Can you make anything of it?"

"It's a message to Park's wife. He knew he was delirious. Mungo Park was a doctor, you know. This note shows he knew he had gone mad."

"What about the treasure? Does he talk about it?"

She didn't answer. She lifted the second note and read it to herself. *"The Bight of Benin is a swampy delta. It will be difficult to transform into a profitable harbor. But one day the white man and woman will come here, and they will tame the land. A pity—and a blessing."*

She refolded the note and inserted it back into the leather band. *He was there, Graeme. Mungo Park was there at the Bight of Benin, just like you thought. He really had made it all the way to the mouth of the Niger.* The third note was barely visible, and she had to dig it out. Would this be the writing of the sane Mungo, as in the last note? Or would this be Mad Mungo again?

Tillie opened the note. Two lines had been inscribed in a shaking hand. *"Well, well, well. It is finished."*

"What does it say, Matilda?" Arthur's voice was impatient.

She read the words again and gave a faint smile. "Arthur, please call in the *amenoukal.*"

The blue-veiled Targui must have been standing just

outside the tent. He walked in, crossed his arms, and waited.

"Is there a well near here?" she asked. "A very old well?"

He frowned and turned to the short turbaned man at his side. They had a rapid exchange.

"Many old wells," he told her. "Great Well of Timbuktu. Very full in rainy season. Many wells."

"Is there an old, dry well near Timbuktu? One that has been dry for a long, long time. Dry before the days of your grandfather's grandfather."

The Targui spoke at length with the man at his side; then he thumped his spear on the tent floor.

"Old Tuareg well on path of gold and salt caravan. Well finished long, long, long time." The *amenoukal* grabbed the chain around her neck and pulled the amulet out of her shirt. "Long ago Tuareg people find this at well."

"You found the amulet at the well?"

The chieftain nodded. "We take. We read. We wait for Tree-Planting Woman. You come, you say go to well again. Well of Waran."

"Well of Waran," she repeated. So that was it. She wrapped her hands around the amulet and lifted her eyes to his. "Ahodu Ag Amastane, the treasure of Timbuktu is inside the Well of Waran."

Sixteen

The *amenoukal* stared at Tillie without comprehension. "Treasure in Well of Waran?"

"Inside the well."

The Tuareg men turned to one another in animated discussion. Tillie placed the green hat back into the chest and snapped the brass clasp. Evening sun slanted through the tent's opening, and she wondered if they would leave immediately. For her, it was all over. The *amenoukal* would go off to the well, find his treasure, and abandon his two captives to their fate. Somehow, she and Arthur would make it back to Timbuktu and from there fly to Bamako.

"Tree-Planting Woman." The *amenoukal* faced her. "Come with Ahodu Ag Amastane."

She glanced at Arthur. "Why? I told you where the treasure is."

"Tree-Planting Woman come now."

A stiff prod from the *amenoukal*'s spear butt was enough to make her scramble to her feet. Surrounded by his Tuareg warriors, the chieftain led her into the waning sunlight. Someone pushed her toward the caravan. Someone else lifted her onto her familiar, cantankerous old dromedary.

"Wait a minute." She grabbed the three-pronged saddle horn and closed her eyes as the camel lurched to its feet.

"I told you where the treasure is. You don't need me anymore. Where are you taking me?"

"Well of Waran." The *amenoukal* gave a haughty smile. "Tree-Planting Woman find treasure for Ahodu Ag Amastane."

He lifted his spear, and the caravan set off. Women rushed to hang the last of their belongings on the saddles. A pot, a cloth bag, a basket. Children raced to their favorite places in the caravan. An *imzad* began to play, and voices lifted one by one to join the song.

Numb, Tillie let the camel's plodding gait hypnotize her. She couldn't imagine a future. She couldn't bear to remember the past. She couldn't pray beyond the wordless pleading in her spirit.

Evening descended, and she stared with an empty heart at the windblown grains of sand that sifted onto her saddle and collected in the folds of her clothing. She tried to close her eyes and sleep. Instead, her mind wandered to the image of Graeme crouching empty-handed in the bottom of the mine. The *amenoukal's* broadsword arced down toward his head. She jerked upright.

"Matilda, darling." Arthur urged his dromedary alongside hers. "You must try to stay alert."

"I can't stop thinking. Remembering."

"There, listen to that. Some woman's just begun a song on her *imzad*. Let your mind dwell on the music."

She focused on the haunting melody and closed her eyes again. The music had a gentle rhythm, one that soothed and comforted while evoking a nameless sorrow. The notes were high and plaintive, beckoning, calling to her almost as though she had heard them before. . . .

"Khatty." She grabbed his arm. "Arthur, that's Khatty's song. She wrote it for me."

"Now, darling, the *amenoukal* told you his wife was dead. You said he'd killed her."

"No, no. That's her voice. Her song. I would know it anywhere, Arthur. It's a song about Graeme McLeod."

"Matilda, for heaven's sake!"

"Come, oh, desert lion," she whispered as she listened to the gentle sounds drift across the night air. "Son of *waran*, man of strength and great wisdom. Your hair blows like ropes of sand in black night. Song of *djenoun* blows your sand-dune locks. Oh, man of black hair, man who sees heart of Tree-Planting Woman, come." She fell silent for a moment. "Khatty's wrong," she murmured finally. "He's not coming back."

"How can that be the voice of this Targui you said was dead, Matilda?"

"Maybe it's the *djenoun*. Maybe they learned Khatty's song, and they're singing it through the desert."

"*Djenoun?*" Arthur gripped her hand. "Matilda, pull yourself together. Now, look! Tomorrow this is all going to end one way or another. We'll arrive at the Well of Waran, and the journal will either be there or it won't."

Unable to feel beyond the emptiness inside her, Tillie stared into Arthur's face.

"Listen to me, Matilda. Listen carefully to what I'm going to tell you. I know you imagined yourself in love with Graeme McLeod. I know you think you cared for him, but I can only believe this infatuation grew out of your exhaustion, lack of proper food, and the constant pressure you've been subjected to. You were under terrible duress, forced to rely on this unscrupulous man during the most horribly difficult situations. Of course you looked to him for protection. It stands to reason you fell under certain delusions about him."

He touched her cheek. "Listen to me, darling. No matter what you felt for Graeme McLeod, no matter what happened, you must recognize that it's finished now. And I want to go on as we had planned. I want you to concentrate on what I tell you. I want you to do something for me. Something for us. It will make everything right again, I know it. I want you to do it to repair our dreams."

She studied his moonlit face. Pale eyes. Pale skin. "What is it, Arthur?"

"When you arrive at the Well of Waran, you will be faced with two possible actions. You must do either or both of them. Do you understand?"

She nodded.

"The first regards the journal." He went on, "It should be in a chest, probably like the one the hat was in. I want you to take the journal out of the container. Hide it in your clothing. We shall make certain you have on a burnous. The Tuareg will never know what you've done."

"Hide the journal?"

"It's an extremely valuable document, Matilda. Second, I want you to take all the treasure you can. Take the gold out of the chest, and hide it in your burnous."

"Gold?"

"I'm certain it's gold. It must be. Timbuktu was full of gold in those days. Take some of it, darling. Take it for us."

"But how can I? The *amenoukal* will search—"

She knew the answer. She reached up and touched the

amulet around her neck. The Tuareg people's fear of the amulet would protect her from the *amenoukal*'s search. She could pretend to invoke its superstitious power and prevent the chieftain from looking for anything she might have concealed. Khatty had been terrified when Tillie called on the power of the cursed document. It would work again. She felt certain of it.

"Take some of the treasure," Arthur whispered, "and take the journal. Give the *amenoukal* a few coins, enough to satisfy him and perhaps buy him a trinket or two at the Timbuktu market. Once he has what he's been wanting, we'll be free to go on our way. We'll return to Bamako and catch the first flight to London. There we can marry just as we planned, and we'll have the gold to support us, darling. We can do whatever we like with it. We'll have everything we could ever want or need—"

"Stop, Arthur. Stop talking." Tillie pulled away. "Just give me time to think."

"Of course, darling." He leaned closer and placed a kiss on her cheek. "Think about it as long as you like. But I'm trusting you'll see the wisdom in my words soon enough. It's all going to be perfect for us."

Tillie's heart throbbed with a dull ache that no promises of future happiness could erase. As she gave herself to the swaying gait of her dromedary, she closed her eyes and wept again.

The long ride to the well continued through the night. At sunup, the caravan stopped for everyone to light fires, heat coffee and tea, and eat a hurried breakfast. Arthur came to life, the military man with a mission. He demanded burnouses and turbans against the sun for himself and Tillie, and he insisted on hearty meals for the two of them.

"You're the tree-planting woman, Tillie," he reminded her as he rode alongside after the march resumed. "Play the part. I know these people. You've got to intimidate them. Keep them afraid, make them cower so you can carry out our plan."

"I'm not into intimidation," she said. "And I don't like watching people cower. Look, you said I had two options at the Well of Waran. Take the journal or take the treasure. Preferably both. I see another option. Assuming I find anything, I could just hand it over to the *amenoukal*. It's what he wants. He believes it will help his people. Why not let him have it?"

"You can't be serious."

"I care about these Tuareg, Arthur. They're poor. They live in the desert. They survive on next to nothing, yet they have such pride."

"How can you possibly have any feeling for the *amenoukal?* Just since you've known him, the chieftain has killed at least two people."

"You shot more than two of his people."

"I was protecting you!"

"Ahodu Ag Amastane believes he's protecting his drum group. He's cruel, even brutal, but no one can deny he wants the best for his caravan. So do I. Maybe they ought to have the treasure."

"I cannot believe I'm hearing this."

"Let's drop the subject." She patted her dromedary's shaggy neck. "I don't know what I'm going to do yet." *I really don't, Lord. Help me.*

They crested silky sand dunes one after the next, skirted stone wadis, followed faint, windblown trails. Tillie searched the caravan for any sign of Khatty. She knew the song she had heard in the night. It couldn't have been *djenoun*—she knew that—but how could it have been Khatty?

She used the hours of silence to consider Arthur's request, but she couldn't find peace. She studied him, his familiar back swaying ahead of her, his light brown hair lifting and scattering in the breeze, his shoulders squared like the corners of a box. He looked foreign to her now. As she turned his plan over in her mind, she knew it was wrong. Something was missing.

In the early afternoon a ripple of excitement ran through the caravan. Through a wavering, watery haze across the hot sands, she saw a giant mound of solid rock. The fierce sunlight bathed it in a white glow, making it look like an altar to some desert god. A stone outcrop lifted toward the sky in a pronged image that suggested a lizard's open mouth.

The Well of Waran.

Like two fingers from an outstretched hand, a shadow spilled across the sand. The line of camels filed into its shade. Tillie's throat tightened as the caravan pulled to a halt at the base of the rock. The *amenoukal*'s camel plodded from the head of the line back toward her. Arthur gave her a reassuring nod. "Just do what I told you."

"Tree-Planting Woman." The *amenoukal* spoke through the folds of his turban. "Well of Waran."

"Show me the entrance to the well."

The *amenoukal* called to the rider ahead of Arthur. The veiled man approached, and Tillie repeated her message.

Upon hearing the muffled translation, the *amenoukal* nodded and tapped his camel to its knees.

At this sign, all the camels in the caravan went down, and their riders slipped to the sandy ground. Tillie followed the *amenoukal* along the base of the wadi. Arthur trailed a few steps behind.

Women and children parted to let them pass, then surged in behind, murmuring and jostling with excitement. By the time the *amenoukal* worked his way across the shifting sands and between the two stone fingers, the whole band of Tuareg had joined the expedition. The rock lost its white glow and turned black and pockmarked. Countless sandstorms had smoothed some of the jagged pinnacles into round columns of stone, but they had clawed others into distorted shapes that bore a remarkable resemblance to medieval gargoyles.

Tillie followed the *amenoukal* through the stone sculptures and into an inner ravine. He stopped and held up a hand. Jockeying for position, the Tuareg surrounded their leader.

"Tree-Planting Woman," he said. "Well of Waran."

He stepped aside, and she looked down into a jagged crack in the stone that resembled a snaggletoothed mouth.

"This is a well?" She hadn't expected Snow White's wishing well with its round wall, neat roof, and cute little wooden bucket, but she wasn't prepared for this either.

The *amenoukal* pointed a long finger at the hole. "Well of Waran. Get treasure."

She edged past him and looked down into the darkness. "I need a rope and a lamp."

After the *amenoukal*'s translator explained, the chieftain

waded into the crowd, shouting orders to his men. Tuareg swarmed into action, tying tent rope to tent rope and combing their supplies for a suitable lamp and fuel. Tillie fingered her amulet, trying to pray as the *amenoukal* personally supervised the search.

"Tree-Planting Woman." A whispered voice at her shoulder brought her around in surprise. The *amenoukal*'s translator took a step closer.

"Yes?" Tillie felt her irritation mounting. "What do you want?"

The translator said nothing. His eyes blinked, deep brown, almond eyes, heavily rimmed with kohl. Not the eyes of a Targui man, but the eyes of—

"Khatty!"

"Quiet, Tree-Planting Woman," Khatty whispered. "He must not see."

"But he told me you were dead. And the turban, the veil—they're men's clothes."

The dark eyes clouded. "Ahodu Ag Amastane, *amenoukal* of Tuareg people, is angry with me. I help you escape with black-haired man. He cast me away. I am dead to him. He puts me into men's clothing to pretend I do not exist."

"I'm so sorry."

"Never to worry, one day soon he takes me again. Of course, even now he needs me for talking to you." She smiled slyly and whispered. "Among Tuareg people, inheritance passes through female line. Now, in my stomach, I carry child of Ahodu Ag Amastane. He will need me again. I am his beloved wife."

"That's wonderful, Khatty." Tillie couldn't hold back a

hug. "I'm so thankful to see you again. When I heard your song in the night, I told Arthur it must be the *djenoun.*"

The young woman's laugh tinkled across the afternoon like a wind chime, and Tillie felt her heart lift. "Not *djenoun!* Khatty make that song for you and your man. You sing black-haired man back into your heart. You love him always and never let him go."

"Khatty, you don't understand."

"I understand you very sad. Khatty sees everything." She leaned closer. "In Tuareg camp, you teach me something about how to be strong. Already I told you I believe Jesus Christ is son of God, born of virgin, died on cross, alive again." A frown creased her forehead. "But I see Christ make you different. I not know how to be this kind of different. I want to know more. You will come back to Tuareg, Tree-Planting Woman? Come back to teach me one day?"

Tillie nodded. "If I survive this . . . and if your husband will let me, I'll find you again, Khatty. I'll teach you the path to a new life."

"I am glad," Khatty said, her eyes shining. "Even in Tuareg camp where everyone is Muslim, even now when husband cast me away and I live like man, I pray to this Jesus Christ and I find happy." She touched her heart. "Happy is here, inside. Hope is here. Love is here. You know Jesus very well, Tree-Planting Woman. In him, you find happy. Yes?"

"You're right, Khatty. You're right."

"Tree-Planting Woman, come." The *amenoukal*'s summons stopped Tillie's response in her throat. Khatty fell back and melted into the crowd.

A length of rope was coiled around the chieftain's fore-arm. He thrust one end at Tillie and distributed the remainder to the row of men he had assembled. She looked skeptically at the series of knots, wondering if they could hold her as she descended into the well. The *amenoukal* tied her end of the rope into a loop and tested the knot. Seizing her arm, he led her toward the black hole.

She slipped the loop into position around her hips so she could sit on it as they lowered her. The heavy burnous would protect her from the rope's friction, and she tucked the cotton fabric under her hips. The *amenoukal* handed her a lighted brass lamp that swung from a slender chain.

Arthur's guard shoved him to his knees in front of the *amenoukal*. Then he drew a long knife and held it to the Englishman's throat. Arthur let out a strangled cry. Tillie gasped and stepped forward, but a pair of Tuareg men clamped her arms. The *amenoukal* shouted a string of words at Khatty.

"Ahodu Ag Amastane, *amenoukal* of Tuareg people," she translated, "tells Tree-Planting Woman to find treasure of Timbuktu and bring to him. In this way, she breaks curse of amulet and saves her life. If she does not bring treasure from Well of Waran and if she does not give treasure to *amenoukal,* he will cut throat of this pale English scorpion."

Sudden anger sent a wash of adrenaline through Tillie's veins. "Tree-Planting Woman has a message for Ahodu Ag Amastane, the *amenoukal* of the Tuareg people. He must not harm the Englishman. He must let the man go free at once. Tree-Planting Woman commands this by the power of the amulet."

As Khatty translated the message, Tillie spread open her

burnous and held up the silver locket. The words ended, and a ripple of fear ran through the crowd. A shadow of indecision crossed the *amenoukal*'s face. In one quick movement, he released Arthur and bellowed at his guards to stand back.

"Now," she said quietly, "I'll see if there's anything in this well."

Holding the rope in one hand and the lamp in the other, she walked to the edge of the gaping black hole. She sat on the barren rock and let her legs dangle over the abyss. With a glance into the sapphire sky, she slid over the ledge.

For an instant Tillie believed the rope's knots had pulled apart or the Tuareg men had dropped her. Free-falling through the black void like Alice in the white rabbit's hole, she heard the air hiss from her lungs and saw the lamplight fade to nothing. Then the rope snapped tight around her hips, and she came to a jolting stop that yanked the brass lamp from her hand. She gripped the rope and listened for a clatter that would signal the lamp's landing place. Nothing.

Her first impulse was to shout for help, to demand to be pulled up into the fresh air and light. The *amenoukal* would probably ignore her. As if to confirm that conclusion, she felt herself being lowered, this time more slowly. A distant echo sounded from below—the lamp clanging on the bottom of the well.

As Tillie continued her descent, she was forced to use her free hand to push away from the rough rock sides of the craggy hole. More than once her burnous caught and tore.

Above, she could see the jagged circle of light. She could also make out the dark shape of a man's head as he peered down at her. Clenching her teeth, she closed her eyes and felt her way down the shaft. She would make it. She would get to the bottom of this pit, and she would find the treasure, and she would find the—

The journal. Graeme's quest. All the Targui's talk of treasure had numbed her mind to Graeme's goal. His motives may not have been pure, but she knew he wanted the journal for the information it contained about Mungo Park. That had been his crusade. The thought that she somehow could fulfill it lightened her heart. A surge of resolve flowed back into her at the memory of the man with whom she had shared so much.

"Graeme," she called up to the *amenoukal*. "This is for Graeme."

As the words drifted up, echoing back and forth along the tunnel's walls, a shower of pebbles and sand rained down on her head. She continued down, conscious of bruised elbows and scraped knuckles. When her feet met something solid, she let out a gasp, and another cascade of sand spilled onto her.

The darkness around her was total. Was this the bottom of the well? Or a ledge? It was so dark she began to think she saw spots of light. She rubbed her eyes, released the rope with one hand, and knelt to let her fingers slide across the sandy surface. When they touched something hard and cold, she jerked her hand to her mouth.

"The lamp," she whispered. "It's the lamp."

Again she ventured out, letting her fingers wander over the smooth, cold surface of the brass lantern. "Relax, Tillie," she told herself. "Uncurl those legs."

Her heart hammering in her temples, she took her other hand from the rope. Beads of sweat popped out on her forehead. The hair on the nape of her neck rose to attention.

Where was the treasure chest?

Her fingers roamed across every inch of the narrow floor. The sand was smooth and even. Her hands moved over the untouched ground, around the perimeter, up the craggy walls. Nothing. No sign of disturbance. Nothing lived here, no monitor lizards, no snakes, not even a scorpion. There was no trace of water, as if even the most essential element of life had been swept away by the desert.

Frustrated, she clamped her teeth shut. Where was it? She sat back on her heels. What would Graeme have done? How would he have reasoned it out? Unless she had been mistaken in her reading of Mungo Park's note, the chest had to be here.

"Ahmadi Fatouma, where did you hide that chest?" Her question echoed upward and sent a trickle of sand drifting onto her head. A chill washed through her.

That was it. Sand. It had been two centuries since the chest had been placed at the bottom of this well. Two centuries, with more than a thousand sandstorms and more than a hundred rains. The chest was buried.

She sank her hands into the sand. Her fingers tore at grit and stones and shoved them away. How deep would it be? How far would she have to dig to find it?

After ten minutes of digging, her fingertips grazed something hard. She paused, heart racing; then she began to brush back the sand. A straight, hard edge emerged. Smooth wood studded with nails. Carvings. She scrabbled with her bare fingers until she had exposed one whole side of the box.

After a minute's rest, she resumed digging. She found a clasp—the same kind of clasp Graeme had opened on the first chest. This was it. She had found the chest.

She clawed at the sand until she could slide her bleeding fingers under the wooden box. With a grunt, she lifted the chest onto her lap. Breathing hard, she sat alone in the darkness and realized her cheeks were wet. She'd been crying as she dug. Crying over Graeme. He should be the one holding Mungo Park's final legacy.

Crying for herself, too. She had given herself into God's hands the moment she had tumbled into Graeme's Land Rover. She had pledged herself to trust God one moment at a time, but she had failed him in so many ways.

With Khatty, she had tried to set an example. She had encouraged the Targui woman in her simple, childlike quest. Yet it was Khatty—forced to live in a Muslim world, the wife of a man who had rejected, abandoned, and humiliated her—who had been compelled to admonish Tillie in the end. "You find happy," Khatty had said.

Happy? How could she be happy when she had failed so miserably with Graeme?

God had allowed him into her life, a man she could care about, perhaps even lead toward the Lord. Instead—against all she knew was right—she had fallen in love with him. Even though she had told Graeme they could have no future, she had never stopped loving him. And now he was dead, without God. For eternity. Sharp grief washed over her, and she wondered if life would ever be the same.

Find happy? It seemed impossible.

She brushed the heel of her palm over her damp cheek. It was time to bring this to an end.

Fumbling with the clasp, she felt it give. The lid swung open. Sightless, she peered into the blackness. A dry, musky smell rose from the chest, the odor of an attic closed up too long. Her fingers trailed over two items inside the chest. Under her left hand lay a small, thin book. She slid her hand around it and held it to her nose, breathing the rich leather scent. The journal of Mungo Park. Graeme's Holy Grail.

Under her right hand lay a large pouch made of dry, crusty fabric. She could feel small round lumps inside it. Gold nuggets, she supposed, or coins. The treasure of Timbuktu.

She could close the box, jerk the rope, and carry the treasure up to Ahodu Ag Amastane. It might help his people. Or it might set up a tradition of greed. She imagined it sending the Tuareg into Timbuktu to trade, to start selling their trinkets and broadswords to fat, pink tourists. They had been desert nomads for centuries. Long before Mungo Park's time and long after. Did they really need his treasure to survive?

What about Arthur? His instructions sifted down like the sand that trickled into her hair. Hidden in blackness, she could open the pouch. No one would see. She could take out some of the gold and hide it under her burnous. The gold would help give Arthur the life he thought he wanted.

A prayer formed on Tillie's lips. She curled on her knees and touched her forehead to the sand. "Father, I love you. I see you working all around me. In Khatty's life. Through Robert and Mary McHugh. Through Hannah. Maybe you were working in Graeme's life, too. I want to join you in your work. Work through me, Father. Amen."

She lifted her head and took a deep breath. Now what? The gold. The journal. The *amenoukal*. Arthur. Who should have what?

"Where your treasure is, there will your heart be also."

The answer was easy after all.

She took the journal out of the chest, snapped the lid shut, and fastened the clasp. The small book slipped easily under her burnous and inside Graeme's shirt. Robert McHugh would know what to do with it.

Tillie shifted the chest into the crook of her arm and adjusted the rope around her hips. With a tug, she signaled her readiness to leave the well. Immediately the rope tightened.

Ascending was harder than going down had been, but she hardly felt the bumps and scrapes. Her heart was light, and a song played at her lips.

"Come, oh, desert lion." Tillie whispered the lilting tune as she rose through the darkness. "Son of the waran, man of strength and mighty wisdom. Come, oh, desert lion. . . . Come, oh, desert lion. . . ."

Hands reached down to pull her from the well. When her head lifted into the fresh air, she saw the last rays of the sun sliding beneath the horizon. Pale stars were scattered like random cross-stitch on a blue-gray cloth. A full moon smiled overhead.

Tillie climbed over the lip of the well and stood on solid rock. "Ahodu Ag Amastane, the tree-planting woman has returned from the Well of Waran." She handed him the chest. "Take this. It is the treasure of Timbuktu."

She walked past him down the rock. As she brushed by Arthur, he grabbed her arm. "Did you do what I told you?" he hissed. "Did you get the treasure? the journal?"

"The *amenoukal* has the gold, Arthur. You and I don't need earthly treasure, remember? Our wealth is in heaven."

"Don't be ridiculous, Matilda! You gave it all to him?

What about the journal? On the black market it'll fetch a small fortune."

She turned back slowly. "The black market, Arthur?"

Suddenly Hannah's cryptic message on the telephone made sense. Like a mango growing on a banana stalk, things were not as they ought to be. Arthur was the thing in Tillie's clothing that would sting her. Hannah had seen into his heart, and she knew.

"You've been stealing the books from the Sankore Mosque, haven't you, Arthur?"

The answer was written in his expression. His eyes washed a pale empty blue as her words registered. The color drained from his face, and he grabbed for her arm. His Tuareg guards jerked him back. The Englishman struggled and called her name, but she turned away.

Tillie could see the *amenoukal* surrounded by his men. They were carrying the chest to a higher platform of rock to open it in view of the whole caravan. Khatty was at her husband's side, where no doubt she would remain.

In the distance a sound like thunder rolled across the night. Remembering the sandstorm, Tillie glanced into the sky. No lightning flickered on the horizon. No dust swirled toward the well. She wandered across the uneven terrain.

She was free. They had all forgotten her, Tree-Planting Woman. Even Arthur had struggled into the mass of swarming Tuareg, hoping for a glimpse of his lost dreams. In silence, she surveyed the deserted well. Her focus fell on the box that had held Mungo Park's hat. The little chest lay abandoned, so she picked it up.

The thunder was louder now, and she stared at a low formation of silver-lined clouds that billowed over the horizon. Wanting to feel the desert breeze wash away the memory of the well, she climbed onto one of the two stone fingers that formed the *waran*'s open mouth. She threw off her burnous and gripped the jagged rock, her well-worn boots finding sure footing.

When she had climbed to the tip of the peak, she looked down at the bustling hive of Tuareg. Blue-clad backs pressed and writhed; turbaned heads craned to see. She smiled, the weight of the search lifted from her shoulders.

Thank you, Father. Thank you for showing me the real treasure.

She tucked Mungo Park's hatbox under her arm. Suddenly the *amenoukal* leapt to his feet, his shrill cry piercing the air. He raised his broadsword and brought it down on the wooden chest. It shattered into a hundred fragments across the stone. He flung the treasure pouch into the air, and its contents spilled out in the fading light.

It wasn't golden nuggets that flew in every direction. Or gold coins. It was seashells. Cowrie shells. Ahmadi Fatouma's treasure was nothing more than hundreds upon hundreds of cowrie shells.

"Mansong, the king of Segou," Tillie whispered. "Graeme said Mansong gave Mungo Park five thousand cowrie shells. *That's* the treasure of Timbuktu!"

A laugh bubbled up in her throat. She tossed back her head, and the breeze caught her hair. Cowrie shells! Thunder rolled over her laughter, drowning out the sound.

"Tillie!" someone shouted.

She swung around toward the voice. It had come from the west, across the desert. Was she imagining the *djenoun* again? Peering into the setting sun, she shielded her eyes against the glare. A loud rumble roared toward her. That sound . . . it wasn't thunder at all. It was the roar of an airplane's engines.

A wing dipped as a battered old two-seater with a single propeller flew past the rock. A hand shot out of the open cockpit. She saw a ripple of black hair and the flash of a boyish grin.

"Graeme!" she shouted.

"Hang on, Tillie-girl. I'm coming to get you."

Seventeen

The airplane circled the Well of Waran and began a descent to the desert. Heart racing, Tillie slid down the stone. Loose rocks scattered under her feet. She fell, her ankle twisted, her palm split. She rolled onto her knees and leapt back to her feet. The old wooden chest tucked under her arm, she ran on. She jumped over a crevice and slid on her bottom down a narrow ravine.

Behind her, the Tuareg spotted the plane and gave chase. The enraged *amenoukal* raised his spear and led his men over the stone away from their scattered treasure. Shouting, screaming, they raced after her.

The rusty old airplane came to a stop on the strip of level road. Graeme rose out of the cockpit to beckon Tillie. His black hair blew away from his face, and she could see a strip of cloth tied around his head. He was wounded, but he was alive. Alive.

Her feet hit the sand. Racing up one dune and down the next, she glanced to her side as the *amenoukal*'s spear dug into the sand. The tattered banner of her skirt flapped in the breeze. The spear's shaft swung back and forth and then toppled over.

Graeme climbed half out of the cockpit, and Tillie could see that the propeller was still humming. He stepped out onto the wing. She smelled diesel fuel, hot metal, smoke. Tillie reached the aircraft and lifted her hands. Graeme leaned toward her. In a replay of their first meeting, his arm swung out over the edge of the wing and snapped around her waist like an iron band. Lifted horizontally into the air, she saw the blue-black sky sprinkled with stars spin overhead, the dunes whirl below. Her breath was knocked from her lungs, and her hair floated over her face like a fan. Mungo Park's box tumbled from her arms into the cockpit. She followed it into a tiny space where her knees met her chin.

The airplane's engine *thunk-thunked* from idle to full rev. In the seat ahead of her Graeme worked the controls. The plane rolled forward over the sand, a deathly slow start. The Tuareg poured over a dune and swarmed toward them.

"Keep 'em busy!" Graeme shouted.

Tillie tore off a boot and hurled it at a Targui who reached for the plane's wing. Stunned, he stumbled backward, but another warrior took his place. Tillie's second boot glanced off his chin, tangled in his veil, and made him lose his grip.

"I got it now," Graeme shouted. "Hang onto your hat. We're going for a ride."

The plane's forward thrust pressed Tillie against the brown leather seat. Graeme accelerated as the aircraft bounced across the sandy road, dipped and surged and half floated into the air before slamming onto the road again. Behind them, the Tuareg swarmed over the plane's tracks as they tried to keep up.

When Tillie was sure her eardrums would burst from the engine's roar, the plane lifted into the cobalt sky.

"Graeme!" she cried. "You did it."

"*We* did it." His voice was filled with elation. "Look at our pal down there."

She leaned over the side of the airplane and saw the *amenoukal* standing on a dune. His spear was at his side again; his broadsword hung loose in one hand. "Look, Graeme. There's Khatty."

Graeme hung one arm out and waved at the two figures. "*Maktoub!*" he shouted. "*Maktoub.*" It was God's will.

Khatty pulled off her turban and waved it in farewell. Then the tall, blue-veiled Targui beside her lifted his spear in salute.

"Did you see that?" Tillie called. "The *amenoukal* waved at us."

"He's saying we were worthy adversaries."

"So was he." She slumped back in the crumbling leather seat. How could this all be happening? Graeme had been killed. But here he was. Alive.

The plane veered into a sweeping turn. "There's Arthur," he called over one shoulder.

Below the plane, the Englishman sat dejected at the lip of the Well of Waran. The splintered chest and the treasure pouch lay beside him. He was running his fingers through the piles of tiny round opalescent shells that were the legacy of Mungo Park's guide, Ahmadi Fatouma.

"Shall we go get him?" Graeme yelled.

Tillie considered for a moment. "No," she shouted back. "He got what he wanted. Leave him with it."

He turned to her. "The journal? Did he get his hands on it?"

"No." She touched the slender book hidden under her shirt. "Graeme, at the Sankore Mosque, I saw—"

"There they come!" He let out a whoop that cut off
Tillie's words. The plane swooped down to buzz a line of
Land Rovers headed for the wadi of the Well of Waran.
Police Land Rovers.

The officials smiled and waved as the airplane blasted
over them. When Graeme lifted the plane's nose again,
Tillie slid forward and draped her arms around his neck. His
black hair blew across her cheek, and she laid her head
against his.

Despite the breeze, the night was warm. The stars seemed
brighter from up here; the full moon began a gradual ascent.
Bright silver-white, it lit up the sand until each grain glit-
tered like a diamond and each dune wore a shining halo.
The flight was not long, and as the plane began to lose alti-
tude, Tillie spotted what looked like an alabaster snake
winding across the desert.

"What's that?" she called.

"The Niger."

"Mungo Park's river." She gazed down at the curling
channel and smiled. From here it was the stuff of dreams.
"And that glittering spot in the sand?"

"Timbuktu."

The plane descended, and the lights grew closer, chang-
ing from silver to gold and red and blue—the colors of lamp
flames, cooking fires, coals warming thick black coffee,
braziers roasting kabobs of goat. The river rippled in the
wind, drifting shoreward to lap at the banks where egrets
stood. Hippos rose from the water and waddled out to
munch on reeds and papyrus, while crocodiles crawled
along the shore in search of a stretch of warm sand.

As the plane bumped down onto an expanse of barren,

moonlit track between the river and the town, Tillie drank in the dry smell of the sand she had come to know so well. The breeze died to a gentle caress as Graeme eased the plane to a halt and cut the engine. The propeller slowed to a tired whirl and stopped.

He climbed out of the cockpit and helped Tillie across the wing. The amulet tumbled from her shirt and clanked on the cool metal. When she dropped into Graeme's arms, he held her close against his chest, and she could hear his heart thudding against his ribs.

"I was scared to death for you," he whispered. His breath warmed her cheek. "I was sure I'd lost you."

"But I thought the *amenoukal* had killed you. In the mine—I saw his broadsword. You were down in the water, and he swung it at you."

"You thought I'd been killed?"

"The last thing I saw before they knocked me out was the sword coming down on your neck."

He groaned and looked up into the sky. "I thought you knew what happened. We were on a ledge, remember? At the last instant, I dove off it into the water. The *amenoukal* grabbed me and nicked my head with his sword. I squirmed between his feet and swam underwater. I was sure he wouldn't follow me. You know how the Tuareg feel about water. I was swimming blindly, down one tunnel after another, and when I finally came up, I was lost. It took me hours to find my way back to the entrance of the mine— I'm still not even sure how I did it. By that time, the police had arrived. I guess you were gone by then?"

"Someone hit the back of my head, and when I woke

up, I was in the *amenoukal*'s tent a long way from the mine."

"All this time you thought I was dead? Tillie, I'm sorry." He cupped her face in his hands and brushed her cheeks with his thumbs. "The police took me straight to the clinic in Timbuktu and had my head and leg patched up. Then they located an old plane down in Mopti and ordered it flown up here for me. They've been out with their Land Rovers, and I've been flying from Timbuktu halfway to Algeria looking for you."

"Graeme," she shook her head, "why would the police do that for you? At the Sankore Mosque, I saw you put the three books Mahamane Samouda had shown us into your shirt."

"You did?" He shook his head. "You're a better detective than I realized. No wonder you were spooked in Timbuktu. Remember the smuggling ring that has been taking rare books and selling them on the European black market?"

"Arthur told me. He was working on it."

"He sure was." Graeme gave a wry chuckle. "When the police and Mahamane Samouda found out I was writing a book on Mungo Park, they asked me to do whatever I could to help protect the books. I've been helping them for several months now. Mahamane Samouda has been sending me the library's most valuable books a few at a time, and I've been keeping them safe until we could assemble enough evidence to crack the smuggling ring. We suspected the old doorkeeper had something to do with it. A couple of days ago we connected him with Arthur Robinson."

She looked away. She'd been hoping she was wrong

about Arthur's involvement. Dismay filled her at his deception. "He mentioned the black market."

"He was the link with the exporters, through his position in the embassy. I didn't make the connection until you told me what he had said about the journal's value." He searched her face for a reaction. "Look, I know you cared about him. I don't think he was a bad guy. He just let greed seduce him. It was easy work, and the money was too good."

"He wanted to lay up treasures on earth, 'where moth and rust destroy, and where thieves break in and steal,'" she repeated softly. "It's from the Bible."

"About that." He raked a hand through his hair. Then he looked up into the sky, remembering. "I want to tell you what happened to me when I was searching for you, Tillie-girl."

Graeme closed his eyes for a moment, remembering that desperate night he'd landed the plane in the desert after another futile day of searching for the Tuareg caravan.

He looked down at Tillie, still barely able to believe he'd finally found her. *She needs to know what happened. All of it.*

"I spent days looking for the Tuareg caravan," he began, "and found nothing. Finally one night, I was sitting there in the desert. I knew I had to get back to the Timbuktu airstrip, that I didn't have much fuel—" he broke off and looked at her, and in his eyes she could see the pain he'd felt— "but I didn't care. How could I? I figured you were dead."

"Oh, Graeme . . ."

He shook his head. "It only made sense. I knew the *amenoukal* wouldn't keep you alive once he realized you couldn't find the treasure. And when I thought of you lying dead in the desert, I felt empty inside. Empty and hopeless." His voice was choked, but he continued doggedly. "My gut twisted into a knot. I hadn't eaten much of anything for days. I didn't want to stop looking. As for sleep—" he gave a rueful laugh— "that was pretty much out of the question. I just knew I needed to think. So I brought the plane down on a stretch of open desert, cut the engine, climbed out of the cockpit, and collapsed."

He looked up at the sky, a faraway look in his eyes, and felt Tillie tighten her hold around him. He could do this. He could tell her.

"I can still feel the sand under my back. It was cold and hard. And there were millions of stars. I lay there and watched them and realized I'd only been in that much pain once before—"

He broke off, echoes of that pain washing over him. Tillie waited in silence. Grateful, he drew a deep, steadying breath and went on. "It was when I was a boy, watching my mother's face, her eyes wide with fear because my father was holding a gun to her head. I couldn't let him hurt her. So I did the only thing I could. I didn't even think about it, I just acted."

Graeme jerked as he recalled how he had grabbed a kitchen knife . . . swung at his father . . . heard the cry of shock . . . seen the blood. "I killed my father, Tillie. He died in my arms. I was only a boy, and because of the circumstances, I wasn't charged. But that hardly mattered. My life was changed. I swore I would never trust anyone again, never let anyone close enough to hurt me. I would never love another human being as long as I lived. And then . . . ." He looked down at her, his heart filling with tenderness. "Then you came along, Tillie-girl. And you turned everything around. You taught me to hope, made me want to open up again. You showed me how to have faith." He cupped her face with one hand, almost afraid to believe she was really there. "Then I lost you, too."

He felt again the desperation that had swept over him that night, remembered how he had turned over on his stomach and clutched two handfuls of sand. Tillie had called herself water and him sand. She had said they were on two separate paths.

"God!" The word had been wrenched aloud from his heart. "God, I want to find Tillie's path! I'm lost. I can't find my own way anymore. Show me the way."

That was when her words had come to him, swirling around and through him. *"Anyone who's lost can be found,"* she'd told him. *"Anyone who's blind can see. Anyone who's willing to let his old self die can be born again. All it takes is surrender."*

Looking down into Tillie's shining eyes as she watched him now, he wondered what he had ever done to deserve her. "I was devastated. I lay there, my face in the sand, and knew I couldn't feel any emptier. All my life, I'd relied on my wits. I'd never trusted anyone. That night in the desert, I wanted nothing more than to surrender everything and hand my life over to someone I could trust."

"Graeme," she whispered, and he heard the cautious excitement in her voice. "What are you saying?"

"Remember what you told me? That Jesus touched you,

that his spirit lived inside you, that even when you struggled you knew God's power was real because you could feel it? You could rely on it?" She nodded, and he saw tears glimmering in her eyes—and felt his throat constrict with sudden tears as well. "I wanted to know that for myself. So I asked God to touch me."

He could hear those words he'd spoken echoing in his heart: *"Touch me,"* he'd murmured into the sand. *"Touch me . . . Father."*

How many years had it been since he had called anyone by that name?

"Father," he'd said again, and he'd felt the power in that word. For the first time in his life, he had begun to understand its true meaning. Father. In that moment, lying in the cold sand, he'd been able to let go of his earthly parent, release his bitter memories of the man who had beaten and tormented him. Instead, he'd found himself wrapping his arms around a heavenly Father who loved him, who gave up his own life for him, who wanted to embrace him as a son.

"I told God I'd done a lot of wrong things in my life," he whispered, watching the emotions wash over Tillie's beautiful face. "I asked him to forgive me, and I surrendered everything to him. I gave him my life, *your* life. Everything. I wanted my old self to die, to be born again, just the way you'd said, Tillie. I asked my Father to make me a new man."

She leaned back in his arms, and he'd never seen such complete joy in anyone's eyes before. She reached up to touch his face tenderly, and he pressed his cheek into her warm palm as he went on.

"I lay silently for a long time, feeling the breeze ripple

over my skin, almost as though it were cooling and cleansing me. An incredible peace filled my heart. I asked Jesus to show me how to walk on his path, how to do his work. I asked him to touch me, fill me, teach me. I knew, without a doubt, that the great Creator of the universe loved me. That no one is ever abandoned by God. And for the first time in my life, I understood the meaning of faith." He paused, smiling at the woman who watched him with such wonder, and shrugged slightly. "That's how it happened, Tillie-girl. That's how I found my heavenly Father."

Tillie stood there, her heart overflowing with praise to God, feeling the warm tears run down her face.

"I'm so glad for you," she whispered, struggling for control. Joy swept through her, filling the places that had seemed dead only hours ago.

"I'm on God's path," Graeme said, his voice strong and sure. "Though I'm a long way behind you." He lifted his head and smiled. "But I'm a quick learner."

She turned the beaded ring on her left hand. "When I thought you were dead, I didn't see how I could go on. Something made me keep going through the motions. I took the notes from Mungo Park's hat and figured out Ahmadi Fatouma had hidden the chest inside the Well of Waran."

Remembering her descent into the darkness, she pulled out of his arms and wandered toward the river. When she glanced back, she saw his tall figure outlined in moonlight. His shirt had taken on a luminescent quality. His face wore a pensive expression.

"What's the matter, Tillie?" He walked to her side and took her hand. "Did something happen in the well?"

"It's where I made my own decision. Ever since I was a little girl, my goal has been to find God's will for my life. I was sure agroforestry in Mali was it. It fit perfectly into all my plans. *My* plans."

She shoved her hands into her pockets. "In the well I finally understood that I'm not supposed to be looking for God's will for my life. I'm just supposed to look for God's will. Period. Wherever I happen to be, when I see him working—like he is with Khatty—I'm supposed to go there and let him do his work through me. And along the way, I need to let go of my own plans and trust him one day at a time."

Graeme kissed her forehead. "You're a beautiful woman," he whispered. "Come here and see what I brought you."

At the plane, he reached into the cockpit and took out a small, brown-paper parcel tied with twine. She loosened the bow, and the paper fell aside to reveal a soft pink fabric embroidered with tiny rosebuds.

"My dress," she whispered. "How did you get it back?"

"The steamer arrived in Timbuktu yesterday. The steward sent it to me at the police station. I tossed it into the plane, still hoping I'd find you somehow. Do you want it?"

Gazing down at the soft dress, her thoughts went back to the steamer and the brief hours of peace they had shared there. In that respite—when she'd seen him as more than her rescuer and more than her partner in adventure—she had realized she loved Graeme McLeod.

"Yes, I want to keep my dress. And my ring. And you." She held out her hand, and he took it gently. Turning it over, he traced a fingertip from her wrist to her palm and back—the sign of acceptance—then kissed each finger and her wrist.

"I don't have a lot to offer a woman, Tillie. But what I've got is yours."

"You know, Arthur wanted me to take some of the treasure. He thought it could build a happy life. Did you see what the treasure turned out to be?"

"I saw the chest smashed on the rocks."

She smiled. "Cowrie shells. Hundreds of them."

A chuckle escaped his lips, and he grinned wryly. "The treasure of Mansong. We should have guessed it. The king had given Mungo shells on his first trip. Five thousand of them, worth a lot back then. Ahmadi Fatouma must have thought he'd gotten his hands on a great treasure, or he never would have gone to so much trouble to hide it."

"Mungo must have thought the shells were worth something, too, the way he spoke to Ailie in the notes. He loved her very much, I think."

"And I love you." He brushed a kiss across her cheek. "Are you ready to head back to Timbuktu?"

"Wait, Graeme." She held him at arm's length. "What about the journal? Don't you care what happened to it?"

"If there even was a book in that chest, I know its pages are probably scattered across miles of desert by now. The main thing is that I found you. Mungo Park's story was important to me. It was my life's dream. I'll have his hat to remind me how close we came, but I can go on with my other ideas. I have three or four story assignments waiting for me—" He broke off in confusion when she turned away from him and began unbuttoning her shirt. "Um . . ." he shifted uncomfortably. "What are you doing?"

She glanced at him over her shoulder, tears glistening in her eyes. "You gave me my pink dress. Now I have something for you." She slipped the little book from its warm hiding place, rebuttoned her blouse, then turned and held her offering out to him. "Mungo Park's journal. I took it out of the chest while I was down in the well."

He stared at the book for a moment, as though he didn't dare move. His gaze rose to meet hers, and the wonder she saw there lifted her heart. Slowly he reached out, took the book, lifted its stiff cover, and stared down at the scrawled handwriting. He released his breath in a soft whoosh of amazement. "This is it. It's the last journal." He gave a loud whoop and swept her up into his arms. "You're incredible. I can't believe this!"

As he spun her around and around, Tillie laughed aloud. She could hardly wait to tell Hannah everything. Graeme held her tight against him, then pressed his lips to hers. Her response was warm, filled with happiness.

"I love you, Tillie. Nothing matters now but our new life. Not the treasure, not Mungo Park or his journal—nothing but us and this path we're on." He paused and stepped back, taking both her hands in his. "Tillie Thornton," he said, his voice somber, "I want you to be my wife. Will you do that?"

"Partners," she whispered. She slid her hands behind his neck and feathered her fingers in his hair. It was sprinkled with stars, and the moon had dusted his skin with silver. "Partners for life."

He tucked her under his arm, and they started toward the

sparkling jewel of the desert, knowing they held in their hearts the greatest treasure of all.

> THE ALMIGHTY WILL BE YOUR GOLD AND CHOICE SILVER TO YOU. FOR THEN YOU WILL DELIGHT IN THE ALMIGHTY, AND LIFT UP YOUR FACE TO GOD. YOU WILL PRAY TO HIM, AND HE WILL HEAR YOU.
>
> *Job 22:25-27*

Afterword

The story of Mungo Park, from his birth to his disappearance on the Niger River, is true. The Scottish explorer was known for his physical endurance, spiritual forbearance, and hunger for learning. He was described as a dry, prickly man with fine features, wavy hair, and Byronic good looks. In 1794, Park was instructed by the African Association to gather information on "the rise, the course, and the termination of the Niger, as well as of the various nations that inhabit its borders."

After a journey that included a sandstorm, attack by natives, hunger, and disease, Park returned to Scotland to pen his memoir, *Travels in the Interior of Africa*. He had written notes for the book on scraps of paper and stored them in the crown of his hat.

In 1805, Park went back to Africa to follow the mysterious Niger. To purchase a boat, he spent some of the five thousand cowrie shells he had been given by Mansong, the King of Segou. Again Park was beset with a variety of plagues that decimated three-fourths of his party. On November 20, Park disappeared. The story of the attack on the explorer's boat and his death by drowning was reported by his guide, Ahmadi Fatouma.

Several questions were raised. How did Ahmadi Fatouma

survive the attack? How could Yauri troops (who supposedly led the attack) have been permitted into the kingdom of Bussa, the land of their sworn enemy? How could Mungo Park have drowned when he was known to be an excellent swimmer? In Bussa in 1830, the Lander brothers were shown a book that had belonged to Park. Today this book can be seen in the Royal Geographic Society Museum in London. Oddly enough, it shows no sign of water damage.

On May 3, 1819, *The Times* of London reported of Park: "The death of this intrepid traveler is now placed [proven] beyond any doubt." It was also reported that the "journal of his long excursion down the Niger to Bussa disappeared with most of his other belongings."

The fictional mystery in this novel of the finding of the amulet, the journal, and the treasure evolved from my imagination and the true story of Mungo Park.

For further reading about topics mentioned in *A Kiss of Adventure,* please see the reading list that follows.

Reading List

De Gramont, Sanche. *The Strong Brown God: The Story of the Niger River.* Houghton Mifflin Company: Boston. 1976.

July, Robert W. *A History of the African People.* Charles Scribner's Sons: New York. 1980.

Moorhouse, Griffin. *The Fearful Void.* J. B. Lippincott Company: New York. 1974.

Oliver, Roland and Caroline, eds. *Africa in the Days of Exploration.* Prentice-Hall, Inc.: Englewood Cliffs, N. J. 1965.

Porch, Douglas. *The Conquest of the Sahara.* Alfred A. Knopf: New York. 1984.

The World and Its Peoples: Africa South and West. Greystone Press: New York. 1967.

A Note from the Author

Dear friends,

My deepest thanks to those of you who faithfully read each of my books and to those who write to share such wonderful words of encouragement. I praise God that my stories touch your lives and help you grow in your faith walk.

Watch for my first mainstream novel, A DANGEROUS SILENCE, due out in the spring of 2001. Meanwhile, be sure to read the rest of the books in the Treasures of the Heart series, as well as my other HeartQuest novels and novellas. (A complete list appears on page 350.)

May God bless you with peace of mind and heart,

Catherine Palmer

About the Author

Catherine Palmer lives in Missouri with her husband, Tim, and sons, Geoffrey and Andrei. She is a graduate of Southwest Baptist University and has a master's degree in English from Baylor University. Her first book was published in 1988. Since then she has published more than twenty novels. Catherine has won numerous awards for her writing, including Most Exotic Historical Romance Novel from *Romantic Times* magazine. Most recently she has been nominated for the *Romantic Times* Career Achievement Award. Total sales of her novels number more than one million copies.

Her HeartQuest books include both series of full-length novels and novellas in several anthologies. Her first mainstream novel, *A Dangerous Silence,* was released in the spring of 2001.

Catherine welcomes letters written to her in care of Tyndale House Author Relations, P.O. Box 80, Wheaton, IL 60189-0080.

Visit www.HeartQuest.com for lots of info on
HeartQuest books and authors and more!

www.HeartQuest.com

Books by Catherine Palmer

A Town Called Hope series

Prairie Rose

Prairie Fire

Prairie Storm

Prairie Christmas (anthology)

Treasures of the Heart series

A Kiss of Adventure (original title: *The Treasure of Timbuktu*)

A Whisper of Danger (original title: *The Treasure of Zanzibar*)

A Touch of Betrayal

Finders Keepers series

Finders Keepers

Hide and Seek

Anthologies

Prairie Christmas

A Victorian Christmas Cottage

A Victorian Christmas Quilt

A Victorian Christmas Tea

Current HeartQuest Releases

- *Magnolia*, Ginny Aiken
- *Lark*, Ginny Aiken
- *Camellia*, Ginny Aiken

- *Sweet Delights*, Terri Blackstock, Ranee McCollum, and Elizabeth White

- *Awakening Mercy*, Angela Benson
- *Abiding Hope*, Angela Benson

- *Faith*, Lori Copeland
- *Hope*, Lori Copeland
- *June*, Lori Copeland
- *Glory*, Lori Copeland

- *Freedom's Promise*, Dianna Crawford
- *Freedom's Hope*, Dianna Crawford
- *Freedom's Belle*, Dianna Crawford

- *Prairie Fire*, Catherine Palmer
- *Prairie Rose*, Catherine Palmer
- *Prairie Storm*, Catherine Palmer
- *Prairie Christmas*, Catherine Palmer, Elizabeth White, and Peggy Stoks

- *Finders Keepers*, Catherine Palmer
- *Hide and Seek*, Catherine Palmer
- *A Kiss of Adventure*, Catherine Palmer (original title: *The Treasure of Timbuktu*)
- *A Whisper of Danger*, Catherine Palmer (original title: *The Treasure of Zanzibar*)
- *A Touch of Betrayal*, Catherine Palmer
- *A Victorian Christmas Cottage*, Catherine Palmer, Debra White Smith, Jeri Odell, and Peggy Stoks
- *A Victorian Christmas Quilt*, Catherine Palmer, Debra White Smith, Ginny Aiken, and Peggy Stoks
- *A Victorian Christmas Tea*, Catherine Palmer, Dianna Crawford, Peggy Stoks, and Katherine Chute

- *Olivia's Touch*, Peggy Stoks
- *Romy's Walk*, Peggy Stoks

HEART QUEST®

Other Great Tyndale House Fiction

- *Jenny's Story*, Judy Baer
- *Libby's Story*, Judy Baer

- *Out of the Shadows*, Sigmund Brouwer

- *Ashes and Lace*, B. J. Hoff
- *Cloth of Heaven*, B. J. Hoff

- *The Price*, Jim and Terri Kraus
- *The Treasure*, Jim and Terri Kraus
- *The Promise*, Jim and Terri Kraus

- *Winter Passing*, Cindy McCormick Martinusen

- *Rift in Time*, Michael Phillips
- *Hidden in Time*, Michael Phillips

- *Unveiled*, Francine Rivers
- *Unashamed*, Francine Rivers
- *Unshaken*, Francine Rivers
- *A Voice in the Wind*, Francine Rivers
- *An Echo in the Darkness*, Francine Rivers
- *As Sure As the Dawn*, Francine Rivers
- *The Last Sin Eater*, Francine Rivers
- *Leota's Garden*, Francine Rivers
- *The Scarlet Thread*, Francine Rivers
- *The Atonement Child*, Francine Rivers

- *The Promise Remains*, Travis Thrasher

HeartQuest Books by Catherine Palmer

A Town Called Hope series
Prairie Rose—Kansas holds their future, but only faith can mend their past. Hope and love blossom on the untamed prairie as a young woman, searching for a place to call home, happens upon a Kansas homestead during the 1860s.

Prairie Fire—Will a burning secret extinguish the spark of love between Jack and Caitrin? The town of Hope discovers the importance of forgiveness, overcoming prejudice, and the dangers of keeping unhealthy family secrets.

Prairie Storm—Can one tiny baby calm the brewing storm between Lily's past and Elijah's future? United in their concern for an orphaned infant, Eli and Lily are forced to set aside their differences and learn to trust God's plan to see them through the storms of life.

Prairie Christmas (anthology)—In "The Christmas Bride," by Catherine Palmer, Rolf Rustemeyer can hardly wait for the arrival of his Christmas bride, all the way from Germany. You'll love this heartwarming Christmas visit with friends old and new from A Town Called Hope. Anthology also includes novellas by Elizabeth White and Peggy Stoks.

Treasures of the Heart series
A Kiss of Adventure (original title: *The Treasure of Timbuktu*)—Abducted by a treasure hunter, Tillie becomes a pawn in a dangerous game.

A Whisper of Danger (original title: *The Treasure of Zanzibar*)—Jessica's unexpected inheritance turns out to be an ancient house filled with secrets, an unknown enemy . . . and a lost love.

A Touch of Betrayal—Stranded in a dangerous land, Alexandra must face her fear . . . and escape the man determined to ruin her life.

Finders Keepers series
Finders Keepers—Blue-eyed, fiery-tempered Elizabeth Hayes is working hard to preserve Chalmers House, the Victorian mansion next to her growing antiques business. But Zachary Chalmers, heir to the mansion, has very different plans for the site. And Elizabeth's eight-year-old son, adopted from Romania three years earlier, has plans of his own: He wants a daddy—and this tall, handsome man is the perfect candidate.

Hide and Seek—Luke Easton wants to be left alone to nurse his broken heart, raise his daughter in peace, and complete the renovation of the Chalmers Mansion. Jo Callaway prizes her privacy too. She doesn't want her new friends to ask too many questions about her mysterious past. But fighting for common goals begins to forge a bond between Luke and Jo that neither expected—or welcomes.

Anthologies

A Victorian Christmas Cottage—Four novellas centering around hearth and home at Christmastime. Stories by Catherine Palmer, Jeri Odell, Debra White Smith, and Peggy Stoks.

A Victorian Christmas Quilt—A patchwork of four novellas about love and joy at Christmastime. Stories by Catherine Palmer, Ginny Aiken, Peggy Stoks, and Debra White Smith.

A Victorian Christmas Tea—Four novellas about life and love at Christmastime. Stories by Catherine Palmer, Dianna Crawford, Peggy Stoks, and Katherine Chute.